Praise for t

"A perfectly enjoyable action filled ....
—*Publishers Weekly*

"Kennealy makes San Francisco one of his main characters. His other characters ring true partly because of the realistic dialogue. I can't wait 'til Kennealy's next novel hits the bookstores."
—*San Francisco Examiner*

"His best novel to date. A crime thriller that has prize-winner written all over it. A gritty work. Enthralling."
—*Harriet Klausner*

"A gleeful cat-and-mouse game. Bullets fly, bombs explode, sex is plentiful, double-crosses abound and there's enough insider cop jargon to satisfy any procedural fan."
—*San Francisco Sunday Chronicle Examiner*

"Kennealy writes colorful, authentic novels."
—*Philadelphia Inquirer*

THE
HUNTED

Jerry Kennealy

A SIGNET BOOK

SIGNET
Published by New American Library, a division of
Penguin Putnam Inc., 375 Hudson Street,
New York, New York 10014, U.S.A.
Penguin Books Ltd, 27 Wrights Lane,
London W8 5TZ, England
Penguin Books Australia Ltd, Ringwood,
Victoria, Australia
Penguin Books Canada Ltd, 10 Alcorn Avenue,
Toronto, Ontario, Canada M4V 3B2
Penguin Books (N.Z.) Ltd, 182–190 Wairau Road,
Auckland 10, New Zealand

Penguin Books Ltd, Registered Offices:
Harmondsworth, Middlesex, England

First published by Signet, an imprint of New American Library,
a division of Penguin Putnam Inc.

First Printing, July 1999
10 9 8 7 6 5 4 3 2 1

Copyright © Jerry Kennealy, 1999
All rights reserved

 REGISTERED TRADEMARK—MARCA REGISTRADA

Printed in the United States of America

Without limiting the rights under copyright reserved above, no part of
this publication may be reproduced, stored in or introduced into a
retrieval system, or transmitted, in any form, or by any means (electronic, mechanical, photocopying, recording, or otherwise), without
the prior written permission of both the copyright owner and the above
publisher of this book.

PUBLISHER'S NOTE
This is a work of fiction. Names, characters, places, and incidents either
are the product of the author's imagination or are used fictitiously,
and any resemblance to actual persons, living or dead, events, or locales
is entirely coincidental.

BOOKS ARE AVAILABLE AT QUANTITY DISCOUNTS WHEN USED TO PROMOTE
PRODUCTS OR SERVICES. FOR INFORMATION PLEASE WRITE TO PREMIUM
MARKETING DIVISION, PENGUIN PUTNAM INC., 375 HUDSON STREET, NEW YORK,
NEW YORK 10014.

If you purchased this book without a cover you should be aware that
this book is stolen property. It was reported as "unsold and destroyed" to the publisher and neither the author nor the publisher has
received any payment for this "stripped book."

For my grandson Jake

Welcome to the world
Young Blue Eyes

I hope I can pass some things along

There are some things which cannot be learned quickly, and time, which is all we have, must be paid heavily for their acquiring. They are the very simplest things and because it takes a man's life to know them, the little new that each man gets from life is very costly and the only heritage he has to leave.

—*Ernest Hemingway*

Prologue

Philip Bovard stomped his feet on the ice-cold concrete floor and rubbed his gloved hands together as he watched the sinister shape of the one-hundred-sixty-seven-meter Delta IV nuclear submarine emerge from the dark, oily waters of the Murmansk harbor and slowly, seemingly reluctantly, inch up the tracks leading to the cavernous shipping dock.

The submarine looked like a monstrous whale to Bovard: sleek, black, a sea creature being led to slaughter.

Once the sub was inside the abysmal, cavernous dock, a gang of men, dressed in knit caps, ragged coveralls, and heavy boots, descended upon it, anxious to cut up what was left of the carcass. The conning tower had already been removed, as were the nuclear warheads, the sophisticated electronics stations, the kitchen services, and the bathroom fixtures. There were just two items of value left in the belly of the ship. Two very precious items.

While the whalers of old had used razor-sharp spears to hack away at the blubber of their victim, these shipmen brandished cutting torches. Their blue-arced flames contrasted with the sub's inky steel skin.

"Shouldn't they be wearing protective clothing?" Bovard asked the Russian bureaucrat standing alongside him. "Isn't it dangerous for them?"

"Who cares," Gregor Zinovsky grunted. Zinovsky was short and stout, his figure enveloped in a fur coat and hat. All that was visible was a close-cropped beard, and dark, espresso-colored eyes shielded behind a pair of glasses of the style favored by American pilots and motorcycle policemen. "They're *chernozhopyi*. Black-assed bastards from Kazakhstan. They're lucky to have the work."

Bovard slipped a metal flask from the pocket of his fur coat and handed it to the Russian. "When will I have the reactors?"

The Russian removed the flask's cap with his bare fingers, then took a long swallow before passing it back to Bovard. "Oh, two weeks. We want enough time for them to be properly lost."

Bovard sipped from the flask. The brandy made a temporary pool of warmth in his stomach. He was glad he wouldn't have to endure a night in town. Murmansk was Russia's principal port on the Arctic Ocean. Somehow its five hundred thousand inhabitants endured the dark and sub-zero temperatures. Its only attraction was the fact that the harbor was ice-free all year.

"I need a firm date. My clients are very anxious," Bovard said.

The Russian looked at his watch, a gold Cartier "Panther" that Bovard had presented to him last night. "Today is the twenty-seventh. You want delivery in Cyprus, no?"

"Cyprus, yes," Bovard agreed. "The harbor at Limassol."

Zinovsky chuckled knowingly. "A good choice. Very near your clients—and their target, no?"

Bovard didn't respond to the question. It was none of the bastard's business who his clients were. He drained what remained in the flask as he looked out at the harbor. There had to be thirty submarines and half that many nuclear-powered icebreakers waiting their turn to be dismantled. Each submarine and icebreaker housed a minimum of two nuclear reactors. "Floating Chernobyls" Yeltzin had once dubbed them, no doubt in an attempt to encourage the United States to help pay for their dismantling.

The Russian pointed toward one of the subs moored in

the harbor. "That's yours, too. When do I get the rest of the money?"

"As we agreed. A million when the reactors are removed, another million when you've hijacked them from the train, and the rest when I take delivery."

"There is the money for our Swedish captain. That has to be advanced right away."

"Not a problem," Bovard assured him.

"Good. Delivery will be on April the tenth. Satisfactory?"

"Yes," Bovard confirmed. "Quite satisfactory."

Gregor Zinovsky slapped a broad hand on Bovard's back. "Come now, let's get out of this shit hole and back to Moscow. I want to show you a new casino. I feel lucky."

"I don't believe in luck," Bovard said, turning to take one last look at the gutting of the nuclear submarine.

Chapter 1

San Francisco
Golden Gate Park
March 30

The sky was cloudless, a pure, solid cobalt blue, except for a brassy haze ringing the sun.

Janna Drovana watched as birds with sickle-shaped wings bolted from a towering palm tree to avoid the stones being thrown by two young boys dressed in cutoff jeans and matching red T-shirts.

Janna was thirteen years old, but looked younger: thin-boned and small for her age, her shoulder-length hair so black it had hints of blue in it. Her face was heart-shaped, like her mother's had been. She tilted her head upward to the sun, closing her eyes, enjoying the warmth, remembering how cold and damp she had been last night.

"There she is!" a familiar, harsh voice shouted.

Janna jerked her head around and spotted her mother's cousin, Yuri Stoylar, less than fifty yards away, standing at the foot of the steps leading to the De Young Museum.

Janna leaped over a low-lying sphinxlike statue, threaded her way through a throng of tourists, darted into a road that was choked with cars and double-parked buses, then raced toward the Japanese Tea Gardens.

Yuri Stoylar's shouts of "Get her! Get her!" rang in her ears as she tried to pick his companions out of the crowd.

She narrowly missed running directly into one: a broad-shouldered, slab-faced man with a droopy mustache. She recognized him. He'd been to the flat, to drink with

Cousin Yuri after her mother's death. She'd overheard someone say that he was a weight lifter who once had been a member of the Russian Olympic team. She did not know his name, but she remembered how he had looked at her. Just like Yuri and his other friends had. Even before Mama died.

He held out his arms, about to encircle her.

Janna immediately dove to the ground, then rolled into the legs of a woman wearing a knee-length plaid skirt, who let out a startled yelp at the contact.

Janna quickly regained her feet and sprinted away, her head swiveling back and forth, catching a glimpse of the man with the droopy mustache using his massive arms to shove a group of Chinese students out of his way.

Janna scrambled past the long line of people waiting to pay for admittance to the Tea Gardens. She dropped down, skittering on her palms and toes, like a frightened cat, as she approached the kiosk.

There were some laughs and some indignant shouts, but she ignored them, getting back to her feet, weaving through the overhanging cherry trees and taking refuge behind a stand of timber bamboo.

Yuri Stoylar bulled his way into the gardens, the Mustache Man at his heels. There was a commotion and finally Stoylar fumbled his wallet from his pocket, threw a handful of bills at the woman in the kiosk, then began gesturing wildly with his hands, directing the other man.

They split up, Stoylar standing guard near the ten-foot bronze Buddha that he so closely resembled: bald head, bulging belly. He was dressed as usual—a soiled black leather jacket and ragged jeans. The top of his head was sheened with sweat. The Mustache Man moved off, elbowing his way through the tourists and kimono-clad women serving Jasmine tea and fortune cookies.

Yesterday, Janna had managed to pick up enough of the abandoned, half-eaten cookies to make a breakfast.

She edged away from the bamboo, slipping into the center of a bevy of young girls, who were being chaperoned by a Catholic nun.

The girls were somewhat younger than Janna. Nine or ten, she estimated. She bent her knees and hunched her shoulders, hoping to go unnoticed.

The Catholic nun gave her a curious look and was about to say something when Janna felt the strong, painful grip of a hand on her shoulder.

"Come with me," the Mustache Man said in guttural Russian. "Your friends are looking for you."

Janna tried pulling away, but his fingers dug in deeper. She twisted her head, struggling to latch her teeth on to that hand, but she couldn't reach it.

"What's going on?" the nun demanded. She was fair-skinned, her smooth forehead disappearing into the cowl of her starched white habit.

"He's hurting me," Janna cried. "He's hurting me."

The Mustache Man was waving with his free hand toward Yuri Stoylar.

"Let her go," the nun insisted.

The man gave her a hard look. "Go mind your own business!" he shouted in heavily accented English.

The nun hesitated for a moment.

"Help!" Janna yelled. "He made me touch him. Touch him down there. Look! His pants are unzipped!"

Janna considered the accusation a white lie. The Mustache Man had never tried to make her touch him, but Cousin Yuri had.

The man released his grip momentarily. Janna squirmed free, reaching for the protection of the nun's flowing robe.

"Don't let him take me," she pleaded.

The nun's pale face reddened. "Someone call the police," she ordered in a loud classroom voice.

Janna could see Cousin Yuri standing at the fringe of the gathering crowd. She looked directly into his piglike eyes, gave him a quick, triumphant smile, then darted over a narrow wooden bridge spanning a stone-laden creek, past the three-story orange-and-gold pagoda, and finally through the head-high turnstile exit at the rear of the gardens.

Janna ran nonstop for fifteen minutes, zigzagging up

the incline to Stow Lake, easily passing older, dedicated joggers and flashily dressed roller-bladers, scattering squadrons of squatting seagulls and pigeons, not slowing her pace until she was beyond Rainbow Fall and the stables by the Polo Field, finally stopping at her favorite spot by tiny Speckles Lake, where people came to sail their model boats.

She paused in the shade of the antlerlike branches of a cypress tree, bent over at the hips, hands on her knees, sucking in great gulps of air. It had been close. Too close. She was going to have to find another hiding place. But where else could she go? Her mother had brought her to Golden Gate Park almost every day. She'd gotten to know most of the nooks and crannies of the thousand-acre park, which was located just five blocks from their flat. The flat they had shared for four long months with Cousin Yuri Stoylar. And his friends. Every few weeks one man would leave, then another one, or two, would move in. Cousin Yuri had told her that she would have to be "nice" to the men to pay for her keep. "Like your mother, before she took sick, Janna."

Janna straightened up and scanned the irregular-shaped little lake. Its stone-flagged border path was rimmed with towering eucalyptus, pine, and cypress trees.

She liked to watch the people who came to sail their elaborate model boats on the murky, olive-green pond waters. They were mostly older men, who brought their own folding chairs. They sat with their transmitters on their laps, the long, telescoping antennas resembling fishing rods, while they orchestrated the activities of the flotilla of boats, which ranged from models to snub-nosed tug boats, to fully rigged, long-masted schooners, to menacing-looking battleships.

Janna also enjoyed watching the hand-sized turtles bask in the sun. They would struggle clumsily to climb up on the back of a giant, half-submerged concrete turtle, then gently slide back into the lake.

The boats and the turtles weren't her main interests today. Her eyes were fixed on the woman who was sitting alone on the green wooden bench by the path leading to Fulton Street.

She was feeding the squirrels. The woman was older than her mother had been. And quite fat. Her face was chalk-white, thick with makeup. Her hair was the color of a ripe orange. Yesterday she'd worn a beautiful yellow sweater and matching skirt. Today she was wearing a tobacco-brown suede coat. Her plump legs were encased in dark brown pants. Brightly polished boots reached up to her knees. The boots reminded Janna of the type she'd seen rich people wear in the movies when they rode horses. She smiled at the thought of the fat woman on a horse.

The fat woman had a wicker basket stuffed with food. Yesterday she ate a lunch of sandwiches, cake, pie, and candy. There seemed to be too much food for one person in the basket. She threw pieces of the pastry to the birds, and then lobbed peanuts at a family of squirrels, who sat on their haunches, waving their paws, begging for the nuts.

Yesterday she'd left behind a sandwich, thick creamy egg and sweet pickle, Janna's favorite. Along with an apple and a banana. It had made a wonderful dinner. Janna wondered if the woman would leave her any food today.

The woman rummaged through her basket and took out a small black plastic computer. Janna had watched her play with it yesterday. She looked up at Janna and smiled.

Janna pivoted around, looking for Yuri Stoylar and the Mustache Man. When she turned back, the woman was still smiling.

"Did you enjoy the sandwich I left for you yesterday, young lady?" Her voice was soft, slightly husky. "I hope someone else didn't get to it first. You looked so hungry."

Janna edged closer, noticing the rings on the woman's fingers. Were they real diamonds? If they were real, she must be very rich. "I got the sandwich," she acknowledged.

The woman began clicking away at the mini-computer.

"You speak English very well. Your accent. It's Russian. Let me guess. St. Petersburg?"

"Yes," Janna answered curtly. "How did you know?"

"Because I was born there! My name is Angela. Do you like to play games? I love playing checkers, solitaire, and blackjack." She tilted the small computer screen toward Janna. "I'm playing blackjack now." She giggled lightly. "And not doing very well. It's a good thing I'm not playing for money. Would you like to join me for lunch today?"

Janna jammed her hands into her jacket pockets. "Why do you have so much food?"

Angela dug a box of candy out of the basket. "I cook for my two nieces, who are just about your age. Their mother died, so every day I bring them food." Her eyes drifted toward the lake. A motorized replica of a Mississippi riverboat nearly collided with a graceful, blue-hulled sailing model. "I like to stop here. It's so peaceful. Do you live nearby?"

Janna nodded her head. Very nearby. Her sleeping bag and one change of clothing, all that she'd been able to take from the flat, were hidden across the road in a thicket of rhododendrons.

She had no other choice. She'd overheard Cousin Yuri on the phone, discussing his plans for her. He was going to sell her! Sell her, as if she were some kind of animal, a pet that belonged to him.

Janna sat down cautiously on the edge of the bench, ready to jump up at the first sign of Cousin Yuri or the Mustache Man.

The woman handed the small computer to her. "Here, see if you have any luck. Have you ever played blackjack?"

"No," Janna admitted. The game was unfamiliar to her. "But I like to play chess. My father taught me to play chess on a computer back home."

"Wonderful," Angela cheered, clapping her hands together. "Perhaps you can teach me. Come. Eat. Try the candy," the woman urged. "I made it myself."

Janna snatched one of the chocolate-covered bonbons, popped it into her mouth, and quickly took another one.

She'd been hiding in the park for the last four days, and had learned that one of the lessons of survival was to eat all you could, when you could.

The woman patted the bench. "Come. Don't be so frightened. Sit down with me. I have some chicken and pie. Blueberry pie." She smiled, her face fanning into hundreds of wrinkles. "Blueberry. Like the color of your eyes. Sit. Eat. I want to be your friend."

Chapter 2

Maureen "Mo" Connah grabbed the phone on the first ring.

"Homicide, Inspector Connah."

"Given yourself a promotion already have you, Mo?" came the caustic reply. "You're still an assistant inspector. This is Captain Neil. Is our hero there?"

"Who's that, Captain?"

"Your new partner. Inspector Jack Kordic, our very own combination of James Bond and Arnold Schwarzenegger," Neil mocked sarcastically. "The chief wants to see him before he takes off for London."

"He's not here at the moment, Captain. I expect him back shortly."

"How do you like Homicide so far?"

"I've only been here a few days, Captain."

Neil's voice softened. "You don't have to be so formal, Mo. If you need any help feeling your way around while Kordic is away, we could get together."

Connah leaned back in her chair and lifted her feet up on the desk. It was ten minutes after noon, everyone had gone to lunch. The office was deserted.

She was careful with her reply. The Captain of Detectives had been responsible for getting her assigned to the Homicide detail. "I appreciate that, Captain. How are Jo-Anne, and the twins?"

Captain Neil's tone became officious. "They're fine. Tell Kordic to call Chief Fletcher ASAP. We want to go over a few things with him before he takes off for London."

Connah dropped the receiver into its cradle with a

smile. Bill Neil. Her boss of bosses. A horny kiss-ass with a wife who was too good for him, and adorable eight-year-old twin boys. "If you need any help feeling your way around." Maureen pushed herself away from the desk, got to her feet, and walked over to a window that overlooked the dreary Bayshore Freeway, which even at noontime was clogged with cars, trucks, buses, massive eighteen-wheelers, all inching their way toward the Bay Bridge.

She swiveled around to make sure that she was still alone, then put her hands on her hips and arched her back.

Maureen had been named after her mother's favorite actress, Maureen O'Hara. She stood five feet ten in her bare feet. Her hair was a deep red-gold, her creamy skin lightly dusted with freckles. She was long-legged, with a figure that had caused her trouble since the seventh grade. She'd blossomed early, and soon found herself being chased by fellow students, as well as a couple of her teachers.

At about the time of her twelfth birthday, boys she'd played baseball and soccer with suddenly became tongue-tied, their eyes riveted on her breasts.

Maureen was careful in her selection of clothes for work: loose-fitting slacks, bulky sweaters. Her shoulder-length hair was simply finger-combed and held back with a rubber band.

Still, the Bill Neils in the department never stopped trying.

Maureen was well aware that there was still some resentment over her promotion to the Homicide detail. The fact that she'd never walked a beat or driven a patrol car didn't sit well with the men and women she'd jumped over to get the assistant inspector's job.

Shortly after she'd graduated from the police academy, she'd been detailed to the Vice squad, outfitted in a tight miniskirt and low-cut blouse, and put to work as a decoy on the dark, crime-ridden streets of the Tenderloin District.

She'd drawn the attention of hundreds of street-cruising johns, including one very embarrassed lieutenant of the nearby Santa Rosa Police Department.

Maureen had also drawn the attention of a coke-high pimp who'd gone after her with a baseball bat. Sergeant Tom Flavio had been her backup, and had ended the pimp's career with a well-placed bullet in the buttocks.

"Another crack in his ass," had been the way Flavio described the incident to his buddies.

Maureen and Flavio started dating after that. It seemed a perfect matchup. He was slightly shorter than she, but muscular, dark, sullenly handsome. They were married six months later.

Her husband was never jealous over her strutting around the streets of the Tenderloin in "ho-threads." Tom Flavio had liked seeing her in those hooker outfits. He began buying her skimpy clothing, right out of the Frederick's of Hollywood catalogue, chastising her when she wouldn't wear them when they went out socially.

"Irish Catholic prude," he'd protest in a mocking brogue accent.

Then he started bringing his cop buddies home on the spur of the moment, or they'd suddenly appear at the door with their girlfriends for an impromptu party. The hints started: "Is Joey a good-looking dude? What do you think? Hung like a horse, I bet." "Dick and JoAnne. Are they a hot couple, or what? I think they swing a little."

Maureen made it clear that she wanted no part of any of it. Then one night, Tom's friend Joey came over to the apartment and after a round of shoptalk, Maureen went to bed, leaving them at the kitchen table working on a bottle of Jack Daniel's.

She had been sound asleep when her husband had crawled into bed. His hands were suddenly all over her, his whiskey breath hot in her ear. She struggled to a sitting position and spotted Joey leaning in the doorway, his pants dropped down to his ankles, his erection pointed directly at her.

"Come on, Mo," Flavio had pleaded, cupping her

breasts from behind. "Let's have a little fun. I've been telling Joey how hot you are."

Maureen's screams and threats with her off-duty gun had sobered up both of the men. She filed for a divorce immediately.

Tom Flavio didn't fight the divorce, but he did make it painful. He spread the word around the department that Maureen was frigid. A closet dyke. Then there were the phone calls. Sometimes just heavy breathing. She knew it was Flavio, but there wasn't much she could do about it. Her number was unlisted, but it was available to her bosses at work. And Flavio had a way of finding it.

There were calls from drunks in the middle of the night. She had a trap put on the phone. The calling number was traced to a bar in the Mission District. Among the penciled messages on the graffitied wall near the pay phone was one in red ink with her number and: "Want a blow? Call redhead Mo. She loves it!!!"

The calls had eventually stopped. But Tom Flavio was still in the department. Still a sergeant, working Vice, which was located on the same floor as the Homicide detail. Every once in a while she'd spot him. Driving by her new apartment. At the neighborhood bar. At the local supermarket. He'd just smirk at her and move off.

There hadn't been enough contact for her to file a formal complaint. He wasn't stalking her. Just letting her know that he was still there. Still a threat.

After two years in Vice, Maureen had been transferred to the Office of Citizen Complaints, where she spent a frustrating year and a half handling claims of misconduct against her fellow officers. Connah hated the job and had reluctantly called on her father, "Big John" Connah, who, as the result of a stroke, had retired as a deputy chief two months before Maureen had entered the department. Her father lobbied his old friend, Captain of Detectives Bill Neil, for a transfer for his daughter. Now she was in Homicide. It was the assignment she'd always wanted.

Maureen was bent over, touching her toes, trying to relieve the tension in her back, when she heard footsteps.

She straightened up quickly and pivoted around.

"I thought you might be hungry," Inspector Jack Kordic said, holding a brown paper bag out in front of him. "You've got your choice. Ham and Swiss on rye, or tuna on wheat."

"Either one's fine."

Kordic emptied the contents of the bag on his desk. "Let's split 'em," he suggested, sliding a can of Coke across the desk to her.

Maureen nodded her thanks as she snapped open the soda and took a swig. She studied Kordic over the rim of the can as he went about his chores. She'd been curious about Kordic, and had gone through the trouble of checking his DMV record out on the computer. Forty-three years of age. Forty-four in two months. He was tall, six feet one at least. She was thankful for that. There was something about a woman cop towering over her male partner that rang the wrong bells.

He had all his hair, a shaggy, salt-and-pepper mane. She liked the lines in his face: craggy, with deep clefts between his eyes, slash marks on the cheeks, and another cleft in the chin. Character lines. And those eyes. Green eyes. Jade-green, a shade she'd never seen before. His voice was soft, raspy, and sometimes she had to lean close to hear just what he was saying.

Department scuttlebutt had him hooked up with an attorney, whose life he'd saved by killing the terrorist Rene Santos.

But Maureen had seen no sign of the attorney, or any other women in Kordic's life in the last seven days.

He had the look of a loner, and Maureen could easily picture him in another time, another era: the strong, silent cowboy who rode into town and shot up all the bad guys before hitching up with the schoolmarm.

Maureen had heard several versions of the death of Kordic's wife and young son while on their way to meet him in San Francisco for dinner and Christmas shopping, their being stopped on the street, shot and killed, by a carjacker who'd never been caught, never even been identified.

She also heard that he'd had a drinking problem brought on by the murders, as well as a mental break-down and a suicide attempt. She had doubted the rumors of the suicide attempt until she'd spotted the narrow, rag-ged scars under both of his wrists.

They were still feeling each other out, and Maureen had a hunch that Captain Neil had deliberately put them to-gether, hoping that Kordic would back away, and then Maureen would be on her own, and dependent on Neil again.

Would Kordic back away? Or would she? She knew that for a partnership to work, both sides had to contrib-ute. She didn't have a whole hell of a lot to contribute as far as investigative experience was concerned, but she was willing, hell, damn eager, she admitted, to learn. Both sides had to give a little. Would Kordic pass on his experi-ence? What would he expect in return? The same thing Bill Neil wanted?

She told Kordic about the phone call from Captain Neil.

He shrugged his shoulders. "I'll be glad to get the damn trip over with."

"Have you ever been to London?" Maureen asked.

Kordic flapped open the tuna sandwich and scrutinized the contents. "No. How about you?"

"Oh, sure. Several times. Pop took us to Ireland on va-cation every other year. While he prowled the countryside looking for long-lost relatives, Mom and I would sneak off to London. 'Enemy territory' according to Pop. I loved it. Are you going to have any time to yourself?"

"Not much. I'd like to squeeze in a day of sightseeing, but the chief wants me back here as soon as the conference is over. Someone from Scotland Yard is supposed to give me a quick cook's tour. Any suggestions?"

"Oh, yes," Maureen said enthusiastically. "It's the greatest shopping town in the world, Jack. Harrods. Bur-berry's. Mom tried like crazy to get Pop to go to one of those Savile Row tailors, Hardy Ames, but he wanted no part of it. She bought him a great suit, Savile Row off the rack, at a place called Hacketts."

Kordic ripped open a bag of potato chips, then looked at his frayed shirt cuffs. "Are you trying to tell me something?"

"No, no," she protested lightly. "I was just—"

Kordic held up his hand like the traffic officer he'd been some twenty years before. "I guess it is about time I bought some new duds." He picked up a pencil and scribbled down the names of the clothing stores.

"You must be excited, Jack. Where are you staying?"

"The Savoy. That's where they're holding the banquet."

"The Savoy! Who's paying for all of this? Not you, I hope. And I can't see Chief Fletcher opening up the department purse strings for the Savoy."

"No. The people sponsoring the convention are picking up the tab. The Law Enforcement Anti-Terrorism Network."

"Sounds impressive," Connah said. "And that's when you'll get the award?"

"That's when I get the award," Kordic acknowledged with a grunt.

Maureen fixed her eyes on her new partner. "What really happened, Jack? All I know is what I read in the papers, and what I've heard around here."

Kordic loosened his tie and leaned back in his chair. "There was this terrorist. A real bastard by the name of Rene Santos. He was known as *el Cabecilla*—The Conductor, because he usually stage-managed his operations. He came to San Francisco to kidnap Paul Abrams."

"The oil billionaire," Maureen supplied.

"Right. An attorney by the name of Mary Ariza got caught in the middle. Santos was trying to have her killed. That's how I originally got involved. There was a man from Israeli Intelligence, a Mossad agent, Anatoly Weeks, who did most of the heavy lifting. Santos nearly ended up killing Weeks. Actually, Anatoly should be getting the award."

"But you're the one who killed Santos, right?"

Kordic held up his palm, then made a mock gun of his fist. "That was the first time I'd ever fired a gun on the job, outside of going to the practice range. Santos murdered over a dozen innocent people, including Lieutenant Chris Sullivan. Chris was murdered right in this room." He pointed the imaginary gun at the floor. "We found Chris's body right there." His voice lowered a notch. "Ancient history now." He shook his head slowly from side to side. "Any calls other than Neil's?"

"Nope. That was it," Maureen said, reaching for a bag of potato chips.

"After lunch, I'll take you down to the coroner's office and introduce you around." He took a bite of the sandwich, then said, "I appreciate you giving me a lift to the airport tomorrow night."

"No problem," Connah responded with a slight sense of guilt. Driving Kordic to the airport would guarantee her the use of his unmarked car while he was away in London.

Chapter 3

Janna slowly blinked her eyes open. She could hear voices. They sounded far away. She flinched as her vision cleared and she saw the bald, sweaty head of Cousin Yuri Stoylar hovering over him, smiling like a Halloween lantern, exposing his jagged, nicotine-stained teeth.

"We caught you, you little bitch," Stoylar boasted, drops of spittle flying from between his teeth. "You think you're so smart. Smarter than anyone, huh? Not so smart now, are you, Janna?"

Janna tried to move to avoid his hand, but she couldn't. Her arms were numb. She barely felt his thumb and index finger pinch her cheeks.

Another hand appeared, moving as if in slow motion.

"Enough," she heard a woman say.

Yuri Stoylar leaned down, so that his face was inches from Janna's. "Janna, the 'little genius.' Did you know that's what her mother called her, Angela? 'Little genius.' Her father was a scientist, yes, a pompous bastard. She got her brains from him. Fortunately she got her looks from her mother. Now you're going to be a little whore, just like your mother was, Janna. I was going to teach you to be a whore, Little Genius." He yanked his hand away, his huge face splitting into an obscene grin. "But someone else will have that privilege now. Maybe when Angela is through with you, you can come back to me, and you can make the money your mother should have made for me."

Yuri Stoylar leered at the woman. "Isn't that right, Little Angel?" He opened both hands and wiggled his fingers. "After you pay me, of course." He glanced back at Janna.

"She's small for her age, and looks younger than she is. That should make her worth even more to you."

"Out, out," the woman said shrilly. "Go to the kitchen, and I'll bring you your money."

Stoylar peered down at Janna, pursed his lips and made loud kissing sounds, then spun on his heel and strode briskly from the room.

Janna was having trouble keeping her eyes open. The woman's face floated in and out of view. It was the fat woman from the park. The one with the food. She'd said her name was Angela. Little angel. Janna remembered sitting with her on the bench. Eating the candy. Then feeling sick, drowsy. Then nothing, until now. Until seeing Cousin Yuri Stoylar. Her stomach contracted, and for a moment she thought she would vomit. Yuri Stoylar, the man who was supposed to help her and her mother, to protect them, but who had betrayed them both.

She tried to say something, but her tongue felt as if it were glued to the roof of her mouth.

The fat woman sat down alongside Janna and stroked her damp hair. "You do not have to worry about him anymore, dear. He will never bother you again." Her puffy hand trailed down Janna's forehead, the fingers spreading to slide over her eyes, then down to her neck.

"You and I are going to be great friends. I'm going to introduce you to some nice people. Very nice people. And you will have friends to play with." Her pale, pastry-dough face beamed. "Friends your own age. My Tina and Amber. They will teach you all kinds of new games."

Janna barely felt the woman's hands glide back up to her eyes, rolling the lids shut.

"Go back to sleep now," Angela crooned softly. "When you wake up, we'll start your lessons."

Janna's chin dropped to her chest. She heard herself let out an involuntary snore. There was the sound of footsteps moving away. Then a scraping sound. Janna managed to force one eye open. The fat woman was crouched over in front of a dark wooden bureau. On her knees, as if she were cleaning the floor. Janna saw her retrieve a metal box from a hole in the floor. She was wondering what was in the box when she fell asleep again.

March 31

Patrick Lynam entered the glass-fronted laundromat, his eyes searching for a change machine.

Two women wearing heavy coats and bandannas wrapped around their heads were sitting in front of churning washing machines. They both lowered their magazines and gave him a brief glare before returning to their reading material.

The heavy smell of detergent and bleach assaulted his nostrils as he slid two ten-dollar bills into the change machine, then scooped up the handfuls of quarters. There was a pay phone on the wall at the back of the room.

He kept his eyes on the two women as he punched in the fifteen digits of the London telephone number.

"That will be ten dollars and seventy-five cents for the first three minutes," the overseas operator informed him.

He fed in the necessary coinage. After the first ring there was the buzzing sound of connection, then a series of clicks.

"It's Old Friend. I'm at 415 555-9995." Lynam hung up, sat down on a folding chair, and took his notebook computer from his suit coat pocket, slipped it from its leather case, and activated the screen. He wanted to have all the information Bovard would ask about when the call came in. He used the tip of a gold Bulgari pen to click the machine's small keyboard.

It somewhat amused Lynam that Bovard had instructed him to always use public pay phones. Bovard was a sophisticated, astute man. It would have been much easier, in Lynam's estimation, to limit their transactions to coded E-mail, but Bovard had insisted on the phone calls. A throwback to Bovard's career as an intelligence officer, he assumed, and, now that he would have to ask for Bovard's assistance, perhaps a good idea. The procedure was that if the call was not returned within ten minutes, Lynam was to go to another location and call within the hour.

The phone rang at the very end of the ten-minute deadline, just as Lynam was preparing to leave the laundromat.

"What is it?" Philip Bovard demanded, his voice thick, irritated. "Is there a problem?"

"Yes," Lynam confirmed. "The Syrians want to pay in gold."

"Gold! Shit. They promised me dollars. I don't want to have to convert that much gold. How much would we lose?"

Lynam had already calculated the amount. "If we have to convert the gold into dollars quickly, the amount may be more than three million. Next month's gold futures are down fourteen dollars, and as you know, gold is much more difficult to launder than dollars."

"Unacceptable," Bovard barked. "Those bastards. They always haggle right up to the end. I can't afford to take that kind of a loss. All right, all right," he said sullenly. "I'll talk to them. I received some good news this morning. Delivery is guaranteed. The package will be delivered via a Swedish freighter, the *Sjogang*. It means 'high sea.' Send the Russian his one million."

Lynam's fingers flicked at the computer, entering the amount alongside the account number and the words "high sea."

"The *Sjogang* will be in Cyprus on the tenth of April. Tomorrow morning, transfer three hundred thousand American dollars to this number at Credit Suisse." Bovard read off a string of numbers, followed by four letters. "That's for Eric Nordeman, the captain of the *Sjogang*."

"I'll forward the money," Lynam said, entering the bank account number, and Nordeman's and the ship's names alongside the figures. "There . . . there is one thing more. Do you remember that conversation we had a few weeks ago about my . . . possible appointment?"

"Yes. Certainly."

"It may be very soon."

Bovard's voice harshened. "This cannot interfere with the Cyprus delivery."

"No, no," Lynam assured him. "It definitely will not, but I need some assistance. There are people who have become a liability."

"How much of a liability?" Bovard inquired sharply.

"I'd need to have them eliminated."

"Where are the targets?"

"Here, in San Francisco. A woman and two girls."

Bovard said, "Whores?"

Lynam winced inwardly at the blunt description. "Yes, you see—"

"Are they all at the same location?" Bovard asked.

"Yes. All in the same house."

"Then it should be simple. Call the whores. Make an appointment for tomorrow night. Say it's for a business friend of yours. Is that feasible?"

"Yes, that would certainly be possible."

"Then do it," Bovard ordered. "Call me in the morning. London morning time, Patrick. I'll have a man for you. It will be taken care of."

"You're sure you can get someone to—"

"Of course. They're as good as dead. I need your full attention on the delivery of the nuclear reactors to Cyprus eleven days from now." Bovard's voice dropped to a confidential whisper. "Your appointment. I've been thinking about it. It could be quite profitable. For both of us."

"Yes, yes, I'm sure it will be," Lynam answered solemnly.

"Your father would be proud of you, Patrick."

They said their good-byes, then Lynam fingered the remaining quarters in his coat pocket. One last time? he debated with himself. Why not?

He slotted coins into the phone and dialed a familiar number.

"Yes, can I help you?" the soft, sultry voice cooed.

He was always amazed at how young and sexy Angela sounded on the phone. How many people had been fooled by that voice? Then sickened when they saw her in person? But then, no one who called Angela was interested in her personally.

"Angela. It's Paul, August eleven."

"Ahh, Paul. We have missed you. Are you coming soon?"

"I was thinking of it. I called to let you know that I'm sending you a new client. Tomorrow. A business associate of mine."

"I will make sure he's welcomed."

"He'll use my code to identify himself." Lynam hesitated a moment, then said, "Who's with you now?"

A light giggle. "Amber and Tina are here. And . . ." She paused dramatically. "Someone new. Brand-*new*. Janna. I was hoping you would be *the* very first one to meet her. Tina and I have been instructing our new darling."

"Brand-new? You mean that she . . ."

"Absolutely," Angela Lolley assured him. "She's younger than Amber or Tina. And very, very pretty. I have someone coming later tonight, so if you want to be the first, you will have to hurry. Of course, there will be an additional fee for her services."

"How much?" he asked, trying to keep the excitement out of his voice.

"Mmmmm. Two thousand, I think." She waited for him to protest, and when he didn't, she quickly added, "And the usual five hundred for Tina and Amber. You do want them all, don't you?"

Lynam glanced at his watch. Twenty after five. There was no time to return to the bank, or the garage for his car. He'd have to use a cab or public transit. "It'll be about an hour before I get there."

"Marvelous. That will give us time to prepare. Do you have anything special you want them to wear?"

He shook the quarters in his pants pocket. "I think, I think something from school."

Angela laughed impishly. "Yes, naughty schoolgirls. Perfect. We look forward to seeing you."

He leaned against the wall, the receiver tucked under his chin, one finger holding down the phone's disconnect bar, his mind running over the possibilities of what was about to happen at Angela's, deciding it was a fitting way to end the relationship.

Chapter 4

London

Douglas Lancer leaned over the drafting table and studied the blueprints.

"Where'd you get them?" asked the nervous man fidgeting alongside him. "I couldn't have done it without those blueprints, Doug. There's a ton of pipes under that floor. I really had to wiggle my way through them."

"From the Building Inspection Department. They remodeled that wing of the hotel a year ago. Good job, Mouse," Lancer praised in the manner of a teacher bestowing accolades on his favorite student.

Denis "Mouse" Fennesy bobbed his elfin head up and down in appreciation. He was jockey-sized, barely five feet tall, with pointy features and mud-gray hair cut in monklike bangs. His arms were unusually long and leanly muscled.

Lancer often wondered if Mouse had gotten his nickname because of his appearance, or because of his expertise. Maybe it was a combination of the two: mousey looks and his ability as a "tunnel rat."

"What about the explosives?" Lancer queried.

"They've been in place for two days."

Lancer scrutinized the blueprints again, dragging his finger along the line that Mouse had highlighted in red, indicating the electrical pipes leading to the stage area of the hotel's conference room. It certainly didn't appear that there was enough room for a man to move between the maze of pipes, beams, and studs shown on the prints.

But somehow Mouse Fennesy had succeeded in molding a pound of PETN, the plastic explosive that had become a standard for terrorists worldwide, to the pipes directly under the podium.

Fennesy's stories about how he'd planted bombs for the IRA during the construction of the Chunnel leading from England to France had convinced Lancer to travel by sea or air whenever a trip between the two countries was necessary.

"Great job, Mouse," he praised. "Great job."

Fennesy grinned and wrapped his long arms around his chest, the fingertips of both hands meeting in the middle of his back. He didn't mind it when the big Australian called him Mouse. He said it like a compliment. Not like the others, who made fun of him. He watched closely as Lancer went over the blueprints. Lancer reminded him of a pirate. A Viking pirate, his skin sunburned, his long hair so blond it was almost white, his eyebrows so pale as to not be noticeable in certain light.

Fennesy lifted a scuffed briefcase onto the drafting table. He extracted a crude diagram of the conference room. He had penciled in the names of the guests in circles to signify their seating positions at the main table.

"It's a hell of a lineup, Doug," Fennesy joked, digging back into the briefcase for a brochure listing the notable attenders. "We're going to be responsible for a great many civil service job openings."

Lancer nonchalantly turned the pages of the slick brochure. There were representatives from the major intelligence services of Great Britain, France, Belgium, Germany, the Netherlands, Italy, Spain, Greece, and Israel. He hadn't paid any attention to the lot of them. The Israeli was their target. The others who would be blown to bits were a bonus.

Lancer tapped his knuckle against the circle indicating where the Israeli would be seated. "We've got to make sure he's taken out, Mouse."

"I know. I got it fixed. Even if he switches seats, he won't survive." Mouse removed his glasses and polished them with the sleeve of his baggy cardigan sweater. "The whole table will go, Doug. All of those bloody—"

The chirping of Lancer's cellular phone cut Fennesy off. Only one person had the number to the phone. His employer, Philip Bovard.

"I need someone for an assignment in San Francisco, Douglas," Bovard said over a faint wash of static.

"What kind of—"

"Elimination," Bovard replied abruptly. "I'd send you, but I want you to finish the Savoy job."

"I'll find someone. When do you—"

"Right away. Get back to me with a name."

There was a click and the buzz of a disconnected line.

Lancer slipped the tiny phone into his pocket, then turned his attention to Mouse Fennesy. "Do you know any reliable people in San Francisco? It's a wet job."

Fennesy cocked his head and looked up at the big Australian. "I do. I do, indeed. Frank Dunbar. Kill a priest for a communion wafer, Frank would."

Chapter 5

Patrick Lynam grimaced as he squeezed into the cramped confines of the pay phone. He angrily punched in the numbers for Angela Lolley's house. "This is Paul, August eleven. I left something behind last night," he said when they were connected.

"I want to apologize again," Angela Lolley said in a soft, childlike whisper. "Believe me, Janna is being punished. Your next visit will be no charge. I will make it up to you, really I will."

"Good, Angela. But I left something behind. A notebook computer. You must have found it."

"No. A notebook you say? What does it look like?"

"A wallet. A long black wallet."

"You must have left it somewhere else," Angela answered sincerely, holding the very computer in front of her face. It did resemble an oversize wallet. "Perhaps in your car?"

"No." Lynam bit down on his lower lip to keep from screaming at the old whore. "Please look. It's important to me."

"I will," Angela promised. "I will check everywhere. Your business associate called. He is coming over later this evening."

"Yes. When you find the computer, give it to him. It has to be there, Angela."

"I will look, Paul, but . . . you know, you had several

drinks last night. Perhaps you lost your item on the way home."

"Look for it, Angela. I will pay a reward for its return. A very generous one. I'll be in touch."

Angela cradled the receiver gently, then withdrew the notebook computer from its leather case. It was very expensive looking. What secrets did it hold? Certainly Paul's real name, his home address. Perhaps even a hint as to how much he was worth.

Angela had been able to access the computer's extensive address book. Whoever Paul was, he had the names, telephone numbers, and E-mail addresses for banks all over the world. And there were the mysterious initials with only addresses and numbers. Who were they? There was one E-mail—a jumble of numbers and letters that made no sense at all to her. She knew enough not to delete the E-mail, it might tip Paul off that she had the computer.

Angela had given Janna, the supposed "little genius," a chance at accessing the files she herself could not retrieve. The girl had found only an "entertainment" icon that opened up to games: poker, dominoes, chess, and an encyclopedia.

Somehow Angela couldn't picture Paul, August eleven, playing solitaire. Paul appeared to be the wealthiest of her clients. His clothes were beautifully made. A stockbroker, she guessed. Or an attorney. A very successful attorney. During prior visits, she had gone through his suit pockets, never finding a wallet or a business card. He had always been very careful, until last night. Again, no business cards—his wallet had been wrapped up and knotted inside a handkerchief. She'd been tempted to unwrap it, but feared that Paul had it tied in such a way that he would know if it had been tampered with. Then she'd found the tiny computer.

Paul was a very successful man at whatever it was that he did, but like all of her clients, a naughty little boy when his pants were down.

Paul always had a drink or two before joining the girls. Scotch. He had been furious after Janna bit him. Angela punishing the girl in front of him had calmed him down a bit. Then he had several more drinks. She made certain that Tina and Amber were especially nice to him.

He was still angry and upset when he left. Upset enough not to notice the notebook computer was missing.

Angela's stubby fingers played with the small keyboard. Her computer service was sending out a man tomorrow morning, to download everything onto her computer. Then she would do some exploring. Once she had the notebook's secrets, she could tell Paul that she'd found it, under the crib or the couch. Or, she could say that she found it in Janna's possession, and allow him to punish her. Janna had to be broken. Paul would enjoy participating in that.

She slid the computer back into its leather case. In a year, Tina would be too old to interest her clients. Amber was still young enough, but she was too passive. Without the drugs, Amber would just sit and mope. And Janna. A major disappointment. She might never respond to her training—she was the type to find a way out, to run away, to cause trouble. It was time to retire. Perhaps the information on Paul's computer was the answer. Blackmailing a rich man seemed a much easier task than coming up with a new stable of girls.

Damascus, Syria
The Pardoss Tower Hotel

Philip Bovard ran his eye around the Al-Bash restaurant dining room. He spotted Colonel Rashid Awad, the head of Mukhabarat, Syrian Military Intelligence, at the far end of the room, his table situated on a slightly raised platform, the colonel's head buried in a newspaper. Rashid was a short, heavyset man, with thick black hair, smooth skin, a cherubic face, and heavy-lidded eyes.

A uniformed soldier gave Bovard a hard look as he began weaving his way between the tables. "It's all right," Bovard assured him. "The colonel is expecting me."

The soldier turned toward Rashid, who lowered his paper and nodded permission for Bovard to proceed.

"Philip, you appear to be tired," Rashid said when Bovard settled into a chair.

"I've been busy, Colonel."

"You have the merchandise?"

"Yes. Now I need American dollars, not gold, Colonel."

Rashid jumbled up the newspaper in both hands and dropped it to the floor. He selected an apple from the table's fruit bowl and began skinning the peel off with a small, sharp-pointed knife. "There can be no mistake this time, Philip. You know how upset we were when the nerve gas was hijacked by the Mossad."

"I have the reactors, and to thank you for past favors, I'm including a special bonus."

Rashid's droopy eyelids widened. "Bonus?"

"Yes. Ira Heiser."

"You've killed the Jew?"

"Tomorrow, Colonel."

Rashid studied Bovard's features for a long moment, then his face broke out into a rare smile. "Good. Now, how about fifty percent in gold and the rest in dollars?"

Bovard sighed inwardly. Haggle. Rashid always wanted to haggle. "Our agreement was for American dollars, Colonel."

"My superiors were hoping you'd be agreeable to a compromise."

"Dollars, Colonel. I must have dollars."

Rashid dangled the long, single curling strand of apple peel in front of Bovard's face. "If you fail, I will not be able to protect you."

"I won't fail," Bovard vowed. "You will get the nuclear reactors."

Janna purposely bit down on her lower lip hard enough to draw blood. Her shoulders gave a quick jerk, as if she'd gotten a chill.

"I'm sick," she implored. "I need a doctor."

The two girls, both bigger and older than Janna, had

her bracketed. Tina, dark-haired with twin ponytails, the more domineering one, slapped Janna across the face with an open palm. "Liar! You're faking. We're having a visitor in a little while. I'm telling Angela. You're faking."

Janna blotted her lips with the back of her hand as Tina stormed from the room.

The other girl, Amber, had short blond hair worn in loose ringlets. Her hazel eyes were dull and glassy. She shook her head sadly. "You'll get Angela mad. Then we will all be in trouble."

Janna cupped her hand around Amber's elbow. "Why do you stay here?" she asked in a frightened whisper. "Why don't you run away? Help me, and I will—"

The door slapped open and the fat woman walked directly over to Janna. She had a metal ruler in one hand. The same ruler she'd used on Janna's buttocks and the bottoms of her feet after the man called Paul had left. Janna edged away, stopping only when her back made contact with the wall.

"What did you do to yourself?" Angela demanded, slapping the ruler lightly against Janna's stomach.

"I'm sick!" Janna protested, shivering uncontrollably as she folded her arms across her chest.

The woman moved the ruler up until its sharp edge was resting on Janna's chin.

"I believe that you are faking. I will not tolerate another performance like your first one. If you ever bite another of our guests, I'm going to pull out all of your teeth! Do you understand that, my little darling?"

Janna swallowed hard. "Yes. But please, I am sick. I think it's the pills you gave—"

The sound of the doorbell brought a silencing gesture from the fat woman. "All right. Tina, take Janna to the crib room." Her eyes racheted onto Janna's. "Do not make a sound, understand? When our guest has gone, I'm going to give you a thorough examination. If you are lying to me, you will be very, very sorry."

"She's faking," Tina insisted, grabbing Janna by her hair and pulling her toward a door at the rear of the room.

Janna let herself be shoved into the crib room, the walls of which were painted a pale pink. Red corduroy curtains covered the barred windows. Disney character mobiles hung from the ceiling. Dozens of red, white, and blue pillows were scattered across the red-carpeted floor and piled up three deep around the perimeter of the room. An oversized crib sat against one wall. Janna sank to the floor, sighing with relief as the door clicked shut.

Frank Dunbar could hear the locks being disengaged, then the door opened a few scant inches, still secured by a chain.

"Yes, who is it?"

Sexy voice, he thought. He could just make out an eye, a nose, a section of chin.

"It's me. I talked to you this afternoon. Paul, August eleven, called you on my behalf."

"Oh, yes. Just a moment, please."

He tried to place her accent. Russian? Polish?

The door closed and there was the scraping sound of the chain sliding loose.

The woman opened the door and stepped back into the darkness. Dunbar entered the room and quickly understood why the darkness was necessary. She was in her sixties, with a lumpish figure shrouded in a floral print dress. Her improbable red hair was a wig, and a poor one at that. Her powdered face glowed in the dim lighting.

She gave him a lopsided smile. "It's so nice to meet you. Relax, take off your hat and coat. Your friend spoke highly of you. He said you wanted to see all of my girls. Is that right?"

"Right you are, love. All three of them." He ran his eyes around the room. There was a couch, a TV, a desk with a computer and printer.

The woman stretched on her tiptoes to retrieve a red binder from a shelf above the computer. Dunbar saw the small black computer alongside the binder and smiled. This was going to be much easier than he'd thought.

"Here are some photographs of my two little darlings,

in different costumes. It may give you some ideas. I'm sorry to say that my newest darling is unavailable. Your friend had some difficulty with her. I'm afraid she needs a little more training. But I'm sure you will be delighted with the two girls I have to offer. Your friend always is."

Dunbar dropped his tweed hat on the couch, then flipped through the binder while the woman walked to the desk and sank into a plush maroon leather chair. He wasn't worried about leaving fingerprints. He was wearing a pair of his favorite "working gloves"—light tan, soft leather golfing gloves. The tannish color almost looked like flesh, and the leather was flexible. He'd switched from the disposable plastic gloves that everyone from coppers to killers were wearing, after he'd heard of a burglar who, after doing his night's work, had peeled off the gloves and dropped them on the street. The coppers had been able to pull a set of his prints from the inside of the gloves.

Angela Lolley clicked a few keys on the computer keyboard, then entered the date and time. "I will ask a few questions," she proposed. "A code name. Just a first name and a month and day, perhaps your birthday." She smiled up at him, showing a broad range of oversized teeth. "Of course it doesn't have to be your real birthday; however, make sure it is a date you will remember for your next visit."

As Angela turned her attention back to the bright blue screen, Dunbar bent down, set the binder on the floor, then reached into his jacket pockets, pulling out a gun from the right pocket, then a hollowed-out potato from the left.

He wished he'd had more time to do some proper shopping. Acquiring the gun hadn't been a problem, but he hadn't been able to locate a proper silencer. So he'd had to resort to an old IRA standby. He twisted the potato onto the six-inch barrel of the Ruger semiautomatic pistol.

"Have you decided on a name and a date?" the woman queried.

"Make it Frank, December twenty-fifth. Where are the little darlin's?"

"Ah, December twenty-fifth. A Christmas baby. Don't be hasty," she chided with a giggle. "They are in the bedroom waiting. Impatiently," she added with another giggle. She paused, her fingers perched over the keyboard. "Now, tell me just a little of what you like. Costumes, fantasies, the kind of—"

Dunbar placed the tip of the potato against her head and pulled the trigger. There was a soft squishy sound as her face banged into the computer screen.

He slipped off the splattered potato and dropped it into his pocket, then moved swiftly toward the door on the far side of the room.

He cracked the door open. The two girls were sitting together on a round, bright red vinyl ottoman. They stood up when they heard him enter. They were both wearing black patent leather shoes, short pleated skirts, and white blouses with broad Pilgrim collars. They looked as if they were dressed to make their first communion.

"Sure'n the both of ya should be ashamed of yourselves," Dunbar preached as he screwed another hollowed-out potato onto the gun's barrel.

Janna was at the door, on her knees, in the adjoining room, peering through the keyhole when the man entered the outer room. She'd wondered if he would be the same man. The man that Angela and Tina had helped touch her. Hurt her. The man they'd tried to make her do disgusting things to. Paul, Angela had called him. Paul, August eleven. Amber had told her about the reason for the month and day, but warned her never to call the men by anything but their first names, or Angela would punish her. She would never forget the look of rage on his face when she'd bitten him.

She'd been relieved, yet frightened when she saw the man in the blue jacket. He was not the same man. Not silver-haired. This man was taller, with long sideburns, scraggly brown hair, and a big red nose.

Janna gasped as she realized he was holding a gun. Her scream was masked by those of Tina and Amber.

The man raised his arm and slipped something onto the barrel of the gun. There was a coughing sound, then Tina stiffened and dropped to the floor. She landed on her back and Janna could see a mushroom of red blood on her starched white blouse.

Amber was screaming, her hands cupped over her ears. She was running toward the door! Toward her! Janna held the knob tightly in both hands. The man again slipped something onto the gun. Janna recognized it now. A potato. He shot Amber in the back. Amber stumbled to her knees, and began crawling. Janna watched in horror, her hands frozen on the doorknob as the man calmly strode over to Amber, screwed anther potato onto his gun barrel, jammed it in the back of Amber's head, and once again pulled the trigger.

There was another muffled explosion and Amber's arms jerked outward, her face smashed into the floor.

The man stood motionless for a few seconds, then swept the obscene barrel of the gun around the room, as if searching for another target.

Janna crept backward. He was coming for her! She could hear his footsteps. She looked around for a hiding place. The closet was too far away. She sprinted over to a corner of the room and burrowed herself under a pile of the oversized red, white, and blue pillows.

She took a deep breath as she heard the click of the knob, then the creaking sound of the door swinging open.

Chapter 6

Maureen Connah was waiting out on the sidewalk when Kordic drove up to her apartment house.

"It looks like we've got a messy one," Kordic said once she was settled into the passenger's seat.

Maureen looked over her shoulder at the suitcase in the backseat. "Are you sure you're going to have time to get to the airport?"

Kordic glanced at his watch and nodded. "Yeah. Lots of time. My flight doesn't take off until ten after midnight."

"Communications told me it's a triple," she said, rolling the window up to shut out the cold night air.

"Yes. An older woman and two kids. Fifty-four Tara Street."

"Tara? Like in *Gone with the Wind?*"

Kordic gave a grim smile. "Yep. Right out of Scarlett O'Hara's plantation."

"Where the hell is Tara Street?"

Kordic slowed down momentarily for a red light, gunning the motor when he saw no cross traffic. Sunset Boulevard was deserted. The bordering cypress trees were filigreed by an opalescent fog. "The Ingleside District. Off Ocean Avenue, by the Balboa Park BART transit station."

"Any ID on the victims, Jack?"

"No. An anonymous caller dialed 911 from the BART station. All he said was that there'd been a murder at Fifty-four Tara." He frowned at Connah. "I hate to leave this in your lap while I'm out of town."

"I'll be okay," Maureen answered with more confidence

than she really felt. "You're only going to be away for a few days."

Kordic frowned. The Homicide detail had been under-staffed for some time. Half the personnel was assigned to assist an FBI task force investigating the murder of a prominent local attorney with ties to a ruthless Vietnam-ese gang who were in a war with the old-established Chinatown mob. The lieutenant's spot was vacant, the last occupant off on disability leave and not expected to return. One of the inspectors, Ray Tracey, was the acting lieutenant. "I can ask Tracey to have someone give you a hand," Kordic offered.

"If I need help, I'll ask, Jack."

Kordic took a left on Ocean Avenue, driving past rows of well-kept homes, then crossed Nineteenth Avenue, speeding through a business district where every other shop had its windows covered with raw sheets of plywood.

Connah was glad Kordic was driving. This part of San Francisco was as unfamiliar to her as Berlin.

"Here we are," Kordic announced as they approached an intersection blocked by two radio cars, their red lights circling endlessly in the misty fog.

54 Tara was a bay-windowed single-family residence typical of the area. Built in the thirties, when a single car garage seemed more than adequate, since not many people owned even that one car.

Now the street was jammed with vehicles, some parked on the sidewalk, straddling runt gardens. Most were in a state of disrepair: shattered windows, missing fenders, bumpers, or doors.

Kordic hustled over to one of the radio cars, leaning down to talk to the driver through the open window.

Maureen started for the front steps. A uniformed motor-cycle officer, his leathers slick and gleaming from the drizzle, called out to her.

"Hey, lady, get out of there, you ain't—"

"I ain't no lady," Connah flared, pulling her badge from her shapeless black parka.

"Sorry. No offense," the officer countered with outstretched arms.

The front steps were speckled terrazzo, the centers worn down to crescents from years of use. The front door stood ajar, emitting a slice of light. A crime-lab technician in hospital-white coveralls was dusting the door for prints.

As they pounded up the steps, Kordic handed Maureen a pair of rubber gloves. Another technician was vacuuming the area around the desk.

Maureen purposely stood back and took mental notes as she watched Kordic communicate with the technicians and the uniformed officers. She liked the way he handled himself: his voice was full of confidence and authority, and he called almost everyone by their first name, adding a personal comment or small joke, the way people whose jobs bring them into constant contact with dead bodies do, to ease the tension.

One of the victims was lying on the rug in the front room. A woman. Her jaw hanging open, her eyes wide, almost bursting from their sockets. Her throat was a coagulated mass of jellied blood.

"Well, I'll be damned," Maureen said, louder than she'd meant to, when she got a closer look at the corpse.

She felt Kordic's hand on her shoulder. "You know the victim?" he queried.

"She's an old madam. Her name is Angela Lolley. 'Lollipop' is what she was called. She specialized in young kids."

A uniformed sergeant approached them. He took off his hat and wiped his forehead with the back of his hand. "There are two more victims in the next room. The oldest looks like she couldn't be more than thirteen or fourteen, Jack."

Kordic nodded his thanks. "We'll be right there."

He turned his attention back to Connah. "Where did you know her from, Mo?"

"We had Lolley in a few times, when I worked Vice. She was scum, Jack. Real scum. I mean she ran kids. Boys, girls, it didn't much matter to her. Or to her customers. God, it broke my heart to see those poor kids. They were scared to death."

"Did you ever bust her?"

Maureen shrugged her shoulders in disgust. "We were never able to arrest her, though we sure as hell tried. Lolley was clever. She came on like a sweet little old lady, all smiles and giggles. The kids were usually illegals. So were their parents. They never wanted to press charges, or they had left the country. The kids had nowhere to go. No one to turn to. And we never did get to any of her johns." She flicked her eyes around the room. "It'd be nice to find her john list."

Kordic motioned to the desk. "I'm afraid we may be out of luck there. A computer screen, but the computer base is missing. The killer took it with him. Come on, let's look at the other victims."

A crime-lab technician delayed their journey. He waved two plastic bags at Kordic.

"We found these in the master bedroom, Inspector. Next to a section of the floor that had been cut out."

Kordic examined the largest bag, which contained a gray rectangular metal box, approximately two feet long, half that in height.

"It was empty," the technician explained. "These were lying on the floor right alongside it."

Kordic reached for the second bag. He held it up to the light.

"Computer disks," Maureen said with obvious excitement. "Let's hope they have Lollipop's john list on them."

Kordic twisted the bag around. There were three disks, three and a half inches square: one each in red, blue, yellow, along with four one-hundred-dollar bills and a leather case. He smoothed the plastic bag around the case to get a better look at it. "There's an inscription. HV2500. What the hell is that?"

Maureen peered into the bag. "HV. Probably Helmut-Victor, the computer manufacturer."

"Show me just where you found these," Kordic instructed the technician.

Both Kordic and Maureen dropped to their knees to examine the cutout in the bedroom floor.

Maureen said, "I bet there was a lot of money in this box, Jack."

"Right. But something doesn't make sense here. The leather case held some kind of small computer. The killer strips the case off. A few of the bills fall to the floor. He's in a hurry, so he leaves them behind, too. But the disks. Why would the killer take all of Angela's computer stuff and leave the disks behind?"

It was a little after eleven by the time Maureen Connah dropped Kordic off at the airport for his London flight.

"Thanks for the ride, Maureen. I appreciate it," Kordic said, yanking his suitcase from the back of the unmarked police car.

"Have a good trip, Jack."

"Will do." Kordic hesitated a moment, then leaned down so his head was level with Connah's. "Maybe you should talk to Ray Tracey and—"

"I can handle it," Maureen insisted. "I know how Lollipop operated better than anyone in the detail, Jack. I'll handle it."

"Okay, keep me posted." He patted his coat pockets. "Did I give you my itinerary?"

"Yeah, I've got it. Relax, enjoy the grip. The medical examiner's report should be in by the morning. And I'll get the lab working on those disks right away. I'll call you at the hotel in London." She leaned across the bench seat and gave him a smile. "And do some shopping?"

"See you in a few days," Kordic responded with a weary grin, then hoisted up his luggage and disappeared into the airport terminal.

Janna Drovana squeezed the red leather purse between her legs when she saw the waitress clearing the dishes from a table nearby.

The bag was stuffed with money. More money than Janna had been able to count. And the small computer. Paul, the man who had hurt her, his computer.

She couldn't get what had happened out of her mind. It

had been so frightening. The man with the gun had come into the crib room, he even kicked at the pile of pillows she'd been hiding under, then he tore through the closet. She heard him tramping from room to room. Heard him curse. Even after she'd heard the front door slam shut, she remained under the pillows frozen in fear, finally crawling free, like a soldier leaving a trench in the battlefield.

A battlefield is what the house resembled. Tina, Amber, and Angela, all dead. Janna said a quick prayer for Amber, but not for the other two, then she undressed, throwing her blouse and skirt over Amber's bloody head. She found her old clothes in the closet, the ones she'd been wearing the day she'd met Angela in Golden Gate Park. Her slender body shivered uncontrollably as she dressed.

She realized she had to get out of the house. The police could arrive at any moment. Or the man with the gun might return.

The police would either send her back to Russia, put her in prison, or turn her over to Cousin Yuri.

Her days and nights of hiding in the park, after she'd run away from Cousin Yuri, had made it clear to her that she needed money to exist.

She located Angela's purse in her bedroom. The wallet held only a handful of change. She pocketed the coins and looked wildly around the room.

Drawers were gaping open. Clothes had been dragged from the closet and dropped onto the bed, along with a tangled pile of Angela's jewelry. She was tempted to grab a handful of the jewelry, but decided not to. Was it real? Even if it was, who could she sell it to?

She started for the front door, stopping in midstride, remembering the day she'd woken up in the house. Cousin Yuri had been demanding money. Angela kicking Yuri out of the room, then digging a metal box out from beneath the floorboards in her bedroom. Maybe there was still some money hidden in the box.

She dropped to her knees, her hands exploring the hardwood until she found the small open crack in the wood. She wormed a fingernail in the crack and wriggled the boards free. The metal box was still hidden there. It was much like the box a fisherman keeps his tackle in. She opened the lid and let out a loud gasp.

Paul's computer sat on a stack of bills. Piles and piles of money, some loose, others bundled together with rubber bands. She tossed the computer on the bed, then ran to the closet. There were several pieces of luggage strewn on the floor. She grabbed a large leather purse, stretched it wide open, and upended the metal box.

At the bottom of the metal box were three brightly colored plastic computer disks: red, yellow, and blue. She fingered them curiously, hesitated a moment, then dropped them to the floor. At the last moment she reached back for the computer, sliding it from its case, letting the case fall to the floor. Angela had been so excited about the computer, as if it were worth a lot of money. She stuffed the computer in the purse, then raced from the room, pausing only to take a final look at Angela, careful not to step in the puddle that had formed near the body.

Her stomach and throat constricted when she noticed that Angela's ring fingers had been cut off.

"Are you all right, honey? You're not going to be sick, are you?"

The voice startled Janna. She started to jump to her feet, then she realized it was only the waitress.

"I . . . I'm fine. Some more hot chocolate please."

The waitress, a narrow-faced woman of fifty with crisp black hair, leaned over the table. "Are you waiting for someone, honey? It's awful late for you to be—"

"My mother will be here shortly," Janna responded quickly. "And pie. A piece of apple pie, please."

The waitress hesitated a moment. "Okay. But in case your mother doesn't show up, are you sure you've got enough money to pay for everything?"

"Oh, yes," Janna assured her, squeezing the purse between her legs. "I have more than enough."

Chapter 7

April 2

Maureen Connah was back at 54 Tara Street early the following morning. She had mixed emotions about Jack Kordic taking off for London and leaving her on her own. In the short time she'd been working with Kordic, she'd already grown to respect him: his low-key manner, his obvious street smarts.

Still, it felt good to be on her own. With no one looking over her shoulder.

The bright morning sunlight hammered the rusting roofs of the abandoned cars.

The neighborhood was even more depressing in the daylight: the sidewalks were cracked, the cracks choked with weeds. A chain of graffiti ran around the walls of the two neighboring houses, one of which was fronted by an armoring of wear-stained shingles, the other with crinkled aluminum foil blanketing the windows.

Squadrons of flies dive-bombed at an open garbage can leaning against the garage door of Angela Lolley's house.

Maureen could understand why Lollipop had chosen this location. Tara Street bordered the 280 freeway. Her customers only had to drive a half block to gain access to the freeway approaches for the Peninsula or San Francisco. Or they could use public transportation: There was a bus stop across from the BART station, although Maureen couldn't imagine the type of client that would be attracted to Lollypop's house of evil stooping to use a Mini bus. They could easily hop on a BART train and in a few min-

utes be in downtown San Francisco, or a slightly longer
trip would take them under the bay waters, over to the
East Bay.

Maureen stooped to pick up a newspaper lying on the
front steps. *The Wall Street Journal.* There were neatly bundled stacks of the newspaper in Lolley's basement, along
with past copies of *Forbes, Fortune,* and *Money* magazine.
Lolley's reading materials had leaned heavily toward financial publications. Maureen limboed under the banner
of yellow crime-scene tape stretched across the front steps,
fingering the keys she'd found in Lollipop's purse. Two
keys only. One to the front door, the other to her car,
which was parked in the garage, a sparkling new mint-
green Lexus with less than four thousand miles on the
odometer.

Maureen pushed the door open and stood motionless
for a moment, trying to imagine the killer's entrance.
There was no sign of damage to the door, so he'd been
expected. A customer. Welcome, welcome.

Angela Lolley had been shot while sitting at her desk,
directly in front of the spot where the computer had been
stationed. So, she let the killer in, then sat down to enter
information into the computer.

Did she record each of the johns' visits? Did she enter
the date, time, price, and sexual preferences each time a
john showed up? Surely she collected the money before
she sent the pervert into the room with the girls.

Was he a new customer? Someone she had to log on?

Maureen and Kordic had gone through the desk and
adjoining bookcases the night of the murders. They'd
found nothing there relating to the computer except its
disconnected screen. No printer, keyboard, no documents
of any kind, not even an operating manual. Everything
gone, and yet the three disks were left on the floor in the
bedroom. Jack was right. It made no sense.

Maureen walked around the chalk outline of Angela
Lolley's body. The black-gray tweed rug was still saturated with the old madam's blood. She'd taken one shot

to the back of the head. So she had trusted her john, right up to the end.

The killer then dragged the body away from the desk. Why? To get the computer. Or was there something else on the desk that had interested him?

The evidence pointed to Angela Lolley being shot first. The two girls were fully clothed when they were killed. Maureen hadn't seen the autopsies yet, but she was willing to bet that they hadn't been sexually assaulted before they died. The sequence seemed obvious. After shooting Lolley, he'd made his way to the bedroom and killed the dark-haired girl first. She was the tallest, and also appeared to be the oldest of the two. She'd taken a bullet right in the chest. The blond girl had started to run and the killer had to shoot her in the back, then he'd finished her off with a coup de grâce to the head. The blond girl's head was draped with a blouse and skirt. Why would he bother to go to the closet and get the skirt and blouse? Why cover the one girl and not the other? Did the blond victim have a personal connection to the killer? Was she the main target, and the others killed simply because they were there? Could the killer be a relative? Her father, who found out what she was doing—then want on a killing spree?

Unlikely, Mo decided, but certainly not out of the realm of possibilities.

Maureen entered the bedroom where the two girls had been killed, her attention first drawn to the chalked outlines of their small bodies on the scuffed white-and-black checkered linoleum floor. The walls were padded with mattresses that had been overlaid with strips of black imitation leather, fastened at the seams with black electrical tape.

Half the ceiling was mirrored, the other half was festooned with an assortment of eye bolts from which hung bars and ropes, like a trapeze setup at a circus.

Maureen used her foot to nudge open the door that led to the next room. Dozens of red, white, and blue pillows were strewn around the red-carpeted floor. The walls were pink, the ceiling papered with bright red, gold, and blue flowers that had loopy-winged butterflies perched on their petals.

The furniture was painted white: a pint-sized table and chairs. The table was littered with comics and coloring books. A white coffee mug that still held several crayons had been knocked off the table, the rest of the crayons lay scattered across the floor.

An oversized crib stood against one wall. A mobile of Disney characters dangled from the ceiling directly over the crib. Next to the crib was a child's portable toilet.

A closet with mirrored sliding doors extended across one wall. Again Maureen used her foot to nudge the closet door open, hesitant to touch anything—not because of the possibility of leaving prints, the crime lab had finished with that aspect of the investigation—but reluctant to come into physical contact with anything in the room until she had to.

She moaned out loud. It was time. She had to.

She started with the closet, going through the clothing: young girls' dresses and slips. Then there were the undergarments—training bras, push-up bras, crotchless panties. Shoes ranging from patent leather Mary Janes to thigh-high leather boots. And all in sizes that she herself had outgrown by the time she was ten.

Lollipop's bedroom was next. Maureen stood with her hands crossed over her chest and surveyed the results of what money and bad taste had accomplished. It looked as if it didn't belong in the same house: gilt-trimmed wall panels, a pair of circular-shaped, silvery-white, deep-pile throw rugs. A brass four-poster bed canopied by gauzy material the color of a rain cloud squatted in the center of the room.

Crammed against the east wall was a sofa done entirely in leopard skin. Two chairs bracketed the sofa, the wood carved in a woven pattern that resembled snake skin. The seats were covered with more of the leopard skin.

A floor-to-ceiling armoire of burlwood with mother-of-pearl inlays and a matching dresser commanded the remaining space. The cutout section of hardwood floor was lying next to the now empty hole. The crime lab had taken the metal box and the computer disks that had been hidden there.

How had the killer known about the metal box? Had he tortured Lollipop before he killed her? Made her tell him where her stash was hidden. Was that the reason for the amputation of her fingers? Or had he simply cut them off to get at her rings?

Maureen closed her eyes and concentrated on the image of Angela Lolley. She'd seen her what? Three, maybe four times when she'd worked Vice. One of the first things she'd noticed was Lolley's jewelry. Her rings in particular. Big, gaudy. Maureen had joked to her lieutenant about them being junk, cubic zirconium, but no, he'd assured her that they were the real thing. Diamonds. The old madam treated herself royally with the money she made from the luckless kids she lured into her house of perversion.

The crime lab had dumped the contents of the closet and dresser drawers onto the bed. Dresses, fur coats, slacks, cashmere sweaters, dozens of expensive Italian shoes. A small rosewood jewelry case lay open and empty. There was a foot-high pile of glittering costume jewelry: bracelets, rings, and necklaces, looking like the booty from a movie pirate ship's chest.

The killer had known the real thing. He'd hacked off Lolley's fingers to get her expensive rings, and had taken whatever of value was in the rosewood case. She grabbed the bedspread by one end and yanked hard, sending the jewelry flying through the air.

The buzzing of her pager interrupted her thoughts. She unhooked it from her belt, immediately recognizing the numbers popping up on the display screen: the crime lab.

Maureen kicked her way through the debris on the floor and grabbed the phone on the bed stand, grateful to hear the dial tone.

"This is Inspector Connah," she said after being connected.

"Oh, yeah, Inspector. Al Balardi. Hang on. I've got something for you."

Maureen could hear the rustling of papers, then the phone being picked up.

"Here we go," Balardi said. "Those homicides on Tara Street, they're your package, right?"

"Right. What have you got?"

"Well, so far we've got thirty-six unidentified sets or partials. I ran everything through our AFIS and sent them to the FBI. It'll take a couple of days for the FBI results to come through. The only matchups we came up with are for the woman, Angela Lolley, and the two young victims. Unfortunately, we didn't get anything on the kids when we ran them through the computer."

Connah groaned out loud. AFIS, the automatic fingerprint identification system, was the department's crown jewel. She'd been hoping for a positive ID on at least one of the young victims. An ID that would lead to their parents or guardians. Or sadly, perhaps to their former pimps.

"So you got nothing," Maureen said, not bothering to disguise her disappointment.

"No, I've got something," Balardi corrected. "The metal box and the computer disks. Lolley's prints were all over them, and so was someone else's. I was able to pull a full palm print and four fingers of the left hand from the box."

Connah said, "Great. The killer's. But you weren't able to get a hit with them, right?"

"Right," Balardi conceded. "But I'm not so sure they're the killers. I can tell you this. The prints belong to a kid. Either a kid or a midget."

The back of Maureen's neck went cold. "How old a kid are you talking about?"

"No way to tell for sure. When I first saw them, I figured they would match up with one of the two young victims: same general size. If it was just the fingerprints, I wouldn't be so positive. But the palm print, that's a kid's, no doubt about it, so it looks like there was a third kid in the house.

"I did find these same prints in the room where the two girls were killed, in the adjoining room and the bathrooms and also in the Lexus in the basement."

"Nowhere else?" Connah pressed. "How about in the office? Or on those circus setups hanging from the ceiling?"

Balardi's voice turned frosty. "Listen, Inspector. I have two girls of my own, ten and twelve years old. I went over that house millimeter by millimeter. Those prints show up on the metal box, in the room with the dead girls' bodies, the room with the crib, both bathrooms, and on the interior window of the rear, right side passenger door of the Lexus in the basement. Nowhere else. The frequency patterns tell me that victim number one, Angela Lolley, had been in the house the longest period of time, her prints are everywhere. Victim number two, the young brunette, also has mega-multiple pattern prints, so she was there for some time; the third victim, the young blond, also had multiple prints, but not nearly as many as victim number two. My guess is the small set of prints on the metal box belong to a kid, and that she, or he, was in the house for a very short time."

"How short a time?" Maureen asked.

"It's impossible to say for sure, but my guess is not more than a few days."

"How about the printouts from these computer disks? When can I have them?"

Balardi sighed. "I sent them out to a private agency. They should be back this afternoon." He sighed again. "I'm doing the beset I can, Inspector. We're swamped."

"I know," Maureen responded sincerely. The last thing she wanted to do was make an enemy in the crime lab. "And I appreciate it, Al. I really do."

Chapter 8

London

Jack Kordic was hurrying across the plush lobby of the Savoy Hotel, a shopping bag in tow, his new raincoat draped over one shoulder, when he heard a familiar voice inquire: "New suit?"

Kordic wheeled around, grinning when he spotted the sardonic expression on the face of the Israeli Mossad agent Anatoly Weeks.

"Anatoly, what the hell are you doing here?" Kordic beamed. "Have they come to their senses and decided to give the award to you instead of me?"

Weeks pressed his lips into a kiss of disapproval. "Thank God, no. You take the glory. I'll stay in the background."

Kordic stepped back to get a better look at his friend.

Weeks had taken a bullet in his left shoulder during those last frantic minutes before Kordic had killed the terrorist Rene Santos. The intelligence agent didn't look much the worse for wear: a full crop of steel-wool hair, his skin tanned the color of tree bark. It wasn't until Weeks walked closer that Kordic noticed that his left arm hung straight down, motionless along his side.

"You're looking good, Anatoly. How's the arm?"

Weeks gave an unintelligible grunt, then reached over and ran a thumb and forefinger along the lapel of Kordic's dark blue suit jacket. "Not bad. You've been doing some shopping, huh?"

"Yes," Kordic laughed. "Orders from my partner."

"Are you and that attorney, Mary Ariza, still seeing each other?" Weeks asked.

"No," Kordic said, frowning. Ariza had been the first woman that Kordic had had any interest in after his son's and wife's tragic deaths. They had dated for some time after Rene Santos was killed. For a while Kordic had hopes that their relationship would lead to something permanent, but the trauma Mary had gone through—the attempts on her life, a co-worker being murdered, her boss's wife taking a bullet that had been meant for her—had left scars, scars that never completely healed.

"She's moved down to San Diego. We still talk, but . . ."

Weeks shrugged his good shoulder. "Hey, a cop and an attorney. That's a tough combo. I hope you're not going to give a long, boring speech at the banquet tonight."

"You'll be there?"

"Why not?"

Kordic flexed his arm and looked at his watch. "How about a drink?"

"Absolutely," Weeks accepted. "Let's go to the Grill."

Weeks led Kordic around the High Tea in the Thaymes Foyer, with its tailcoated waiters and tuxedoed pianist, who was playing a soft Cole Porter medley, then into the renowned, yew-paneled Savoy Grill.

There was a line of impatient diners waiting to be seated. The maître d' greeted Weeks with a raised eyebrow.

Kordic wasn't sure what the Mossad agent whispered into the man's ear, but whatever it was, it got his immediate attention. They were quickly escorted to a corner table.

When they were seated, and had their drinks in hand, Weeks took an appreciative sip of the vodka martini, then said, "I've got something that's connected to your neck of the woods, San Francisco, Jack. Does the name Philip Bovard ring any bells?"

Kordic sampled his beer before responding. "Bovard. No, should it?"

"Probably not. He's ex-Swiss Intelligence."

"Switzerland has an intelligence service?" Kordic asked, grinning a little.

"Indeed. Two of them actually: a very efficient military unit, and their banks. You Americans seem to think that the Swiss do nothing but speak French, make clocks, and climb mountains. German is the preferred language. Their army has six hundred and fifty thousand troops—ten percent of the population. Civilians who spend one day out of every ten in uniform. They march around the Alps with top-flight American weapons at the ready. The bankers handle most of the intelligence work—when they're doing their army time and when they're back behind their desks at Credit Suisse, the Bank of Switzerland, and a handful of very private, very influential banks. That's where the real work gets done. Those bankers have access to stuff your CIA and FBI would kill to get their hands on." Weeks gave a wolfish smile, then added, "Us, too. They do their own recruiting. Friends recommend friends, who recommend friends. It's run like an English gentleman's club. Only these guys ain't no gentlemen. Bovard wasn't a banker, he just worked for them as a *kammerjager*. A vermin killer."

"Vermin killer? What kind of vermin?"

"Jews. Jews with money. A few old Nazis, too, probably. Those who stuffed away stolen money, gold, works of art, in the Swiss vaults during the war."

"You're talking about World War II?" Kordic asked.

"Sure, sure. Those stories you're reading about now, the claims for the millions of dollars of gold, jewels, artwork, that's nothing. The poor schmucks with the really big stuff were taken care of over the last fifteen, twenty years by bastards like Bovard. *Gamein Behandeln.* The dirty duty. Eliminate them before they had any chance of making a claim on their holdings. Everything neat and tidy.

"Bovard left Switzerland about ten years ago. He now describes himself as an import-export consultant."

Weeks leaned across the table. "Did you read about the plant at Hamerling Industries in Germany blowing up last year? They're the outfit that had been shipping weapons to the Iranians."

Kordic shifted uncomfortably in his chair. "Yes. The spin the newspapers gave us was that your people may have been involved."

"We weren't," Weeks responded angrily. "But you're right. The papers did spin it that way. Because there was evidence planted that made it look like we were dirty. What wasn't in the papers was that there were several cases of canisters of Sarin taken from the plant before the explosion." He saw the puzzled look on Kordic's face. "Sarin is a nerve gas used in chemical warfare. Colorless, odorless, extremely volatile. We were able to track it down before it got to its destination, Libya." He took another sip of his drink. "That's ancient history. Eight days ago, on March twenty-fifth, Bovard was in Moscow. He dropped a bundle of cash, over sixty thousand at a casino, the one that's owned by the American actor. What's his name? The little guy that karate kicks everyone?"

"You got me," Kordic said.

"Norris. Chuck Norris. He owns the biggest operation in Moscow. The Beverly Hills Casino. Plush joint. You have to have an invitation to get in."

Kordic shook his head in disbelief at the thought of an American action actor operating a casino in Russia.

"Anyway," Weeks continued, "the next day, Bovard leaves Moscow. He journeys north, to Murmansk, on the Barents Sea, where the Russians have mothballed all their nuclear subs, then flies back to Moscow.

"The nuclear reactors are supposed to be taken from the subs, then shipped by train to Mayak, in Siberia. Probably the most dangerous place on earth, Mayak. They've got all kinds of nuclear waste piling up there. They were expecting a shipment of thirty submarine reactors this week. Only twenty-six showed up."

"And you think this Bovard character has the missing four?" Kordic asked skeptically.

"Yes. We do."

"I'm not really up on nuclear reactors," Kordic admitted. "Just how serious is this?"

"Lethal. The Russians' much more so than the ones used on your subs. Each liquid metal reactor holds fifteen hundred kilograms of highly enriched uranium. Ninety-seven point three percent enrichment, to be exact. Commercial reactors are enriched to only four or five percent, so you can see that these babies are potent. In August of 1995 a Victor I class sub was docked in the Chazma Bay naval yard near Vladivostok. The reactor went critical during refueling and contaminated six squares miles on the Shotovto Peninsula. Close to a thousand people were killed." Weeks took a black-and-white photograph from his pocket and passed it to Kordic. "That's Bovard. Unfortunately, outside of Mossad, no one else is paying him any attention."

Kordic examined the grainy photograph. A harsh-featured middle-aged man caught walking down a crowded street, his head glowering in the direction of the camera. There was nothing remarkable about him.

"What about the CIA? NATO?" Kordic asked.

"They all think that Mossad is like the little boy who cried wolf once too often, Jack. Bovard's a very careful *momzer*. He's got an office on Old Broad Street, near the London Stock Exchange. We've wired in his private office line. Calls come in, but no real names are given, just short, cryptic messages, asking Bovard to contact them. The telephone numbers left are always to a pay phone."

"Anatoly, this is all fascinating, but what's the connection to San Francisco?"

"Four days ago someone—male, middle-aged, American accent—called from a laundromat on Larkin Street in San Francisco." Weeks pulled an ordinary-looking ballpoint pen from his coat pocket. "Get a load of this," he said, then clicked the pen three times and handed it to Kordic.

Kordic listened to the recorded message: "It's Old Friend. I'm at 415 555-4210."

"The voice means nothing to me, Anatoly," Kordic said, admiring the pen. "But I like this gadget."

"Not bad, huh? Just rotate the top portion and the recording device is activated. You can even write with it while you're taping something. We didn't have time to put a tap on that telephone line, but we did find out that it's a public phone in the laundromat. Two days later, March thirty-first, another call came in. Just click the pen," Weeks instructed.

Kordic clicked the pen and the miniature tape recorder activated: "This is Old Friend. I'm at 415 555–9995."

Kordic said, "It's the same voice."

"Right. Another laundromat. This one's in San Francisco too. On Chestnut Street. You know why he uses laundromats, Jack?"

"I haven't a clue," Kordic admitted.

"Coin machines. He loaded up on quarters to pay for the international calls. He's a very careful man. Over the past month, 'Old Friend' has called Bovard nine times, and always from some Frisco laundromat."

Kordic handed the pen back to Weeks. "I can check out these places when I get back, but I don't think it'll do much good."

"Neither do I," Weeks confirmed. His eyebrows knitted. "So, tell me, how does it feel to be a hero?"

"Believe me, I wanted nothing to do with this," Kordic assured him. "The new mayor is a publicity hound. He ordered the chief to send me. So here I am."

Weeks rolled the olive around in his glass. "Are you doing any real police work, Jack?"

"Some," Kordic sighed. "Nothing as exotic as what you're used to. My partner called me with the preliminary results from the medical examiner on a new homicide case. The victims were a madam and two girls in their early teens."

"There's a lot of that going around," Weeks granted glumly. "You were solo the last time I was in San Francisco. Who's your partner?"

"Maureen Connah. She's new."

"What else is she?" Weeks asked.

"Young, gorgeous, ambitious."

"Married?"

"Nope. Not at the moment."

"She sounds interesting, Jack. Tell me about the case."

"Here's a twist, something I've never run into. They found bits of solanum tuberson, plain old raw potato, in all three of the victims' bullet wounds."

"Tell me more," Weeks said, leaning back and listening with his eyes half-closed.

Kordic relayed everything that Maureen Connah had learned from the medical report, and all that he knew about the victims.

"Angela Lolley. Lollipop," Weeks snorted. "Ain't that cute. The potato's nothing new, Jack. An 'Irish silencer.' The IRA used them all the time before they got the real thing from Qaddafi and those other *shtarkers*."

Kordic had picked up quite a bit of Yiddish slang from Weeks while they worked together chasing after Rene Santos. He knew *momzer* was bastard, but this was a new one to him.

"*Shtarker*, a strong man, a big shot," Weeks explained. "Did the killer leave a mess? Cartridge casings? The potatoes?"

"No, he swept everything up real well. I wouldn't have known about the potatoes if it wasn't for the autopsies."

Weeks rubbed the tips of his fingers across his thumb. "Then he came prepared. You said what? Four shots fired? That means four potatoes. Each one would have to have been carefully hollowed out, to fit the gun barrel. Curious. He's a pro, but he doesn't have a silencer for his gun, so he comes with a pocketful of potatoes. What do you know about the kids that were killed?"

"Not much," Kordic admitted. "Both were Caucasian, one dark, the other light-skinned and blond. The killer took the madam's computer base, the printer, and all its paraphernalia. We found a metal box that had been hidden in the bedroom floor. It was empty, but there were three computer disks lying alongside it, you know, the kind you use to make backups of the hard drive. I don't know yet what was on the disks, but I'm hoping it's the madam's john list."

Weeks drained what remained of his drink and signaled to a waiter for a refill. "You've got a pretty big Irish community in San Francisco, don't you?"

"Sure."

"Well, look for a Harp hitman. Someone from the old sod. The potatoes. That's definitely one of their trademarks. And the one-shot kills on the woman and the one kid, then the coup de grâce to the second kid. Sounds like a real pro to me. You ready for a refill?"

Kordic picked up his half-finished glass of dark beer. The butterflies were already dancing in his stomach in anticipation of his giving an acceptance speech at the banquet.

"Why not? Are you going to be at the head table tonight?"

"No. I'll be way in the back. My boss, Ira Heiser, will be presenting you with your award. Just do me a couple of favors, Jack. Don't mention my name in your speech, and don't spill any wine on Heiser, okay?"

Chapter 9

Janna Drovana had spent the night searching for a safe place to sleep, finally curling up on a layer of newspapers on the ground near the rear exit of a restaurant with the curious name of House of Pancakes.

Later, she had boarded a bus, not knowing where it would take her, grateful for the somewhat soft padding on the bus seats, and dozed off, until the bus driver rudely shook her awake.

"End of the line, kid. Get off the bus," he ordered.

Janna found herself in downtown San Francisco. The angry bay waters crashed into the sea wall. She found herself at a depot where large white ferry boats dropped off passengers. There were newspapers scattered on the floor and benches. She dug through the papers and found a photograph of Angela's house. There was a short article under the photo.

> The bodies of Angela Lolley and two young unidentified girls were found shot to death in a house in the Ingleside District. Inspector Maureen Connah of the Homicide detail stated that Lolley had a record for prostitution.
>
> Anyone with information regarding the two unidentified girls should contact Connah at 555-1361.

Janna reread the article several times. Should she call the police? Give them Amber's and Tina's names?

Cousin Yuri had often warned her to stay away from the police. If they learned she was here illegally, she'd be thrown in prison. Raped. Used by the prison guards and not set free until she was old and ugly. Janna had tried to talk Amber into running away from Angela's house, but Amber had been frightened of the police, too. She debated with herself for several minutes, then went to a pay telephone, carefully reading the instructions before dropping coins into the slot.

Charlotte, the Homicide detail secretary, hurried over to Maureen Connah's desk. "There's a call on line four. It's about the Tara Street killings. A young girl. She sounds scared as hell."

Maureen grabbed the phone with one hand and activated the tape recorder with the other. "Hello, this is Inspector Connah."

"Have you found the killer yet?"

Maureen lowered her voice. The girl did sound frightened. "No. Can you help us?"

"The girls' names are Tina and Amber."

"Which was which. One had dark hair, and—"

"Tina. Amber was blond. I do not know their last names.'

"Thank you for calling. That helps a lot. What's your name?"

"Good-bye."

"No, wait," Mo pleaded. "I need your help. Don't be afraid, please, I want—"

There was a click, then the droning of a dead line.

"Shit!" Mo swore, slamming the receiver down.

Inspector Dave Grandanos, the office romeo, winced and raised his eyes. "Having a bad day, kid?"

She gave Grandanos a look that caused him to decide to wait for another time to ask her out for a drink after work.

Maureen leaned her elbow on the desk and buried her hands in her hair. Damn. She'd scared the kid off. She should have waited and got some more information before asking for her name. At least she'd gotten the names of the two dead girls. Amber and Tina. Did that third set of small fingerprints belong to the caller? If so, she may have draped the blouse over the blonde's bloody head. How the hell had she avoided the killer? And where was she now? Somewhere out on the streets. Alone. And scared to death from the sound of her voice.

Maureen said a short, informal prayer. Come on, God. Make her call again. Give me another chance with the kid.

Janna stared at the telephone. The policewoman had sounded friendly. Maybe she should call her back and give her a description of the killer. It was important to catch him. He'd kicked at the pillows where she was hiding. She'd gotten a better look at him through a tiny crack in the pillows. His face was ugly, scarred, his skin a pale white, except for his nose. Could he still be after her? Hunting for her right now?

Janna's stomach made a rumbling noise. She was hungry. She selected a restaurant with a wonderful view of a marina filled with boats, real boats, not like the models floating aimlessly in the pond at Golden Gate Park.

The waiter had looked at her suspiciously, but did a turnaround after Janna had placed a hundred-dollar bill on the table.

She went to the women's rest room and when she returned to her table an enormous platter of eggs and ham was waiting for her.

Janna picked at her food while she fiddled with the computer she'd taken from Angela's. It snapped open—exposing the screen and a miniature keyboard. She turned it on. An icon of a mailbox was blinking. Janna touched the icon with her finger and a message appeared. Numbers and letters in no recognizable sequence. Then in plain English a request: Reply most urgent. It meant nothing to her. It must mean something to Paul, August eleven. A message from someone who didn't know what kind of man he really is.

Janna pecked at the keyboard. Her three-word message said: Paul is evil. She clicked the reply icon and the screen flashed a message: Your mail has been sent.

*   *   *

The light streaming through the dusty, half-curtained saloon's windows gave off a gauzelike effect as it mingled with the smoke that curled from the cigarettes clamped between the fingers of the sullen band of dedicated morning drinkers.

The walls were festooned with yellowing wanted posters of old IRA outlaws and faded green, white, and orange Republic of Ireland flags.

Frank Dunbar circled the spoon in his coffee cup while eyeing the neon BUD LITE clock positioned over the cash register. He was a shade under six feet, full-jawed and long-faced, with thinning brown hair. His forehead and cheeks were pitted with acne scars and his nose noticeably reddened by rosacea. Ten minutes until the expected phone call. Nine minutes, to be precise, and Dunbar considered himself a precise, trustworthy man. But he couldn't say the same for his latest client. Paul, August eleven. Paulie Boy. He didn't know the man's real name— yet. For now he'd call him Paulie Boy, the baby fucker. Any man that preferred having sex with a skinny *cailín beag*, a little girl, instead of a real woman, couldn't be trusted in Dunbar's mind.

Killing the two young girls and the old woman had been a job. Nothing more than that. He felt a slight bit of remorse about the girls, but only very slight. They had jumped up when he'd walked into the room. As if they couldn't wait to start fucking him. Or whatever it was that they did with the twisted bastards that paid for their time.

He sampled his coffee, then smacked his lips in distaste. "Kelty," he called to the bartender. "Sweeten this bloody mud up for me, will ya, man."

The bartender was a barrel-chested man, bald, but for some grayish strands combed sideways, like pencil lines across his scalp. He wiped his hands on the smudged apron draped over his protruding stomach, then reached into the well for a bottle of Paddy's Irish Whiskey. He poured a shot freehand into Dunbar's coffee cup.

"You're lookin' pretty chipper this morning, Frank."

"I'll be a lot more chipper if we can do business, Mr. Sean Kelty."

The bartender stamped his meaty elbows on the bar top and leaned forward. "When do I see the work?"

Dunbar lowered his voice to a whisper. "And great work it is, bucko. Six rings, all diamonds, one has to be two plus carats. A sable mink coat. A gold Tiffany watch with diamonds sprinkled like sugar across the face, a half-dozen bracelets, all gold, and—"

Sean Kelty held up his hand. "They sound wonderful, Frank, but I've got to see them before I can give you a price."

"Sure'n you can have the whole kit for fifty grand," Dunbar offered.

The bartender frowned, leaned over Dunbar's coffee cup, and sniffed loudly. "Did I put too much whiskey in this, Frank? Fifty thousand dollars?"

"You'll be drooling when you see it," Dunbar predicted. "Tonight. Closing time."

"I'll be here."

Dunbar took a long sip of the coffee royal and smacked his lips again before informing Kelty: "I'll be using your office for a few minutes."

He walked to the back of the bar and into Sean Kelty's private office. The room's dimensions were ten feet by twelve, but floor space had been squeezed down by the ceiling-high stacks of boxes of hard liquor, beer, and cigarettes.

Dunbar settled into the battered rattan rocking chair behind the cluttered desk and took a cellular phone from his coat pocket. He rooted in his pockets for the tube of medicine the dermatologist had prescribed for his rosacea, found it, and dabbed a teardrop size of the ointment on his index finger, rubbing it into his nose and humming to himself as he watched the patrons through the one-way mirror Kelty had installed.

His nose was throbbing. The doctor had told him that stress and alcohol were "major contributing factors" to the rosacea. Dunbar was tempted to tell him that killing people was a stressful job. As for the alcohol, well, he wasn't going to give that up, either.

Sean Kelty was jawing with a uniformed cop who tipped his cap back as Kelty dumped a good double shot of booze into the copper's coffee cup.

Dunbar had to admit that Kelty was good with the cops. Fed them all the free booze they could swallow, then had a good gossip, Kelty picking the dumb copper's whiskey-addled brain.

Sean Kelty was a "wannabe." He wanted to be thought of as an important man in "The Cause." His donations, which he believed went to buy supplies and weapons for the gallant warriors of the IRA, were swallowed up quickly, spent by a few political ruffians on dope and women. The real hardmen laughed at people like Sean Kelty. Accepted their money gratefully, but laughed all the same.

Still, Kelty was useful. A lot more useful to people like Frank Dunbar than he was to "The Cause." He was a reliable fence, and his bar was a clearinghouse for the boyos who jumped ship in Vancouver, then made their way down to San Francisco.

Kelty made an unholy profit washing the checks of those unskilled men who worked as laborers and wood-butchering carpenters under assumed names and phony IDs, scared shitless that every time they opened their front doors, they'd be looking right into the eyes of a copper.

His cellular phone rang at exactly eleven o'clock.

"Paulie Boy, the baby fucker," Dunbar whispered to himself before he activated the receiver.

"I'm very disappointed in you, Mr. Dunbar." The voice was icy cold, bland, impersonal. Like a bloody computer-recorded answering machine, Dunbar thought.

"How so? You got the packages, didn't you?"

Dunbar had followed his client's orders. After the killings, he'd taken the old whore's small computer, then the big one's computer base, her printer, keyboard, and all the computer disks and paraphernalia he could find on her desk, along with the red binder of photos. He'd jammed everything into two of the large suitcases he'd found in the bedroom and dropped them off early that morning at the specified downtown hotel lobby.

"I told you to get the notebook computer!"

"I did," Dunbar protested, his fingers unconsciously rubbing at his nose. "The old whore had it right by her desk and I—"

"You took a toy, Mr. Dunbar. A silly little toy, used to play games. Not my notebook computer!"

Dunbar shook a Camel lose from its pack and plucked it free with his lips. "What are you talking about?"

"I told you what I wanted. The notebook computer is vital! You left it behind!"

"I tore the place apart. I took everything that was to be took."

"No. You didn't. And there's still the third girl. The one you didn't eliminate. The news said there were three victims, Angela Lolley and two unknown girls. Two, not three!"

"There were just two of the little darlin's," Dunbar insisted. "I gave the place a thorough look. No one else was there. The old whore told me the one who gave you the trouble, 'needed more trainin'.' She must have shipped her out someplace."

"Did she tell you that before or after you mutilated her? The newspaper said her fingers had been cut off."

"Sure'n I wanted it to look like a robbery," Dunbar explained.

"What about the camera?"

Dunbar sucked in his breath. Had the baby fucker somehow spotted him at the hotel? "You didn't say you wanted the damn camera."

"The new girl's photographs weren't in the photo album. Angela told me she had taken photos of her. The film's probably still in the camera. I hope you didn't leave it behind."

It was an expensive camera. A Leica that Dunbar figured he could easily get three hundred dollars for. "There's nothing in the camera. I checked."

"I want that girl killed. I want the job finished. And I want it done now! Don't you understand? She was there. She's missing. The notebook computer is missing! She has it."

"Maybe the police have them both," Dunbar suggested. "The little girl and the computer."

"No," Lynam insisted, though he didn't explain his reasoning. If the police had the computer, they would have already traced it back to him. "Someone used it this morning. That someone has to be Janna!"

Dunbar scraped a match across the top of Kelty's desk and lit his cigarette. Jesus. What if the third little bitch had been there? Had seen him? Where the hell could she have been hiding? "It's not going to be easy finding her."

"You'll receive an additional twenty thousand dollars after you've killed her. And twenty thousand more when you get the computer. Her name is Janna. Her mother died within the last couple of weeks. Her last name may be Stoylar. There's a name of Y. Stoylar in Angela's records."

"That's not much to go on," Dunbar said, coughing as he inhaled. "I think—"

"Don't think. Just do as I tell you."

Dunbar's jaws bunched. He blew a stream of smoke at the one-way mirror. Some Australian he'd never heard of, named Lancer, had given him the job. Mouse Fennesy had called him at Kelty's bar and vouched for the Aussie. "He can send a lot of work your way. He's the best I ever worked for."

From what Dunbar knew of Mouse Fennesy, that wasn't a hell of a recommendation. But Dunbar needed work. Needed it badly, so he'd given the number of his cell phone to Lancer. Then the Aussie called back and told him that someone else would be making contact soon.

"Do what he tells you, and you'll be well paid," the Aussie had promised. And so far, Paulie Boy had met that promise. But he was a pompous asshole, Paulie was.

"I'll try and find the girl, but it won't be easy," Dunbar said through a smoker's cough.

"Check with your fellow criminal friends," Lynam said sarcastically. "Y. Stoylar. It's an unusual name. Find him. Has it dawned on you, Mr. Dunbar, that Janna was at the house, and that she saw you? And can identify you? Angela told me the girl was there when I called to make your appointment. The police are undoubtedly looking for Janna, too, so I suggest for both our sakes that you do find her first. I'll call you. Eleven o'clock tonight."

"Why don't you give me a number where I can reach you?"

"I'll call you. Get the girl. And the computer!"

Dunbar cursed and dropped the phone into his coat pocket. Cheeky bastard. The girl, Janna, she couldn't have been at the house. Couldn't have seen him. He squinted and pulled at his nose. Unless there was some secret spot, some little cupboard the girls were locked up in, or where they could play hide-and-seek with the likes of Paulie Boy.

Y. Stoylar. Not even a first name. The little *cailin's* mother dying. Where did the baby fucker get all his information? From the whore's bloody computer? Or did the little girl tell him about her mother before she bit his prick? At least Dunbar hoped that was what had happened to the pervert. The old whore had said that "your friend" had some difficulty with the girl.

Trouble was just what Dunbar planned to give the baby fucker. The bastard thought he was bloody clever. Half the men he knew in the nick were there because they were too damn clever. At least Paulie Boy had been smart about the money he'd delivered so far. A simple FedEx package sent to Dunbar in care of Kelty's bar. But the transfer at the hotel. That's where he'd made his mistake.

The instructions had been specific. Leave the suitcases near the espresso stand by the elevator at exactly five minutes after eight that morning. A little over three hours ago.

Dunbar paid one of the drunks that hung out at Kelty's saloon twenty dollars to place the suitcases, jammed with all the computer materials and the red plastic binder filled with glossy photographs of Angela's girls, at the designated spot, while he stood in line at the hotel's check-in counter, under the whopping, cigar-shaped crystal chandelier, the Leica camera dangling around his neck, like so many of the tourists he was in line with. He was able to click off a half-dozen shots of the well-dressed gray-haired man grabbing the suitcases and hurrying over to the nearby bank of elevators.

Dunbar hadn't bothered following him. Paulie Boy must have thought that it was a real smart move, going up the elevator with the suitcases, rather than hurrying out onto Market Street, or using the hotel's Fifth Street exit. Maybe Paulie had taken a room at the hotel. Dunbar didn't much care. He had him on film. He knew what Paulie Boy looked like.

Dunbar crisscrossed the butt end of his cigarette in an overflowing ashtray, then immediately shook another Camel from its pack. He'd find Janna. And kill her. Then, after he got his money, he'd deal with the baby fucker. Find out who he was. Where he lived. Then squeeze him bloody dry.

Patrick Lynam dry-washed his face, moaned, then glared at the telephone, as if it were responsible for the tragedies that had suddenly entered his life. Dunbar. Why had Philip Bovard sent him such an incompetent? He picked up the tiny black toy computer that Dunbar had mistaken for his notebook, hurled it across the room, then turned his attention to his desk, staring at the blank seventeen-inch screen of his powerful IBM. He'd had the notebook set up so that it could access his home computer. It had seemed like such a good idea at the time—he could cross-reference anything he wanted, pull in a report, a spreadsheet, a phone number, check his E-mail.

He groaned again. A bank manager in Switzerland, who had control of Bovard's Russian ally's account, had sent a coded E-mail message while Lynam had been at the hotel picking up the suitcases. The nervous bank manager later made a phone call, something he had always been reluctant to do, inquiring about the strange response: Paul is evil.

Lynam had informed him that there was an error in transmission or that some hacker had somehow stumbled into his E-mail.

That explanation had done little to soothe the banker's nerves. New codes had to be set up, new account numbers assigned.

Lynam had gone through his files thoroughly, copying everything onto backup disks, then deleting each and every item. The machine's hard drive was blank, nothing there for the notebook computer to couple with now, other than the machine itself.

Paul is evil. God, the little bitch!

Lynam closed his eyes and massaged his temples with the heels of his hands. He'd have to call Bovard now. Tell him about the missing notebook. If Dunbar had just done his job, killed them all, found the notebook, then Lynam would never have had to mention the incident to Bovard. But now there was no choice. If the police were somehow to come into possession of the notebook, it would be the end of Bovard's deal involving the nuclear reactors. He got unsteadily to his feet, wondering just how violently Bovard would react to the news. The man was a killer, like Dunbar, he suddenly realized, only much more professional.

Chapter 10

April 3

Janna Drovana burst out of the door to the lobby of the Travelodge motel. She had given up on securing a room. The clerk hadn't been convinced by her story that her mother would be arriving later in the day. He'd accused her of being a prostitute and threatened to call the police.

She sighed at the irony of it, making sure the newly purchased tan canvas backpack holding the money she'd taken from Angela's house was securely strapped over her shoulder and snug against her side. She'd gotten rid of Angela's expensive red purse. It made too inviting a target for a thief. All that money. Over forty-eight thousand dollars! Mostly in hundred-dollar bills. She had counted it several times to be sure she hadn't made a mistake. It was staggering! She was rich. Unbelievably rich.

For the last year of her young, eventful life, money had been in short supply. It hadn't always been like that. Her father, Ivan Drovana, had been a highly respected scientist, and commanded a large St. Petersburg apartment. She'd had her own bedroom, complete with a television set and computer. They'd spent weekends at Petrodvorets, the former Imperial Palace, picnicking among the vast fountains and cascades in the lush park. She remembered summers when they'd enjoyed a full month in a spacious dacha on Lake Logoda. They'd been able to shop at the best stores; Janna had attended a private school for gifted students, where the ratio was one teacher for every six students. English and math were stressed, and Janna was always at the top of her class. In addition, her father had provided a private tutor to work on English: "The language of science," he had often preached.

Then there had been an explosion at her father's plant. He was killed, along with fourteen co-workers.

Their apartment was taken away. She and her mother were moved to Moscow, to a small single room in a prison-like blockhouse on the eastern edge of the city.

Janna was enrolled in a public school, full of rowdy beggars. The lone teacher was a vodka-drenched old man who rambled on and on before dozing off at his desk.

Janna was immediately despised by her fellow students for her superior language and mathematical skills.

One winter in that icy apartment had been enough for her mother. She'd vowed to get them out of there.

Janna sat down on a bus stop bench, her eyes tearing at the thought of her beautiful mother, Irina. Janna never asked her mother how she'd scraped together enough money for their trip to America, but one day, when Janna had been out wandering the streets, she'd spotted her mother, wearing her best party dress, standing on Tverskaya Street, near Red Square. Janna started to run to her, but stopped short when her mother strolled over to a long black limousine parked at the curb. She'd spoken to the driver for a brief moment, then scampered around and hopped into the passenger side door.

Sometime after that, her mother announced that they would be leaving on a trip. The first leg of their journey took them back to St. Petersburg, where they boarded a small wooden fishing boat and sailed across the Gulf of Finland, through the Baltic Sea and eventually to Bergen, Norway, where they lived for a month before being smuggled onto the rusty freighter that began the long, monotonous trip to South America, and eventually around Cape Horn to San Francisco and Cousin Yuri Stoylar's flat.

The ship had made several stops in South America, loading and unloading cargo. She and her mother, along with eight other Russian illegals with whom they shared a room, were forced to stay in a damp, diesel-smelling hold in the belly of the ship on those occasions.

Her mother had been sick, even before they'd left Russia. The illness had worsened, until at the end, she'd not been able to leave their cramped room in Stoylar's flat.

Their roles were reversed for those last few painful weeks of her mother's life, with Janna being the caregiver, the protector, while her mother lay helplessly in bed. Cousin Yuri had ranted and raved about how much money the medicine was costing, how much money he was losing, and making it plain that he thought that Janna would have to remedy that by "being nice" to his friends.

Janna often wondered if they would have been better off if they had stayed in Russia.

She felt exhausted. She needed a safe place to sleep. It was so frustrating, having all that money and not being able to use it for a room to sleep in.

She'd spent the day shopping, shopping as she'd never done before, even when her father had taken her to the great department store, *Gostiny Dvor*, in St. Petersburg for her birthday.

Even *Gostiny Dvor* couldn't compete with the unbelievable variety of stores in San Francisco. The clerks had been more than happy to accept the cash she'd taken from Angela's metal box in exchange for a new, shorter haircut, then Levi's, tennis shoes with the name of a famous athlete sewn into the leather, a warm red woolen sweater, a knit cap, several pairs of socks and sets of underwear, and a black anorak with zipper pockets in the fake fur collar and lining, a perfect place to hide some of her money.

Her thoughts once again returned to Russia, the happy days with her parents, then she shrugged her narrow shoulders. It was foolish to have those thoughts now. She hugged the backpack close to her. She still hadn't been able to use the computer properly, and she knew no one she could ask for help. The police. They must be looking for the killer. Would the computer help them find the killer, and the man who had hurt her?

She got to her feet, walking aimlessly, finally stopping

at a petrol station, where she purchased a map of San Francisco. There was a phone on the wall in the petrol station's office. She stared at the phone for several moments, then made her decision. Another call to the policewoman.

Maureen Connah had the phone's receiver cradled between her ear and shoulder, her feet resting on an open desk drawer. "All I want to know is if you've sold a HV2500 notebook computer to someone by the name of Angela Lolley or Y. Stoylar."

The Helmut-Victor executive on the other end of the line was the fourth person Mo had spoken to since she called their offices fifteen minutes ago. "It's a police matter. An urgent police matter. If you want me to go through all the red tape of getting a subpoena, I'll do it, but it's just going to make more work for both of us, Mr. Gevertz."

"Yes, yes, I realize that. Company policy, though, you know, Inspector. Still, I don't see what harm there can be in checking the records. Hold on a moment."

Maureen waited for close to four minutes. She was about to disconnect and call back when Gevertz came back on the line.

"I've checked thoroughly, Inspector Connah. There have been over a hundred thousand units sold throughout the world, the majority in the United States of course, and no one under the names you provided has registered with us."

"Would they have to do that?" Mo queried. "Couldn't they just buy it at a store and not notify you?"

"Oh, yes. But then the unit wouldn't be under warranty, and if the HV2500 was lost, and we were contacted, we couldn't notify the owner."

"How would you know who purchased it?"

"The serial number," Gevertz replied with a superior tone. "Every unit has a serial number, Inspector."

Maureen swung her feet to the floor and sat up straight. "So, if I find the notebook, I could check back with you to see who it belonged to?"

"If they registered, Inspector. If not, at least we would know the retailer who ordered the machine from us."

"I'd appreciate it if you'd let me know immediately if anyone reports a stolen or missing notebook, Mr. Gevertz, and could you fax me some information on the HV2500? Something that would show me just what it can do."

Maureen gave Gevertz the Homicide detail fax number.

"I'll be happy to."

Charlotte, the secretary, was waving her arm at Maureen. "There's another call on the Tara Street case. I think it's that same young girl. Line three."

Maureen thanked Gevertz and said she'd get back to him, activated the tape recorder hooked up to the phone, then punched line three. "Hi, Inspector Connah speaking."

"Have you found the murderer?"

"Not yet. But I want to thank you again for giving me the names of the two girls. I still haven't found their families. Do you have any more information that could help us?"

"I do not know their last names."

"Listen, I know you're scared, but please don't hang up. Let me give you my direct number. If you call and I'm not here, someone will get in touch with me right away, or you can leave a message. They'll page me. Do you have a pencil?" Maureen recited the phone number. "You can call me. Anytime. Day or night, okay?"

"I saw the man," Janna said.

"You mean the man who shot Angela and the girls?"

"Yes. He had brown hair. And a red nose."

"Red nose, huh. Where did you see him? Was he—"

"He put something on his gun before he shot them. It looked like a potato."

"Jesus," Maureen whispered to herself, wishing that real police work was like it was in the movies, where they could trace incoming calls in a matter of seconds. The actual procedure took several minutes, and only after the phone company had been alerted to the call. "Yes, yes.

He did. Tell me, honey. Shall I call you honey? Don't you want me to know your name?''

"Janna. My name is Janna."

Mo heaved a silent sigh of relief. The girl was starting to trust her. "Janna. Did the killer see you? Does he know you saw him?"

"No," Janna said in a shaky voice. "I hid myself."

"Where . . . where were you? I was at the house, and I was wondering where you would have been able—"

"In the next room. I saw him through a keyhole. Then I hid under the pillows."

Mo hunched forward, scribbling notes on a yellow foolscap notepad, even though she could see the blinking red button on the tape recorder. "Can you tell me anything else about the way the man looked? Did he say anything?"

"Yes. He said something strange. It was like . . . 'Sure and the both of you should be ashamed of yourselves.' He . . . he had an accent, and . . ."

"Janna. Can you guess what type of accent?"

"It was like . . . not English, but . . ."

"Irish? A brogue?" Maureen suggested, deepening her voice. " 'Sure'n the both of you should be ashamed of yourselves.' Like that? An Irish accent?"

"Yes, just like that. I have to go now."

"Wait, Janna," Maureen pleaded. "Wait. Please. Are you all right? If the killer knows you saw him, he may come after you. Let me help you."

There was a long silence. Maureen could sense the girl's fear. "Call me anytime, Janna. Anytime at all. I really do want to help you."

There was a click, then the receiver purred in Mo's ear. Maureen closed her eyes, picturing the house on Tara Street. The killing room. The room next door. The girl on the other side of the door, peeking through the keyhole. Seeing the murders, then hiding under the pillows.

Maureen shifted uneasily in her chair and thought back to when she was Janna's age. Her home life had been reasonably happy. She wondered how she would have fared if she'd had to face what Janna had. Somehow being taken in by the likes of Angela Lolley, forced into prostitution, then witnessing two gruesome murders. And now, living God knows where in the streets of San Francisco, perhaps being chased by the killer, or another Angela Lolley.

Mo reached out to the phone, tapping her fingernails nervously against the receiver. Call back, Janna. Please call back.

Janna began running, wondering what to do next. The policewoman sounded sincere. Sounded like she wanted to help. But so had Cousin Yuri Stoylar when they first arrived at the flat. Was it a mistake to give Maureen her name? Was she someone she could trust? She hopped up on a brick bulkhead separating a food market from a parking lot and unfolded the map across her lap. Where to go? Where? She studied the map for several minutes. There was only one spot on the map that was familiar to her. Golden Gate Park.

Janna neatly refolded the map and slipped it in her jacket pocket.

"Hey, sugar, you want some juice?"

A dark-faced man with hair like greased snakes was smiling at her.

He held out his hand, opened the palm, and flashed a small cellophane bag.

"How 'bout it? Five dollars. Tell you what. I'll give it to you free. We can go to my car. I got some more. How 'bout it, sugar?"

Janna jumped down to the sidewalk, nimbly skirted the man, and sprinted away.

Chapter 11

April 3

The leaves made crunching sounds under his feet as Yuri Stoylar edged his way under the sheltering branches of a thicket of trees.

He was less than a hundred yards from where he'd found Janna's sleeping bag. Was she still alive? Would she come back for it? Stoylar was furious that someone had used his idea to rob Angela Lolley, and taken Janna away to boot. Or could Janna have killed Angela and the girls? No. The "little genius" didn't have the stomach for that. But if she was alive, and somehow the police got hold of her, she'd tell them all about his smuggling, the drug deals, the stolen property. She was a smart little bitch, always listening in when he had someone at the flat, talking over a deal. She'd blurt it all out to the police. He couldn't let her do that.

After reading the story in the newspaper about the murders at 54 Tara Street, Stoylar had gone to the morgue and given the coroner a sob story about his daughter being missing.

The lie had worked. The two young murder victims' bodies were shown to him. He remembered seeing them both at Angela's, the day he and the old whore had trapped Janna in the park.

Yes, Janna, a real smart little bitch, but not smart enough to get away from the trap he and Lolley had set for her. The drugged candy had been his idea. And a good one it had been.

He'd gone along to Angela's house that day, in her car,

sitting in the backseat with Janna, her drugged body limp, her pretty, unconscious head lying right in his lap.

He hadn't paid much attention to the two other girls at the time—it was the house he'd been interested in. He'd planned to go back and rob Lolley, and take Janna back to the flat with him. Why should Lolley make all the money? Yuri knew plenty of men who wanted to spend some time with Janna. And this time he'd make sure she'd have no chance to run away. He'd tie her to the bed, treat her like an animal. Train her like a pet—perhaps a dog. A grateful dog who would do tricks for him.

He chuckled at his own joke, then slipped his hand into his shirt pocket and extracted a postage stamp. He held it carefully between two fingers as he slowly ran his tongue across the back.

It was a United States postage stamp, with a picture of the American flag. He licked some more, then rolled the stamp into a ball, put it between his teeth, and bit down, feeling the kick of the PCP that had been layered over the stamp's glue.

It was an ingenious idea, he conceded. The man who sold him the stamps had called them "juiced."

Yuri had invested all the money Angela paid him for Janna in sheets of the drug-laced stamps. Seven thousand dollars for a thousand of the stamps. He knew he could triple his investment in a short time.

A thin line of fog began rolling in. In minutes the meadow was obscured.

Janna. Where could she be? All she knew was his flat, and Golden Gate Park.

He pulled up his coat collar and rubbed his hands briskly. "Janna," he whispered. "If you're alive, I'm going to find you."

London

Although Jack Kordic had paid what he considered to be an outrageous price for his off-the-rack suit from the

London tailor Maureen Connah had recommended, he felt considerably underdressed as he approached the dais in the conference room at the Savoy Hotel.

The majority of those in the audience were in black tie, as were most of the men Kordic would be sharing the dais with.

He had met many of them at a welcoming breakfast that morning and now he nodded his hellos, finessing names he didn't completely remember.

Kordic recalled once reading a magazine article in a dentist's waiting room. The author's premise was that the two things Americans feared most were public speaking and death—in that order. He'd been amused at the time. But not now. He was nervous, more nervous than he'd ever been testifying at a murder trial. He'd worked for hours on his speech, the results tucked away on three-by-five index cards in the inside pocket of his new suit.

"You look like you need a drink," a short man with an unruly black beard said, thrusting a glass at Kordic.

"Ira Heiser," the man announced. He wore gunmetal-rimmed glasses. One lens was noticeably thicker than the other. "Anatoly told me you might be feeling a bit nervous. Champane's just the thing for the nerves."

Kordic accepted the wine gratefully, holding the glass out to see if his hand was shaking.

"Weeks told me to be careful not to spill any of this on you."

Heiser barked out a loud laugh. "Anatoly's been a little testy, lately. He's been chained to a desk for too long."

There was a loud banging sound. Kordic looked around and spotted one of the hotel staff pounding a mallet against a large circle of brass.

Heiser drained what little champagne was left in his glass. "The dinner gong, I'm afraid. Come on, Inspector. You're sitting next to me."

The meal was elaborately prepared and formally delivered: a delicious soup Kordic couldn't recognize, a poached fish dish, a salad swimming with prawns and scallops, and a slab of rare roast beef as thick as first base.

The sommelier arrived at each serving with a different wine, announcing its vintage and heritage in the hushed tones of a priest giving the last rites to his bishop.

Heiser was sitting on Kordic's left. He cut his food with the precision of a surgeon and kept a running conversation on a variety of subjects.

The man on Kordic's right was named Gilbeax. The scent of gin drifted over the table when he explained his position in the Belgian government.

Heiser looked up at Kordic with a twinkle in his eye. "Almost ready, Inspector? After dessert, I start the ball rolling. Then you give your acceptance speech."

"As ready as I'll ever be, I guess," Kordic said, patting his coat pocket for his speech notes. He murmured a curse. The notes weren't there. He'd left the damn notes in his room.

Kordic pushed his chair from the table and got to his feet. "Be right back," he told Heiser.

Uniformed security guards, armed with weapons and metal detectors, ringed the entrances to the ballroom. Kordic explained his predicament to one of the guards. "I left my speech notes in my room. I'll be right back."

He was crossing the lobby to the elevators when there was the thunderous sound of an explosion.

Chapter 12

The fluorescent table lamp splashed light over Maureen Connah's desk. It was the lone light in the Homicide detail. She sat hunched over her desk, grateful for the silence.

Maureen laboriously worked her way through the computer printouts the lab had finally obtained from the disks found at Angela Lolley's house.

Lolley had been methodical in her record keeping. Each disk covered a fiscal three-month time period: July through September, October to December, January through March.

The murders had taken place on April the first. April Fool's Day. She wondered what the killer's reaction had been when he checked Lolley's computer. Had she erased all of her files when she made the backups? Or was everything still there, on the hard disk?

Maureen had hoped for better IDs on Lolley's johns, but the madam had been careful about that. All the entries were made under a first name and then a month and day: Bill, August 1. Ronald, November 4. John, June 6. There were a lot of Johns, all listed as having sessions with Amber or Tina—sometimes Amber and Tina.

The income figures were neatly listed in the far right column. For the period from January 1 to March 31, Lolley had taken in sixty-seven thousand dollars.

"Dear God," Maureen murmured under her breath. A quarter million dollars a year. And she had no doubt that it had all been paid in cash.

There was just one large expenditure listed on the printouts. March 30: $7M to Y. Stoylar for Janna.

Lolley had paid Y. Stoylar for a new girl. Janna. Who was Stoylar? Would Janna bolt if she brought the name up during the next phone call? She had to treat Janna carefully, gently, not scare her away. There was just one listing for Janna—the last day of the month, the same day that Paul, August eleven, was shown as paying $2500— for Janna, Tina, and Amber.

Maureen had listened to the 911 tape of the call reporting the killing on Tara Street several times. The call had been made from a pay phone at the nearby BART station. The voice was male, and sounded to be Caucasian—he was definitely nervous, close to panic: "There are . . . Oh, God. They're dead. Three of them. Fifty-four Tara Street. God, it's . . ."

She was certain it wasn't the voice of the killer. There was no reason for the killer to call the police. It had to have been one of Lollipop's regular customers, arriving for an evening of child molesting, and instead finding all that carnage.

How had the caller gotten into the house? Certainly Angela hadn't passed out keys. No, the door must have been left open. The killer never would have done that. Janna. Frightened Janna, fleeing, in too much of a hurry, or just too damn scared to think about the door. Which meant she left the house after the killer had.

Maureen went back to the printouts.

There were numerous other listings for Paul, August eleven, in amounts of two hundred fifty dollars, and five hundred dollars. Two fifty for each girl. Was the extra two thousand for Janna joining in? Why so much? Because she was new? Someone different? Younger than the other girls? Maureen grimaced and shook her head. A virgin? Could Janna have been a virgin? God, the poor kid. What a hell of a thing that would be.

She leaned back and rubbed her toe across her shin, then turned to the preliminary crime-lab report.

London
April 4

The ringing of the telephone dragged Jack Kordic from a damp, groggy sleep. At first he had no idea where he was. He blinked his eyes rapidly, his hands searching across the unfamiliar bed for the source of the noise.

He finally found the phone and elbowed himself into a sitting position.

"Kordic," he growled, the heel of one hand rubbing at his forehead.

"Inspector, Commander Gresham here. We've solved our problem. You're free to go home at any time."

Kordic was suddenly wide awake. "What happened, Commander?"

"We got our man. An old IRA villain. He was tinkering with another bomb in his flat in Holborn. It went off in his hands. Killed him and the poor chap in the lower flat."

"You're sure it was the same man?"

"Positive," the commander assured him. "Some maps survived the explosion. Detailed maps of the construction work done recently at the Savoy Hotel. Fennesy was the man's name. Denis Fennesy. Most of his comrades called him Mouse. Does his name mean anything to you, Inspector?"

Kordic squeezed his eyes shut and concentrated. Denis Mouse Fennesy. He was sure he'd never come across anyone by that name. "No, Commander. I've never heard of him."

"Well, we won't need you any longer, Inspector," the Scotland Yard commander proclaimed. "I imagine you're anxious to get back home. I've taken the liberty of confirming your flight. Your plane leaves Heathrow at three forty-five this afternoon. You'd better get there a couple of hours early, just to be safe. We'll be in touch, Inspector. Good-bye."

Kordic bounced the receiver in his hand. It was heavy. Too heavy to be plastic. Metal coated with enamel, in an art deco style, like the rest of the furniture in the suite.

He dropped the receiver on its cradle and switched on the brass lamp in the shape of a nude balancing a globe in her hands. The clock in the base of the lamp showed it was a little after ten in the morning.

Commander Hugh Gresham was anxious for him to leave London. Gresham. The same high-ranking Scotland Yard official who'd greeted him so warmly at Heathrow Airport on his arrival in London, and who had assigned Detective Sergeant Holtzer to give him the first-class treatment: a hurried cruise down the Thames on a police cruiser, a tour of the Tower of London, with none of that waiting in the long queues to see the crown jewels. He'd been escorted right to the front of the line, then he'd been driven to Scotland Yard and given a private tour of the famed Black Museum.

Holtzer, a cannon-voiced man with a weather-creased face, had been stiff and formal at first, but he'd warmed up after Kordic got the message across that they were both working-class cops, and that an inspector in the San Francisco Police Department was only one civil-service rank up from sergeant.

Holtzer had then shown Kordic the real London, the streets and alleyways to avoid, the wharfs where the Great Britain version of Mafia chiefs hung out, then, at Kordic's request, dropped him off at one of the stores Maureen Connah had recommended, staying long enough to advise the salesman that he was dealing with a special friend of the Yard.

But that had all changed after the explosion. Eleven men had been killed, including the Israeli, Ira Heiser, and the former head of MI5, the British Security Service.

After the smoke had cleared, Kordic had been hurried down to Scotland Yard, and this time treated more like a suspect than a visiting brother officer.

Commander Hugh Gresham, a tall, balding man with blood vessels spiderwebbed across his hollowed cheeks, had conducted the interrogation personally, at first almost implying that there was some connection between Kordic and the bomb. "Damn fortunate you forgot those notes, isn't it, Inspector?"

"You'd have been crisped if you hadn't gotten out of the ballroom," Sergeant Holtzer added solemnly.

Kordic couldn't argue with that. Gresham had dismissed Kordic with a curt warning about not leaving town. The escort service was over. Kordic took a cab back to the Savoy and had tumbled into bed less than three hours ago. And now Scotland Yard wanted him out of London. And in a hurry.

He yawned, swung his legs over the mattress, and got to his feet.

The windows overlooked what he assumed the English would call a "smashing" view of the River Thames. The river gleamed like dark ice in the weak morning sunlight. The rooster-tail wake of a motorboat cut in front of one of Her Majesty's warships. The Royal Navy craft reminded Kordic of a model that he'd worked on with his son, Danny. Danny had been so proud of the finished results that he'd convinced his mother that it belonged on the mantel over the living-room fireplace.

Kordic suddenly felt the need of a strong Scotch. Maybe Scotch because he was in London. After Danny and Linda had been killed, it hadn't mattered what it was: Scotch, bourbon, vodka, gin, wine, or beer. He upturned his palms and stared at the scars across both wrists. He didn't remember drinking himself into oblivion, or climbing into the bathtub that day, then trying to kill himself.

Kordic wheeled around and went to the huge, rounded Cuban mahogany closet, dug his suitcase free, and began packing. He tossed his old suit and the sport coat he'd traveled to London in into the wastebasket, packing only the new clothes, thinking that at least Maureen Connah would be happy about his purchases.

Kordic had just finished packing when there was a knock at the door. He opened it cautiously, yanking it wider when he saw the grim face of Anatoly Weeks.

"Skipping out of town, Jack?" Weeks accused, barging into the room.

"Anatoly. I'm really sorry about your boss, Ira Heiser. He and I were—"

"Yeah, yeah. I know." Weeks marched over to the bed stand. "It was that *momzer* Bovard."

"I just heard from Commander Gresham. He says they've got—"

"They've got shit," Weeks said with little enthusiasm.

There were three silver-dollar-sized call lights on the wall: red, to summon the waiter, yellow for the maid, and green for the valet. Eve floor of the Savoy had one of each ready and waiting around the clock.

Weeks pushed the red light, then flopped down on the bed.

"Did Fresham tell you that Mouse Fennesy blew himself to hell?"

"Yes. He said they found some maps of the Savoy at Fennesy's place."

"Fennesy was a *shmeker*," Weeks protested. "A coke-head. A nothing. He was a freelancer. He'd work for anyone. He could make a bomb, and tunnel his way into a rat hole, but he didn't have the moxie to figure out an operation like this. Someone hired him. Used him." Weeks rapped his knuckles on Kordic's suitcase. "What's your hurry?"

"I don't have any choice. Gresham made it crystal clear he wants me out of here. I wouldn't be surprised if he had someone from the Yard waiting in the lobby to make sure I follow orders. You still think this Bovard guy is involved?"

"I'm positive. Ira was getting too close to him. Those nukes from the subs I told you about? Well, we got word that they're already celebrating in Beirut. I've got to find—"

A discreet knock at the door announced the waiter.

Weeks ordered breakfast for two while Kordic slipped into the vast blue tiled bathroom. He was soaping himself when the glass shower door clicked open.

Weeks said, "Did Gresham show you the videos?"

Kordic knuckled the soap out of his eyes. "What videos?"

"Scotland Yard had video cameras in the ballroom and in the Savoy lobby. I won't be able to get my hands on a copy of the videos until later today."

"Gresham didn't mention anything about videos."

"Shit," Weeks snorted. "The Brits. They're okay in a fight, but worthless in anything else. They blame the Irish for everything. That's their standard operating procedure. Any robber, homicide, or mob scene they can't solve in ten minutes, they throw it on the Irish. They expect us to believe that Mouse Fennesy tunnels his way through the poshest hotel in London, plants a bomb at the precise spot where it will wipe out a table full of some of the top intelligence officers in the world, then he goes home and accidentally blows himself up. Give me a break."

Kordic pointed the scented bar of soap at Weeks's feet. "Close the door, damn it. You're getting the floor wet."

"So what?" Weeks flared. "This is the Savoy. Push the yellow button and twenty maids in dancing shoes will be here with mink towels to clean the place up. I want you to do everything you can to find that 'Old Friend' of Bovard's in San Francisco. Check out those laundromats, the phones, anything you can think of, Jack."

Chapter 13

San Francisco

"Sure'n it's a joke, isn't it, Sean?" Frank Dunbar suggested softly, fighting to keep his temper in check. "Fifteen thousand dollars for the whole kit? It has to be a joke."

Sean Kelty shook his head slowly from side to side as he scrutinized the loot spread across his desk. "It's no joke, Frank." His stubby fingers flicked through the bracelets, watches, and rings, finally selecting a pear-cut diamond ring.

He screwed a jeweler's loupe in his eye and examined the diamond under the desk lamp.

"Beautiful stone," Kelty conceded. "I thought it might have a touch of pink to it, but no. It's just a speck of blood on the setting." He pocketed the loupe and winked at Dunbar. "A speck of blood, imagine that, Frank."

Dunbar flicked his nose with his thumb. "Fifteen is not in the ballpark."

"Then keep the work. It's hot as hell, we both know that, man. I couldn't shop it here. It'll all have to go to New York."

Dunbar reached over and picked up a thick gold bracelet in the shape of a coiled snake, with two ruby eyes. He knew a woman in Berkeley who'd screw his bloody brains out for that bracelet. "All right, you fuckin' bandit. Fifteen. Cash." He grunted a curse and pocketed the bracelet. "But I'm keepin' this one."

Kelty pushed his beefy hand across the desk. "Done."

"Done," Dunbar agreed. He watched as Sean Kelty shoveled the jewelry into a brown paper bag.

Kelty said, "You heard we lost a good man, did ya?"

Dunbar didn't know what Kelty was talking about. "Who might that be?"

"Denis Fennesy. The Brits say he blew himself up in his room." Kelty looked at Dunbar in disbelief. "Can you imagine Mouse blowing himself up? A finer explosives man I've never seen. The Brits killed him, I've no doubt."

"Did you ever really meet Mouse?" Dunbar asked.

"No, but I—"

"He was a doper. His arms were like pincushions. Never trust a man who uses drugs, Sean. Or one who doesn't drink. Fennesy was probably full of coke and dropped a bloody bomb between his legs."

Kelty squirmed in his chair. He didn't think it right for Dunbar to talk about Fennesy that way. "I'll have the cash for you tomorrow, Frank."

"All right. Did you find out anything about that name I gave you? Y. Stoylar?"

"Nothin'. And I didn't expect to. It's a damn strange name. No one I'm likely to have dealin's with."

Dunbar grunted an acknowledgment, then made his way out of the bar and onto Taraval Street. He hunched his shoulders against the strong wind, whistling to himself as he stalked off in the general direction of his apartment. He made several abrupt stops along the way to make sure he wasn't being followed.

He calculated his cash flow as he walked. Fifteen thousand from Kelty for the goods he'd taken from Lolley's house. Add that to the twenty thousand he'd already gotten from Paulie Boy for the killings, along with the money he'd get for taking care of this third little darlin', and it came to a tidy sum. Not enough to go home and buy a tavern, a real tavern, not a dump like Kelty's, but by the time he got through with the baby fucker, he'd have all he needed. Janna. He had to find the little whore, all right. Find her before the coppers did.

Dunbar's apartment was a square-shaped single room

in the basement of a house owned by Mrs. Abernathy, an old widow whose only interest in life was the dozens of cats that shared the upper portion of the house with her.

Dunbar put up with the smell and the cat hairs because the woman was half-blind and nearly deaf—in his situation an ideal landlady.

He walked around the side of the house and used his key on the door to his unit, first checking to make sure that the sprawl of junk mail half sticking out from the bottom of the door was in the same position as when he'd left. As soon as he was inside, the phone in his coat pocket started ringing.

Eleven o'clock. Exactly. He studied his watch, a Timex, with a cracked crystal and an imitation leather band. He wondered what type watch the baby fucker had. Probably a big, thick gold one with special dials to tell the phase of the moon. The thought of killing the baby fucker and taking his watch made him smile.

He tugged the phone from his pocket.

"Have you finished the job, Mr. Dunbar?"

"No. I can't find anyone who ever heard of this Stoylar asshole."

"I want you to go back to the house. The photographs that Angela took of Janna went out from a photo lab in yesterday's mail. They should be at the house now."

"You think I'm daft? I'm not goin' back to the bloody house," Dunbar blurted belligerently.

"The police have finished there. The maildrop is right alongside the garage door. You can be in and out in a minute. If you're going to find Janna, you'll have to know what she looks like. And, just as importantly, we don't want the police knowing. Remember, she was there. She must have seen you. If the police get to her first, she'll give them a description of you."

"You better take a—"

"Ten thousand dollars extra. Cash. For the photographs."

"It's too dangerous," Dunbar said between tight-together lips.

"Ten thousand dollars," the calm voice repeated. "Easy money, Mr. Dunbar. Very easy money. I'll call when I have an address for Stoylar."

Dunbar squeezed the phone in his hand. The baby fucker's voice was getting on his nerves. "I'll take a look, but I ain't makin' no promises. If it don't look right, I'm not going in."

"I'll have the money delivered to you as soon as you've got the pictures. That's a promise. Don't disappoint me."

Jack Kordic was surprised at how alert he was feeling.

Anatoly Weeks, the Mossad agent, had peppered him with questions during their room-service breakfast at the Savoy Hotel, right up until Kordic's plane departed Heathrow Airport at 7:45 A.M., San Francisco time.

Weeks had pressed a small red capsule in Kordic's hand as he was boarding the plane.

"Don't have any booze to drink, and swallow this as soon as you're in the air. I guarantee it will make for a pleasant flight," Weeks predicted.

Kordic had followed instructions, and except for a couple of times when the man sitting alongside him in the cramped tourist section of the 747 jumbo jet had angrily dug his elbow into Kordic's side in attempts to stifle his snoring, he'd slept peacefully the entire trip, gratefully missing the in-flight movie and cellophane-wrapped meals.

Now he was clearheaded, refreshed, and hungry. His good luck continued as he carried his luggage to the United States Customs Inspector, who he recognized as having worked with on a couple of cases.

The man cleared his luggage without bothering to open it, a complete reversal of what had taken place when Kordic had landed at Heathrow. The Great Britain Customs Inspector had laboriously checked everything, going so far as to disassemble Kordic's electric shaver before finally granting him permission to proceed into the airport.

He spotted Maureen Connah's solemn face in the thick-pressed crowd waiting to greet the London passengers.

"You took my advice," Connah said after they'd shaken hands.

Kordic arched his eyes in a questioning gesture.

"The sport coat. And the raincoat. Very nice."

Kordic grimaced. "This was supposed to be a free trip. It ended up costing me a bundle. What's new on the Lollipop case?"

Maureen's hands moved as if to explain, then dropped to her sides. "Quite a bit, Jack. You want to stop for a cup of coffee somewhere?"

Kordic decided he needed more than just coffee. He chose Gulliver's, a restaurant near the airport that specialized in prime rib.

They ordered a bottle of California merlot and Kordic brought Connah up-to-date on what had happened in London.

Connah listened with rapt attention, her chin cupped in her hand.

"God, you were lucky, Jack."

"Yes, I guess I was. Now, bring me up-to-date on the Lollipop murders. I'm anxious to get a look at those computer printouts."

Maureen reached down and picked through her purse. She pulled out a small tape recorder. "Listen to this first. There was a third girl in the house. Janna. She's called me twice."

When the recording was finished, Kordic said, "Jesus Christ. The kid saw the whole damn thing. Red nose. What do you make of that? Sunburn, a boozer, a rash, or just the kid's imagination?"

"I don't know. That, and the way she says he talks. 'Sure'n.' That's definitely Irish."

"Yeah. That would make Anatoly Weeks's theory a lot more plausible."

"Weeks. The Mossad agent you told me about?"

"Yep. He was in London. I told him about the homicides on Tara Street. He said that the hollowed-out potato trick was an old IRA specialty."

Maureen frowned. "What would an IRA man have to do with Angela Lolley?"

"I don't know, Mo. It's just a theory. But from what Janna says, the killer had an Irish accent. We've got to find this kid. She speaks English quite well, but you can sense she's groping for words. She hasn't been here long, would be my guess. The accent—Polish? Russian? The Baltics? I can't tell."

"Take a look at the printouts, Jack. They're not as much as I hoped for. There's no positive ID on Lollypop's clients, just first names, which are probably fictitious, and a series of numbers, which appear to be a month and day. No first number higher than twelve, no second number over thirty-one. Their birthdays probably."

Kordic rearranged the table setting so he could get at the documents. His eyes zeroed in on the figures Maureen had highlighted in yellow. "Lolley was really raking in big bucks, wasn't she?"

"Yes. I had a meeting with Al Balardi in the crime lab today."

"Al's a good man," Kordic said, his forehead knitting as he read through the printouts.

"Balardi said that there was a third kid in Lolley's house. He picked up her prints off the computer disks, the money box, in several of the rooms, and the Lexus. They have to be Janna's."

"Al's sure the prints are a kid's?"

"Positive. Balardi also says that the frequency pattern of the prints suggest that this kid wasn't in the house for very long." Maureen reached across the table and tapped her fingernail on the printouts. "Look at this. Lolley paid someone named Y. Stoylar seven thousand dollars for Janna."

"That could explain the backup disks being left behind. The killer didn't find the metal box, but maybe Janna did."

"The kid sure had a good view of the killings. She saw the bastard put the potatoes on the gun. And she must have gotten a pretty good look at him. Brown hair and a red nose."

"That doesn't narrow it down a hell of a lot, Mo. I wonder just how much we can believe of what Janna tells us."

The waitress came with their dinner orders. The slab of beef reminded Kordic of the one he'd left on his plate at the Savoy Hotel conference room.

"What about this Y. Stoylar. Did you run him?"

"Yep. He's negative. Or she is. We don't know if it's a man or woman. Without a full name or date of birth, I couldn't pick anything up in DMV, criminal, or reports. A complete blank. And there's more bad news on the HV2500 computer case. I talked to an exec at Helmut-Victor. They manufactured over a hundred thousand of the damn things, and they retail at close to ten thousand bucks. No record of Angela Lolley or Y. Stoylar buying one, or at least registering the sale with Helmut-Victor, and they say that almost everyone registers the machine's serial number to cover the warranty, in case it's lost or stolen. They faxed me some information on the HV2500. It does everything but feed and burp you."

Kordic drummed his fingers on the stem of his wineglass. "So, if we find the damn thing, we can trace the owner." He gave a halfhearted smile. "That's good news."

Maureen studied Kordic as he chewed thoughtfully on a piece of prime rib. He seemed amazingly calm for a man who'd nearly been killed in a bombing incident.

Kordic sawed off another hunk of the meat, then said, "So what have we got? This third kid, Janna, was there at the time of the shooting, hiding in the adjoining room, and when the shooter left, she went to the metal box and found the cash. There's no telling how much money Lollipop had stashed there—it could be thousands of dollars. The computer disks wouldn't have been of any interest to her, so she takes the money, and probably the notebook, and runs."

"It seems to make sense, Jack."

Kordic pushed his plate away, his appetite suddenly

gone. "Some of it, anyway. We may be reading too much into the girl having the notebook computer. The killer could have found it and just dropped the case in Lolley's bedroom."

"The case was lying right alongside the metal box and the money," Maureen reminded him. "If Janna did take it, then the killer could still be after it, and her. Janna's somewhere in the city now, and scared as hell."

"I don't blame her for that. If Balardi is right, and Janna wasn't at the house for very long, how the hell did she know about the metal box? Lollipop had it well hidden under the floorboards. Maybe Janna knew the killer, let him into the house, and . . ." His voice trailed off. "No, if she was in on it with the killer, she never would have made those calls to you."

Maureen began pushing the food around her plate with her fork, repositioning it rather than eating. "Al Balardi sent a group of unidentified fingerprints he picked up at the house to the FBI. Stoylar's could be among them."

"Let's hope so," Kordic concurred, his eyes focusing back on the printouts. "At least we've got first names for the two young victims—Tina and Amber. Christ, look at the number of dates for them."

"Check the last one. The last day of the month. March thirty-first. Paul, August eleven. Tina, Amber, and Janna. It's the only listing for Janna."

Kordic made a clucking sound of disapproval. "Twenty-five hundred dollars." He paged through the printouts. "Paul, August eleven was a regular. Usually five hundred dollars a visit. He must have been spending two grand a month at Lolley's place. Then the sudden jump to twenty-five hundred a visit. It had to be for the new girl, Janna, for all three of them."

"Let's hope we get lucky and this Paul, August eleven's prints will match up with something at the FBI lab."

Kordic grunted contemptuously. He had never had a great deal of respect for the FBI in general, and now their once-revered labs had been tarnished so badly that local police departments were using private forensic agencies.

Still, the Bureau had the largest collection of fingerprints in the world. "Y. Stoylar. He could be the killer. He sold Janna to Lollipops, then came back for more money. And the girl."

Maureen's forehead knitted. "It could have been a new client. Someone who was disgusted with the whole scene. Or someone who saw the kind of jewelry Lolley wore and decided it was worth his while to take her out."

"Possible," Kordic conceded. "But that someone used a small caliber semiautomatic pistol with a makeshift silencer."

Maureen's interest was immediate. Had she missed something in the crime lab's report? "How do you know the gun was a semiautomatic? We didn't find any cartridge casings in the house."

"No. The killer picked them up, another sign we're dealing with a pro. It had to be a semiautomatic. It's not possible to silence a revolver, even with a state-of-the-art silencer, it's just the way the guns are designed. Whoever our killer is, he's resourceful, using a potato like that." Kordic handed the waitress his credit card. "Come on, let's stop back at Lolley's house on the way home."

"You think I missed something?" Connah said defensively.

"No, but thre should be something there now that wasn't there when you last looked."

Connah looked at him blankly.

"The mail," Kordic explained. "Always go back and check the mail. We don't know a hell of a lot about Lolley, other than she was a kiddy madam, and was obviously pulling in a lot of money. You saw all those financial magazines. She was probably playing the market, and may have a big fat bank account and a safe-deposit box full of cash. And she may have some relatives out there. If so, you can be sure an attorney will show up, open a probate, and make things difficult for us, so we might as well get as much as we can, while we can. So we look through the mail, and anything we find that might help us, we keep. And we don't tell the Post Office." Kordic grabbed the arms of the chair and hauled himself to his feet. "Technically, the mail that comes in is now under their jurisdiction. And they can get touchy as hell about it."

Chapter 14

The weather suited Frank Dunbar just fine. The dense, murky fog cut visibility down to half a block and the chill, ocean-scented wind was strong enough to limit pedestrian traffic. He took a final slow ride past 54 Tara Street. He was satisfied that the house was empty and that there were no police surveillance vehicles in the area.

He'd had the property under observation for the last three hours. The possibility that the police were waiting inside the house was remote. Paulie Boy was right about that. There was no reason for them to be there.

Still, he hadn't taken any chances. He'd used the pay phone at the nearby BART station to call the police emergency line and reported a hit-and-run accident at Tara and Geneva, fifty yards from Lolley's house.

Two black-and-white cars and an ambulance had responded in a matter of minutes, searching for the supposed victim.

Dunbar paid little attention to their activities. His undivided interest was on Angela Lolley's house. Cops are naturally nosey, they hate to be left out of anything. No lights went on, no one came to the door.

He remembered a piece of work in Dublin years earlier.

The target had been a ritzy jewelry store on Grafton Street. His partner, a dim-witted Orangeman weighed down by three pints of Guinness, wanted to smash the window and grab what was there. But Dunbar had used the same ploy, calling in a phony accident. When the local coppers showed up with their sirens blowing, three plainclothesmen had bolted out of the apartment across the street from the jewelry store, guns and flashlights in hand.

If Dunbar hadn't made the call, he and his half-drunk friend would have gone right into the nick.

He drove up the ski-slope-inclined hill, made a tight U-turn, and parked the car in front of an abandoned house, its windows broken, the muddy front yard clogged with old newspapers. He sat listening to the engine crackle from its heat, his eyes on the garage doors. He waited five minutes, then reached for the crowbar under the front seat.

"Show time," he muttered softly as he exited the car. He tugged the brim of his battered tweed hat down, lifted the collar of his dark blue windbreaker, and started walking, his rubber-soled shoes making faint kissing sounds on the wet sidewalk.

"I feel like I'm in a time warp," Jack Kordic said, looking at the weather through the car's windshield wipers. "It's just like London."

"Nothing's like London," Maureen Connah said adamantly.

"How's your father doing?" Kordic asked.

"Pretty well, considering he suffered a pretty bad stroke. He can get out on his own now. Mom hates it when he drives by himself, but he's stubborn." She glanced at Kordic. "I guess you know that."

Kordic nodded his agreement. He had never been a fan of former Deputy Chief "Big John" Connah. Nor Connah of him. John Connah had once been a force to be reckoned with. He had a clique of loyal friends, most of whom were Irish, and he had rewarded them with promotions and details to choice assignments.

He'd also cultivated friendships with the local politicians and press, and he no doubt still had close ties to many powerful people in the Irish community.

Kordic had never fit into Big John's profile, and while Connah hadn't actively opposed Kordic's promotion to the Homicide detail, he hadn't given him any support, either.

"You might run this Irish hit man scenario by your father, Mo."

Maureen coasted to a stop at a traffic light. "I can ask, but—"

She let out a string of curses as a battered pickup truck ran the red light on Geneva Street.

"Makes you wish you were a cop with a ticket book, doesn't it?" Kordic said with some nostalgia.

Connah jammed the car into low and the tires briefly hydroplaned on the slick pavement.

"You know, I've actually never written a ticket."

"You didn't miss much," Kordic assured her. "Here we are, Mo. Tara Street."

Connah was halfway into her turn when Kordic shouted: "A man! At Lolley's garage door! Get him!"

The sound of the squealing tires caused Frank Dunbar's head to hook around. He squinted at the headlights, dropping the crowbar when he saw the car's spotlight flick on, his hand clawing for the gun in his waistband. He dove to the ground and rolled over to the protection of a dark sedan, hugging the fender, before cautiously raising his head.

Maureen hit the brakes and the unmarked police car veered momentarily out of control.

"Call for backup," Kordic ordered, opening the door before the car came to a complete stop.

Dunbar snapped off two quick shots at the man in the car's passenger seat, then started running, his chest heaving after he'd gone no more than a few yards.

He took a quick look over his shoulder. A man in a tan raincoat was out of the car, running after him. Gaining ground.

Dunbar swiveled around, fell to one knee, and steadied the gun in the palm of his left hand. He fired two more shots. The man in the tan raincoat belly-flopped to the pavement.

Dunbar scrambled to his feet and started running, careening off a streetlight post as he reached the corner.

He could hear the rush of traffic below him as he hurried across the pedestrian overpass. The freeway was a caterpillar of lights. He felt a sudden pain in his chest and his legs turned rubbery. Fuckin' cigarettes, he told himself. If I get out of this, no more fuckin' cigarettes. He looked over his shoulder again. The copper in the raincoat was still after him, just turning the corner. Dunbar dropped his head to his chest and ran hard, as hard as he could, expecting to hear the sound of a gunshot any second, expecting to feel the impact before he heard the sound.

A grouping of eight or nine people were clustered around a glass-partitioned bus stop. Dunbar zigzagged his way through them and plunged down the steps, into the Balboa Park BART station.

Maureen Connah gripped the steering wheel with one hand, the other clutched the radio microphone: "This is unit Five-H, four-oh-six, shots are fired! Four-oh-six," she blared, repeating the emergency code for officer needs help. "Geneva and Tara Streets, near BART."

Connah let go of the microphone, her right hand digging for the 9mm Beretta holstered under her left shoulder. She slowed down briefly when she came level with Kordic, then punched the accelerator when she saw the man in the tweed hat barrel through a group of people, then disappear down the steps to the BART station.

The car jumped the curb and skidded along the sidewalk, knocking down a string of newspaper racks before bucking to a halt. She opened the door, swearing viciously when the seat belt restraints dug into her stomach. Her fingers grappled frantically at the release latch. By the time she was free, Kordic was alongside and they descended the brick stairs two at a time.

The sirens from the police units responding to the 406 call were ululating in the distance.

They stopped at the landing. The interior of the station resembled a bunker: raw concrete walls and floors. Strings of ticket dispensers and money changers lined the walls. An attractive black woman sat behind a glass-walled information booth, her face paralyzed, her mouth open in a wide circle, her eyes transfixed on Maureen's gun. A half-dozen statue-figured citizens stared back at Connah and Kordic.

"Police," Kordic shouted. "A man in a tweed hat and dark jacket just ran down the stairs. Did anyone see him?"

Maureen leaned over the railing, looking down some fifteen feet to the station's second level, where the BART trains ran. One of the smooth-skinned silver-colored trains was just pulling away.

Kordic caught her eye. "I don't think he had time to get on the train."

"I saw a man in a tweed hat run out that way," a tall, gaunt woman in a yellow rain slicker yelled out.

Kordic and Connah followed her hand to an exit that led to an escalator ascending back up to Geneva Avenue, and an outdoor stairway that skirted under the freeway toward City College. A six-foot anchor fence was the only barrier to the Muni Railway's Car Barn, which was filled with over a hundred empty, dark-windowed buses and streetcars.

Kordic turned full circle surveying the possibilities. "The bastard could be anywhere, Mo."

Connah holstered her weapon. She sighed and drew a deep breath into her lungs. "Are you all right, Jack? Some of those shots looked like they came pretty damn close."

"Yeah." Kordic held out the folds of his new raincoat, poking a finger through the bullet hole in the plaid lining. "Too damn close." He patted his right hip, the location where his gun had been positioned for twenty years. "I could have had the bastard, Mo. I left my goddamn gun at home. I couldn't take it on the trip to London."

"Did you get a good look at him?"

"Not much of one. White, in his thirties or forties. Five ten or eleven. Thin. Tweed hat. His jacket was black or dark blue. I couldn't tell if he had a red nose, but I did get a real good look at his gun. A revolver this time."

"Maybe he wasn't the killer," Maureen said, her breath exploding like little clouds in front of her face in the cold night air. "The killer used an automatic on Lollipop and the girls."

"Yeah, which shows he's a pro. He disposed of that gun right away. The killer. Returning to the scene of the crime. How's that for a cliché? Let's go back to the house and see what he came back for."

Chapter 15

England

Doug Lancer downshifted as he curled the silver BMW through a village of cottages with low thatched roofs and whitened, softly rounded walls. He accelerated when he reached a long stretch of overgrown ridge-and-furrow fields filled with grazing sheep, only to brake down to loitering speed when he approached the chain of hawthorn hedgerows shielding Philip Bovard's house from the road.

He stopped at the hulking ten-foot-high medieval iron gate, reached through the car's window, and punched in the security code numbers he'd been given. The well-oiled gates swung open slowly, noiselessly.

Lancer motored up the cobbled road to an ancient stone bridge that arched over a deep-banked river bordered by stands of pale pink pimpernel and yellow asphodel wildflowers.

Lancer had never been to this particular piece of property. He was impressed when the house came into view. Three stories of narrow bricks that had been salvaged from a long-lost Roman ruin filled in the timbered framework.

Rows of leaded casement windows jutted out from the bricks.

Philip Bovard stood on the lichened steps leading to the front doors, his thumbs tucked in the slash pockets of his houndstooth sport coat. Twill trousers, Wellington boots, and a canvas fishing hat completed his outfit.

The perfect English gentleman farmer, thought Lancer. Though Bovard was anything but English. His philosophy was talk American, dress English, eat French, and think German.

"Welcome," Bovard called with little enthusiasm as Lancer exited the BMW.

"Afternoon, sir," he responded, noticing that there was mud on Bovard's boots and a fishing creel at his feet.

"Come on in," Bovard said abruptly, picking up his creel, turning his back on Lancer, and entering the house.

Lancer followed in his host's footsteps, across a highly polished rosewood floor. The walls were paneled in dark walnut and festooned with paintings of pompous-looking men with long beards.

Bovard's boots left a trail of mud droppings on the floor. He bumped his way through a door that led them into the kitchen. A stout, stern-eyed woman wearing a white apron stood in front of an industrial-sized stove stirring a wooden spoon in a cast-iron pot.

Bovard shooed her away with a hand, then upended his creel into the sink, sending a half-dozen silvery trout slithering around the enamel. He slid a boning knife from a drawer and started gutting the fish.

Lancer said nothing, watching Bovard go about his task.

It had been five years since he'd first met Philip Bovard. Five very prosperous years. Bovard was an average-looking man, at least when first observed. In his late fifties, of medium height, with dark hair that curled around his ears and a stomach that bulged over his belt buckle. Lancer had almost brushed him off when Bovard first approached him in a pub in Covent Gardens, figuring the man was a poof, trying to pick him up.

When Bovard spoke, there was a trace of French: street-hard, gutter French. Later, Lancer learned that Bovard spoke seven languages, and was adept at expressing himself as a polished scholar or a coarse-mouthed thug in all of them. Bovard had started that first conversation by bringing up details about Lancer's life, some of which even Lancer had long forgotten.

"Well?" Bovard finally called over his shoulder.

"Everything worked out just right," Doug Lancer said.

Bovard began rinsing the fish under the kitchen faucet, the water turning red after contact. "Scotland Yard seems satisfied that our friend Mouse Fennesy was responsible for the bomb."

"Yes," Bovard agreed. "They do like to settle these things on the Irish."

Bovard turned to face Lancer, shaking the water from his hands before drying them off with a kitchen towel. "Have you ever been to San Francisco?"

"A long time ago. When I was in the Australian navy."

Bovard bunched the towel up and tossed it over his shoulder. "You're going back. Right away. This is urgent. That man you recommended. Dunbar. He botched the job."

"Mouse Fennesy told me Dunbar was reliable."

"Well, the dearly departed Mr. Fennesy was wrong."

"We haven't done much in the United States," Lancer reminded. "Outside of Boston. Nothing on the West Coast. There wasn't enough time to send someone we trust to San Francisco."

"Don't get your hackles up, Douglas, I'm not blaming you. Dunbar killed three of the targets, but there was an additional one that he missed. A young girl. Her name is Janna. That's all we know now. Except that she got away with a notebook computer. It's vital that we get it back. I want you to do whatever it takes to get the notebook, and eliminate her. This has priority over anything else you're involved in. Use Dunbar any way you wish. Whether or not he finds the girl and kills her before you get to San Francisco, I want you to eliminate him. Totally. The man, his possessions. Make it all disappear. As if he'd never existed." Bovard twitched his head toward the butcher-block table. "Everything you need to know is in that folder."

"I'll handle it," Lancer assured him. "Who's the client?"

Bovard picked up the boning knife and ran the blade under the faucet. "Patrick Lynam."

"Lawrence Lynam's son?" Lancer asked.

"Yes. He'll contact you, using the name 'Old Friend.' Don't let him know that you know who he is. It may be necessary for you to kill him, too."

"I thought Lynam was valuable to us."

Bovard grasped the knife by the tip of the blade and flung it toward a kitchen cabinet. It made a thunking sound as the blade penetrated the wood. "*Was* may be the operable word, Douglas. Patrick Lynam did something incredibly stupid. It's his notebook we have to find. The fool left it at this bordello, and the young girl took off with it. This could jeopardize the Russian nuclear reactor deal. If the notebook falls into the wrong hands, if she's arrested and the police piece things together, we are finished. I need Lynam for this deal, it can't be concluded without him. Our clients are expecting delivery in Cyprus on April the tenth. The reactors are in transit. If I fail them this time, they'll be after my ass. You're booked on the Concorde out of Heathrow at six this evening. Leave your car here. My helicopter will deliver you right to the airport. I'll be flying to San Francisco tomorrow. Don't disappoint me, Douglas. There's too much at stake. For both of us."

"I'll take care of it, boss," Lancer replied confidently. He had never seen Bovard this nervous, this upset.

Bovard grunted, then asked: "Are you hungry?"

Lancer kept his face passive. Bovard had never asked him to eat with him before. A quick drink in celebration of a successful operation, but not a formal meal.

"Yes, I missed lunch," he disclosed.

Bovard turned his attention back to the trout. "I'll have Hilda pack you something. You can eat in the helicopter on the way to the airport."

Janna Drovana balanced nimbly on one leg as she stretched her arms to reach the narrow, weather-torn window ledge. The windows had been broken so many times that the city had stopped replacing them years ago. Her fingers dug into the soggy wood and she leaped upward,

pulling herself up high enough so that she could peer
inside the darkened stable.

She hung there for several moments. The only sounds
were the occasional shuffling of a horse's hoofs. It was
risky, she knew, hiding in the stable that housed the police
horses. The presence of the police so nearby would keep
the others away. The filthy ones who roamed the park at
night. They could be as dangerous as Cousin Yuri—men
who slept in makeshift tents, alongside small campfires
and drank or took drugs. They had tried to lure her into
one of their camps that first night she'd spent in the park.
One had threatened her with a knife, another with a
hatchet.

Janna adjusted the backpack, hooked her elbow over
the window's sill, swung her legs up slowly, then slith-
ered through the opening, falling noiselessly onto the hay-
covered flooring.

She got to her hands and knees, her head cocked to
one side, while her eyes slowly adjusted to the darkness.
She could make out the bulky figures of two dozing
horses.

She edged her way to the far corner of the stall where
bales of hay were haphazardly stacked in random
heights. She took out the small flashlight she'd purchased, flicked on the beam, and wormed her way
through a narrow opening, the dry scent triggering
memories of the stables near Moskovsky Park where her
father had often taken her to ride the horses. As she
pushed her way forward, the gaps in the hay stacks
widened and she found the same tiny cocoon where
she'd spent the night before Cousin Yuri and the fat
woman had captured her.

Janna laid down on her side, and took the notebook
computer from her jacket pocket, positioning the flashlight
between her knees so she could see the keyboard clearly.
She began fiddling with the controls, and the screen
brightened.

The mailbox icon was blinking. She clicked into the read
mail file. Her heartbeat quickened when she saw the E-

mail message: Janna, are you all right? Do you need help? Money?

Janna quickly deleted the message and turned the computer off. Somehow Paul knew she had the computer. How? Could he trace her through the computer? Find out where she was? Where she was sleeping? She decided to throw the computer away. In the morning.

She pulled the knit hat down over her ears and snuggled up against the hay, pulling her legs up against her chest. Safe. I'm safe, she told herself. For now. But for how long? She thought of her mother. Her father. Of Russia. Of home, and began sobbing, jamming the heel of her hand against her lips to muffle the sound.

Doug Lancer wasn't looking forward to flying the Concorde, despite the fact that it would deposit him in New York in approximately three and a half hours.

The sleek airplane was overrated in Lancer's estimation: noisy, narrow, and cramped, and there was no real first-class section. The entire passenger list of one hundred thirty-two were supposedly treated as first class. He shuffled along with the prosperous-looking crowd waiting in line to board the plane, most of whom were grumbling about a twenty-five-minute takeoff delay.

His assigned seat was up front, in the second row, so at least he'd be able to disembark quickly when they landed in New York.

Lancer was traveling under a forged passport that Philip Bovard had provided. John David. A nice common name, with the added plus of being reversible: John David—David John. Lancer preferred names like that: William George—George William, Allen Charles—Charles Allen. The simple switch of the first and last name had proved useful in the past, when checking into hotels or at airports: desk clerks, ticket clerks, security guards, even customs officials most often barely glanced at a passport's signature. Most preferred wasting their time checking out the resemblance of the man to the passport photograph. Additional false identity cards, an assortment of weapons, and communications equipment would be waiting for him in New York on the chartered jet taking him to San Francisco.

His lone piece of luggage, a nylon suitcase he kept in the trunk of the BMW, contained a small assortment of clothing: socks, underwear, shirts, slacks, all void of labels or laundry marks, along with a map of San Francisco that Bovard had supplied with his instructions, which had included a detailed dossier on Francis Aloysius Dunbar: his criminal record as recorded in Irish police files: four arrests—two convictions, both for misdemeanors, and the information Bovard had been able to dig up on Dunbar's suspected terrorist activities— seven known assassinations, which meant there were probably at least a dozen that even Bovard couldn't confirm. Dunbar's mug shot was obviously taken after he'd been roughed up by the police: a cut over his right eye, nose out of plumb, and swollen lips. Dunbar had migrated to America two years ago, and so far had avoided any contact with the police.

Lancer hated being dropped into an unknown area on the spur of the moment. All he could recall of his prior visit to San Francisco was the pier where his ship had docked and that waterfront bar.

What was it? Twelve or fifteen years ago? It had been a bar he had later heard referred to in American slang as "a bucket of blood."

A bucket might have been a bit of an overstatement, but there had been a pint or two of spilled blood on the floor. Some of it his own.

He nodded vaguely to the flight attendant as he took his assigned seat, squirming in the chair to get comfortable as he opened the suitcase and began unfolding a map of San Francisco.

As soon as the plane was airborne, Lancer flagged a steward and ordered a double vodka. He studied the map for a while, then dozed off. The announcement that they would be landing in New York in fifteen minutes dragged him from a groggy sleep. He felt the need to visit the men's room, but decided it would be better to wait until after they had docked at the airport—the pint-sized lavatories were another one of his grievances against the Concorde. Had he taken that trip down the aisle, he would have seen a fellow traveler in the back of the plane: a man with gray hair like steel wool and skin tanned the color of tree bark.

Chapter 16

Captain of Detectives Bill Neil shut the door behind Inspector Jack Kordic and waved him to a seat. "Sit down, Jack," he said as he walked around his surfboard-shaped desk. "Scotland Yard called, just to make sure you arrived home okay."

Kordic settled himself into a hard-as-marble chair positioned in front of Neil's desk.

Neil was heavyset, with wavy, mahogany-brown hair. His face was crisscrossed with the lines of a lifelong worrier. His most pronounced feature was his long, jutting chin, a chin that made a tempting target for the many enemies he'd made during his career. Neil wasn't worried about his enemies now. He was one of the mayor's "apostles," and in charge of the mayor's pet project, turning San Francisco into Hollywood North. The office walls were slathered with photographs of Neil in concert with movie and television personalities who had come to town to make their films.

Anything the producers wanted, be it shutting down a street, or a bridge, or City Hall, or the Hall of Justice itself to allow filming a scene was quickly agreed to. And Bill Neil was quite often there for the filming, schmoozing with the Hollywood crowd, his reward an occasional spot in a scene, and, if the rumors Kordic heard were true, "tokens of appreciation" such as elaborate dinners, lunch with a movie personality, and the companionship of aspiring actresses.

Neil perched one hip of his well-tailored suit on the edge of his desk and beamed at Kordic. "Man, that was some stroke of luck, you getting out of the room before the big bang. The top dog over there. What the hell's his name?" He snapped his fingers rapidly as if that act would jar his memory.

"Commander Hugh Gresham," Kordic supplied.

"Yeah, right. Gresham. He says they haven't come up with any additional suspects on the bombing. Just this Mouse Fennesy guy."

"Gresham made no bones about wanting me out of London in a hurry. He damn near kicked me out of town. I don't think they want to find anyone else, Captain."

Neil walked behind his desk and plopped into the overstuffed executive chair. "What the hell do you mean by that?"

"Someone I know in the Mossad thinks that Fennesy was just a fall guy."

Neil hunched his shoulders. "Yeah? Well, that's their problem, Jack. Not ours. How are you getting along with Maureen Connah?"

"So far, so good, Cap."

Neil nodded and edged forward in his chair. "Do you know Tom Flavio, Maureen's ex? He works out of vice."

"I met him a couple of times," Kordic said, "but I don't really know him."

"He swears that Maureen's a closet dyke. That would be a shame, wouldn't it? Built like she is, and a lesbo. I've known her since she was a little kid. Big John Connah is a good buddy of mine, Jack. A damn good buddy. As a favor to him, I put Maureen in Homicide." Neil leaned back in his chair and crossed his legs delicately, smoothing the crease to avoid wrinkles. "I kind of hated to drop her on you. Maureen really hasn't done any real cop work. Her father once had a lot of clout, but all his friends are long gone. Except for me. I went out on a limb for Maureen. So far she hasn't shown much appreciation, so keep me posted, you know what I mean? If she can't hack it, I want to know about it. If she hasn't got what it takes to handle Homicide, then it's better to know it now, so I can put her someplace else, you know what I mean, Jack?"

Kordic knew only too well what Neil meant. Neil wanted him to pass along the threat, that if Maureen didn't show some "appreciation" she'd be transferred out of Homicide, and he wanted Kordic to back him by saying she couldn't do the job. He pushed his chair back, the legs making scraping sounds on the linoleum floor. "Is that all, Captain?"

"Relax, Jack. Don't get all uptight. I just want you to know that if you feel she's not qualified, not packing her weight, I'll transfer her to another detail. Now tell me, what's going on in the Lollipop case?"

Kordic gave Neil a briefing on the information that was on the computer disks and what had taken place at the BART station the night before. "I didn't get a very good look at him. White, wearing a tweed hat. I was ducking most of the time he was shooting at me."

"The bombing in London and now this guy. That's two close calls in a short period of time. Why do you think he went back to the house?"

"The mail. We found photographs of a young girl, one who survived the massacre. We think Lolley took the pictures. She probably showed them to her clients. The girl's name is Janna. She saw the murderer kill the two other girls. She called Maureen and gave her a description of the killer. Brown hair and a red nose."

"And Mo didn't rope the kid in?"

"I listened to the tape recordings. Maureen handled it well. I think the girl will call back."

"Great," Neil scoffed. "Why would the shooter go back for the photographs? How did he know they'd be there?"

"Maybe he just wanted the mail. Any mail. Or maybe there's something he knows is coming in. Something that can identify him."

Neil walked over and wrapped his arm around Kordic's shoulder. "Okay, but if you need help, just ask. The mayor has expressed an interest in the case. He hates kids being used like that. So keep me up-to-date on the investigation."

Kordic gave a quick nod and Neil patted him on the back. "Hey, nice coat, Jack. New?"

"A London souvenir."

Neil's mouth twisted into a sour grin. "So, you had a little time over there before they kicked you out, huh? At least to shop."

Janna was sitting on a bench drinking a cup of hot chocolate she'd bought from the concession stand in Golden Gate Park. The merry-go-round hadn't opened yet. She'd decided not to throw the computer away. She had found a way to access the entertainment section, and was enjoying a game of chess, lost in concentration as she maneuvered the pieces on the black-and-white board with just a click of a key.

The mail icon came on. She sat up straight, and looked over her shoulder, to see if she was being watched. It was another message from Paul.

Janna. Please let me help you. I read about the terrible things that happened. Are you all right? Do you need money? Please respond.

Janna's fingers hovered over the keyboard a moment, then clicked in: yes, no. Leave me alone or I will go to the police!

Maureen Connah had propped the dozen glossy eight-by-ten colored photographs across a row of procedural textbooks on her desk. Janna. It had to be Janna. Her long dark hair was twisted into pigtails. God, she was a beauty. She had a clean, well-defined nose and mouth. A firm chin. Her eyes were a bright blue.

In one picture she was wearing a short skirt and starched white blouse, the very same outfit the two dead girls were wearing when they were murdered. The photographs showed her in a variety of poses: in one she wore a slip, in another a two-piece bathing suit, and in another, just a pair of white panties.

One thing was constant in the photographs—the look of discomfort or fear on her face. Maureen wondered at first why she wasn't coached, or perhaps drugged to look happier, more seductive, then it dawned on her—Lollipop's customers must have preferred the children that way—fearful, vulnerable.

"More work for you, Inspector."

Maureen looked up to see the concerned face of Al Balardi from the crime lab looking down at her. Balardi was a heavyset man with pouchy eyes and long-lobed ears. His dark hair was straight and neatly parted. The breast pocket of his white smock drooped under the weight of an array of ballpoint pens.

"The FBI finally got off their duffs and sent in those prints from Tara Street." He dropped the packet on Maureen's desk, then nodded somberly and said: "Four hits. I hope they help."

Maureen tipped over the photographs of the girl, swept them into a pile, and quickly started digging through the FBI reports.

It was almost an hour later when she leaned back and parked a pencil in her hair. She had to tell Kordic about this. Where the hell was he?

Maureen bolted out of her chair when she saw Kordic striding toward her desk.

"Jack. We just got the FBI report on the prints our lab couldn't identify. Four hits! Four of them!"

"Great," Kordic responded enthusiastically. "Come on, let's celebrate. I'll buy lunch."

Maureen looked at the phone on her desk. She was hoping for a call from Janna.

"We'll be back in half an hour," Kordic said. "Charlotte will beep you if anything comes in." He leaned over to look at the photographs of Janna. "Why don't you pick out the one you think is best, have the lab make some copies, and we'll send them out to the district stations."

They took the elevator to the main floor, crossed Bryant Street, then walked down Sixth, past the wholesale flower stands bursting with brilliantly multicolored blooms and into the Flower Mart Coffee Shop.

It was ten-thirty, between the breakfast and lunch crowd, and the restaurant was practically deserted.

Kordic selected a booth that gave them a bird's-eye view of the activity at the flower stands. He picked up a menu and ordered a steak sandwich and coffee.

"I'm still not sure what time zone I'm in," he explained with a forced smile.

When the waitress brought their coffee, Kordic gave a long sigh, then said: "Now, let's see those FBI reports."

Maureen extracted the envelope from her purse. "Four positive hits. One, Arnold Devlin, a dentist who lives in Mill Valley. Another, an attorney, Richard Bekker, lives in San Mateo. Their prints were all over the room where we found the two dead girls—on the walls, the floors, those trapeze things hanging from the ceiling, and on the baby crib in the adjoining room."

She slid the documents over to Kordic. "No criminal records on either of them. The FBI matched their prints to old service records: the army and the coast guard."

Kordic took a bite of his sandwich, then went through the documents. Both men were Caucasians. Devlin was forty-five years old, Bekker fifty-six. "Lollipop's customers. It's going to be fun grilling the bastards. What about the other two hits?"

Connah allowed herself a thin little smile before passing the final reports to Kordic. "Number three is a man named Daryl Houng. He lives here in San Francisco. On Moneta Way. That's only about a half mile from Lolley's house on Tara Street. His prints are on the computer screen and the desk in Lolley's office, Jack. Nowhere else."

Kordic studied the printout on Houng. "Thirty-two years of age. He's younger than the others. No rap sheet?"

"No. The FBI picked him up on a Department of Defense employment application. He worked for the Pentagon until about a year ago."

"It's hard to believe the killer would be that sloppy, leaving prints on the computer screen." Kordic turned his attention to the last report. "And who's behind curtain number four?"

"I saved the best 'til last. Yuri Stoylar. According to Lolley's records, the guy who sold Janna to her was Y. Stoylar. The FBI shows him with just one arrest, for armed robbery back in Brooklyn three years ago. The charges were dismissed. Now we've got his full name and date of birth, his social security number, but he's still negative— no local rap sheet, no DMV record. Nothing. I called the Brooklyn P.D. They're going to fax me everything they've got."

"Where did we find his prints at Lolley's place?"

"Just one print, Jack, a thumb, under the toilet seat."

Kordic dropped the reports and turned his head slowly to look out at the activity in the Flower Mart parking lot. A delivery van was unloading a cargo of richly colored, long-stemmed gladiolus to one of the vendors. He focused in on a spray of yellow flowers. They'd been his wife's favorite. He'd gotten into the habit of buying her a dozen yellow gladiolus every Friday, before driving home across the bridge to Walnut Creek.

Maureen saw his face tighten, his eyes turn watery. "Are you all right, Jack," she asked.

"Yeah, sure," Kordic responded. "Old memories. You say only one print on the toilet seat. Stoylar was probably at the house just that one time, when he delivered the girl."

"Unless he's the killer, and wore gloves when we went back."

Kordic rubbed his forehead as if soothing away a pain. "I've got a feeling about this one. The shooter we encountered at the house last night. Let's say he wasn't this Stoylar guy. Stoylar wouldn't be interested in the photographs. He sold the girl to Lolley. But the shooter was the one who killed Lolley and the two girls. I'm betting he went back for the photographs. Why take that kind of a risk? Because he needed them to ID the girl, or because he didn't want us to see them? I think we better find your Janna before he does."

Chapter 17

Yuri Stoylar bobbed along in the middle of the crowd like a fishing float. He was amazed at the number of people mulling around the Whale Fountain in front of the Steinhart Aquarium.

Men, women, and children stuffing their faces with cotton candy, popcorn, hot dogs. He wondered if he could sell his PCP-laced stamps here. So far he'd seen one policeman—a young, moon-faced Asian in blue shirt, pants, and a baseball cap, who didn't appear to be carrying a gun.

Stoylar himself had been approached twice by young men, men in their twenties, dressed in jeans and leather.

One wanted to sell him some high-grade marijuana: "Just down from Humboldt County, man. The best shit on the street."

The second man, cadaver thin with a mustache that looked like melted chocolate over his lip, flashed a cellophane bag at him. "Nickel bag, man. How about it?"

Yuri had been tempted to try to sell him one of the stamps, but he wasn't sure. Maybe the man was a policeman. An undercover policeman. Either that, or the man was stupid, because Stoylar considered himself to now look like a cheap version of the television policeman in the clothes he'd picked up from a secondhand store on Clement Street: a raincoat, a felt hat, and large-lensed sunglasses. A black woolen scarf covered his neck and the lower half of his face.

He bought himself a Coca-Cola, settled on a bench near the fountain, and monitored the area. The two drug dealers worked the crowd well. He'd seen the skinny one make five sales, so he couldn't be a policeman.

Stoylar leaned his arms back against the bench and swept his eyes over steps leading up to the aquarium and the Morrison Planetarium. He'd been wandering through Golden Gate Park for several hours, stopping at all the places he knew Janna liked: the merry-go-round, the Tea Garden, and the aquarium. She had often bored him with stories about the fish, the alligators, and especially the penguins. Penguins. What good was a penguin? Especially in San Francisco?

There was no sign of Janna. He would have considered the afternoon a complete waste of time if it weren't for the drug dealers. He'd found a good place to sell his drug-laced stamps.

The killer, after he had taken care of Angela and the two girls, may have decided to take Janna with him. Use her, then kill her, dump her body somewhere.

Or maybe the killer was in the same business as Angela. There was money to be made with Janna. No doubt about it. And if he ever did find her, he—

Stoylar dropped the can of Coke, the dark liquid splashing on his pants leg and shoes. That girl! The girl running up the steps. It looked like Janna.

The San Francisco Hall of Justice is a squat, seven-story concrete block building that takes up a full square block of prime south of Market property. It is consistently ranked number one in the polls rating the ugliest buildings in the city.

The detective bureaus are situated on the fourth floor, the Homicide detail is located just around the corner from the central elevators. It is a large L-shaped room, separated from the hallway by a partition sealing off the receptionist's desk. There are rows of mismatched gray metal desks, the desk tops cluttered with phones, computer screens, file holders, and the detective's personal collection of family photographs and memorabilia from former cases: a piece of iron pipe, bullet casings, hammers, and a mixed bag of blunt instruments.

Ray Tracey, the Homicide detail's temporary lieutenant, kept a set of six FaberCastell number two lead pencils in an enclosed lucite case on his desk, to remind him of a serial killer who murdered his victims, all female schoolteachers, by jamming one of the pencils in their ears. Tracey had finally caught the man, a retired public school janitor, while he was stalking his seventh victim.

Two twin-sized interrogation rooms, nothing more than cramped cubicles, are positioned against the northern part of the room, smack up against the elevator shafts.

The walls and ceiling are paneled with acoustical tile that have taken on a locker-room yellow coloring over the years.

The furnishings consist of a narrow wooden table, the top of which is crosscrossed with cigarette burns and knife carvings, and three plain wooden chairs, with nearly as many scars as the table.

Daryl Houng was sitting in one of the chairs. His prints had been found on Lolley's computer screen and her desk. His explanation was a simple one—he worked for the retailer that had sold and serviced Angela Lolley's computer. He had been sent to update the machine's hard disk and software when Lolley moved into the house on Tara Street some five months ago.

Houng was a soft-voiced man. He looked at Kordic and Maureen with an apologetic smile on his face. "If I had known it had anything to do with the murders, I'd have called you right away, Inspectors, but I really didn't think—"

Kordic nodded his understanding. "You say that Angela Lolley called you the day of the murders?"

"April first, right. Actually, I didn't talk to her. She spoke to the manager. She wanted someone to come out and help her access and download some files from another computer into hers." Houng dug a service order slip from his briefcase. "Here it is."

Maureen and Kordic leaned over to study the pink-colored work order. Angela Lolley's name and address were neatly printed in block letters across the top of the form. Below was a one-line description of the work to be done: Client wants more speed on her Compaq computer and download capabilities for HV2500 to Compaq.

"I guess she needed to pump up her power, 'cause she was using the Internet, and playing games. She had a lot of games: Doom, Risk, Creep Night, Tomb Raider. You know, those capture and action games. I put in a CD ROM drive for her last time I was there."

Maureen frowned at the irony of it: the madam playing childish video games while her dirty old johns were in the back rooms with the girls.

"I really didn't know what kind of business Miss Lolley was running until I saw the story in the newspaper," Houng explained. "I just upgraded her computer."

Kordic said, "We believe you, Mr. Houng. Our problem is that the killer took the computer with him. We found some backup disks. They list her clients for the last several months. We want to know what else was on that computer."

Houng spread his hands. "Just about everything. I think she did her banking on-line, and I know she had a hookup with the web, so there would be E-mail. She could have saved the E-mail, and she might have had her own web page."

Kordic said, "E-mail, web page. Lolley was using the Internet like the yellow pages of a phone book."

"Sure," Houng said. "And she could have gone into a chat room and talked one-to-one. There are chat rooms devoted to just about everything you can think of, including sex. There's a lot of sex of every kind on the web."

Maureen's face creased in disgust. "So Lolley could just go into one of these chat rooms and say she had some twelve-year-old girls available."

"Not directly, maybe," Houng replied, shifting uneasily in his chair. "But there are code words. You just take a look at what goes on in a 'teen romance' chat room. A bunch of dirty old men trying to make contact with kids."

Kordic said, "So, any record of these chats or E-mail could have been on Lolley's computer?"

"Sure. Unless she deleted them."

Maureen showed Houng the coroner's photographs of the two dead girls.

Houng seemed shaken when he examined the photos. "The only person I ever saw at the house was Mrs. Lolley."

Maureen handed Houng the HV2500 leather notebook computer case. "We found this at the house. I checked with the company. They have no record of Lolley owning an HV2500."

Houng's eyebrows rose. " 'Miniature miracle,' that's how they advertise it. I don't know why Mrs. Lolley would have much use for an HV2500, Inspector."

"Why not?" Kordic asked.

Houng picked up the leather case. "It's too much machine for her. It's got everything. Built-in modem, hard disk drive, LAN compatibility, PC card—"

"Hold it," Maureen broke in. "You're losing me. Who would use such a computer?"

"Business people. Someone with a need for a fast, powerful machine, so they could carry their files, their spreadsheets, whatever, and communicate back to their office. And of course there's E-mail, Internet access, all the bells and whistles. Even things like chess games, and poker, so the user can while away his time if he's stuck at an airport or someplace."

Kordic rubbed his chin thoughtfully. "So there was really no reason for Lolley to own one."

"Nope. Overkill. She could have gotten all that she needed for a lot less, and Mrs. Lolley was careful with a dollar. She checked our prices alongside those that she got from a web site." Houng paused, nibbling at a fingernail. "I remember she had a small handheld computer that she used to play games, you know, simple stuff, checkers, blackjack, that kind of thing."

Maureen cleared her throat, then said, "So, if the notebook computer was yours, and it was lost or stolen, how would you go about getting it back, Mr. Houng?"

"First, I'd contact Helmut-Victor and—"

"That's been done," Mo said. "What next?"

"I'd make contact with the notebook, E-mail myself, from my main computer. Offer a reward for returning it."

"Is there some way you could trace it electronically? Like it had a transmitter in it and you—"

"No. It's not like a bug, Inspector." He smiled. "Not yet, anyway. But I'm sure that's coming on-line soon."

Maureen leaned back in her chair and folded her arms across her chest. "Angela Lolley needed your help to access and download the notebook computer, so it must be fairly difficult to operate."

"Well, she'd need a docking cable to download it into her main computer, then it all depends on just what type software is loaded on the machine. Some of it would be pretty simple to get into, other files might be coded, or access restricted."

Kordic's eyes locked on Maureen's. "Suppose, Mr. Houng, suppose a young girl, oh, between eleven and fourteen, found the notebook. Would she have any chance of accessing it?"

Daryl Houng smiled widely. "Depends on the girl, Inspector. My eleven-year-old daughter is a whiz. There're things she knows that even I don't."

Kordic got to his feet and stretched out his hand. "Okay, thanks for coming in."

Maureen added her thanks. "You've been very helpful, Mr. Houng. We may call on you if anything else comes up."

Houng scrambled around the narrow confines and exited the interrogation room.

"What do you think, Mo?" Kordic asked, raising his leg to the chair and tying his shoe.

"I think that expensive notebook probably belonged to one of Lollipop's clients. We find the notebook, we may have the murderer. Who's next?"

Kordic looked at the list on his clipboard. "Arnold Devlin."

"I checked Devlin and the third man whose prints we found at the house, Richard Bekker, with Helmut-Victor. Neither has ever purchased a HV2500, or any other kind of computer from them."

Arnold Devlin was an overweight, sorrowful-faced dentist who looked as if he was close to suffering a heart attack. He carried his disheveled suit jacket in his hands, twisting the material as if trying to wring it dry.

Maureen had contacted Devlin by phone, explaining the circumstances. He had sworn he'd never been to Angela Lolley's house and, at first, tried to say that he was far too busy to come to the Hall of Justice.

Maureen's threats of going to his home and bringing the matter up with his family present had quickly turned Devlin around.

The interrogation was blunt and brief—Kordic dropped a videocassette on the table, but didn't say a word about what was on it. He wanted to leave its contents up to Devlin's imagination. Devlin's reaction was immediate. His face turned beet-red and loops of perspiration sprouted under each arm of his shirt. Kordic then showed Devlin his fingerprints that had been lifted from 54 Tara Street, and the photographs of all three victims.

"That . . . that's Tina," Devlin responded, using a shaking finger to identify the dark-haired girl. "The other is Amber."

"What about Janna?" Maureen asked.

"I . . . I don't know a Janna, I . . . "

Kordic hammered away at Devlin for several minutes, barking out another question before Devlin had time to answer the previous one. They didn't learn much of value, other than to confirm the fact that Angela Lolley had been a heavy user of the Internet sex chat rooms. Devlin had gotten into a "chat" with her, and eventually obtained her E-mail address. Lolley had arranged a meeting between the two of them before granting Devlin access to her house, and the girls: Tina and Amber. Devlin was adamant about the fact that he'd never met Janna, that he'd never heard Angela Lolley mention her name.

Devlin seemed genuinely bewildered when they showed him the notebook computer's leather case. "I have a computer at home, and one at the office, that's all."

As Devlin plodded out of the room, Maureen noticed that there was a large wet spot at the back of his pants.

"What do you think?" Kordic queried.

Maureen found plenty of reasons to despise Devlin for his sexual preferences, but she thought it unlikely he had had anything to do with the murders. "He's a weasel, Jack. Not a killer."

Richard Bekker, the attorney, had put up a tougher fight before agreeing to come to the Hall of Justice. He'd insisted that his only contact with Angela Lolley was as her lawyer, but when Kordic pressed for details on the legal matters he'd handled for the madam, Bekker became evasive, but he eventually succumbed to Kordic's threats of a confrontation at his office.

Houng, Devlin, and Bekker had all been instructed to arrive at the Homicide detail at two in the afternoon. Devlin and Houng had been prompt, almost bumping into each other as they approached the office.

Richard Bekker had arrived predictably late, sauntering in forty-five minutes after two.

Bekker pushed the sleeve of his suit coat back from his wrist after he was escorted into the interrogation room, flashing a chunky gold wristwatch.

"I hope you realize that you're causing me to miss some very important meetings," he protested, his nose wrinkling as he scrutinized his surroundings.

"Sit down," Kordic commanded, pointing to the chair that Arnold Devlin had just vacated. "This is Inspector Connah."

Bekker settled his eyes briefly on Maureen, then slid down into the chair and carefully crossed one leg over the other.

Bekker was smooth-faced and narrow-lipped. His longish pale hair flopped over his forehead. He was wearing a dark suit and a somber tie.

Maureen handed him the notebook case. "You left this behind on your last visit to Angela's, Counselor."

The attorney examined the leather case, then dropped it on the table. "I have no idea what this is, now let's get this over with, I have no intention of—"

Kordic slammed the videocassette on the table. "What brand of law do you practice, Richard?"

Bekker's eyes kept bouncing back and froth from the cassette to Kordic, just the way Devlin's had. The tape could mean only one thing. Angela Lolley had made videos of him with the girls.

Bekker coughed into his hand. "Mostly civil cases. My partners and I—"

"Did your partners go to Lolley's place, too?" Kordic asked bluntly.

"No. No they did not. I handled one or two things for Mrs. Lolley, and I—"

Again Kordic interrupted. "What two things? Tell me one thing you did for her. Have you any documentation to prove that you did legal work for her?"

"See here," Bekker protested. "I don't have to—"

"Yes you do," Kordic warned. He rapped his knuckles against the videocassette. "Having sex with a minor is a criminal offense, Counselor. You must have studied some criminal law in school: sexual exploitation, sexual assault, molestation, statutory rape. Serious crimes. Very serious crimes."

Bekker dusted his hair back with the flat of his hand.

"I had no idea Mrs. Lolley was involved with . . . with minors until you telephoned me."

Maureen made her presence known. "Exactly what legal work involved getting your fingerprints on the circus paraphernalia hanging from the ceiling? Or the baby crib?" She slid the victim's photographs in front of Bekker. "Recognize your former playmates?"

Bekker gave a vulturelike smile. "I'm not going to answer any more questions until I contact an attorney." He looked up at Kordic. "A criminal attorney, who has more expertise than I do in this type of thing."

Kordic picked up the videocassette and patted it against his hip. "I suggest you find a lawyer with some expertise in defending child molesters."

Bekker rose slowly from his chair. "Either I call an attorney this instant, or I walk away from here, Inspector. It's your choice."

Kordic kicked a chair out of the way and moved in on Bekker, so that their faces were just inches apart. "My choice is to throw you in the holding cell, Bekker. And tell all your fellow inmates what you do for kicks. Maybe they can show you a few new tricks. You can be Tina. Or Amber. Or Janna."

The attorney's head rocked back. "I don't even know a Janna, and I think you—"

Kordic grabbed Bekker by his expensive lapels and herded him to the door. "We'll be in touch, Counselor. Before you call your attorney, remember the video. I don't think you'd want anyone you know watching it."

Bekker brushed his jacket sleeves and smoothed his tie in place. "I want to cooperate with you, Inspector, but you must realize—"

"We'll be in touch," Kordic repeated, waving the videocassette like a fan in front of his face.

Bekker opened his mouth to say something, then snapped it shut, swiveled on his heel, and marched away with as much dignity as he could muster.

When he was out of sight, Maureen said, "What's on that cassette, Jack?"

"Last year's Forty-Niner–Dallas Cowboy game," Kordic grinned.

Chapter 18

Philip Bovard watched anxiously as the paper crept slowly through the fax machine. He ripped off the page, his lips inching into a smile as he deciphered the coded message from Gregor Zinovsky: The packages are afloat. Delivery date guaranteed. Send money.

Bovard crumpled up the paper and dropped it into an ashtray, using a rolled gold Dunhill lighter to set it ablaze. The nuclear reactors being safely transferred to the Swedish freighter had been a major concern. Zinovsky had explained the cargo's torturous route—from Murmansk, halfway to Myak in Siberia, where the hijacking would take place. The reactors would then be loaded onto massive trucks, and begin a hazardous zigzag journey to Finland and the port at Kota, where the Swedish freighter would be waiting.

The danger wasn't from the Russian government, but from local Mafia groups who would have loved to have gotten their hands on the reactors. Now it was simply a matter of delivering the cargo to Cyprus.

Simple, if it hadn't been for Patrick Lynam's unbelievable stupidity. Lynam losing his computer, with all the details of the shipment, at a whorehouse!

There was a discreet knock at the door. An airline employee edged the door open. "Your flight is boarding now, sir."

Bovard thanked him politely, snapped shut the case holding the fax machine and telephone, and pushed himself to his feet. He was not happy about having to travel to America. He hated the United States. Hated everything about it. Except its currency.

Frank Dunbar layered his throbbing nose with a glob of ointment, then lit a cigarette as he gazed at the photographs spread across his rumpled bedspread, the ones he'd taken of Paulie Boy in the lobby of the Marriott Hotel.

He leaned over to study the images of Paul, August eleven, picking up the old whore's luggage. Ashes from his cigarette dropped down onto a picture that had caught Paulie Boy staring in the direction of the camera. Dunbar brushed the ashes away, leaving a gray smear.

The photo was a little blurry, but it was clear enough to show the man's face: high forehead, thin lips, thin nose—the better for looking down at someone. Lots of neatly barbered gray hair. Dark coat, white shirt, dark tie. A businessman, Dunbar figured. And a bloody rich one. A rich perverted baby fucker.

Paulie Boy hadn't taken the news about the police being at the old whore's house when Dunbar went back for the wee girl's photographs very well. From his tone, you'd think it was him that had been chased by the coppers.

The cellular phone rang. Dunbar lit a cigarette from the dog end of his old one. The ringing stopped for a half minute, then started again. He derived small pleasure from making Paulie Boy wait, though Dunbar had no real quarrel with his client. Paulie Boy had been damn prompt with his money.

Dunbar picked up the palm-sized phone, hefting it in his hand. How he would have liked to have had one during his days working for the *Fliuch* wing of the Sinn Fein, the wet wing—the assassins. All those times he was stuck hiding out in a bloody countryside barn, or in some filthy warren hutch in Belfast, with no way of communicating with his so-called leaders—hiding out from the coppers, not knowing if it was safe to surface, finally getting the word, which, when it finally came, was scribbled on the back of a bar napkin, delivered by some toothless rummy who Dunbar wouldn't trust to take out the garbage.

He reckoned the IRA was the most backward, ill-prepared, underfinanced, totally fucked-up terrorist organization in the world. The only thing that kept them going was their ruthlessness—and the *Fliuch* were the most ruthless of them all. "Kill hard" was the battle cry, be it man, woman, child, dog, or horse. The biggest uproar against them came when they blew up half a dozen of Her Majesty's Royal Horsemen. The Brits wept a tear or two over the dead soldiers, but cried a bloody river over the stupid horses.

Dunbar brought the phone to his mouth and bellowed a loud: "Hello, there."

"Where have you been? I've been calling you for hours," Lynam demanded angrily.

"I left the phone off by mistake," Dunbar said casually.

There was a scornful grunt on the other end of the line. "I've found Stoylar. Yuri Stoylar. The address is one-two-five-six Cabrillo Street. Stoylar sold Janna to Angela Lolley. Janna may be with him, or he may know where she is."

"Sold the little darlin', did he?" Dunbar couldn't hold back a chest-rattling smoker's cough. "Imagine that. The man's a bloody pervert."

Dr. Alvin Phillips, the medical examiner's chief physician, was a tall, thin man who moved like a bird, head on skinny neck bobbing with each step.

He waved a lanky arm at Jack Kordic, inviting him back to his private office.

Phillips and Kordic had developed a solid relationship over the years. The doctor was in the habit of summoning Kordic to his office, rather than giving him information on the phone or shuffling reports to the Homicide detail.

Kordic correctly surmised that one of the reasons for the personal meetings was that both men shared a common bond. Dr. Phillips's wife and son had been killed in a boating accident shortly before Kordic's family was murdered.

Phillips's office was a standard civil service enclave: gray metal desk and matching file cabinets, two wooden chairs, an office clock, and an old stand-up refrigerator, bare metal showing through around the handle.

The only difference Kordic noticed from his last visit was that the St. Pauli's Beer calendar had been replaced by one featuring a photograph of the Grand Canyon.

Phillips opened the refrigerator and pulled out two shot glasses and a pint-sized bottle labeled *Imperium Super-Concentrated Embalming Fluid.*

Phillips used the embalming bottle to disguise his stash of manhattans from the cleaning crews.

"The lab tests came back on those two young victims at Tara Street, Jack. Bad news."

Kordic sniffed at his glass before taking a sip. "They're dead, Doc. What could be worse?"

"STDs. Sexually transmitted diseases."

"Shit," Kordic said, wincing as if in pain. "AIDS?"

"No. Chlamydia trachomatis. Very infectious. Easily transmitted."

Kordic knocked back the rest of his drink, then asked, "Deadly?"

"Not if treated properly. And promptly. Antibiotics usually do the trick. I say usually, because we're coming across more and more strains of the disease that don't respond to the medication."

Kordic gently settled his empty glass on the doctor's desk. "What are the symptoms?"

"Itching, burning, whitish discharge from the penis, sometimes a lot of pain, sometimes no pain at all at first. Chlamydia and gonorrhea are often transmitted simultaneously, but there was no evidence of gonorrhea on either of the victims, Jack."

"Any idea just how long ago the two girls were infected?"

"No, that we don't know. I can tell you that the one

victim, the brunette, was more sexually active than the other. I found numerous—"

"I'll get those details from the report, Doc," Kordic broke in. He jammed his hands into his pockets. "We now know that there was a third girl at the house the night of the murders. She got away. She saw the killer, and she's somewhere out on the streets right now, on her own."

Dr. Phillips clicked his teeth. "A few years ago, chlamydia, while the most common sexually transmitted disease in the United States, was relatively easy to diagnose and treat. Not anymore. These new strains I mentioned have brought with them additional risks: meningitis, infertility, liver damage, and can cause serious injury to the heart, blood vessels, and nervous system. You better find her soon, Jack."

The address that Paulie Boy had given Dunbar for Yuri Stoylar, 1256 Cabrillo, was the lower flat of a two-unit stucco-front building. The stucco was a dingy gray, streaked with brownish rivulets where the rust from the window frames had washed down the walls. An old faded maroon Buick, the chrome freckled with rust, was nosed right up against the garage doors, forcing pedestrian traffic to veer out into the street to pass around it. Newspapers, still encased in their cellophane bags, were strewn across the two steps leading to the warped, weather-blistered door. There was a tarnished aluminum bellplate alongside the door, but no names were listed in the slots.

Frank Dunbar slipped on his gloves. The front door was locked, but he jimmied it with a putty knife in less than fifteen seconds.

The stairs were covered with rotting cocoa matting.

Dunbar spread his legs and climbed the stairs slowly, his feet hugging the edges of the risers so as not to make any noise.

He paused in front of Yuri Stoylar's unit, his ear to the door. He could hear water running, then heavy footsteps and someone humming.

Dunbar took off his hat, then removed the .25-caliber pistol from his front pants pocket and covered the gun with the hat.

He mused that he was changing guns faster than he was changing his underwear. The pistol he'd killed the old whore and the two girls with had been thrown down a sewer. The gun he'd shot at the policeman with had gone to a watery grave in the ocean. The weapon now in his hand was a cheap Italian piece. What the newspapers referred to as a Saturday Night Special. Dunbar didn't think there was anything special about it, but it was the only firepower Sean Kelty had available on short notice.

He rapped on the door with his knuckles, took a step backward, and clicked back the gun's hammer.

The door opened with a slap, startling Dunbar.

"Who you?" demanded the man with a bushy, drooping mustache.

Dunbar was taken back by the man's size. He wasn't very tall, under six feet, but his body filled the doorway. He was wearing a black T-shirt and gray shorts. His legs looked like tree trunks. His hands were covered with sweat-stained gloves. The gloves were cut off at the knuckles revealing thick, fur-lined fingers.

"Ah. I'm looking for Yuri Stoylar," Dunbar explained, wishing that he'd brought a bigger gun. "Are you Yuri?"

"No. Me Erik. Who you?" the big man repeated, his eyes narrowing.

"A man with some money for Yuri. It's about Janna. Do you know Janna?"

"Yah," the man beamed, holding out his hand in a greeting.

Dunbar took a short step forward and suddenly one of those massive hands grabbed him by the neck, lifting him from the ground and hoisting him into the flat.

The tips of Dunbar's shoes made scraping sounds as they dragged against the linoleum. He was carted inside, then thrown against the wall.

The big man slammed the door shut, then pointed a finger like a truncheon at Dunbar.

"Who you?"

Dunbar hacked out a cough, trying to clear his head. "I told you, it's about Janna, and I— "

Again one of the gloved hands shot out at Dunbar. He was raised off the floor. He could smell garlic and cabbage on the bastard's breath.

"I want to know—"

Dunbar jammed his hat against the man's massive chest and pulled the small gun's trigger rapidly. He wasn't sure if he'd fired three or four shots.

Erik's head jerked back at the first shot. He gave Dunbar an astonished look, releasing his grip when he saw the dark spots oozing through his shirt.

Dunbar held the gun steady in both hands, ready to empty the rest of the clip into the bloody target in front of him.

Bigger gun, damn it, bigger gun. I'm never going to use a piss-ass gun like this again.

Erik took a shaky step forward, then teetered on his heels before collapsing to the ground in a loud thud.

Dunbar stood frozen in place, opening his mouth so his breathing wouldn't interfere with his hearing. Nothing. No sounds at all. Which meant no one else was in the flat. If the sounds of the gunshots hadn't alerted anyone, the noise the big bugger made hitting the floor would have.

Dunbar looked down at the body. There was a look of total shock on the man's face. He lashed out furiously with his foot, sending the tip of his shoes into the hulking stomach several times.

Now what? Cut and run? Would someone report the noises? He surveyed the area. The flat was a shambles. Bottles of beer and vodka standing upright on the floor. Half-empty glasses. A sandwich with one bite taken out of it lying on top of the radiator.

In the next room he found a workout bench, patched with strips of duct tape. Dirty towels were draped over the exercise equipment. The wooden flooring was gouged and scraped from taking the punishment of the barbells being dropped on it. Whoever lived upstairs or next door would be used to hearing loud noises. Dunbar pocketed the pistol and scanned the room.

Clothes were heaped on a cot in the corner. Dunbar picked up a pair of pants, dug through the pockets, and found a wallet containing a wad of twenty-dollar bills, two foil-wrapped condoms, and a State of California driver's license. The photograph on the license showed the basketball-sized head of the man he'd just killed. His name was listed as Erik Urizar.

Dunbar removed the money before dropping the wallet on the cot, then made his way to the adjoining room. Another mess. There was a lone walnut dresser in the corner. He began going through the drawers, using the burglar's technique of starting at the bottom and working up, thus saving the time of closing the drawer after it had been searched. He sifted through underwear, shirts, and sweaters, then in the top drawer he found a jumble of inexpensive men's jewelry, a photo album, and a thick stack of United States postage stamps.

He examined the stamps. There must be hundreds of them. Who the hell needed that many stamps? He laid the photo album on the dresser top and began turning the pages. Some of the black-and-white photographs were obviously professionally done, and featured a short, bald, big-bellied man in various staged poses, along with a group of like-aged men bundled in heavy clothing. The backdrop was immediately recognizable. The Kremlin. Russia. Dunbar turned over the photos. They were labeled with the photographer's name and address—Vetvocik's— St. Petersburg.

The big one was there, Erik, the one he'd just killed.

One washed-out color photograph showed the bald, big-bellied man standing in front of a log cabin, with another man and a woman. The woman was holding a baby.

Dunbar dropped the album on the floor, scratched his itching nose, and dug in his pocket for the ointment, then walked into the next room. He didn't bother to remove his glove before dabbing his nose with the soothing medicine.

There was a single bed, stripped down to a bare mattress. Clothing was piled on the bed. A stack of books rose from the floor to mattress height. He stooped down, pushed a small screen TV with a bent antenna out of the way, then tilted his head to read one of the faded book jackets. The print was foreign, Russian he concluded. He couldn't decipher the title, but the author's name was familiar. Tolstoy. An old Russian bastard.

Dunbar fingered through the clothing. A heavy black woolen coat. Women's dresses. Slips. He freed a rumpled, flower-print dress from one of the boxes and held it up in front of him. The woman who wore this was tall and, judging from the size of the garment, slim. He quickly rummaged through the rest of the clothing. Little girl's clothes. He stroked a sweater as if it were a dog's coat. Janna's?

Dunbar dropped to his knees. There was a slim canvas suitcase under the bed. He dragged the suitcase free. Inside, he found a cachet of photographs of a woman and a young girl. There were several close-ups of the girl. Her pretty face smiling at the lens. The background was a mass of trees, a small lake. It had to be her. He turned the photo over. The names Janna and Irvina, along with a date, were neatly printed on the back. Janna. The date was less than a month ago.

"Janna, I've got you now, you little darlin'. You won't get away this time."

Yuri Stoylar shouldered his way through a pack of slow-moving Japanese tourists to gain entrance to the aquarium. He stumbled, then regained his balance. By the time he'd gotten inside the building, she was gone.

Janna. He hadn't gotten a good look at her face. Just her profile. Her hair was different. Shorter. And the clothes were new. But the way she stood, the way she ran. It had to be her! Where the devil did she go?

After an hour of milling around, he gave up. Janna. How did you get the money to pay for your haircut and your new clothes? Did Angela teach you how to make money? Is that it, little bitch? Are you living with one of Angela's clients? Or did you steal Angela's money? Was that what you did? Stole all her money and jewels. The money and jewels that I should have now? Is that what was in your backpack?

Stoylar didn't know whether he should feel elated or depressed at having spotted Janna. She was still a threat to him.

He suddenly felt tired. He made his way back to the alligator pit. Using the railing for support, he slid one of the stamps from his shirt pocket and licked it slowly, waiting for the drug to kick in. Janna. You came back to the park. Now come home. Come home to me.

Douglas Lancer tipped the bellboy, then checked out the room. The Hilton Hotel's suite Bovard had secured for him was spacious, nicely furnished, and had a spectacular view of the city's skyline.

None of this impressed Lancer. The drawbacks were too numerous. He was on the eleventh floor—it would take much too long to get to the street. And once there, it was either wait several minutes for a rental car to be delivered or use a taxi.

Neither of those choices was acceptable. He decided to keep the room as a message center and find another accommodation that was better suited to his purposes.

Lancer found a local telephone directory in the nightstand. He spread out the maps and tour guides he'd studied on the airplane onto a highly polished cherrywood table next to the window and began thumbing through the phone book's listings of hotels and motels, finding their location on the maps and scoring the spots with a red marking pen.

54 Tara Street and Kelty's, the bar where Frank Dunbar hung out, had been marked on the map during his flight from London.

Denis Fennesy hadn't known where Dunbar lived, but he'd been certain that Dunbar could always be contacted at Kelty's saloon.

Lancer was anxious to meet with Dunbar and find out just how far he'd progressed in finding the target. But before he called Dunbar, Lancer wanted to talk with the client, Patrick Lynam—"Old Friend."

His mouth approximated a smile at the choice of the code name—it was hard to imagine Philip Bovard ever having a real friend.

He felt grimy from the flight, but didn't want to take the chance that the client would call while he was showering.

He unzipped the suitcase that had been waiting for him when he'd arrived in New York, and rechecked the contents. A shoulder holster cradling a custom-crafted, Teflon-coated, fully automatic pistol complete with a built-in silencer, and a box of shells, an assortment of detonators, a two-inch blade combat knife originally designed for the United States Army Green berets, and a cell phone, complete with charger and two spare battery packs.

Lancer was dry-firing the weapon, using the tip of the TransAmerica tower as a target when the cell phone rang.

"This is an old friend," the crisp, icy voice disclosed.

"I've been waiting for your call. Has Dunbar had any success in finding the target?"

"Not yet. I sent him to see Yuri Stoylar, at twelve fifty-six Cabrillo Street. Stoylar knows the girl."

Lancer wrote the address down on a piece of the hotel's stationery. "What else can you tell me about Stoylar?"

"Not much. He's a cautious man and my only connection to the target, so treat him accordingly."

Chapter 19

Yuri Stoylar trudged up the steps to his flat. He paused and let out a loud burp before continuing the trek, pulling a pint of Stolichnaya vodka from his back pocket and taking a long drink.

He saw no reason to share the excellent vodka with Erik. He wasn't looking forward to another night with Erik and his exercise weights. He was tired of the noise and the smell of the man. Once he found Janna, he'd get rid of Erik.

He took no particular notice of the fact that the front door was unlocked. Erik was probably down the street at a bar or buying some groceries. God, how the man could eat.

Stoylar banged the door shut behind him and bellowed a curse in Russian. "Shithead. Are you home?"

There was no response, and Stoylar staggered toward the kitchen. His foot landed on something slick and his legs went out from under him. He grabbed the wall to keep from falling down.

Frank Dunbar emerged out of the shadows of the kitchen, gun in hand. "Stoylar!"

"What? What . . . I—"

"Careful where you step. You might hurt yourself."

The Russian's eyes bounced from the gun to the floor. Blood. There was a narrow, weaving stream of blood on the floor.

He held up his hands defensively. Please, I don't have any money. I don't know what you want, but—"

"I want Janna," Dunbar responded, gesturing with the

gun for Stoylar to follow him into the kitchen. "Come on, let's have a little chat."

Jack Kordic nodded and grunted a "How's it going?" greeting to the dark-haired man with taut muscles straining at the confines of a white tennis shirt. The man responded with a wink and a snide grin.

Who the hell was that? Kordic wondered as he turned into the Homicide detail. A plainclothes cop, in jeans, his empty shoulder holster standing out against the tight-fitting shirt. The name came to him when he spotted Maureen Connah at her desk. Sergeant Tom Flavio. Maureen's ex-husband.

Maureen gave him a weary look. Janna's photographs and the printouts from Angela Lolley's computer were spread across her desk.

"Let's get out of here and call it a day," Kordic suggested.

Maureen leaned back and stretched her hands over her head, the action causing her blouse to bunch up under her breasts.

"I think I'll stick around for a while, Jack. Maybe Janna will call again."

Kordic lowered his voice so no one else in the room could hear him. "We can't wait around for Janna to call us, Mo. She might not *ever* call again. We've got to find her, not hope that she just drops into our laps. I had a talk with Doc Phillips, Mo. Tina and Amber both had chlamydia trachomatis. It's—"

"I know exactly what it is," Maureen said angrily. "Jesus. Those poor kids. And Janna. God, what if she's infected, too?"

"It's a possibility." Kordic gnawed at his lower lip. "I wonder how Misters Devlin and Bekker are going to react to the news. Come on, let's go somewhere comfortable where we can both go through the hard copies."

Maureen began gathering the printouts, and tapping them into a neat bundle. "Where'd you have in mind?"

"My place," Kordic said casually. "Or yours." He

smiled ruefully. "Sounds like an old pickup line, doesn't it?"

"Yes," Maureen agreed. "It certainly does."

Yuri Stoylar knew that whether he was going to live or die would be decided in the next few seconds. The man with the gun was studying him, the expression on his long, red-nosed face was one of contemplation. Stoylar had looked at a man that same way once in Moscow, weighing whether or not the sniveling coward, who had been a conduit for forged credit cards, was of more use to him dead or alive. Stoylar had pulled the trigger. He didn't want this one to make the same decision, because there was no doubt—this one was a killer. He must have been the man who killed Angela and the two girls. And missed Janna. Now he wanted to find her, kill her, and somehow Stoylar had to prove that he could help him.

Stoylar squirmed in the chair. His hands had been looped through the arms of the chair, then bound behind his back with the thick, silver-colored adhesive tape that that fool Erik had used to keep his workout bench together.

His ankles were taped to the chair's legs. Another strip of tape had been plastered across his mouth.

His eyes tracked the man, who left the room for a few moments, then came back grinning, holding an iron in his hand! Irvina Drovana's iron.

Frank Dunbar plugged the iron's cord into an electrical socket, then leaned over Stoylar and slid it across the top of his bald skull. "Sure'n you know the drill now, don't you, bucko? I'm going to ask you a few questions. Either you give me the right answers, or I butcher you. Now, just so you understand that I mean what I'm sayin', I'll give you a little taste of what's coming if you don't tell me what I want to know."

Stoylar tried to speak, his lips gurgling indecipherable mumblings against the tape.

Dunbar rolled his shoulders, then patted the business end of the iron. "Gettin' hot," he advised Stoylar.

The Russian was trembling, sweat was coursing down his ugly face. He was scared shitless. Just the way Dunbar wanted him. He waved the iron in front of Stoylar's eyes, then quickly jammed it against the Russian's left ear.

Stoylar's screams were muffled by the tape across his mouth.

Dunbar clamped his free hand around Stoylar's right ear and pushed his head into the hot iron, then he backed away for a moment, only to suddenly slap the red-hot iron back on Stoylar's singed ear.

"I want to know where Janna is. Understand?" he snarled, pulling the iron back. "Are you going to tell me?"

Stoylar bobbed his head frantically, wincing as the tape was ripped from his mouth.

"Where is she?" Dunbar demanded.

"Please," Stoylar pleaded. "I will tell you. Let me tell you!" He ran the tip of his tongue around his swollen lips. "I can find her. Let me help you. I want to find her as much as you do. She knows too much about me, let me—"

Dunbar jabbed the tip of the iron at Stoylar's face. "Where's Janna?"

"I don't know. I swear, but I can find her. I can do it!" Stoylar's Adam's apple bobbed up and down several times. "I could use a drink," he added, his nostrils contracting as he smelled his own burned flesh. "Please."

Dunbar settled the iron upside down on Stoylar's lap, then went to the kitchen counter and retrieved the pint bottle of vodka he'd taken from him earlier. The bottle lay among the rest of the junk Stoylar had stuffed in his pockets: a thin wad of currency held together by a paper clip, a few coins, a soiled handkerchief, a pocketknife and a key ring with three keys, and a few postage stamps. No wallet, no identification of any kind. Dunbar approved of that.

He tilted the vodka over Stoylar's mouth and watched as the Russian swallowed greedily, then coughed.

"Where are we going to find Janna?" Dunbar asked when the coughing subsided.

"I saw her just hours ago. In the park, an—"

Dunbar glided the iron along Stoylar's bald scalp. "What park?"

"Golden Gate Park. She got away from me, but I—" He stammered to a stop when Dunbar pressed the hot iron into his head. "I know what she looks like, and I—"

"Have you any pictures of the lass?"

"No," Stoylar said quickly. "Just when she was a baby. And she's changed! She cut her hair. Dresses differently. If it wasn't for her gestures, I wouldn't have known her."

Dunbar cocked his head to one side and studied Stoylar as a biologist might study a frog he was about to dissect. "You sold her to the old whore?"

Stoylar lifted his eyes to the grease-stained kitchen ceiling. "A temporary arrangement. I was going to get her back, but someone—"

"Someone beat you to her, huh?" Dunbar waved the liquor bottle over Stoylar's shaky head. "What were you going to do when you got her back?"

The Russian's heavy face crimsoned. "I . . . I was going to help Janna. She is family to me. The 'little genius.' She's family. I wanted to help her."

"Little genius. What the fuck's that mean?"

"She's smart, Janna is. Very smart. Her mother always called her that. Little genius."

Dunbar dribbled some vodka onto Stoylar's scorched ear, then wiped the neck of the bottle along his jacket sleeve before taking a sip himself. Family. The bloody Russian was a bigger pig than Paulie Boy.

He dropped the bottle to the floor and tested the iron with a finger, hissing an "ouch" on contact. "You were goin' to put her out whorin' again, weren't you? What did the old whore pay you for her?"

"Seven . . . seven thousand dollars."

"Shit," Dunbar snorted. "Tell me more about Janna."

"There . . . there's nothing to tell, she—"

Stoylar's head rocked back as Dunbar dropped the iron inches from his crotch.

"You lying piece of shit," Dunbar cursed. "This is her,

isn't it?" He shoved one of the photographs he'd found into Stoylar's face. "This is her!"

"Yes, yes, but she's changed a lot, like I—"

"You said you just saw Janna in the park. Did she see you?"

"No, no. I'm sure she didn't. She likes the park. She slept there after she left here. After her mother died and—"

"Where in the park?"

"I can show—"

Stoylar squeezed back in the chair as the tip of the iron was positioned in front of his right eye.

"You're not going to be able to show me anything," Dunbar hissed in his damaged ear, "because I'm goin' to burn out both your eyes, if you don't tell me exactly where you saw Janna."

"The aquarium," Stoylar stammered. "Not an hour ago. She likes to go there. Janna used to go there with her mother. The aquarium and the merry-go-round, that's where they always went."

Dunbar backed away and Stoylar heaved a sigh of relief when the red-nosed man bent down and laid the iron on the floor.

"I will help you," he promised. "Why . . . why do you want Janna?"

"One of her admirers just wants to have a little party with her."

Stoylar swallowed, his throat feeling like sandpaper as the red-nosed man whipped a knife out from his sock. Stoylar was familiar with the style of knife, a butterfly. A flick of the wrist and the blade magically appeared from the handle. "Please. I can find Janna for you. Let me help you."

"Tell me everything you know about the lass. Now! Or I'll gut you," Dunbar threatened.

Stoylar's voice veered up and down the scale as he described how Janna looked, and exactly where he'd last seen her. "The park. She's living in the park. I'll find her for you!"

"Sure'n you'll be a real help," Dunbar said amiably. He patted Stoylar's scalded head lightly, then cupped his chin in one hand and brutally ran the blade of the knife from one ear to the other.

The numbered avenues ran north to south in sequence, from Second all the way out to Forty-eighth. Douglas Lancer circled the block searching for a parking spot, finally curbing the rented Ford Taurus in front of a fire hydrant at the corner of Tenth and Cabrillo.

He hunched his shoulders against the cold wind. The narrow houses were wedged together, shoulder to shoulder, their entrances glimmering dully in the rays of the streetlights.

There was nothing to single out 1256 Cabrillo from its undistinguished neighbors. He edged into the sheltering alcove of the building directly across the street, scarfing himself in the shadows, wanting to get a feel for the surroundings before going into action.

He kept his eyes on Yuri Stoylar's address as he took a mental inventory of the weapons he was carrying, silenced gun in its shoulder holster, knife strapped on his left forearm, five mercury detonators strapped to his inner left thigh.

He started across the street when he noticed the lights in Stoylar's place go dark. Lancer retreated back into the shadows and waited.

A thin man wearing a dark blue jacket and tweed hat hurried out of the building. Lancer recognized him immediately. Francis Aloysius Dunbar, a little older than his mug shot, but there was no doubt it was him.

Lancer watched as Dunbar walked east on Cabrillo, stopping at a white Saab sedan. He was able to get a quick look at the Irishman's face as the car cruised by. There was a smug grin of accomplishment on Dunbar's homely features.

He jogged across the street, hoping that Dunbar had found and eliminated Janna. If so, he could finish off Dunbar and be back in England tomorrow, which would give him plenty of time to get to Cyprus and oversee the transfer of the nuclear reactors on April tenth.

For the first time since he'd gone to work for the man, Lancer was concerned about Philip Bovard. His implacable, bulletproof air had been dented. Lancer knew that Bovard had taken some heavy financial losses lately, both at the casinos and as a result of the botched delivery of the nerve gas last year.

Lancer's money was safely tucked away in Australia. Enough money to live comfortably for a long time. But not a lifetime. He needed more, for that. After the reactors changed hands, then he'd have enough. Of course, Bovard would never allow him to leave, not with what he knew of Bovard. There was only one way to dissolve the relationship. Termination. Lancer had always planned on killing Bovard one day. Because he knew that Bovard had the same plans for him.

Chapter 20

"The table's probably our best bet," Jack Kordic said, pointing Maureen Connah toward the dining room. "Do you feel like a drink? Or some coffee?"

Kordic dropped the file containing the printouts and the photographs of Janna onto the tabletop.

"A glass of wine, if you have it," Maureen responded, her eyes roaming around the apartment.

Bare beige walls. The dining-room table was highly polished teak and smelled of lemon oil. A large-screen TV sat in front of a puffy, saddle-brown leather couch.

Floor-to-ceiling teak shelves were lined with books, videocassettes, and CDS.

Everything was neat, clean, in proper order. The beige rug had visible swirl marks from the vacuum cleaner, looking as if the cleaning woman had just left.

"Help yourself," Kordic invited. "White wine in the refrigerator, red in the rack alongside. I'll be right back."

Maureen watched Kordic head to the rear of the apartment, wondering if he would return in a bathrobe or some kind of smoking jacket.

The kitchen was neatly laid out: gas range, refrigerator-freezer, teak cabinets. The countertops were of charcoal granite.

The refrigerator door opened with a soft sucking sound. There were rows of wine bottles, packages of various cheeses, jars of olives and onions, hardly any real food. Out of curiosity she tried the freezer compartment, finding that she and Kordic had at least one thing in common—

the freezer was jammed with stacks of frozen dinners and a bottle of Bombay gin.

A narrow row of earthen drain tiles next to the refrigerator was used as a wine rack. She slid a few bottles out, scanned the labels, selecting a bottle of Turning Leaf Zinfandel, simply because she admired the colorful label.

She rummaged around in the cabinets, found two glasses, a corkscrew, and carried them into the dining room.

Kordic was there to greet her. Maureen was glad to see that he'd removed his tie and rolled up his shirtsleeves. No bathrobe. Yet. "This is a nice place, Jack. How long have you been here?"

Kordic reached for the wine bottle. "After my wife and son were killed, I moved here. We had a big house in Walnut Creek. Too big for one person." The cork made a popping sound.

"Sorry," Maureen said, "I should have—"

"If we're going to be partners, we can't have secrets, Mo. I'm sure you've heard all about it. You checked me out, right? My wife and son were murdered, and I went off the deep end. And I checked you out. Ran you through the computer and talked to a couple of people that I trust in the department."

He poured the wine and slouched comfortably into a chair, looking at Maureen over the rim of his glass. "You're a damn good-looking woman, and I'm a widower. Face it. If we stay partners, there's going to be talk about us. I saw your ex-husband in the hallway today. He gave me a look that all but said he thought you and I were jumping on each other's bones. Captain Neil told me that he's responsible for putting you into the Homicide detail, and he doesn't think you've been 'grateful' enough. You and I both know what Neil thinks grateful should be. Those man-woman detective teams work out swell in the movies, but in real life, they can run into a lot of problems. Sex being the big one."

"Maybe that's why Bill Neil put us together in the first place."

"That crossed my mind," Kordic said warily. "Neil's not a fan of mine. We've had some differences in the past, yet he wants me to keep him posted on how you're doing."

"And what did you tell him?"

"The truth. That you're working hard and doing a good job. Neil's a bastard, Mo. You're still on probation as an assistant inspector. Be damn careful until you've got your full year, or Neil will bounce you to some uniformed job."

Maureen settled down in a chair. "So what do we do now?"

"We work a few cases together, see how we get along. Doing the job, that's what it's all about. Either we work well together, or we don't. And if we don't, we go our separate ways." Kordic lifted his wineglass and took an audible sip. "But if we do split up, it'll be our decision. Not Captain Neil's. If you think I'm a pain in the ass, or if you just don't like the look of my face, you tell me and we quit. Fair enough?"

"Fair enough," Maureen agreed. "The same rules apply for you, right? If you don't like working with me, don't feel comfortable, just say so."

Kordic stretched his hand across the table. "It's a deal, partner. Let's get to work."

"Yuri Stoylar was the right man, but unfortunately, he's no longer among the livin'," Frank Dunbar said casually into the cell phone, trying to imagine the look of outrage on Paulie Boy's face. "I killed the bloody pervert. He was of no more use to us."

"Jesus Christ, man! Did he tell you where Janna is?" The voice was raw, on edge now, the cool confidence long gone.

"Not exactly." Dunbar paused dramatically. He was seated in Sean Kelty's private office, looking out through the one-way mirror into the saloon. Kelty's daughter, Debbie, a prick-teaser in her early twenties with a wide, sensual mouth and perfectly globular breasts, was working behind the bar. "But he said he'd seen her earlier today."

"Where?"

"Golden Gate Park."

"Where in the park?" the raw voice demanded.

"By some bloody fish museum," Dunbar answered calmly, relishing having the upper hand. "It's a favorite spot of hers, it seems. There, and the merry-go-round."

"You shouldn't have killed Stoylar. That was a mistake."

"I don't think so. Quit worryin'. I'm gonna find your little sweetheart for you."

"How? You don't even know what Janna looks like."

"Ah, but I do. I found a couple of her pictures, and before he died, Yuri and I had a good chat. I got everything there was to get from the man. He told me she got herself a haircut and a new jacket, so I'll have no problem findin' her." He shook a cigarette from a pack, then added, "Stoylar called her a little genius. Says she's smart as a whip. Speaks English like a bloody Yank, and knows all about computers and that kind of stuff."

Lynam's interest was immediate. "He specified computers?"

"Sure'n he did," Dunbar confirmed, pleased at the tone of panic in the baby fucker's voice. "A regular little whiz at 'em."

Dunbar could hear the baby fucker take a big breath, hold it, then expel the air.

"I need to have the job completed, and very quickly."

"I understand. I want the little bitch, too," Dunbar said, digging the tube of ointment from his pocket. His eyes were focused on Debbie Kelty. She was wearing her usual tight sweater and a miniskirt that barely reached past her thighs. Now there was a woman, a real handful of woman, not a little child.

"If you can't find her, then—"

"I'm the only one that can," Dunbar countered, squeezing a blob of the ointment on his finger and rubbing it over his itching nose. "I know what she looks like, and where she likes to go. I may need some assistance. Someone else who also knows what she looks like. You."

"Out of the question."

"Hell, man. I don't know who you are. You could walk in front of me, and I wouldn't— "

"Out of the question. But I have someone who—"

"I pick my own men, or I work alone," Dunbar threatened. He was gazing out through the one-way mirror, paying so much attention to Debbie Kelty that he didn't notice the tall, blond man enter the bar.

"Goddamn you, I'm paying the bills. You'll do what I tell you to do!"

Patrick Lynam slammed down the receiver, missing the phone's cradle on the first try.

"I hope that wasn't the president you were so rude to, darling."

Lynam swiveled around, spotting his wife leaning casually against the door frame.

"No, Eleanor. Just business."

Eleanor Lynam sauntered slowly into the room. She was a short, shapely woman with a nipped waist. Her face was delicately featured and framed by a halo of gray-blond hair. She had just come from a tennis lesson and was outfitted in spotless white shorts and a matching Polo shirt. Her narrow waist was highlighted by a braided leather belt.

She admired the room for a quiet moment. The coffered ceiling, parquet floor, and wall panelings were of the same rich French walnut and perfectly complemented the Italian landscape oils she'd found on their last trip to Europe. "When will you know for sure about the appointment?" she asked her husband, who was ensconced behind his massive, intricately carved Sheraton oak desk. She fingered the wood affectionately. It was one of her favorite pieces, and fit in perfectly with the rest of the furniture she'd discovered in local antique shops: the bar-back settee, the curricle chairs, the priceless seventeenth-century long-faced Regency clock, its lifeless hands dangling permanently at six-thirty. The dealer had assured her that repairing the clock would lower its value.

The only jarring notes in the room as far as Eleanor was concerned were the telescope, and the computer, fax machine, and the three telephones spread across the desk. Today the desk was messier than usual—there were parts of electronic equipment stacked on top of one another, snarls of cable cords hooked from one machine to another. Paper curled like an accordion from the printer. She hated it when Patrick let it get messy like that. Perhaps she should call an architect and have him draw up plans for a concealed working area where Patrick could fiddle with his electronic gadgets.

"Soon, Eleanor. Very soon. I spoke to Senator Fawley this morning. He says my appointment is in the bag, so you needn't worry."

Lynam watched his wife circle the room, touching the walls, the drapes, and the furniture as if they were friends that she had made and was now reluctant to leave in the care of her husband.

Lynam hated the whole damn room, but knew that if he complained, Eleanor would retaliate by having everything removed, right down to the bare walls, and then redecorated, at an exorbitant cost, the result no doubt being worse than what it was now.

"You're being discreet, aren't you, darling?" she asked, looking out the windows that afforded a glorious view of Angel Island, the skyline of San Francisco, the Golden Gate Bridge.

Lynam House, as she liked to call it, a three-story tile-roofed Mediterranean villa, was situated on the tip of the duck-head-shaped peninsula of Belvedere. Flowering bougainvillea cascaded down from the salmon-colored walls to the waters of San Francisco Bay.

She bent down to peer through the lens of the 99mm refractor telescope that pointed to the neighboring town of Sausalito. "You're not still peeking into that little girl's bedroom in Sausalito, are you?"

"Don't be ridiculous, Eleanor. And while we're on the subject of being discreet, have you changed tennis pros?"

His wife straightened up and gazed at him with resentment blazing in her eyes. "That was finished long ago. You know that."

"Do I?" Lynam had seen Yvette, the husky tennis pro Eleanor had become infatuated with, tooling around Tiburon just yesterday in a bright red Italian convertible. She had pulled alongside his Jaguar, revved her engine, waved at him, then gave an exaggerated wink.

"That's an expensive toy she drives. I wonder how she can afford the payments?"

"She works hard," Eleanor replied icily. "Just like you do, darling. Don't worry about me, Patrick." Her face softened. "This appointment is going to change things. For both of us. Forever."

Lynam nodded at the peace offering, rose to his feet, and walked over to Eleanor, draping his arm around her sinewy shoulders. "It will be worth it, dear. It really will."

"Yes," Eleanor responded, her face flushing at the thought of the conversations that would take place at the yacht club, the tennis club, the golf course, and at her card parties. It would impress them. It would have to. The fact that Patrick was a banker, an enormously wealthy banker, had not won her any points with the old-money crowd. But the wife of the man the president of the United States had appointed as one of the seven members of the Board of Governors of the Federal Reserve was just the kind of formidable, understated position that would have them all drooling.

"What about dinner, Patrick. Will you be home tonight?"

"No. Business. A friend from Switzerland's in town."

Eleanor Lynam's face did not betray her feeling of relief. "Oh, too bad. I was thinking of taking the boat out, later."

Lynam released her shoulder as they reached the door. Eleanor was a competent sailor, but the thirty-two-foot classic motor yacht was not a one-person vessel. "Good idea, but bring someone who can help you. It might get rough out there later. I may stay over in San Francisco." He leaned down and pecked his wife on the cheek. "See you tomorrow, darling."

Lynam waited until Eleanor was out of sight, then closed the door and hurried back to his desk and dialed Lancer's cell phone number.

"That fool Dunbar killed Stoylar," he said when they were connected. He could hear bagpipe music in the background, and the sound of men singing off-key.

"I know," Lancer said. "I got there just as he was leaving Stoylar's place. I'm at Kelty's saloon now. I figure he'll show up here sooner or later. If not, I'll call him, but I'd rather have it be a surprise meeting."

"Dunbar says he has photographs of the target. She was seen today in Golden Gate Park."

"I'll get the photographs, and after he tells me what he knows, take care of him."

"Not yet," Lynam cautioned. "Use him to find Janna. You can eliminate Dunbar after we've found her."

"Okay," Lancer said indifferently.

"Dunbar may be uncooperative."

"No, I don't think so," Lancer predicted. "I'll let him know he won't be paid unless he does what he's told to do."

Lynam liked the man's blunt confidence. "Good. I'm meeting with your employer tonight. Is there anything you want passed on?"

"No. He has my number. Good night, sir."

Lynam broke the connection and poured himself a stiff draft of Johnnie Walker Blue Label Scotch from a crystal decanter.

He had no regrets about ordering the death of Angela Lolley. Angela had kept up on all the financial news. She would have seen his photograph in one of the journals. The girls, well, he couldn't afford to take any chances, they too could identify him.

Having Philip Bovard provide an assassin had been his only reasonable choice, though Bovard would be a leech now, using Lynam's position at the Fed to his utmost advantage. He could look forward to a lifetime of blackmail. Subtle blackmail no doubt, but just as lethal. If only his father had never met Bovard, never done business with him.

If only he hadn't left the notebook computer at Angela's. Or, more accurately, if Angela hadn't stolen it. The miserable creature must have taken it from his coat pocket. He looked at the silver-framed calendar on his desk. Tomorrow would be April the sixth, and tomorrow was almost here. Four days. If they could get by for four more days, without the notebook falling into the hands of the police, Bovard's nuclear reactor deal would go through. However, Lynam knew he could still be ruined if Janna and the notebook turned up next week, next year. She had to be found and killed, the sooner the better.

Complications. God, how he hated complications. He rapped his knuckles on the base of Angela Lolley's computer. He'd connected the base to his computer screen and then printed out every file on the hard drive.

He'd been startled by the number of Lolley's clients. There were over three dozen regulars, like himself. He had never really thought of the others, he had always pictured himself and perhaps one or two other gentlemen seeing Amber and Tina. It sickened him to think that he had been one among many in a production line.

Angela had proudly told Lynam she'd taken photographs of her new girl. "Janna is so sweet, so innocent, her skin so smooth," the whore had crooned. Lynam had been able to access Lolley's computer checkbook records. He'd found the name of the film developer she used. He'd called the processor, and learned that the photos were sent out in the mail to Tara Street. Dunbar had botched that assignment, and now the police had the photos and would be searching for Janna.

Lolley's records had also provided him with Stoylar's name and first initial, Y. Lynam had utilized the bank's numerous data bases in trying to find Stoylar—frustrated at first by the lack of results. Stoylar had been a very careful man, but luckily, he'd made on greedy mistake that had allowed Lynam to identify him and pick up his address.

Francis A. Dunbar was an enigma. Lynam had run his name through the bank's computers and had come up with absolutely nothing. But Bovard's man could always find him at Kelty's Irish bar.

Lancer sounded tough, and competent. He'd have to be both to work for Philip Bovard. Everything was going to be all right, he told himself. Lancer would find Janna and eliminate her, and get the notebook back. Then he'd kill Dunbar. He sipped at the Scotch reflectively, one hand trailing down to his crotch, fingering his sore penis. Angela had always sworn that the girls were clean, though now that he knew of her numerous clients, he had his doubts.

The thought of Janna, a virgin, of Angela holding her hands while little Tina held her head, started a stirring in his groin.

He'd considered seeing a doctor, but had put it off, anticipating the doctor's questions when he examined the bite wound on his penis. Lynam had always hated the looks, the crude jokes he'd had to endure due to the size of his penis. He'd gone out for the swimming team in high school, and would have been one of the stars, but the juvenile taunting in the shower and in the locker room had driven him to quit the team.

Then there were the dates, groping around in the backseat of his father's Cadillac, the girls' hands anxiously working at his zippered pants—then the snickers, the embarrassed giggles.

A prostitute had once broken out laughing: "Am I going to have to charge you half price, sonny?"

Eleanor had been much more tactful, murmuring disgusting old homilies about size not mattering, yet it hadn't been long after their marriage that he'd found the oversized dildos tucked away in her nightstand. The fact that Eleanor had eventually turned to women for her sexual satisfaction infuriated him. He had visions of Eleanor and her tennis pro writhing on a bed, wrestling over the control of an enormous dildo.

He made his way over to the telescope, silently cursing

his wife as he carefully zeroed in on the house with the sun deck over the front garage. The woman who lived there was in her forties, a jiggling-with-fat brunette. She pranced around her apartment half nude most days. It wasn't a very pleasant sight. But the young girl—eleven or twelve years old, thirteen at the most. Golden-haired. The first morning he'd spotted her she was in the kitchen wearing white panties, nothing more, as she sat, eating her breakfast.

He'd seen her dozens of times since then. When she was alone, she'd dance around the apartment in those panties, her hands flying, her young, slender body jerking to music that Lynam couldn't hear.

She was incredibly graceful, lithe, uninhibited. A nymph. A beautiful, unspoiled, untouched nymph.

There she was now! In the kitchen. White shorts and a T-shirt. He winced as his hardened penis rubbed against his pants leg.

Chapter 21

The first wine bottle was empty and they were midway through the second, throwing ideas back and forth as Kordic popped two frozen dinners into the oven.

"Have you ever wondered what kind of a person would go to a place like Lollipops'?"

"Creeps," Maureen responded quickly.

"I talked to a psychiatrist about it."

"I don't have a lot of faith in psychiatrists, Jack."

"I didn't either. Until I needed one. The one who treated me, Dr. Barney Ford, is a damn good man. He probably saved my life. I called Barney this morning, and he put me in touch with another psychiatrist, Dr. Denise Navine, who specializes in sexual dysfunctions. She's well aware of the large numbers of pedophiles on the Internet. It's a huge problem, yet whenever anyone tries to shut them down, there are screams of first amendment rights."

"Did she tell you anything we don't already know, Jack?"

"Maybe. A great many pedophiles are straight, not gay, though there're plenty of man-boy perverts out there—the victims are usually young, real young, seven to ten.

"Lollipop's girls were a little older than that—twelve, thirteen. Dr. Navine says that case studies show that the men who frequent the Lollipops of the world are often Mama's boys, or were dominated by an older sister, who made them dress up in her clothes or humiliated him in front of her friends."

"So what? They're still creeps," Maureen said stiffly.

"You won't get an argument from me on that. Dr. Nav-

ine said that case studies show that the creeps often use
their real first names. It gives them a power high being
called by their real names. The ones who don't use their
name often use the same first initial, if it's a Joe, he'll use
John, that kind of thing. And she had another interesting
theory. Lollipop's customers may suffer from *penis
minutus*."

"Christ," Maureen snorted. "She put it delicately,
didn't she?"

"These are guys that have been put down by girlfriends,
or their wives, all their lives."

Maureen combed her hair with her fingers. "Well, judging from my limited experience, this doesn't help narrow
the list of suspects a hell of a lot, Jack."

"No," Kordic granted, "but it may give us an edge
when we do catch the bastard. Humiliation, Mo. It's a hell
of a powerful tool. You saw Lollipop's income figures.
Her customers were all well off. Rich men, successful businessmen, formidable men in their own fields. Those are
the ones who can't handle humiliation." He rummaged
through the refrigerator bins, holding up a tomato as if it
were a trophy. "So, when we get him, we load him up
with small cock jokes. No lettuce. Sliced tomato okay?"

"Fine," Maureen said. She was feeling the effects of the
wine. "I'm wondering about the killer's timing. What
if—"

The ringing of the doorbell cut her off.

Kordic wiped his hands on a towel on the way to the
door. "I never have any unexpected visitors."

The doorbell rang again. Whoever it was, was impatient
as hell.

Maureen leaned against the kitchen wall, wineglass in
hand, as Kordic opened the door.

"What happened to this town?" a deep, booming
voice asked.

Maureen peeked out and saw a gray-haired man with
a deep tan push his way past Kordic. A black nylon piece
of luggage was strapped over his shoulder, and he held
a pink bakery box in his right hand.

Anatoly Weeks skidded to a halt when he spotted Maureen. He dangled the pink box by its strings. "Croissants, cookies, muffins, and bagels, bagels all over the place, but doughnuts? I had to go to a half-dozen places before I could find doughnuts." He smiled widely, his teeth dazzlingly white against his dark skin. "Anatoly Weeks." He darted a glance back at Kordic. "Did I come at a bad time?"

"What's this?" Frank Dunbar asked in an incredulous voice as Kelty poured a double shot of Bushmills into an old-fashioned glass. "Usually you buy me that cheap swill from the well."

"I'm not buying," Sean Kelty informed him. "It's your friend sitting over there." He leaned his belly against the bar top. "The cute-lookin' blond guy."

Dunbar pivoted around, squinting through the smoke. The saloon was packed—there were several card games in progress and a group of old-timers were playing dominoes. Two middle-aged women wearing bright print dresses were holding the attention of the dozen or so men at the bar. The jukebox was playing Irish tunes. He spotted the blond man sitting alone, with his back to the wall, raising a glass of beer in a saluting gesture.

Dunbar turned back to Kelty. "He used my name?"

"That's what Debbie said." He called down the far end of the bar to his daughter. "Get over here."

Debbie finished pouring a round of drinks, then sashayed over to them.

"Didn't that blondie fella order a drink for Frank, here?" Kelty asked.

Debbie cocked a hip and licked her lips before replying. "He sure did. Gave me a ten-dollar bill and said to buy Frank Dunbar a double from the best bottle in the house."

Dunbar's stomach rolled over. "Was he here when I came in, Sean?"

"I don't believe so." Sean Kelty dribbled a half shot of the Irish whiskey into a glass and knocked it down in one gulp.

They both watched Debbie saunter back to the far end of the bar, then Dunbar looked back at the man who'd bought him the drink. "Could he be a copper?"

"When's the last time a copper bought you a drink?" Kelty scoffed.

Dunbar left his whiskey on the bar, then threaded his way through the tables.

"I don't drink with men I don't know," he announced, glowering down at the blond man, whose hands were lying flat on the table, alongside a folded newspaper.

"You know me, Frank. Doug Lancer. We spoke on the phone." Lancer kicked an empty chair loose from the table. "Sit down, we've got things to talk about."

Dunbar stood uncertainly for a moment, then swiveled the chair around, straddled it, hands draped over the chair back. "Lancer. You're Mouse's friend."

"Mouse Fennesy is dead."

"Sure'n the world's a better place for it," Dunbar grumbled nastily.

"You did a sloppy job, Frank. I'm disappointed in you."

Dunbar's jaw bunched. "What the fuck are you talkin' about? I didn't—"

"You let one girl get away. And—"

"You're mistaken," Dunbar said defiantly. "She wasn't there that day." His nose wasn't only itching, it was throbbing, and he fought off the urge to reach for the ointment. "So, you're working for the baby fucker, are ya, now?"

Lancer leaned forward, his hands caressing the newspaper. "You're working for me, Frank, and I don't like sloppy work."

"I tell you the girl—" Dunbar bit off his words when Lancer flipped the paper open, revealing a sheaf of stamps.

"You left these behind, at Stoylar's place. You should have licked one, Frank. Some chemical. PCP is my guess. They're probably worth a pretty penny."

Dunbar rubbed the back of his hand violently across his

nose. "I had to kill the stupid Russkies. I told that to Paulie Boy."

Lancer showed no reaction to the name. "The two bodies. I assume the one you tortured was Stoylar?"

"The man took some persuadin'."

"You shouldn't have left the iron plugged in. The stench was bound to bring someone. Let's see the photographs."

"What photographs?" Dunbar croaked, worrying that the bastard somehow had found out about the photos he'd taken of the baby fucker picking up the whore's suitcases at the hotel.

"Of Janna, Frank. You told our client you had them." Lancer snapped his fingers like a man signaling for a waiter. "Let's have a look."

"I don't have them on me. I—"

"Prove it to me, Frank. I figure a man of your talents, you dumped the gun. But just in case, empty your pockets on the table. Slowly."

"Don't push it, bucko. You're in my territory now. All I've got to do is say the word, and you're dead meat."

Lancer tilted his head to one side and narrowed his eyes. "That song. The tune that's playing on the jukebox. 'Danny Boy' isn't it? I was in a bar in Belfast once, and they were playing that same dumb song. I started crying, crying like a baby. The bartender, a big ugly potato-head, like your friend behind the bar, came to me and said, 'You must be Irish.' No, I told him. I'm a music lover."

Dunbar glared silently into the Australian's icy blue eyes.

"The bartender took great offense to that, Frank. He actually threatened me, so I kicked the shit out of him and a half-dozen other potato-heads." Lancer ran his eyes slowly around the bar. "Younger, tougher potato-heads than this crowd. I haven't had that kind of fun in a long time. Now, let's stop fucking around. We're working together on this. The sooner we find Janna, the sooner you're going to get paid."

Dunbar eyed the blond man with barely a blink of the eye for several seconds, then slowly pulled the two photo-

graphs from his pocket, slapping them across the table
like a blackjack dealer.

Lancer picked the photos up, one at a time with his left
hand, his right hand under the table, holding the silenced
pistol. He studied them briefly. "Pretty little girl," was his
only comment.

"The baby fucker must think so," Dunbar snarled, rubbing the back of his hand across his itching nose.

When Anatoly Weeks learned that frozen dinners were
being served, he said he'd stick with the glazed sugar
doughnuts. He browsed through the Angela Lolley file
while Maureen and Kordic ate their meal.

"This guy interests me," Weeks said, waving the Brooklyn rap sheet on Yuri Stoylar across the table. "He sold
one of the girls to the madam, huh?"

Maureen sampled the veal piccata cautiously. "For
seven thousand dollars. And we can't find him. Janna has
called me twice. She was there that night and witnessed
the killings. I'm hoping Janna will call again. She sounded
so scared, so lost."

Weeks glanced back down at Stoylar's rap sheet, which
listed his date of birth, his FBI crim number, and his social
security number. "You've got all this, and you can't get
a hit?"

Kordic said, "No. And we've tried everything."

"Maybe not everything. Let me take a crack at him.
What about the shooter? Anything on him?"

"No," Maureen answered. "We spotted him at Lolley's
house the night Jack came back from London. He shot a
hole in Jack's new raincoat."

Weeks licked some glazed sugar from one of his fingers.
"Did he use the potato gimmick again?"

Kordic shook his head. "No. A revolver this time."

"Did you get a good look at him?"

"Not much of one," Kordic said. "White, thirties, tweed
hat, dark jacket. Janna described him as having a red nose,
but I didn't get close enough to spot that."

Maureen said, "Janna heard the killer speak with an

Irish accent. 'Sure'n the both of you should be ashamed of yourselves' is what he said before he killed the two girls."

Weeks nodded at Kordic. "I told you the potato silencer was an IRA trademark. I know of nine men killed exactly that way, and all by men who were either active or former members of the Irish Republican Army. The Iranians, the Syrians, Saddam, and that *alter kocker* Arafat, before he became a man of peace, they all used IRA hit men. Any time, any place where an Arab might look suspicious, they hired an Irishman. I lost two of my men in Gibraltar to one of the *momzers*."

"*Momzer* is a bastard," Kordic explained to Maureen.

"And *alter kocker* is an even worse bastard," Weeks grinned. "Jack, I brought a video from London for you to look at."

"I think I'll use the bathroom before we start," Maureen announced. "Where is it, Jack?"

"Down the hall, second door on the right," Kordic instructed.

Anatoly Weeks watched Maureen stride out of sight. He sampled the wine in her glass, then said softly, "Was that 'where's the bathroom' line for my benefit?"

"Nope. This is her first visit. Sorry to disappoint you, Weeks, but it's strictly business."

"You're not disappointing me," Weeks assured him. "You did say she was single, right?"

"Divorced."

"Really?"

"Really," Kordic confirmed. "Now what about the video?"

"It's in the luggage. I've a dozen more at the embassy, but this is the one I want you to see tonight."

"You've found something good?"

"Maybe," Weeks answered, getting to his feet when Maureen came back into the room.

Weeks removed a videocassette from his luggage and handed it to Kordic.

Kordic turned on the giant-screen TV and slotted the cassette into place.

The screen sparkled to life. Weeks plopped onto the leather couch and patted the cushion next to him. "Come on, Maureen. I'd like your opinion on this, too."

The video came into focus and Kordic recognized the lobby of the Savoy Hotel.

"Scotland Yard had eight cameras in the ballroom, but one lousy fisheye lens installed in the lobby ceiling," Weeks explained. "It gives everything an off-center look. I wish they'd let us handle the surveillance."

The three of them sat in silence for several minutes.

"I hope it gets better than this," Kordic criticized.

Weeks said, "You already missed one of the star players."

A long minute went by, then Maureen said, "There you are, Jack."

Kordic leaned forward. It was an eerie feeling, seeing himself moving through the crowd, knowing what was about to happen. The camera lens wobbled momentarily, the focus blurred.

"The bomb just went off," Weeks informed them. "No sound, of course. The Yard really did this on the cheap."

The screen showed Kordic look up to the ceiling, take a few confused steps, then start to run toward the banquet room.

Weeks walked over to the screen. "Freeze it, Jack."

Kordic pushed the VCR's pause button.

Weeks walked over and tapped his knuckles against the screen. "Twenty-four people are visible now. Well-dressed, stuffy old farts for the most part." He smiled at Kordic. "Except for you, Jack. Start it up again."

Kordic pushed the play button. Half the people were standing statue-still, the others were mulling about nervously, bumping into each other. They all looked up, almost in unison.

"The chandeliers," Weeks explained. "They were swaying like crazy. One of the Savoy staffers told me he dove under a table. He was afraid one of those crystal monsters would come crashing down on him."

The lobby crowd started moving, slowly at first, then faster, becoming a frightened mob.

"Here someone probably yelled out 'Bomb,'" Weeks said. "Look at 'em go."

One tuxedoes man knocked over an elderly woman with a cane in his haste to reach the exits.

"Everybody hit the panic button," Weeks said, "except that guy coming out of the phone booth, Jack."

Kordic stood up and walked toward the television set. A blond man, his hair almost white, emerged from the booth. He glanced up at the ceiling, directly at the camera, then moved off in an easy, swinging athletic stride, as if he was in no particular hurry.

Weeks said, "Sport coat, turtleneck sweater, not dressed up for a dinner at the Savoy, Jack. You ever see him before?"

Kordic rewound the tape, then pushed the forward button, stopping the frame when the blond man's face came into view again.

"No. Can't say that I have. What makes him so special?"

"His name is John David. At least that's the name he used on his passport on the flight from London. An English passport. He works for Philip Bovard."

Kordic made a noncommittal grunting sound, freezing the video frame on the blond man once again. Tall, rugged-looking, mid-thirties, hair stylishly long, spilling over the collar of his sport coat.

"Is someone going to tell me who these people are?" Maureen invited.

Weeks turned to look at her. She was struck by his eyes, a pale gray, that, like his teeth, stood out in stark contrast to his deeply tanned face. He wasn't handsome, but he had a leathery, world-weary charm that she found somehow appealing.

"Sorry," Weeks said. "Philip Bovard is a financial terrorist. He was behind the explosion at the Savoy. An ex-IRA man planted the bomb, but Bovard hired him for the job."

"Why would Bovard be involved in this?" Kordic queried. "How would he profit by bombing the hotel?"

"He did it to take out my boss, Ira Heiser. Ira was getting too close to Bovard."

Maureen squinted at the TV screen. "Weren't there eight or nine people killed—"

"Eleven," Weeks corrected. "All highly placed current or former intelligent agents. People who Bovard would have no compunction about killing anytime, anywhere. His specific target was Ira Heiser."

Kordic started the videotape again, watching as the blond man strode out of sight.

Weeks said, "On two jobs that we are sure Philip Bovard engineered, there were reports of a man we believe worked for Bovard. We were never able to ID him, but he was described as tall, blond, and tough-looking." He dug a manila folder from his suitcase, upended the contents of the folder onto the coffee table, and fanned out a series of eight-by-ten black-and-white photographs. "This one isn't too good. It was taken with a surveillance lens at a house Bovard has used in England."

The scene showed a sleek silver car parked in front of an impressive iron gate. A man's face was barely visible through the car's window.

"That's the man who calls himself John David," Weeks explained. "The same guy exiting the phone booth in the Savoy lobby."

"I couldn't recognize him from that picture," Mo complained.

"They get better," Weeks promised. "He took a helicopter, directly from Bovard's place. We traced it to Heathrow in London. Here he is climbing out of the helicopter." He pointed to the other photos. "That's him in the airport, waiting to take the Concorde to London. Same guy as in the Savoy, right?"

"Right," Kordic agreed.

"I had to push a lot of buttons to hold the flight 'til I could get there. My gut hunch is that he's the one who pulled the trigger on that bomb, Jack. He wanted to be there to make sure it went off."

"Where is he now?" Maureen asked.

Weeks leaned back in the leather couch and pulled at his chin. "I wish I knew. He lost me at Kennedy Airport in New York. And I'm a hard man to lose. This guy's a pro. He could be anywhere. But guess where Philip Bovard is?" Weeks didn't give Maureen or Kordic a chance at a guess. "En route to San Francisco. Over the last four weeks Bovard's received seven calls from someone in San Francisco who identified himself as 'Old Friend.' Now Bovard's coming here. I want to find that 'Old Friend.' "

Maureen rose slowly to her feet, fighting back a yawn. "This is getting awfully complicated. I'm going home, Jack."

"Okay, I'll drive you, and tomorrow—"

"I'll drop you off," Weeks offered quickly. "Tomorrow you can give me a hand tracking down this Old Friend."

"Tomorrow's going to be tough. Maureen and I are—"

"I'll find Yuri Stoylar, and you help me with Old Friend. Deal?"

Kordic couldn't suppress a grin. "Okay. Deal."

Using his right arm, Weeks assisted Maureen into her coat, then led her out to his car, a dark gray sedan that was parked on the west side of the apartment house, facing the Pacific Ocean.

"Cold damn place," Weeks said as he unlocked the car door. "What is it? Six months of wind and cold, wet fog, and then winter sets in?"

Maureen slid into the passenger seat. "You get used to it. I was born less than a mile from here."

Weeks gave an exaggerated shiver. "I like the heat. Do you feel like stopping somewhere and getting some real food? Or something to drink?"

Maureen wrapped herself in her arms. "Did you and Jack have a little man-to-man talk while I was in the bathroom?"

"He told me you're single, that's about all." Weeks

swiveled to face her. "I'm not proposing marriage, just some food and a drink."

"Do you actually think you can locate Yuri Stoylar?"

Weeks started the car's engine, goosing the accelerator before he responded. "Yes. I think so."

Maureen examined his profile, noticing how easily he manipulated the car's gearshift and steering wheel with only his right hand.

"How?"

"Tricks of the trade," Weeks responded casually. "Where to?"

"Take a right. One drink. The Cliff House is just up the road. Stoylar's the only link I have to Janna. If she's still alive, Stoylar may have her."

"Then I'll find him."

"You find Stoylar, and I'll buy you dinner. And all you can drink."

Weeks flashed his teeth. "Anyplace I choose?"

"If it's in my price range, Mr. Weeks."

"Please, call me Anatoly. Can you cook?"

Chapter 22

Patrick Lynam hesitated, his index finger inches from the doorbell of the St. Mark Hotel's penthouse suite.

His concern was Philip Bovard's reaction to the missing notebook computer. He'd sounded furious on the phone when Lynam first informed him of it. Now there was no continent, no Atlantic Ocean between them. The man was a killer. He not only hired assassins, according to Lynam's father, Bovard had been one himself. A very competent one.

He took a deep breath, squared his shoulders, and pushed the button. The door opened almost immediately, as if Bovard had been there, waiting.

To Lynam's relief, Philip Bovard greeted him warmly, first a firm handshake, then he pulled Lynam to him and hugged him to his chest.

"Patrick. This will turn out all right. I've ordered dinner. It's much more comfortable here than in the restaurant, no?"

"Yes," Lynam agreed, entering the hotel suite. Bovard ushered him into the dining area. The sixteen-foot table was set with stiff napery, crystal glasses, and Wedgwood china.

"Thank you for recommending this hotel," Bovard purred amiably. He pulled a bottle of white burgundy, 1994 Meursault Les Perrieres, from a silver ice bucket and wrapped a small towel around it. Water dripped from its base onto the tablecloth as he poured the wine. "It's quite satisfactory. Two thousand American a night, but satisfactory." He handed Lynam a glass of the wine. His voice hardened. "Now, tell me about the hunt for your misplaced computer."

"Dunbar killed the man called Stoylar and—"

"I know all that," Bovard said. "Tell me about the girl. Do you know that she still has the computer?"

"Yes," Lynam answered nervously. "She definitely has it. I've . . . I've made contact. Through E-mail."

"And she's answered you?"

"Yes. Briefly. Just enough to let me know she has it."

"You had better hope so," Bovard threatened, then quickly did an about-face, smiling and patting Lynam on the shoulder. "What we don't want is for it, or her, to fall into the wrong hands, like those of the police." The smile faded away. "You've told me everything, haven't you? Everything that is on the damn computer?"

"Yes, yes," Lynam swore. He paused, coughing into his hand before continuing. "The personal account numbers, the banking codes, but I've changed them all. There's no danger of anyone—"

"The delivery date? April tenth?"

"Well, yes, but again, no one—"

Bovard cut Lynam off with a curt gesture and moved in close, so that he was inches from Lynam's face when he spoke. "The place of delivery, Patrick. Do not lie to me. Did you enter Cyprus? The harbor at Limassol?"

"Yes," Lynam responded meekly.

Bovard backed off a few inches, and Lynam sank into one of the dining-room chairs. He crossed one leg over the other, then draped an arm over his knee, a psychological defensive gesture that Bovard recognized immediately. "And the name of the ship, and the captain, Patrick. Did you enter that information into your little computer, too?"

"No, no," Lynam assured him. "The Swedish freighter, I couldn't even spell the name if I had wanted to."

Bovard struggled to keep his features passive. The lying little bastard. He'd entered everything into that damn computer. He'd strangle Lynam with his own bare hands if this deal was destroyed because of his incompetence. "All right. How goes the money?"

They spoke for fifteen minutes, Lynam giving Bovard the figures of the monies he'd channeled, first through Buenos Aires, then to the Isle of Jersey, and finally through a bank in Barbados. "The Syrians came up with half, Philip. They still want to pay the rest with gold."

"Impossible," Bovard said testily. "I need the currency to pay off the Russians in Cyprus. I have to have that in American dollars, Patrick. That's all that the Russians will accept."

"I understand. I've done about all I can. You'll have to talk to them," Lynam said, glad to shift some of the problems onto Bovard's shoulders.

Bovard topped off Lynam's wineglass. "I'll do that. They are difficult bargainers. Worse when they're crossed. Have you ever heard of the Mukhabarat, Patrick? Syrian Military Intelligence?"

"No. Never."

Bovard held his wineglass up to the light, examining it as a chemist would checking a formula. "Bad people to cross. They are in the habit of skinning their enemies alive. Actually cutting the skin away from the flesh, in long strips. A man by the name of Colonel Rashid Awad is an expert at this. They videotape the entire operation, and send the tapes to their victims' families, or employers. I saw one once, of a captured CIA agent. The blood. The screams. Incredible." He sniffed at the wine, then said, "Now, let's talk of more pleasant matters. Tell me, have you received confirmation of your appointment?"

"Not yet," Lynam replied softly. "Tomorrow. Friday at the latest."

Lynam tapped his glass against Bovard's. "Your father would have been proud of you."

Lynam took a sip of the wine, thinking that he should be toasting his father. Lawrence Lynam had always dreamed of being appointed to the Federal Reserve Board. "A license to steal, son. Even better, a license to print your own money. Just think, a few days', even a few hours' notice of knowing for certain whether the interest rates are going up, down, or remaining the same. That's better than the Midas Touch."

Lawrence Lynam had never realized his goal, but his ambitions had been passed on to his son. The danger was in tracing the inside information back to its source, thus his father had long ago decided that the buys and sells would be made out of the United States. That's where Philip Bovard came in to his father's plan. He could put the Fed policy information to work in foreign markets: Hong Kong, Paris, Madrid, Japan's Nikkei, the German DAX, Bombay, Taiwan, and every kick-started Third World entry that now had its own stock exchange.

Bovard could drop packets of money into markets around the world. Lynam's money. It had worried Lynam at first, Bovard handling the money.

He had grilled his father thoroughly about this. "Sleep well," his father had advised him patiently. "Philip is in my pocket, I'm not in his."

Bovard reminded Lynam of the Orson Wells character, the black marketer, Harry Lime, in the movie *The Third Man.* Vienna, right after World War II. Wells being scolded by his old friend, Joseph Cotton, for selling tainted penicillin to hospitals. Wells, staring down at the black specks of the war-ravaged crowd from a Ferris wheel. Lynam had memorized Wells's line: "Would you really feel any pity if one of those dots stopped moving . . . forever? If I said you can have twenty thousand pounds for every dot that stops, would you really, old man, tell me to keep my money?"

The movie was made in 1949. There were many more dots clogging the world now.

Lynam didn't hear a phone ring, but Bovard swiveled on his foot and strode to the dining table, snapping open a briefcase. A fax machine inside the case was spewing out paper.

"It's from Lancer," Bovard confided, reading each page as it became available. He studied the two pages, then handed one to Lynam.

"Is this the girl? Janna?"

Lynam examined the grainy black-and-white print. "Yes," he said stiffly. "That's her."

"Good. At least Dunbar was able to obtain two photographs of her before he killed the Russian."

"I don't trust Dunbar. There may be more photographs, something that—"

"My man anticipated that, Patrick. It's been taken care of. Apparently the girl frequents a park here, she may even be sleeping there, according to what Dunbar learned from Stoylar." He delicately extracted the faxed photograph from Lynam's hand. "Very pretty. It's a shame she has to die." Bovard sampled his wine discerningly, then said, "Did you ever do business with Saddam?"

"Saddam?" Lynam asked, somewhat puzzled by the question.

"Yes. The devil himself. He had a . . . thirst for young women. He'd send his bodyguards out to the streets, and they'd pick out one or two of the prettier ones, and take them to one of Saddam's palaces. They enjoyed a splendid life there, for several days, then they're never heard from again."

Bovard patted Lynam on his shoulder. "You don't have that luxury. Especially here in America. You should come to Germany. I know several places where you can find some very young, and very accommodating young ladies." He squeezed Lynam's shoulder. "Your father enjoyed Germany very much. Very much indeed."

Chapter 23

Jack Kordic watched from his kitchen window as Anatoly Weeks escorted Maureen Connah to his car. The Mossad agent looked like he had some spring in his step. He wondered what Maureen's reaction would be when Anatoly made a pass.

He put the dirty dishes into the dishwasher, then opened a cabinet and reached for the bottle of Jack Daniel's, his hand pulling back as if he'd suddenly touched something hot.

The doctors had told him that while technically he wasn't an alcoholic, he was dangerously close.

During the months after his wife and son had been killed, up to the time of his suicide attempt, Kordic had considered himself an alcoholic—a full-fledged, drop-down drunk.

Then, all of a sudden, he'd been able to stop drinking. Cold turkey. The doctors had been skeptical. So had he. It was as if he'd reached the point of no return and had done an abrupt about-face.

After a year or so, he started drinking again, sociably, reasonably, he thought. A glass of wine with dinner, then a second, and now a third glass. Very seldom any more. He began to treat wine as a hobby—visits to the great wineries in nearby Napa and Sonoma County, tasting classes, where the instructors treated the vintages as gifts from the gods.

"Jesus Christ turned water into wine. Not vodka, not bourbon, but wine," one of the over-the-top instructors had preached to the class, which consisted mainly of well-to-do middle-aged couples, who arrived in BMWs, Mercedeses, and Jaguars, and smoked thick dark cigars after the lecture.

He already felt a buzz from the wine. Why the extra drink tonight? Was it because of Maureen? What the hell was he going to do about her? You couldn't ignore her good looks, or that body, no matter how much she tried to hide it. He held no macho views that women couldn't handle police work. He found himself thinking about her, and not as a cop. How much of his wanting to bring her over to his apartment actually had to do with the Lollipop case, and how much of it was just wanting to be alone with her? Out of sight, sharing a drink. Maybe more than a drink?

He was restless, too hyped up to sleep. He had to go out. Somewhere. Anywhere.

That afternoon he'd had a talk with Mike Devine, the lead inspector in the Fraud detail.

Not knowing exactly what type jewelry Angela Lolley had in her house at the time of the murders made tracing any jewelry that showed up on the black market back to her murderer near impossible.

Maureen Connah had been sure that Lolley had owned some very high-grade diamond rings. The killer had cut off her fingers to remove the rings. Judging from what had been left behind at her house: expensive clothing, luggage, there was reason to believe that the killer had found a cache of more jewelry somewhere in the house.

"Nothing really new has popped up," Devine had informed him.

"The killer's a pro, Mike. A hit man. So what would he do with the jewelry? Where would he fence it?"

Devine, a balding man of fifty with thick black-framed glasses and a stomach bay-windowed from a lifetime of abundant food and booze, ran a hand across his bare scalp. "It depends, Jack, on who and what the guy is. A professional hit man usually does his job and leaves, he doesn't bother to take anything with him."

"He took the computer, I think because what was in

the machine could identify him or his employer. Maybe he took the jewelry to make it look like a murder-robbery. Now he's got it, and he wants to get rid of it."

"Okay," Divine conceded, "but what is he? I mean, black, Latin, Asian, white, they all have their own cliques. They go with the people they know."

"Let's say he's Irish," Kordic suggested. "Maybe from the old country. Possible former IRA connections."

Divine tilted his glasses up on top of his head. "Irish. Well, that really narrows it down. We've only one possibility. Sean Kelty. He was always a heavy IRA supporter."

Divine gave Kordic a rundown on Kelty. "He's in his fifties, what hair he has is gray. He's got a drinker's bloated face. He works out of his bar on Taraval Street. I've never been able to pin anything on him, Jack. He deals strictly with the lads just over from the old sod. I think he ships the stuff he fences out to the East Coast, so it's never turned over here in town."

"I'd like to talk to him," Kordic said, "but I don't want to mess up anything you've got going."

Divine sighed, wiped his face, and nodded, all at the same time. "I've got nothing, Jack. Stir him up all you want. It might do some good." He settled his glasses back on his nose, then said, "The only time we came close to busting Kelty was over a gun. He sold a big old U.S. Army forty-five semiautomatic to some young punk from Belfast. The gun probably hadn't been fired since World War Two. The kid tried holding up a drugstore, and luckily for the clerk, the gun jammed. He was still trying to figure out how it worked when the radio cars rolled onto the scene."

"What happened to Kelty?"

"He denied it. His word against the kid's, who wasn't too bright. He clammed up once he was in the slam. Last I heard he was deported back to Ireland. That all took place a couple of years ago, Jack. Since then, nothing on Kelty."

Kordic closed the cabinet door and looked at his watch.

It was almost one in the morning. If he hurried, he could get to Kelty's saloon before closing time.

"Now, damn it, bucko! I want it right fuckin' now," Frank Dunbar roared, banging his balled-up fist on Sean Kelty's desk.

Kelty gave a quick nod, like a hiccup. "Four guns in a week, Frank. That's gettin' expensive. What are you doin'? Starting a war?"

"Bugger the cost, man. I want a fuckin' gun, a real gun, not some pussy gun." He pounded his shoe against Kelty's desk. "Even if it's yours, Sean. I want it."

Kelty held his hands out, like a priest granting benediction. He didn't want to do anything to set Dunbar off. He'd never seen the man so upset. His eyes were wild, his nose so red Kelty could swear he saw the god-awful thing throbbing.

"I don't own a gun, Frank, or you'd be welcome to it. Give me a day, man. I'll get you something. Something good."

"Tomorrow mornin'," Dunbar pressed. "I'll wait no longer." His eyes strayed over to the one-way mirror. Kelty's daughter, Debbie, was working the bar by herself. Dunbar was grateful she'd gotten her looks from her mother, and had promised himself that one night he'd take her home to his place. He wouldn't put it past Sean Kelty to be gettin' a taste of her, himself. Tonight she was wearing a black mini-skirt and a skintight white sweater, her nipples almost poking through the material. He was admiring her profile when he saw the man at the bar.

"What's wrong?" Sean Kelty asked when Dunbar jumped to his feet.

"The bastard at the bar, the one Debbie's shoving her tits at. He's a copper."

Kelty squinted through the mirror. "Don't know the man, Frank. Is he trouble?"

Dunbar scratched at his nose. It was the copper that had showed up at the old whore's house. The one he'd taken a couple of shots at.

"I'd say he's trouble. For both of us. I'm leavin' out the back. I want to know what he's asking Debbie. My car's parked around the block on Forty-third. A white Saab. Send her to me as soon as the copper leaves."

"Now, Frank, I don't—"

Dunbar's accent was thickening as his anger rose. "Send the bloody girl, Sean. She'll come to no harm. And find out who the copper is."

Jack Kordic ordered a beer, in a bottle, from the pretty brunette. He didn't want to drink out of one of the smudged glasses that were pyramided alongside the cash register.

"Any beer, or do you want me to surprise you?" the girl teased.

"I haven't been surprised in a long time. You pick."

He watched as she bent over at the waist, causing her short skirt to ride up as she leaned into the refrigerated cabinet.

"Is Sean around?" Kordic asked when she twisted the cap off the bottle of Harp ale and set it in front of him.

"No. He took off a bit ago." She leaned her elbows on the bar. "It's almost closing time."

"That's why I thought he'd be here. To count the till."

She ran her tongue around her full lips and gave an exaggerated pout. "I guess I'll have to handle it all by myself, tonight. I'm Sean's daughter. My name's Debbie. What's yours?"

"Jack," Kordic said, turning to look over his shoulder as four husky, middle-aged men walked behind him. One of them brushed against Kordic's back, then blew a kiss at the girl, said: "See you tomorrow, love," then paused at the door long enough to give Kordic a hard stare. Their eyes locked for a moment, and Kordic gave the man a small victory by pulling his away first. He didn't look anything like the gunman that had shot at him, and neither did any of his companions. There were just three other customers in the bar now, all men in their sixties or seventies.

"Your boyfriend looks upset."

"Boyfriend," she scoffed, going through that routine with her tongue again. "He should be so lucky. Whatcha want with my pa?"

Kordic took a pull on the beer. "Just to talk."

The girl picked up the five-dollar bill Kordic had laid on the bar, dropped it in the register, and smiled when he waved away the change.

"He's a hell of a talker, Jack. He'll chew your ear off. Maybe I can help you." She clasped her hands behind her back and straightened her shoulders, her breasts thrusting forward.

Kordic slipped a business card from his jacket pocket and handed it to the girl. "I was hoping your father could put me in touch with a man."

Debbie's eyebrows arched as she studied Kordic's card. "What man? Maybe I can help you. What's his name?"

"I haven't got a name. Just a description. Thin, wears a tweed hat. He has a red nose. And a brogue."

Debbie crossed her arms across her ample chest, her thumbs extended upward. "I think you've come to the wrong place. He doesn't sound familiar. What's he done?"

Kordic took another pull on the beer, then slid off his stool. "Maybe your father will know who he is."

"I think you'd be wasting your time, Jack," Debbie advised him. "What did you say this man did? Why do you want him?"

"Just to talk, that's all. Tell your father to call me."

Frank Dunbar slumped down behind the steering wheel of his car as the policeman exited Kelty's saloon. An electric streetcar was doing a turnaround at the end of the line, the screeching of the steel wheels on the damp tracks sounding like wailing elephants.

The copper's head swung around in the direction of the noise. The fog was thick, almost down to the ground.

Dunbar cursed silently. The copper made an inviting target as he stood under the pool of light from Kelty's neon sign. If he had a proper gun, he'd get rid of the bastard here and now.

The copper walked unhurriedly, a half block toward the ocean, his heels clicking rhythmically on the wet pavement. He slipped into the driver's seat of a dark sedan.

He's going to stake Kelty out, Dunbar reasoned. He'd have to kill the copper. Killing coppers was no longer a big deal in Ireland, especially British coppers, but here, in America, it was different. It would be much simpler just to kill Kelty.

He heard the sound of the policeman's car engine turn over, then the headlights cut a path through the fog. The car slowed at the corner, then picked up speed. Dunbar watched until the taillights were swallowed up by the fog.

How the hell had the copper got onto Kelty so fast? Was it the Aussie? Lancer? Both of them showing up like that, within an hour. No, the blond fairy wouldn't want to bring the cops in. The copper must have those photographs of Janna, the one the baby fucker sent him back to the house for. He's got them, he knows what she looks like, and he's after her. And me. He's bloody well after me.

He started across the street for the bar, then suddenly veered away. Debbie was coming toward his car. He'd see her first, then her father.

The thumping sound caused Janna to jump. Then she heard the voices:

"Are you sure this is a safe place?" A woman's voice.

"Yeah. There's just the horses." A man, his tone coarse, excited. "Come on, no one comes around the stable at this time of the morning."

"I think we should find a place—"

"This is a place, baby. Come on."

The hay moved, and for a moment Janna was afraid that she was going to be crushed.

"No, no," the woman's voice was firm. "Not with the horses here. I couldn't—"

"They sure as hell aren't going to tell anyone, babe, here—"

There was a slapping sound, and the man cursed.

Janna crawled slowly on her elbows and knees, carefully poking her head out of the opening to her secret hiding place. She could see the man's boots. Knee-high black leather. He was zipping up his jacket. There was a star on the jacket. A police star! The woman was standing off to the side. She was dressed just as he was. A policewoman. Her white motorcycle helmet dangled from one hand.

The man said something Janna couldn't understand.

The woman responded, "We're just going to have to find a better spot, Roy. Come on, let's get back on the street before the sergeant comes looking for us."

Chapter 24

Jack Kordic woke up in a sweat, the bed sheets tangled tightly around his body. The dream had come back. He hadn't had the dream in a long while.

He'd described it to his psychiatrist as a nightmare. He was home, in the backyard, standing alongside the small swimming pool. His wife, Linda, sunbathing on a towel near the pool, her golden tan vivid against her yellow bikini. Danny, standing on the end of the diving board, his hands together in a prayerlike pose, his knees bent. Kordic was coaxing him. "Dive, son. Dive. Close your eyes and dive."

Danny's eyes were squeezed shut, his legs quivered, as he started tumbling forward. Suddenly Linda screamed, scrambled up from her towel, and began running toward the pool. Danny was in midair, Linda leaping toward him. Only then did Kordic notice the pool was empty of water. Nothing but rough white concrete. He tried moving forward, trying to reach Danny, but his feet wouldn't budge.

The dream always ended with a loud scream. Kordic was never sure if the screaming came from Danny, Linda, or himself.

He lay back on the drenched pillow, grateful the dream had returned. Linda and Danny were so vivid in the dream. He'd been losing them, lately. Not thinking of them as often as he thought he should.

He threw the sheets back, donned a pair of khaki pants, a hooded blue sweatshirt sporting a SFPD insignia, and running shoes, stopping at the last moment to slip his off-duty derringer into the sweatshirt pocket, then made his way out of the apartment, zigzagging across the early morning traffic to the beach.

The sky was pewter gray, the ocean a slightly darker color. Even the sand looked gray.

Kordic often thought of moving, buying a house somewhere. Getting a dog, or a cat. Or maybe a parrot. A parrot he could teach a phrase or two. Like, "No more, you've had enough."

Danny had always wanted a dog, but somehow there had always been some reason or other to postpone the purchase: not enough time to train a pet. Who would care for it when they were away for vacation. Vet bills. Lame excuses. Now he had more than enough time and money to do about anything he pleased. Now. When it didn't mean a damn thing to him. His bimonthly paychecks were automatically deposited in the Police Credit Union. He wrote checks for the rent, for cash, and used a credit card for the rest of his needs, never bothering to tally the checkbook. It just didn't seem to matter to him now.

He moved along at a slow, steady pace, nodding a "good morning" to the regular joggers he passed along the way, his mind drifting, thinking of his visit to Kelty's saloon last night. Kelty's daughter, Debbie, looked like a tough cookie. Was she in on the fencing operation with her father? If not directly involved, she certainly had to know what was going on. Luckily, she didn't appear to be too bright. The description he'd given her of the shooter—thin, tweed hat, red nose, and a brogue—probably could have fit dozens of Kelty's patrons, but Debbie acted as if no such man existed. Maybe Maureen should grill Debbie while he worked Kelty over.

Maureen. And Weeks. An unlikely pair. Maureen and the girl, Janna. That was a pair that had him a little worried. Maureen was becoming obsessed with Janna, hanging around the office, waiting for the girl to call. He couldn't much blame her—those phone calls. The kid sounded scared. She had every right to be scared, but when a cop got too close, too involved with a subject, bad things usually happened. For both of them.

Maureen Connah was brushing her teeth when the doorbell rang. She approached the front door cautiously, squinting to peer through the peephole.

"Jesus, Anatoly," she said with a martyred look after opening the door. "Didn't you bother to go to sleep?"

Their "one drink only" stop at the Cliff House had turned into a three-cognac, hour-plus sojourn.

Anatoly Weeks wasn't at all what she'd expected. She admitted to herself that her expectations came mostly from movies and spy novels. She'd assumed that an Israeli Intelligence agent would be closemouthed, nervous, a chain-smoker with a fanatical edge about him, but Weeks was just the opposite: funny, charming, a great storyteller, and interested in her. He'd made that very clear.

Weeks sidestepped his way into the apartment. He was neatly dressed in a charcoal-gray suit, white shirt, and solid black knit tie. The same outfit he'd worn hours earlier, though everything looked freshly pressed.

He waved a pink bakery box at Maureen. "I brought coffee, too."

"I think you're pushing it a little—"

"I found Yuri Stoylar." His eyes roamed over her figure. "You look fetching, but maybe you'd better get dressed."

Maureen glanced down to see her bathrobe had gaped open at the front, revealing a good portion of her breasts.

"Damn it," she cursed, pointing her still wet toothbrush at Weeks. "Is this for real? You found Stoylar? Just like that. I worked my butt off trying to find him, and if you're kidding about this, I'll—"

"Would I lie? I found Stoylar. Where's the kitchen?"

Maureen showered and dressed in record time—stepping into the corduroy slacks she'd worn yesterday, and slipping into a baggy navy turtleneck, shaking her head, like a swimmer surfacing from the bottom of the pool, finger-combing her still wet hair straight back from her forehead. She found Weeks perched on a dinette chair, dunking a chocolate doughnut into a cardboard cup of coffee.

His suit jacket was draped over the back of the chair. His shirt was crosshatched with laundry marks.

"Okay, how'd you do it?" she asked, reaching for a cup of the coffee, noticing that his left arm hung straight down, wondering if he still suffered any pain from the gunshot wound.

"Stoylar's a beauty. He came to New York, claimed he was a political refugee, and bingo, your Uncle Sam welcomed him with open arms, gave him some ID, including a social security number so he could get his government assistance."

Weeks shook the pastry box in her direction. "The jelly rolls are great."

"Go on, go on," Maureen prodded, deciding the hell with her diet and picking up one of the rolls.

"Stoylar clipped Uncle Sam pretty good back in New York, he signed up for every damn welfare program available. They're coached on that before they get here, did you know that? There are schools that give them pamphlets to study, forms to fill out as soon as their feet hit the docks. Right after Stoylar's arrest in Brooklyn, he drops off the dole. Disappears. Then, like most of them, thank God, he did something stupid."

"What stupid?"

"He went to Reno. Nevada. That's not far from here, is it?"

"No. A little over two hundred miles."

"It's a gambling town, right?"

"Yes," Maureen answered impatiently. "Come on. How did you get to him and where is he?"

"Patience," Weeks preached, devouring the remains of his chocolate doughnut and picking up a jelly roll. "I don't know if Stoylar did any gambling, but he did fill out a contest coupon. You know those type things? The booth with the pretty young girl tempting everyone to fill out a form for a chance to win an expense paid trip to wherever. Well, this particular booth in the Reno gambling casino was hustling a free trip to La Paz, Mexico. List your name, address, date of birth, social security number, then drop it in the barrel for a chance to win first-class airfare to La Paz, free room and board. And Stoylar fell for it."

"He won the trip?"

Weeks smiled, crumpling his face. "Maureen, anyone who is sucker enough to fill out the form wins, then the schnorrers come in and—"

"The what?"

"Schnorrers. Crooks, the chiselers that sponsor this type thing. They started nibbling away at the 'winners,' finding out how much they are worth, how much they have in the bank, how much real estate they own. They found out that Stoylar didn't have diddly, so he was dropped real quick."

Maureen licked a drop of jelly from her lips, then said, "So where is he?"

"Right here in San Francisco. Twelve fifty-six Cabrillo."

"I hope he's still there."

Weeks shrugged his right shoulder. "Let's go find out."

Maureen opened her purse, making sure her badge and gun were there. "Did you call Jack yet?"

"Why don't you call him? Tell him we'll meet him there."

Maureen reached for the phone, but before dialing she asked, "How did you get all that information on Stoylar?"

"The people who run these scams strip every last penny they can out of those forms. They sell the address information to credit companies, banks, and it all goes into their computers. Believe it or not, there're a few Jewish banks in this town."

Maureen deposited what was left of her jelly doughnut back into the box, then pushed her sleeve up to look at her watch.

"You dropped me off here less than seven hours ago. How the hell did you get it so fast?"

Weeks scooped up the remains of her doughnut. "Money never sleeps, kid. Call Jack. Let's get this *momzer*."

Chapter 25

Sean Kelty stared down at his daughter as she wearily made her way up the steps.

"You didn't come home last night," he challenged.

Debbie bounced a hand through her tangled hair. "I ran into some friends, Pa."

Kelty held out his hands to block her passage. "I don't like it when you don't come home. Your mother would have never put up with it."

Debbie's eyes fluttered in annoyance. Her mother had left because she couldn't put up with her father anymore. She had just slipped away in the middle of the night. That was nearly seven years ago. "I'm tired, Pa. I'm going to bed."

Kelty wrapped his beefy arms around her waist and pulled her close. Her eyes were red and smudged with yesterday's makeup.

"Did you see Dunbar? Did you talk to him?"

"I did." She struggled to free herself, but he pulled her closer, squashing her breasts against his chest, rubbing his stubbled chin into her shoulder.

"What did he say?"

"Nothin', Pa. I gave him the policeman's card and told him just what he told me." She pulled her head back to get away from his rough beard.

"He's a dangerous man, Dunbar is. You be careful of him."

"I will, Pa." She tried to wriggle free. "I'm tired. I need some sleep if I'm gonna be able to work for you tonight."

Kelty released his grip, chucking his daughter under

the chin with his thumb and forefinger. "Give your pa a kiss, then."

"No. Not now." She put her fingers to his chest, her nails digging into his soiled T-shirt. "Not now!"

Debbie jerked herself free and gave him a feeble wave.

It was then that Kelty noticed the gold bracelet. A thick gold snake with ruby eyes, coiled around her wrist. It was the one that Dunbar had held on to. He slapped his daughter across the face, then grabbed her arm, twisted it behind her back, and yanked the bracelet off her wrist. "You bloody fool! Dunbar killed a woman for this."

Debbie pulled free, glared at her father, and massaged her wrist. "It's worth a lot of money, Pa. Give it back."

"Money? It'll put you, and me, in jail, is what the bloody bracelet will do." He reached out both arms, advanced slowly, and engulfed his daughter. "I'll make it up to you, honey. Pa will make it up to you."

"I'd feel better if Jack were here," Maureen Connah said, her foot nervously tapping the car's floor mat. "He should have gotten my message to meet us here by now."

"We can wait," Anatoly Weeks assured her. "If we see anyone leave the place, we'll grab him."

Maureen nodded her agreement. They sat in silence for several minutes.

Weeks broke the ice. "How do you like working with Jack?"

Maureen glanced quickly at the mysterious Mossad agent, then focused back on the address Weeks had developed for Yuri Stoylar. "We've only been partners a couple of weeks."

"So I've heard. He's a damn good man, Maureen. Of course, I'm prejudiced. Probably because he saved my life. You'll learn a lot from Jack." Weeks nursed a pause, then added, "If you two can stick together."

Maureen turned her head to one side, the cords on her neck taut. "Any reason to think we won't?"

"None that I'm aware of. I think you two could be great

together. Listen, I don't know how long I'm going to be here. Why don't we—"

"There's Jack now," Maureen said, spotting the unmarked car.

Kordic coasted up alongside them and rolled down the window. "What have we got?"

"Stoylar's at twelve fifty-six Cabrillo," Weeks said. "Just down the block."

"What are we waiting for?" Kordic asked.

"You," Weeks replied. "Let's go."

Seeing no open parking spots, Kordic drove the car up on the sidewalk.

Maureen felt like a rookie as she watched Kordic and Weeks communicate with small nods and head gestures as the three of them approached the door to Stoylar's apartment.

Kordic drew his gun, and Maureen followed suit.

Weeks dropped to one knee, squinting at the door lock.

Kordic's hand was inches from the knob when Weeks slapped it away.

"Smell something odd?"

Kordic stuck his nose to the door and inhaled deeply. "Soap?"

"Or cleaning fluid. Get the fire department, or the bomb squad, or whatever you call it over here." He got to his feet and smiled at Maureen. "I think someone left a surprise for us."

Anatoly Weeks leaned against the gleaming red fender of one of the fire engines that was double-parked in front of 1256 Cabrillo.

There was a commotion as two members of the bomb squad, dressed in silver-colored protective bodysuits and hoods, trooped out to the street, looking to Weeks like space aliens from an old science fiction movie. One of the men carried a metal box in his outstretched arms. His partner opened the rear door of the armored bomb disposal unit and stood by as the explosives were carefully placed inside the van. Both of them yanked off their hods. Their hair was damp, their faces slick with sweat.

Jack Kordic spoke to them for several minutes, then waved Weeks over.

"I'm glad you have a good sense of smell, Anatoly."

Weeks placed a finger on his hawklike nose. "This doesn't let me down very often. What was it? Detergents linked up to a detonator?"

"Yes, detergent, sugar, bleach, some of that stuff used to unclog drain pipes, just about everything that was stored under the kitchen and bathroom sinks. It was spread on trailers made from clothing found in the flat. Just for good measure, our boy sprinkled them with gunpowder."

Weeks's face creased in thought. "And the detonator?"

"Take a look," Kordic suggested as he gingerly opened the metal bomb box. Nestled in the foam-lined container were four aluminum tubes, half the length of a cigarette. "The bomb squad says they're some kind of mercury-activated detonators. Three were in the jamb of the door I nearly opened, the other in one of the dead men's lap."

"You said dead *men.* How many?"

"Two. One's a big bugger. He took three or four shots in the chest and stomach. The other was tortured, then had his throat cut."

"Which one was Yuri Stoylar?" Weeks wanted to know.

"Probably the one who was tortured. No ID on him. The big guy had a brand-new California driver's license under the name Erik Urizar."

Weeks shook a handkerchief free from his breast pocket, then picked up one of the aluminum tubes between his thumb and forefinger, holding it up to the sun. "I've seen more than my share of these, Jack. The aluminum is razor thin and breaks apart if you breathe on it too hard. Mercury fulminate is the ignitor. The main explosive component is PETN, so it gives out a pretty good bang. They're manufactured in China, and not only used for detonators. They're like mini-hand grenades. Throw a handful into a crowded room, and you've got instant chaos."

Weeks replaced the tube, then both men moved toward the doorway as a group of firemen exited the building to reclaim their engine.

Kordic said, "The bomb squad extracted the three detonators from the doorjamb without much difficulty. The fourth one was close to being a nasty surprise. An iron had been used to torture the victim whose throat was slashed, then it was placed on his lap, over the detonator, which was packed in gunpowder and doused with some type of kitchen solvent."

Weeks stopped in his tracks, scratching his chin. "An iron? You mean like to iron clothes with?"

"Yep."

"That sounds familiar."

"Not to me," Kordic conceded. "Something about the victims doesn't look right to me. I'd like your opinion."

"Okay, let's go take a look," Weeks said enthusiastically.

The two men walked shoulder to shoulder across the street.

Weeks said, "There was news from home this morning, Jack. The nuclear reactors are no longer in Russia. We don't know where the hell they are. We do know that Bovard is involved."

"Then why is he in San Francisco? Do you think he's having them delivered somewhere in the United States?"

Weeks pulled to a stop. "No. No way. We have a source in Beirut. That's where the reactors are headed. And I've got to find them before they get there."

Kordic stared into his friend's eyes. "Anatoly, I know you operate under a different . . . code and set of circumstances than I do. I wouldn't want you doing anything to Bovard while he's here, understood?"

"Jack, if I thought killing Bovard here and now would stop the delivery of those reactors, he'd be lying in your morgue." Weeks broke the tension with a smile. "By the way, I called you first, this morning. Before I went to Maureen's place."

"I was out jogging. You didn't leave a message."

"I thought you might already be at work."

Kordic allowed himself a little grin. "But you were sure Maureen was home."

A uniformed officer pushed a mulling crowd back as they entered the building.

"Maureen and I had a drink after we left your place last night, Jack. Not a problem, is it?"

"Not with me." He handed Weeks a pair of plastic gloves. "Watch the floor, it's slick with blood."

Maureen monitored Kordic and Weeks as they approached the corpse in the kitchen. She tried to keep her face calm as Kordic prodded at the dead man's clothes.

His neck had been cut from ear to ear. A river of dry blood had cascaded down his chest and onto the iron on his lap, and then puddled on the floor. His bald scalp was scalded red and one ear was blistered.

"Yuri Stoylar?" Weeks asked.

Maureen said, "The neighbors upstairs are Chinese. John and Mabel Lee. They say someone named Yuri lives here, but they don't know his last name. He was described as short, fat, and bald."

"Hell of a description," Weeks conceded. "I think we can assume this is Mr. Stoylar."

Maureen said, "I showed the neighbors the photos of Janna. They both recognized her. She was living here, with her mother, who died a week or so ago. They haven't seen Janna since then. I found some old photographs of a tall, dark brunette in the kitchen. The neighbors ID'd her as the mother, though they don't know her name."

"Good work, Mo," Kordic said, his hands searching through the dead man's pockets. "We'll check death records and pick up the mother's name."

Weeks moved into the next room. The trailers of saturated clothing snaked along the floor. He wondered how many people knew that their kitchens and bathrooms were filled with potentially lethal substances: cleaning agents, detergents, shoe polish, medicines made up of aluminum nitrates, potassium, sodium. When mixed in the proper proportions with something as readily available as sugar, mayonnaise, or hair cream, they could be deadly. Weeks had once been targeted at his office in Tel Aviv. The would-be bomb had been made up of alcohol, sulfuric acid, and aspirin. Fortunately it had been put together improperly, and just fizzled instead of exploding. "A dozen more aspirins and you'd be a dead man," the explosives expert had later told him.

A crime-lab technician was crouched over the massive body of Erik Urizar. Without bothering to look up at Weeks, he said, "Four shots, close range, in the stomach and chest."

"Caliber?" Weeks asked.

"Small. Probably a twenty-two or twenty-five."

Weeks crouched down beside him and examined the corpse. The man's T-shirt had been cut away by the technician. The four entrance wounds were in a tight, upward tilting pattern, and were star-shaped, with the flaps directed outward, indicating that the weapon had been fired from a distance of eighteen inches or less.

"Check the wound for potato fragments," Weeks advised.

The technician, a lanky, heavy-jawed man, looked over at Weeks and said, "Who the hell are you?"

"He's with me," Maureen Connah answered from the doorway.

She motioned for Weeks to follow her, guiding him down the hallway to the back bedroom. She motioned toward the bed.

"A woman's and a young girl's clothing. Probably Janna's and her mother's."

Weeks began fingering the garments, then picked up one of the books, flipping through the pages. "Russian. Tolstoy. Still a damn good read."

Maureen said, "I guess I owe you that dinner now, Anatoly."

He bulged his lower lip with his tongue. "I did find Stoylar for you, too bad we were a little late."

"I meant the booby-trapped front door. That was awfully close."

"I think all we would have gotten were a few wood splinters. The detonator was meant to start a fire, not kill anyone. The killer should have disguised the smell. He must have been in a hurry."

"He. Who?" Maureen wondered aloud.

Weeks's fingers groped among the garments. "To find out who, we have to figure out why. Why wire this dump? Why shoot the big ugly one, then try to burn Stoylar beyond recognition? His face and hands were saturated with solvents." Weeks ran a thumbnail across his chin. "The big man was shot at close range. I sure as hell wouldn't want to get too close to that bastard. The killer took his time with Stoylar, torturing him with the iron, then finishing him off with a knife. That's another IRA trick. Using irons or boiling teapots. But why a knife? He shot the big guy four times. His gun's not empty. Murderers don't go to a place with the intent to kill and bring a gun with just four bullets. So why didn't he shoot the second victim?"

"The noise," Maureen volunteered. "Or maybe he used up al his cartridges when he sprinkled the gunpowder on the fire trailers."

"If the gun didn't have a silencer, the noise would be a factor. If he's the same shooter that killed your madam and the two girls, maybe he tried the potato gimmick again. He didn't come prepared, Maureen. He found the tape he used to secure Stoylar to the chair right here in the flat. There's another roll of it in the room with the weights. The tape and the iron were spur-of-the-moment stuff. There was nothing amateurish about the firetrap. That showed ingenuity and talent. A real talent for destruction. You can't pick up those detonators in a local hardware store. What you've got here, Maureen, is two sloppy murders and one very sophisticated firetrap."

"Which means what? A team? Or two completely different suspects?"

Weeks shrugged his shoulders. "It could be either, or neither, or both. That's what makes this job so damn interesting."

Chapter 26

"She's back," the stocky waitress whispered eagerly into the fry cook's ear.

The cook, a potbellied man with sad, basset-like eyes, twisted around, an oil-slick spatula in his hand.

"Who? What the hell are you talking about, Gladys?"

"The girl, Leo. The cute one with the accent, and the hundred-dollar bills."

The cook squinted toward the booth in the rear of the narrow restaurant. The girl was cute. She paid for her meals in hundred-dollar bills. She'd been wearing the same clothes for the last few days, and Gladys had caught her taking a mini-bath in the women's rest room yesterday. She'd stripped down to her underwear and splashed herself with water from the basin, her backpack tucked safely between her feet. Gladys said she never lets go of that damn backpack. He figured if she was a hooker, her pimp would have a shower or a bath for her. So maybe she was a runaway, and hooking on her own. She was always playing with an expensive-looking computer. So where was she getting all the dough?

The sizzling of pork sausages on the grill drew his attention back to the stove.

"Pump her a little, Gladys. I'd like to find out where all that moola is coming from, and if there's more of it in that backpack."

Janna poured syrup onto her waffle, watching the thick dark liquid fill the square holes and spill onto the plate.

She cut off a piece of the waffle and began chewing slowly. She wasn't very hungry today. She was cold, tired, and felt queasy. It would be nice to just lie in a real bed, relax, and read. Her mother used to read to her in Russian every night. "You must never lose your native tongue, Janna. Never."

The books were classic Russian literature, Dostoyevsky's *The Brothers Karamazov,* Tolstoy's *War and Peace* and, her mother's favorite, *Anna Karenina.*

Anna Karenina was her favorite, too. She wished she'd taken the book with her when she ran away from Cousin Yuri's place.

Would the books still be there? And the photographs of her and her parents taken in Russia? Was it worth going back to get them?

No. Yuri would be waiting for her. Or would he? He was sometimes gone from the flat for days. If she was sure he was gone, she could jump the neighbor's fence, then climb in through the bathroom window. It was never locked. A few minutes would be all she needed. She could hide outside, wait until she saw him leave, and then go in.

"Is the waffle okay, honey? You're not eating much today."

Janna looked up to see the fleshy face of the waitress.

"I'm just not very hungry this morning," Janna said in an apologetic tone.

"You look a little sick, honey. Do you want me to call your mother? Do you live close by?"

"I'm fine," Janna replied, quickly getting to her feet, snatching up the backpack and groping in her jacket pocket for money. She pushed the bill to the waitress who examined it with a frown.

"Another hundred-dollar bill. Where are you getting these, honey?"

"My . . . my father," Janna replied in a low voice. The majority of the money she'd found in the metal box were hundred-dollar bills. The concession stands in the park had refused to take the large denomination bills, so now she used them in restaurants.

"Is there a problem?" Janna asked nervously.

The waitress threaded the bill through her fingers, then

headed for the cash register. "No, no problem. But I'd like to meet your father one of these days. Why don't you bring him in?"

Frank Dunbar wiped the condensation from the motel room's window and stared at the entrance to the zoo, on Sloat Boulevard.

He'd decided against taking Debbie Kelty back to the room he'd rented from the old, half-blind woman. In fact, he wasn't planning on returning to that room until he got rid of the cocky Australian.

Dunbar staggered to the bathroom and examined his face in the mirror. He'd have to buy a razor. Could Lancer already know his home address? He searched his memory. He'd been away from his room for most of yesterday.

Dunbar had been very careful about his living arrangements. No one knew the address. Not Sean Kelty. Especially not Kelty. He'd always watched his back when he left the bar, and always parked his car two or three blocks from the house. He hadn't given the batty old landlady his real name, and half the time she couldn't remember the one he'd told her.

Lancer had picked him up in Kelty's. There was no mystery to that. Mouse Fennesy had given Lancer Kelty's telephone number. Who else had the stupid little bastard given the information to?

Dunbar walked back into the bedroom. The bedspread was lying in a heap on the floor, the sheets tangled in knots. Debbie had been good. Damn good. But for a price. She was right up front about it—wanting three hundred dollars before she'd even let him feel her up. He'd ended up giving her the gold bracelet from the old whore's house.

The business card the copper gave Debbie in the bar last night was lying on the nightstand. He lifted it up and picked at his teeth with the card's edge. Jack Kordic. Homicide detail. The son of a bitch must have seen him at Tara Street the night he went back for the little *cailin*'s photos. The description Kordic gave Debbie: tweed hat, dark jacket, and red nose. But the brogue. Where the hell did the copper get that? A guess? A bluff? He hadn't said a bloody word that night. So where did the copper get it? Janna? Had she heard him when he was in the house with Angela? Did the coppers have Janna? If they did, they had Paulie Boy's computer. But no, the baby fucker was certain that Janna had the computer. Kordic had to be runnin' a bluff. Had to be.

Dunbar grabbed the bottle of Wild Turkey whiskey Debbie had coaxed him into buying last night and took a long swig, swirling the liquid around his teeth as if it were mouthwash.

Jesus, it was gettin' complicated. Dunbar was never a religious man. Catching the village priest screwing his sister in their kitchen had deleted that aspect of his life at an early age.

But he did believe in luck, especially bad luck. And that luck ran in streaks, be it good or bad. And this copper was bad luck.

The ringing of the motel room's phone interrupted his thoughts. He glanced at his wristwatch. It was hours before checkout time.

He snatched the phone up angrily, ready to give the motel manager a hard time.

"Top of the morning to you, Francis Aloysius," piped the cheerful voice of Douglas Lancer. "Are you ready to go to work?"

Dunbar's fingers tightened around the phone. He'd been sure he wasn't followed last night. Debbie. Debbie had met him at his car, then driven her own car to the motel. Lancer must have tailed the silly bitch!

"You're not too tired, are you?" Lancer chided. "You and Debbie were making quite a racket."

"Where are you?" Dunbar asked, trying to keep his voice under control.

"Downstairs. Let's get going. I want to get to Golden Gate Park early."

"Five minutes," Dunbar responded. He lay the telephone softly back on its cradle and stared at it. Lancer.

The cocky bastard! Flaunting his middle name, Aloysius, letting Dunbar know he knew a lot about him. A lot, but not all, you Aussie prick.

He went back to the bathroom and slathered the prescription ointment across his nose. His reflection in the mirror was smiling back at him.

Lancer. The blond fairy thought he was superior, invincible. In-fucking-vincible. That was all right with Dunbar. Most of his kills were of men who'd underestimated him, looked at his skinny frame, his thinning hair, his nose, and decided he could be handled, could be pushed around, given the last bone on the plate. Lancer was making the same mistake.

Janna had made up her mind—she would go back to Cousin Yuri's house. Just to look. She wasn't sure she had the nerve to actually go inside.

She was careful to stay near the cars parked along the sidewalk so that she could duck behind them if she saw Yuri or the Mustache Man.

She was a block away when she spotted the fire engines and the police cars. There were wooden barricades across the street. A crowd had gathered around the barricades.

Janna stood in place for several minutes, then slowly began edging forward. She could see two bright red fire trucks directly in front of Cousin Yuri's flat. Policemen and firemen were moving in and out of the building.

An old man with wobbly jowls and large bags under his eyes was talking to a uniformed policeman on the other side of the barricade. Janna melted into the crowd, which consisted of mostly Asian men and women.

When the old man had finished his conversation with the policeman, she nudged his shoulder.

"What happened?" she asked.

The old man looked down at her. His eyes were red-rimmed, his breath sour.

"You are too young to know, little one."

Janna recognized his halting accent. "No," she responded quickly in Russian. "I need to know. I have friends on this street." She pointed to Cousin Yuri's flat. "In that building."

The old man crouched down. Janna could hear his bones making popping noises.

"Two men were murdered, little one. I saw them take their bodies out and put them in a truck."

"You saw the bodies? What did they look like?"

The old man straightened up, his hands going to the small of his back. "They were covered by blankets. The policeman says that one was shot and one had his throat cut. He asked if any of us knew Yuri Stoylar or Erik Urizar. They must be the dead men."

Janna's eyes bounced back to the flat. The fire engines were moving. A tall, pretty woman with red hair and a dark man with gray hair exited the building. The woman had something pinned on her jacket. A badge. They were talking excitedly.

"You look sick, little one. Are you all right?"

Janna tore her eyes away from the building. "I'm . . . I'm fine."

"Did you know the dead men? You should tell the police if—"

"No!" Janna shouted, then turned and began running toward Golden Gate Park.

Jack Kordic got the word from the lead lab technician that their work had been completed. The two corpses had been carted out by the medical examiner's team. The forensic experts had taken samples of the explosives, blood, hair, latent prints, dust balls vacuumed up from under the beds, and the array of solvents and cleaning fluids that had been used to saturate the makeshift fire trailer leading from the front door to the dead man in the chair.

The photographers had recorded every inch of the flat, their flash units seemingly popping every few seconds.

Sometimes Kordic thought that the only people who actually profited from a homicide scene was the Kodak company.

Despite the enormous advancements in forensic technology, and computer-aided design software that enabled the investigator to sketch crime scenes in two and three dimensions, Kordic relied on a simple pad on graph paper on a clipboard, a lead pencil, and a twenty-five-foot carpenter's tape measure to painstakingly reconstruct a bird's-eye view of the crime scene.

Photographs, videotapes, computer and laser-produced replicas were all welcomed additions, but Kordic knew from hard-earned experience that when seated in a witness stand and being grilled by a sharp defense attorney, handwritten notes and sketches were what often decided a case.

Some of the twelve members of the jury might be excellent photographers, might be computer whizzes, might have a medical background, others might be hunters or gun owners who knew the difference between the caliber of a weapon and the damage it could do. Might. But all of them, at some point in their lives, had taken up a pen, pencil, or crayon and had drawn a sketch of some kind.

He finished his drawings, dropping the clipboard on the bed in the room where they'd found the woman's and girl's clothing, and began sifting through them. Like Anatoly Weeks, he flipped through all the pages of the Russian novels. The dust jackets were faded. There were passages that had been underlined in pencil, but since the language was Russian, they meant nothing to Kordic. He tossed the last of the books on the bed, then picked up a girl's worn tennis shoe to gain access to the bottom of the cardboard box. Something rattled in the shoe. Kordic shook it, then dumped the contents into his open palm. Three brass rings, the size of a watch face. He slid one of the rings onto his index finger and twirled it around. Too big to be a finger ring, too small to be a bracelet, even for a young kid.

He carried the ring over to the window, holding it up to the natural light. There was a worn decorative scrolling around the edge, a twisting leaflike pattern.

He gnawed at his lower lip for a moment. What the

hell could they be? And why would a kid think they were worth keeping? He slipped the rings into a plain white envelope, scribbled his name and badge number on the envelope, and slipped it in his pocket.

Chapter 27

Anatoly Weeks glided his car to a stop behind a black-and-white patrol car double-parked in front of the Hall of Justice.

"Thanks for the ride," Maureen Connah said, reaching for the door handle.

"Sure, sure. Will I see you later? I seem to remember something about you cooking dinner for me."

Maureen flashed a smile. "You are persistent, aren't you?"

Weeks slipped a card from his breast pocket and handed it to Connah. There was no name, no title on the card, just a phone number.

"If I don't answer the phone myself, whoever does can reach me in a matter of minutes, Maureen. So call me when you know your schedule."

Maureen flicked the card with her fingernail. "I've never met a real spy before. No code name? No watch with a built-in phone and TV screen?"

Weeks's tight lips flexed at the corners. "Nope. Disappointed?"

Maureen dropped the card into hr purse and opened the door. "I'll let you know about dinner one way or the other, Anatoly." She slid off the seat, closed the door, then leaned in the open window. "And thanks again. I really mean it."

The deafening growl of a siren stopped Weeks from responding. A black-and-white radio car had nudged up behind him, tapping his bumper. The scowling face of the policeman behind the wheel was staring daggers at Weeks.

Maureen waved her badge at him and the policeman shrugged and pulled around them.

Maureen's beeper went off. She saw the number for the Homicide detail flashing on the screen. She leaned her head back in through the car window and smiled. "I saved you a ticket. I guess we're even now."

Weeks flashed his teeth. "That's one of the few good things about being a spy, Maureen. We don't exist, so we don't pay tickets."

Maureen entered the Hall of Justice through the front doors, skirting the long line of civilians waiting to pass through the metal detector before being granted entrance into the bowels of the building.

Once again she showed her badge to the officer camped on the other side of the metal detector. Several of the ill-kempt gathering gave her dirty looks. One lanky, sullen-faced man with shoulder-length purple hair mumbled, "How come the bitch gets in?"

There was the usual depressing throng of what her father called "the great unwashed" waiting at the bank of elevators: suspects and their attorneys on their way to the courts on the second and third floors. Battered and bruised victims en route to meetings with inspectors or the district attorney.

Maureen often had to fight off a feeling of claustrophobia when trapped in the elevator with them. There was a thick stench, a combination of unwashed bodies and sweaty fear, that had a smell of its own and had seemingly permeated the steel walls.

The elevator door pinged open and the waiting crowd surged forward before the people inside could exit.

As soon as Maureen had opened the door to the Homicide detail, Charlotte waved her over to her desk.

"The girl called, Mo. I tried to get a number, but she wouldn't give me one. She sounded . . . frightened."

"Did she say she'd call back?"

"She asked if you had red hair. That's all. 'Does detective Maureen have red hair?' When I said yes, she hung up on me."

Goose bumps prickled Maureen's arm. Janna must have seen her at the flat on Cabrillo Street. Jesus. She was right there. Standing in the crowd. Mo cursed herself. Why the hell didn't I think of that? Why didn't I look? Janna. So goddamn close. She slammed her purse on Charlotte's desk, sending a tray full of reports crashing to the floor.

Janna crossed her arms over her chest and shuddered. She felt ill. She wasn't sure what to do. Where to go. Cousin Yuri was dead. Murdered. And a man named Erik. He must have been Yuri's friend, the one with the mustache. Who had killed Cousin Yuri? Could it be the same man who killed Angela and Tina? And Amber? Would she be next?

She'd hated Yuri and had often thought about killing him herself. The way he'd treated Mama, the things he'd tried to get her to do. Yet she somehow felt saddened. There was no one, now. Not a soul in all of America. Not a living soul that she knew.

Janna shuddered again, then picked up her pace, cutting through a bike path bordering the Tenth Avenue entrance to Golden Gate Park. She wandered aimlessly for several minutes, ending up on a bench overlooking the patched-glass Victorian-styled Conservatory of Flowers.

She slipped out of the backpack and held it on her lap, unbuckling the large compartment where the money was stored. All that money. What good was it doing her now? She fastened the buckle, then unzipped the compartment containing Paul, August eleven's computer, which was tangled up in with some underwear and socks. She picked up the computer and turned it on. The mail box icon was blinking. Could Paul have anything to do with the murders? Of Angela, Tina, Amber, and now Cousin Yuri? Could he?

She clicked on the mail. Another message from Paul:

Janna, I read about what happened at Angela's house.

Please let me help you. Tell me where you are. I will help you.

Janna's fingers lingered over the keyboard for several moments, then she abruptly deleted the message, shut off the computer, and jammed it back into her backpack.

A sprinkler racheted slowly back and forth, drenching a field flecked with wildflowers. A steady swarm of joggers, roller-bladers, bikers, and people walking their dogs streamed by, but Janna stared through them, her small hands clutching at the backpack. Tears formed in her eyes, then ebbed down her cheeks. She licked a salty tear away, then blotted her eyes with the sleeve of her jacket.

She started to get to her feet, then slumped back. Perhaps one of Cousin Yuri's gangster friends, one of the *molinas*, had killed him. That could be it. Men like Yuri had enemies. Bad enemies.

The redheaded policewoman, Maureen. It had been her leaving Yuri's flat. She was so tall, taller than Mama, and pretty. She *sounded* so nice on the phone. She wanted to help. Paul wanted to help. Would Detective Maureen change if I went to see her? Janna wondered. Like Cousin Yuri had done. He was so friendly, so helpful, his letters to Mama, promising them a good life once they came to America. That had been a lie. Was Maureen lying, too? Would she put me in prison, like Cousin Yuri said?

The tears started again, and she thought of how her mother had held her tightly at night, wrapping her arms and legs around her when Cousin Yuri or one of his friends entered their bedroom.

She needed those comforting arms now. Those tender kisses on her face.

"Cheer up," her mother would whisper. "It will get better. I promise."

Whenever Janna was feeling sad, Mama would take her to the park. To the merry-go-round or to the aquarium.

The sight of all the young children playing near the merry-go-round always cheered her up. Janna especially liked riding one of the beautiful wooden horses and reaching out to grab one of the brass rings that could be turned in for a free ride, sometimes giving a ring to one of the smaller children.

Now it seemed as if there was nothing that could erase the cloud of her mother's death, and of what had happened at Angela's house. She got to her feet and began walking slowly with no set destination in mind.

"What if she recognizes you?" Doug Lancer asked, leaning back in the driver's seat.

"The *cailin* never bloody saw me," Frank Dunbar insisted.

"That's not what I heard. She was there at the house, so you know damn well she saw you." Lancer twisted in his seat and gave Dunbar an appraising inspection. Dunbar had replaced his dark blue jacket with a brown one, and the tweed hat with a Giants baseball cap. The cap was pulled low on his forehead, but not low enough to cover his crimson nose. "Francis Aloysius Dunbar. You're a Catholic, aren't you? I know you've done your share of killing, but those two young girls. You think you'll burn in hell for that, Francis?"

Dunbar's hand involuntarily went to his nose and scratched. He needed the ointment, but didn't want to give Lancer the satisfaction of seeing him put the gook on.

When Dunbar didn't respond, Lancer came back with: "Maybe you don't believe in hell, is that it? Wormwood Prison, I bet that was a taste of hell, huh? You were there, what? Just six months?"

"A bit more," Dunbar retorted, the anger stuck in his throat like a cork in a bottle. The bloody Aussie was taunting him, letting him know just how much he knew of his background. Six months, two weeks, and four days he'd spent in that miserable British prison. The guards had loved crowding them six to a cell. "What about you, Blondie? You look like you've spent a time or two in the nick. It must have been tough, a pretty boy like you. We had an Aussie in Wormwood. A real beach boy, he was. He spent more time on his knees than a cleanin' woman."

"I've never been in prison," Lancer replied, a bemused smile settling on the corner of his lips. "Never."

"Well, there's always a first time," Dunbar said, slouching into a comfortable position.

Lancer's car was parked on Concourse Drive, directly across from the California Academy of Sciences, the oldest scientific institution west of Chicago. The structure had been remodeled numerous times since its original construction at the turn of the century and housed a natural history museum, the Steinhart Aquarium, the Morrison Planetarium, and a library.

Lancer opened the door and ordered Dunbar to stay in the car while he "reconnoitered" the building.

Reconnoiter. The pompous Australian reminded Dunbar of the Sinn Fein commanders, the bosses, the intellectuals. The ones who knew all the answers, all the time, but when things went wrong, blamed it on the poor *saighdears* who did the bloody work.

Lancer's absence gave Dunbar the opportunity to put some ointment on his nose and to plot his next move. He clearly understood that Lancer had no fear of him. Dunbar also understood his own limitations. He'd be no match for Lancer in any kind of fair physical confrontation. But he had a trump card. Lancer thought that as long as he was holding the purse strings, Dunbar had no reason to try anything until the girl was a done deal and the money was on the table.

When Lancer came back he gave Dunbar a thumbs-up signal. "One entrance in, one exit out. When we spot her, we've got it made."

They had an excellent view of the front entrance. The only disadvantage to their parking spot was the heavy traffic. There would be no way to make a quick getaway in the car.

But that obviously wasn't a worry to Lancer. Dunbar figured that the car was probably stolen or rented under an assumed name. Lancer wore a pair of thin black gloves, so there'd be no prints.

Dunbar wasn't wearing his gloves. He had feigned indifference, but he knew the exact spots his hands had come into contact with. His car was parked several blocks away on Lincoln Avenue, near the Kezar football stadium, bordering Golden Gate Park.

Dunbar had trailed Lancer from the motel to the park. Once he'd parked, and he'd gotten into Lancer's car, the Australian began laying down the rules.

"When we spot her, we follow her, and I take over from there," Lancer instructed. "Do you have a gun?"

"No," Dunbar responded, opening his coat. "And if you don't believe me, you can pat me down. I'm thinkin' you might enjoy it."

Lancer had debated doing just that, but decided against it.

"The client wants me to eliminate her. It makes no difference to you—I'll do the dirty work, we get the computer, and you still get paid, so relax, Francis."

Relaxing was one thing Dunbar wasn't good at, and he was certain that Lancer planned on killing him as soon as Janna was taken care of. Certain, because that's exactly what he would do. He hated not having a gun. His only weapon was the quick-flick butterfly knife wedged in his right sock. He chain-smoked through half a pack, then cracked the door open.

"Where do you think you're going?" Lancer challenged.

"There's a concession stand back a bit. I need a cup of coffee."

Lancer leaned over the seat and picked up a thermos.

"Here. Black, no sugar. We're not moving until we spot the girl."

Dunbar unscrewed the thermos top. "What if she don't show?"

Lancer reached into his jacket and came out with a handful of red ticket stubs. He opened his gloved palm and let the paper flutter like confetti onto Dunbar's lap. "Those are ticket stubs to the aquarium. You left them behind in Stoylar's apartment. I found them in a woman's coat pocket. The coat had a Russian label. *Baginski*. It must have belonged to the girl's mother. You should have spotted it."

Dunbar stared at the scattered pile of pasteboard.

"Twenty-three ticket stubs, Francis. Five adult tickets, and the rest for a child. Janna likes this place. Stoylar saw her here yesterday. She'll be back."

Dunbar blew on the steaming coffee to cool it off. "Stoylar said she liked to ride the merry-go-round. Maybe we should split up, and—"

"No. We stay here," Lancer responded, his tone leaving no room for argument.

They sat in silence for the better part of an hour, Dunbar puffing his way through three more cigarettes and drinking half of the thermos.

"Tell me about Paulie Boy," he said. "I like the color of his money, but I don't much like workin' for a man who fucks little children."

When Lancer didn't respond, he added, "Of course, maybe you and he enjoy the same things, eh, bucko? Are you a baby fucker, too?"

Lancer kept his eyes on the entrance to the building. He sighed deeply, his shoulders raising up to his neck. "Why do you call him Paulie Boy?"

"That's the code name he used with the old whore. Paul, August eleven. Didn't he tell you that, now?"

Lancer turned to look at Dunbar, his pale blue eyes flecked with curiosity. "August eleven. Why the date?"

"That's the way the old whore kept track of her clients. By their birthday. She was askin' me for mine when I shot the bitch."

Dunbar quickly poured himself another cup of coffee. A young girl caught his eye. She was wearing a black jacket. She resembled the girl in the pictures, except for her hair. Stoylar had said that she'd cut her hair and was wearing a black coat with a fur collar. And that she had a tan-colored backpack. It was her! The backpack was hanging in front of her chest, and she had both hands wrapped tightly around it. It was her! Janna.

Lancer noticed something in Dunbar's eyes. His head snapped around. "What's up? You see her?"

"No, I thought it might be her, but she's too young, her hair is wrong, I . . . wait. Over there. By the statue!"

Lancer's hands dropped from the steering wheel, he was reaching for the door when Dunbar said, "Look out!"

The hot coffee hit Lancer in the face. His eyes squeezed shut, one hand blindly groping for his gun.

Dunbar expertly flicked the blade of the butterfly knife open and drove it into Lancer's sternum, giving it a violent upward thrust, leaning forward so he was no more than a few inches from Lancer's shocked features. He smiled wickedly, glaring into Lancer's rapidly glazing eyes.

"You thought you were dealin' with some bloody amateur, did you, pretty boy?"

Lancer's mouth drooped open and blood began spilling over his teeth.

Dunbar withdrew the knife, wiping the blade clean on the Australian's jacket before sliding it back into his sock.

He grabbed Lancer by the neck and lowered him onto the bench seat, then quickly went through his pockets, coming away with a billfold stuffed with cash and Lancer's gun. A proper gun with a silencer.

He patted Lancer's silky blond hair. "Thanks, bucko, this will come in right handy."

Chapter 28

"Congratulations, darling," Eleanor Lynam gushed. "I just heard the good news."

"What?" her husband grumbled. "What did you hear?"

"About your appointment. I was having breakfast at the club. Several people came over and told me that they'd seen the story on TV."

Patrick Lynam gnawed at his lower lip. Damn the news agencies. He'd just gotten the word from the president's chief of staff a few hours ago himself.

"You don't sound very happy for someone who has just been appointed to the Federal Reserve Board, Pat."

"Nominated, not appointed yet," Lynam corrected.

"God, don't be so pessimistic, darling. Of course you'll be appointed. We should celebrate. Dinner at the club. We've got it, we might as well flaunt it."

"I'm not sure just when I'll get home tonight," Lynam informed his wife. "Was my picture on TV?"

"Yes. And a good one, too. Full face, I think they cropped it from one of the fund-raising parties you did for the president. I'm sure you'll make all the newspapers."

Lynam took off his reading glasses and pinched the bridge of his nose. He had figured that *The Wall Street Journal* might run a story, but they never used photographs, just stenciled drawings of the subject. Janna would never read the *Journal*. Local news shows would be of no interest to a child her age. Those thoughts relieved his fears a bit.

"Thank you for calling, Eleanor. If not tonight, then tomorrow night. We'll celebrate, I promise."

"You will be coming home later, though, won't you, Pat?"

"I'll do my best," Lynam promised, thinking it better not to give her a definite answer. If he said he wasn't coming home, she might just invite that butch tennis pro to sleep over. He'd caught them once. In Eleanor's bed. They'd long ago decided it would be more "comfortable" for both of them to have their own rooms. Lynam had returned unexpectedly from a tiring trip to New York. He hadn't gotten to the house until well after midnight. He never would have bothered to stop at Eleanor's door if it wasn't for the noise they were making: grunting, groaning, some terrible rock music playing on the radio.

Lynam had edged the door open and peeked inside to see the back of his wife's head buried between her tennis coach's legs. Yvette saw him and smiled. Lynam would never forget that smile. It covered a wide range of emotions: lust, contentment, confidence, and power. It was the power he resented most, the bitch letting him know that she could do what he couldn't—satisfy his wife.

"Don't drive across the bridge if it's too late, and you've had a few drinks," Eleanor suggested. "The Highway Patrol has been on a tear. We can't have you getting arrested for driving under the influence—not now, certainly. We'll celebrate tomorrow night. It will give everyone at the club time to digest the news. I'm proud of you, darling!"

They said their good-byes and Lynam walked to the office window, which looked out over Chinatown, North Beach, Fisherman's Wharf. The panorama covered both the Bay Bridge and the Golden Gate, and a goodly portion of the bay itself, including Alcatraz and Angel Island.

A wall of fog all but obliterated the Golden Gate Bridge. Smoke-colored clouds scudded over the East Bay hills.

The strong wind had stirred the bay into a muddy, gray-brown color, flecked with whitecaps. There were a few large commercial tankers plowing through the water, but no pleasure crafts.

That was the reason for the call, Lynam knew. It was too blustery for Eleanor to take her friend out for a sail.

They'd have to stay topside because of the weather, rather than disappear down below for their sexual romp, so she wanted the house for her little assignation. Why didn't she just purchase a little pied-à-terre in the wine country and save them both all this subterfuge?

He quickly put Eleanor out of his mind. One of the reasons he was successful in the rough-and-tumble world of commercial banking was that he could compartmentalize his problems—obliterate everything else and concentrate on one issue. The issue now was finding Janna! What had happened to Lancer? He wasn't answering his phone. Neither was Philip Bovard. A small chill went down his back. Something was wrong. Had Bovard called Lancer off? Where the hell was Bovard?

He stared out at the magnificent view with blank eyes, his thoughts on Frank Dunbar. A common criminal with the morals of a jackal according to Philip Bovard. A nobody. A nobody who now had the power to ruin my entire life.

After dropping Maureen off at the Hall of Justice, Anatoly Weeks hurried over to the Israeli Consulate General's office on Bush Street, in the heart of San Francisco's financial district. He waved nonchalantly at the surveillance camera mounted above the front entrance before using his key on the door.

He smiled at the pretty, gamin-faced woman with coppery brown hair drawn back in a tight bun, sitting behind the wavy, bulletproof glass-protected reception area. She pushed the button that unlocked the two-inch-thick steel door leading to the inner-sanctum offices.

There were three additional buttons at her disposal. One dropped a steel curtain down directly in front of the bulletproof glass. Another released a cloud of tear gas from the light fixtures in the waiting room, and the third unleashed a deadly cross-pattern of 10mm cartridges that guaranteed that anyone within the confines of the waiting room would be killed instantly.

"Have you ever been tempted to push the wrong button, Rosalie?" he teased as he passed her desk.

She responded with a blank expression, and went back to clicking her computer keyboard.

No sense of humor, Weeks lamented as he used his key to access the code room. The young ones they were recruiting were all tough, dedicated, but seemingly incapable of expressing joy, humor, or having the slightest zest for life. They drank copious amounts of liquor, but got more morose with each drink. They made love with their teeth clenched.

His attempts at developing a social relationship with Rosalie had gone nowhere. She, like everyone else in the consulate, resented Weeks's presence. His rank as a commander in the elite *Zaddick* unit of the Technical Operations Department of *ha-Mossad le-Modiin ule-Tafkidim Meyuhadim* gave him absolute authority over everyone with the exception of the consulate general himself, and even that worthy gentleman practically snapped to attention every time Weeks spoke to him.

Weeks tried to downplay his importance with smiles and jokes, but it did little good. He was an unwanted big boat in a small pond, and his wake was disturbing the disgruntled cadre of agents attached to the cushy San Francisco duty post.

The three intelligence agents now under his command were older men, veterans working the final few years of their contract, happy to do nothing other than photograph the crowds at anti-Israeli rallies or assist the local police when a temple was defaced.

Weeks had never worked with any of the men before. His review of their personnel files did nothing to bolster his confidence in them. They were too soft, too complacent. He almost added too old, but that was before he realized that he was in the same age group.

Weeks slipped out of his suit coat and flopped into the chair in front of the high-frequency transmitter that was linked directly to the Mossad's intelligence headquarters in Tel Aviv.

Losing the use of his left arm was a constant irritant, and never more so than when he had to use the intricate Mossad transmittal decoder. The injury had led to his giving up his daily intake of two packs of cigarettes. The frustration of slitting the cellophane, digging through the foiled packaging, and then fumbling with a book of matches had been too much.

He reached into his suit jacket, slid out an eight-inch Cuban Cohiba cigar, bit off the end, and lit up with a Zippo lighter, fanning away the smoke before the air conditioner had a chance to suck it away. The Cohibas had been one of the perks that went along with working for Ira Heiser, who seemed to have had an endless supply of the much-sought-after stogies. Now Heiser was gone, and he'd have to find another supplier, or another vice.

He worked the cigar from one end of his mouth to the other, then picked up the phone, buzzing Rosalie at the front desk.

Any word from our boys?" he asked.

"Do you mean your surveillance team?" she responded in a stony voice.

"That's right," Weeks said glumly. She even talked as if her teeth were clenched.

"Michael called in just a few minutes ago. They've lost the man."

Weeks leaned back in his chair and rolled his eyes. "They lost Bovard? The three of them couldn't keep the *momzer* in sight? Get me Michael right away, and I want—"

"He's en route to the office now, Mr. Weeks, I'll have him—"

"Have him on the phone to me in two minutes or I'll have his ass back in Tel Aviv in a day!"

Weeks slammed the phone down and immediately regretted his outburst. Michael Oren was the most experienced of the three agents assigned to the San Francisco office. There was no point in making the man any more upset than he already was. Besides, Weeks was still kicking himself for losing the man who called himself John David in the New York airport.

The phone chirped and Weeks snatched it up.

"Oren reporting, sir. We think we lost the subject, and I—"

"You *think* you lost him?"

"Philip Bovard entered the Bank of America Building at eleven-twenty this morning. We followed him to the thirty-first floor. He went to the offices of the Hong Kong Bank Corporation. He left at ten minutes after noon, went upstairs to the rooftop restaurant. He had lunch with three Asians. Then—"

"Then you lost him," Weeks concluded.

"Yes, sir. The elevators were jammed. We weren't able to—"

"Didn't you have a man waiting in the lobby?"

"Yes, sir. But Bovard wasn't spotted."

"Then he could still be in the building, Michael."

"I left the team stationed in the lobby. There's been no sign of him yet."

Weeks flicked cigar ash on the matted gray carpet, then scattered it with a deft sideways movement of his shoe.

"Okay, Michael. Not to worry. I've lost my share of tails over the years. What about the hotel?"

"Bovard left the St. Mark a little after nine this morning. He took a cab downtown." There was a pause as Oren searched for his notes. "He made stops at the Union Bank of Switzerland, and Credit Lyonnais, before heading for the Hong Kong Bank."

Weeks blew a wobbly smoke ring toward the ceiling. There was nothing unusual with Bovard's visits—he could be checking on his financial dealings—or making contact with his old chums at the Swiss banks, or maybe meeting with "Old Friend." Old Friend could be working for any of the banks. It would be a pain in the butt to have to check out each and every one of his stops, but it would have to be done.

"What about visitors to the St. Mark?"

Oren's voice faded out in a wash of static, then came

back on-line. "Not much luck there, I'm afraid. Bovard's staying in the penthouse. Several banks of elevators service the top floor. We haven't been able to get the hotel to cooperate."

"So we don't know if he's had visitors? We can't monitor his phone?"

"No, sir. The hotel was quite firm about that."

Quite firm. Nice turn of phrase, Weeks acknowledged. Bovard was paying a fortune for his privacy and the hotel was going to make sure he got it. Still, if Bovard was holed up in a penthouse suite in London, Paris, Madrid, or Rome, Weeks would have had no problem getting the access he needed. In Cairo, in exchange for a few gold coins, he could hook into the closed circuit monitoring devices that the luxury hotels had installed in all of their most lavish suites.

It was one of his earliest lessons in the intelligence trade. "Always stay at a cheap hotel. No one bothers to bug them, except the Russians. And they bug everything," Ira Heiser had instructed.

"Did Bovard look like he intentionally slipped the noose?"

"No, sir. It was just one of those things."

Weeks took a long draw on the cigar. "Just one of those things." A nice Cole Porter song, but a lousy excuse. He puffed repeatedly until the cigar's tip glowed red. "Tell me about Bovard. How did he move around?"

"He took a taxi from the hotel, then walked to the other locations. They're all within a few blocks of each other."

Weeks mumbled an "um hmmm." They were also within a few blocks of the Israeli Consulate. Bovard could be walking by the front of the building right now. "How was he dressed? Was he carrying anything?"

"A dark suit. He carried an attaché case in one hand. It looked heavy, but we never saw him open it."

"Did he act nervous? Was he in a hurry? Did he talk to anyone on the street?"

"No. He did stop and use a pay phone three times. He

wasn't on the phone very long. No conversation from his side, so whoever he was calling wasn't there."

Weeks's interest was immediate. "Pay phones. Where were they?"

"On the street. One at Pine and Sansome, another at—"

"How did Bovard pay for the calls? Did he put coins in, or use a credit card? What?"

"Coins. We have that on film, but he screened us off from seeing what numbers he punched in."

"Okay, Michael. Find Bovard. Call me as soon as you've located him."

He lowered a finger, breaking the connection, rattling the line bar until Rosalie responded.

"Yes, sir?"

"I'm hungry. How about you?"

"I beg your pardon?"

"Food, kid. Do you want to go out for lunch?"

"I've had lunch. I always eat at my desk, sir."

Weeks had a sudden vision of her, sandwich in one hand, the other perched over those lethal buttons, that beautiful face grave-digger solemn as she slowly chewed away.

"Was it good?"

Rosalie seemed surprised by the question. "Was what good?"

"Lunch," Weeks said in exasperation. "Whatever the hell you ate. Was it good?"

"Yes. The delicatessen in the lobby makes a very good tuna on rye."

"Great. Have them send up a double order and a Coke, Rosalie. And put a call in for me to Inspector Kordic at the San Francisco Police Department. Homicide detail."

"Yes, sir." The receptionist paused for several moments, then said, "Lunch will probably be around ten dollars."

"I'm good for it, Rosalie," Weeks sighed. "If an Inspector Maureen Connah calls, put her right through to me."

He dropped the phone on its cradle and studied the end of his cigar, which was frayed like a rope end.

Tuna on rye. He wondered what Philip Bovard had had

for lunch. Caviar, champagne, oysters, steak. Weeks hoped that it was something that would give him a stomachache, or high cholesterol. An old Jewish curse popped into his head: May your enemy lose all of his teeth, except for one. So he can have a toothache.

Bovard slipping away like that worried Weeks. The curbside phone calls could be legitimate, or he could have stopped to check to see if he was being tailed. Weeks knew from past experience with the FBI and the CIA that it was not possible to have the calls Bovard made from the pay phones traced. Unless a trap had been put on the phone in advance, or the call was made with a credit card, the phone companies had no way to keep track of the calls.

He drew deeply on the cigar, pulling the smoke slowly through his lips and letting it escape just as slowly through his nostrils.

If Bovard hadn't spotted the tail, he would eventually return to his hotel room. Maybe Kordic had some connections at the St. Mark.

Chapter 29

The condition of Philip Bovard's stomach would have pleased Anatoly Weeks.

Bovard was greatly upset, but not by the Petrali sole and chocolate eclair he'd consumed at lunch.

He'd known he was under surveillance. What puzzled Bovard was the clumsiness with which he was being observed. He'd spotted two men shortly after leaving the hotel, almost physically bumping into one when he stopped to use a phone booth. Bovard had no doubt that the man was a Jew. He prided himself on his ability to identify racial characteristics. The second man was less obvious: Caucasian, a military-style crew cut, an ill-fitting blue suit, the pants legs at least a full inch above the scruffy, brown suede oxfords he plodded around in. The small duffel bag clutched rigidly under his right arm surely concealed a camera of some type.

Were the two of them being intentionally obtuse? Did they want him to know they were there, so that a third or fourth man would escape his attention? After a moment of deliberation he discarded that theory. Their hurried, comical attempts at concealment showed them to be serious. Inept, but serious.

There was no reason for the FBI, CIA, or local police agencies to have any interest in him. The Jews? Mossad? Here in San Francisco? Had they followed him from London? Could they have somehow connected him to the Savoy Hotel bombing? Or were they local agents, called into play by one of Ira Heiser's underlings? Heiser. The Jew bastard was haunting him from his grave.

Once Bovard knew he was being followed, he made no effort to go anywhere near Patrick Lynam. The visits to the other banks had been strictly for the benefit of his pursuers. He did take advantage of the chance to call Moscow. Gregor Zinovsky was in high spirits. The *Sjogang* was on schedule. The nuclear reactors would be in Cyprus right on time.

Eluding his shadows had been an effortless task. Bovard simply thanked his Hong Kong associates for the lunch, then a quick detour from a trip to the men's room into the restaurant's kitchen, the proffer of a fifty-dollar bill to a crafty-faced waiter, along with the explanation: "There's a man waiting for me in the bar who quite rightly thinks that I've been seeing his wife. I'd like to avoid him."

The waiter escorted Bovard to the service elevator, which deposited him in the building's basement. From there it was through the garage and out to Pine Street. The wind had died down, gulls circled endlessly in the cloudless sky, the sidewalks were brimming with businessmen and women hurrying back to work after the lunch hour. He melted in easily with a thick-pressed crowd of garishly dressed tourists.

Bovard had engaged in a classic ladder-box evasion technique—one moment walking briskly, the next notching down to a crawl, changing directions haphazardly.

He found himself in a nicely groomed inner-city park, shadowed by the towering office buildings that ringed its perimeter. He sank down onto a concrete bench alongside a pine tree dripping with baublelike cones, snapped open his briefcase, and removed a foil-wrapped chocolate candy from the case. He peeled the foil away and popped the heart-shaped candy into his mouth.

The surveillance team was a concern, but evading them had been somewhat exhilarating. They'd no doubt be waiting for him back at the hotel. A minor inconvenience. One of the major inconveniences was Douglas Lancer. Lancer had not called in at the scheduled times. And Bovard's calls to Lancer, made in the banker's offices, out of sight of the men following him, had gone unanswered.

Lancer had missed calls before, but on those occasions he was emersed in a difficult assignment in some exotic locale: a Mideast desert, a Bosnian forest, a backward Ukrainian oil field.

There was no excuse for him to miss three contacts while on a simple mission in San Francisco. No excuse, which to Bovard meant one thing only: Lancer was dead, or had been captured by an adversary. The Jews again? Certainly Lancer would never have fallen into the hands of the likes of the two who had followed him around all morning.

He needed the Australian's help on Cyprus for transfer of the reactors. Now he'd have to handle every damn detail himself. If he didn't receive the American dollars from the Syrians in time to pay the Russians, they would turn the ship around. The Syrians would blame him. They were still angry over not receiving the poison gas canisters. One mistake, he could get away with. Two, and they'd be after him. And once the Syrians targeted you, they never let up. He glanced at his Cartier watch, a duplicate to the one he'd given the Russian bureaucrat in Murmansk. The time wasn't his main focus, the day was. April the tenth. Just four days away—and there'd be a half day's travel time to get to Cyprus.

Bovard settled the briefcase on his lap. In addition to a good-sized bag of his favorite chocolates, the case contained a Swiss-made cell phone and fax machine that cost forty thousand dollars and, due to its sophisticated rolling digital code, the manufacturer guaranteed could not be breached by anyone, including the manufacturer, once the machine left their offices.

Bovard had not been impressed by the money-back guarantee. If his transmissions were ever intercepted, the cost of the machine would be the least of his worries. And while the Swiss were confident that their machine could not be breached, there was no assurance that the phone Bovard was calling wasn't bugged. And Lancer's cell phone had a direct link to the Swiss phone. If the Jews had Lancer, they'd have his phone.

His fleshy, well-manicured hand reached for the phone, then abruptly dropped down and selected another chocolate.

His one personal meeting with Patrick Lynam had been at the St. Mark Hotel. If the men who were tailing him had bugged the room, had overheard their conversations during dinner, then the game was over.

Damn Lynam. And damn Lancer.

Bovard flexed his fingers, thinking how he would like to wrap them around Lynam's neck. If it wasn't for Lynam's upcoming appointment, he'd do just that as soon as the nuclear reactors transfer was concluded.

Lynam's joining the United States Federal Reserve Board could be every bit as successful as Lynam's father had prophesied. Bovard had researched the subject. The Fed was its own little kingdom: twenty-five thousand employees; an air force of Lear jets and cargo planes; grandiose, costly relics of buildings in a dozen United States cities, and branches in another twenty-five. The Fed's own five hundred million dollars of assets made it wealthier than most countries. Assets that the American public at large, and Congress itself, knew little about, and had no real power to control.

The power center was, of course, in Washington, D.C., and in the hands of the Fed chairman, a high-profile position that Lawrence Lynam did not want his son to touch. The Fed chairman was a figurehead, a celebrity, with regularly scheduled televised visits to the Congress and Senate.

No, Lynam, as one of the seven Board of Governors, would be sitting in on virtual anonymity, with access to all the daily information: check-clearing, monitoring local banks, distributing currency, settling interbank payments, and, most importantly of all, setting interest rate policy.

Bovard bit down on a chocolate, the cherry brandy center exploding in his mouth. It was too bad Patrick wasn't the man his father had been, though the apple hadn't fallen too far from the tree. Lawrence Bovard had a taste for very young flesh, too. But the old man's preference had been little boys.

He chewed slowly on the chocolate, running his tongue over his teeth to lick away the last morsel of the cherry filling. If Lancer was dead, then it stood to reason that Dunbar was the man who had killed him. Lancer's last phone call had been to inform Bovard that he had followed Dunbar's girlfriend to a dismal motel, where they had spent the night. Lancer had planned to take Dunbar to Golden Gate Park to search for Janna. Perhaps Dunbar wasn't such a dullard after all. Lancer would not be an easy man to kill. Dunbar still needed to be eliminated, and Bovard reluctantly concluded that he would have to perform the chore himself. There was no time to call in someone, and no one he really trusted, now that Lancer was gone. He leaned back, closed his eyes, and thought back to the last time that he'd had to kill a man. Seven years? Eight? The Frenchman, Druve? Or the Spaniard, Lorca? Both very tough, clever men. Certainly of a higher caliber than this ex IRA thug.

The mug shot photo of Francis Dunbar popped into Bovard's mind. Coarse features, thinning hair. Lancer had told him that Dunbar had aged since the mug shot was taken. His hair thinner, his skin scaly, his nose a virtual red beacon. He certainly wouldn't be difficult to spot.

What would Dunbar do? He had a vested interest in killing the girl, she'd no doubt seen him commit the murders, and he'd still want his money. His only connection to the money was Patrick Lynam. Dunbar would wait for Lynam to call him.

Bovard picked through the chocolates, sifting out a dozen of the largest and dropping them into his coat pocket.

He spotted a construction site near the Hyatt Regency Hotel. He strolled casually toward a rusty, scarred debris box with raw pieces of mangled lumber jutting from it, scanned the crowd, activated the explosive mechanism, then casually tossed his case into the huge box. He was half a block away when he heard the muffled explosion.

*   *   *

Maureen Connah was hunched over her desk, her head propped up by her hands when Kordic returned to the Homicide detail.

Temporary lieutenant Ray Tracey, and Inspectors Dave Grandanos and Barry "Putty" Putman, his partner, were gathered around the detail's galley, drinking coffee.

Grandanos was an aging lothario with thick jet-black hair and a pencil-thin mustache. He wore Italian designer suits, two-toned shirts, and expensive silk ties. Putmam was in his thirties, narrow-boned, his nervous, constantly moving body actions in complete contrast to his laid-back partner.

Maureen leaned back in her chair and wrapped herself in her arms. "Janna called again, Jack. She asked Charlotte if I had red hair. She must have seen me out on Cabrillo Street. I can't believe she saw me and I didn't see her!"

"What else did she say?"

"Nothing." Maureen pointed her chin toward the phone. "I'm hoping she'll call back."

Her voice sounded drained to Kordic. "Don't get your hopes up, Mo. The kid is scared, confused, she may never call back. You can't just sit around and wait for her. Why not try running her mother down? Check with the morgue, we may develop some additional leads through her mother's death."

Maureen considered the request. "Okay. Are you going to be here awhile?"

"Yep. I've got a ton of paperwork to catch up on. I'll be here if Janna calls."

"But she won't—"

"Mo. We've got to find her. We can't expect her to come to us."

"Okay," Maureen said without looking up. "I'll check on her mother."

She gathered up her purse and a file folder and walked smartly past Kordic and out of the office.

"How's Maureen doing?" Grandanos asked when Kordic walked back to the coffee machine. Grandanos had suggested that he and Kordic switch partners the first week that Maureen came to work.

"Fine. Real fine."

Tracey loosened his tie and wiped his finger inside his collar. "I could use some paper on those Cabrillo Street victims, Jack."

"Yeah, Ray, I want to show you something that I found—"

Charlotte's shrill yell cut Kordic off. "Work, boss. A two-nineteen in a car parked at Haight and Shrader. A meter maid found the victim. The ME says it looks like a one eighty-seven."

Tracey reacted calmly to the news that a white male adult had been stabbed and found in a parked car and that the medical examiner considered it a homicide.

"Who's up?"

"Grandanos and Putman," Charlotte responded.

Grandanos had his feet up on his desk, sipping his coffee.

"Get going, guys," Tracey bellowed. "Haight and Shrader. The coroner's waiting on you."

Putman was already at the door, moving from one foot to the other as if he had to go to the bathroom.

"Come on, Dave, let's go, let's go," he urged.

Grandanos took a loud slurp of coffee and rose slowly to his feet. "When are you going to learn, Putty? No one's going anywhere until we get there. Especially the stiff."

Tracey knew there was no sense in his saying anything. He hated being the temporary lieutenant, being cooped up in the office all day, devising work schedules, handling payroll sheets. He couldn't wait for the spot to be filled so he could get back to being a working cop. He turned to Kordic. "You wanted to show me something."

"Yeah." He tore open the envelope with the brass rings and shook it loose onto the counter next to the coffeepot. "I found these in one of the missing girl's shoes at the Cabrillo Street flat. Maybe the lab can figure out just what they are."

Tracey picked up one of the rings and grinned. "Jack.

You don't know what these are? That's because you don't have any kids. I . . ." Tracey's face crimsoned. Shit. Sorry, pal, I . . ."

"Relax, Ray. Don't worry about it. What are they?"

Tracey, who had a brood of six children, all boys, smiled apologetically. "This is a merry-go-round ring. From Golden Gate Park. A kid grabs a ring and gets a free ride."

Chapter 30

Frank Dunbar was out of breath by the time he got back to Golden Gate Park. There'd been no time to do a proper job of disposing of Lancer's body, so he'd driven the Australian's car a few blocks and left him there in the front seat, looking like he was taking a nap. He handed the waxen-faced ticket taker at the aquarium a ten-dollar bill and hurried into the building, not bothering to wait for his change.

He was in an upbeat mood. Killing the big Australian like that, with just a knife, that had been better than sex. Even better than sex with Debbie Kelty. Then there were the goodies he'd found in Lancer's pants pockets. Over four thousand dollars. There was a cellular phone that he'd taken, then decided to dump in a park trash can, and the gun. The gun was a beauty. A professional's weapon. It reminded him of the one he'd used on a British sergeant in a dark Belfast alley years ago.

One shot in the ugly bugger's left knee, the next in his right. He had barely heard the soft cough of the bullets. The Brit cried like a baby. Dunbar had put him out of his misery with another pop in the back of the head.

He began searching the aquarium for the little *cailin*, his hand under his coat and wrapped around the grip of the silenced pistol.

He paused briefly to watch a shark cruising around in an oversized tank. He waited, hoping to see the shark take a gulp out of the swarm of smaller fish in the tank, finally moving on after a disappointing few moments.

His cell phone chirped. Paulie Boy must be in a sweat by now.

"Where are you?" the voice demanded.

"Lookin' for your little friend. I spotted her at a hamburger joint, but that big blond fag of an Australian, Lancer, scared her off."

"What happened to him?"

"Blondie? I don't know. I went after the girl. I haven't seen the bugger since."

"Where did the girl go?"

"Sure'n if I knew that, I'd already have her drawn and quartered for you. Maybe Blondie stumbled onto her."

"I want to talk to Lancer. Right away."

Dunbar lit a cigarette from the dog-end of his old one and inhaled deeply. "Who's more important? Blondie or Janna?"

"The girl, obviously," Lynam said between clenched teeth. "Find her, and get that computer!"

Dunbar's phone let out a light chirp and the icon for low battery flashed on. "Talk to you soon," he said abruptly, then pushed the off button.

A six-foot-long slimy gator was lazing under a spiky palm tree on a narrow, man-made beach. He seemed to be staring directly up at Dunbar. Dunbar winked at him, then flipped his cigarette, aiming for the creature's eyes. The cigarette fell a few feet short, dropping into the milky green lagoon waters.

Anatoly Weeks sounded agitated. "Jack. I need help. Do you know anybody in security at the St. Mark Hotel?"

"The St. Mark? Very plush, Anatoly. If you want a discount on a room, I'm not your man."

"This is serious, Jack. I need a favor. Philip Bovard's registered in the penthouse."

Kordic's chair squeaked as he leaned back. "Ah, the mysterious Mr. Bovard. Let me think."

Most of the major hotels in the city hired retired San Francisco policemen for their security staffs. He frisked his memory for someone at the St. Mark. "Yeah, I know a guy there. Al Paramo. You can buy me dinner and I'll introduce you."

"I'm in a hurry, and I may be booked for dinner," Weeks injected quickly. "Can you put me in touch with Paramo. Right away."

"Hang on and let me see if he's working," Kordic said. He put Weeks on hold, then punched the phone for an outside line, then dialed information and got the number for the St. Mark.

Paramo was working. His cautious tone gave Kordic the impression that the phones were monitored by the hotel.

"I just wanted to stop by and say hello," Kordic said. "It shouldn't take long."

"I'll be here 'til eight tonight, Jack. Come on by."

"He's working," Kordic advised Weeks. He pushed his sleeve back and glanced at his watch. "I've got to finish up this report. Meet me there in, oh . . . an hour. Okay?"

"I'll be there. Early."

Janna held the back of her hand to her forehead. It felt warm, slick with sweat. She watched the merry-go-round and listened to the beautiful music and the laughter of the children.

Usually just seeing the magnificently carved horses with their jeweled eyes, the zebras, camels, and ostriches, all moving up and down on their shiny brass poles, cheered her up.

Her favorite horse, a palomino, dressed in armor like a knight's charger, now held a boy no older than four, cradled in its silver saddle, his mother's hand gently holding on to the child's back.

Janna's hand went to her jeans pocket, where she had kept the free-ride brass rings she was so skilled at grabbing.

The merry-go-round operator, a grouchy man with an always-angry face, had scolded her for capturing the rings.

"You're like a monkey. Give the others a chance."

How could a man who worked all day at such a beautiful merry-go-round be so angry? She wondered.

There were no rings in her pockets now. Just money. Lots of money. She wasn't hungry, but she thought that she had better eat something. Soup. Mama had always made her soup when she wasn't feeling well.

Chapter 31

Anatoly Weeks was waiting under the burnished copper canopied entrance to the St. Mark Hotel when Jack Kordic wheeled the unmarked car into the brick-paved plaza.

The doorman, resplendent in a red double-breasted knee-length coat and black fur top hat, was about to admonish Kordic for leaving his car parked near the fire hydrant, and thus eliminating his tip.

Kordic palmed his badge discreetly. "Official business. I'll only be a few minutes."

The door man nodded gruffly, then turned on a high-voltage smile as a stretch Cadillac limousine purred to a stop at his feet.

The hotel lobby was dominated by a series of fifteen-foot columns covered in gold marble. The tesselated flooring soon gave way to a multipatterned carpet of California poppies.

A tuxedoed hotel employee sized Kordic and Weeks up and raised his eyebrows in a question. "Can I help you gentlemen?"

"Al Paramo," Kordic said.

The eyebrows dropped like a curtain. "I'll get him for you," the tuxedo replied with little enthusiasm.

Weeks leaned back on his heels and examined the lofty, frescoed ceiling. "Not bad," he quipped. "But not the Savoy."

Kordic saw Al Paramo's head pop out of a door down by the elevators.

Kordic made the introductions. "Anatoly Weeks, Al. He's a friend. He needs some help."

Paramo was broad and bulky. His outstanding feature was a crushed nose. Paramo had several versions of just how his nose had ended up in that condition—most of them having to do with knock-down-drag-out fights involving motorcycle gangs or drug-crazed homicide suspects.

Actually the cause of the injury was a baseball bat that had slipped out of the hands of a fellow officer during a softball game at the lunch-hour break at the police academy.

Paramo squeezed hard on Weeks's hand, forcing a grin when the suntanned man equaled the pressure, then increased it. When Paramo's hand was released he put it behind his back and wiggled his fingers. "You in the business, Anatoly?"

"Mossad."

Paramo's face sobered. "You shittin' me?"

"No," Kordic assured him. "Maybe we should go somewhere private, Al."

They followed Paramo through a veiled door, down a narrow steel staircase, and into the basement of the hotel.

"Enter the dungeon," Paramo joked, holding the door open to his office.

It was a small room, triangular in shape. There was one ornate walnut desk and four mismatched chairs. The walls were cloaked in thick, sun-streaked drapes. The same poppies carpet used in the hotel lobby covered most of the floor, stopping inches short of the drapes in several spots, revealing dull concrete. A mini-refrigerator sat on a sturdy mahogany end table with claw-and-ball feet. The refrigerator was positioned so as to be within arm's length of the desk.

Hotel castoffs, Weeks correctly assumed.

The desk was cluttered with a computer, printer, fax machine, and a single telephone. In between the electronics were several cardboard cups and a ceramic ashtray in the shape of a horse's hoof holding the remains of two cigar butts. The aroma of old cigar smoke hung heavy in the air.

Paramo quickly crossed to his desk, picked up the phone, dialed a number, then set the receiver on the desk.

Kordic could make out the recorded message of a woman advising that: "At the tone, Pacific Daylight Time will be three-oh-eight and fifty seconds."

Paramo next turned on a radio, adjusting the classical music so that they were barely able to talk over it.

"You guys thirsty?" Paramo asked, reaching over to the refrigerator and coming out with a shoe box full of miniature liquor bottles.

"What's your pleasure?" His fingers rumbled through the bottles. "Stoli, Jack Daniel's, Corvoissier, Black Label, nothing's too good for the guests of the St. Mark."

"The vodka sounds good," Weeks said. "Did a Michael Oren from my office talk to you already?"

"Nope. He may have talked to someone upstairs. If so, it was a mistake. You ask those guys for an extra room towel and they check with New York headquarters."

Weeks frowned. No doubt Oren had gone directly to the front office asking for cooperation. "I'm looking for information on one of your guests. Philip Bovard. He's in the penthouse."

"Good for him," Paramo responded enthusiastically. "I had it myself for one night. February, our worst month. It had been vacant for a week. My wife thought she died and went to heaven."

He tossed Weeks one of the bottles, another to Kordic, selected one for himself, then dug paper cups from the desk.

Paramo took notice of how the Mossad agent used his teeth to crack open the bottle.

"I'd take it as a personal favor if you could help my friend," Kordic said over the chorus of what seemed like hundreds of violins performing a rousing symphony.

Paramo knocked back half of his drink, settled the cup on the desk, flicked on the computer, and clicked in a command.

"Okay, Jack. For you." Paramo owed Kordic a few "chips"—favors that one cop does for another. One of those chips had saved Paramo from a nasty brawl involving a city supervisor who Paramo had inadvertently recorded enjoying himself in a gay bathhouse. Paramo's target had been a vacationing East Coast Mafia lieutenant. The tape could have been dynamite—the Mafia dons didn't much care what their boys did, as long as they didn't do it with other boys.

When the supervisor heard about the tape, which had been planted without benefit of a search warrant, he went ballistic. Kordic had somehow smoothed things over. Paramo was never quite sure how he'd done it, but it was one big chip.

"Philip Bovard," he read from the screen. "His reservation was made from his London address—Old Broad Street. Payment by American Express." He clicked some more keys. "Not much there. No phone calls. Some chow."

"May I look?" Weeks asked politely.

Paramo hit the shift and F7 keys and the printer gurgled to life.

He examined the printed page before passing it over to Weeks.

"Like I said, pal. Not much there."

Weeks examined the printout studiously. "Not much, but a little. He had dinner in his room last night. Dinner for two—double orders of salad, fish, rack of lamb, and two bottles of wine." His eyebrows edged upward. "French white Burgundy at two hundred ten dollars a bottle. I'd like to talk to the waiter who brought the food."

Paramo scowled and sucked in his lips so that they virtually disappeared. "I don't mind helping out a friend of Jack's, but I've got a pretty sweet deal here, pal. I can't just start pumping the waiters, and—"

Weeks tossed a Cuban cigar toward Paramo. "I've got a whole box of these. I can have them delivered to you in an hour." He leaned back and hung his good arm over the back of the chair. "The waiter, the maid, the houseboy, anything you can do would be appreciated. I want to know who had dinner with Bovard. Everything available about him, or her. Age, description, dress. And any future guests. A glass, coffee cups, anything that might hold fingerprints, all of those would be of enormous use to me," Weeks said, raising the volume when he pronounced "enormous."

Al Paramo picked up the cigar and ran it under his nose, inhaling deeply. "I'll see what I can do. I'll call Jack if anything turns up."

Weeks nodded his head, leaned forward, pressed another cigar into Paramo's hand, then whispered softly, "Passkey?"

Paramo's face soured. "No way, if Bovard—"

"Bovard won't be a problem. My men have him under surveillance right now," Weeks said with a poker face. For all he knew Bovard was in the lobby at that moment. "They'll page me if he gets within a mile of your hotel."

Paramo shifted his gaze to Kordic, who gave him a positive nod.

"Five minutes is all I need," Weeks pleaded. "And I'll throw in another box of those beautiful Cubans."

Chapter 32

Frank Dunbar crushed the empty pack of cigarettes and flipped it toward an overflowing garbage can near the tennis courts.

The sight of two well-groomed women in tennis whites, batting a ball lazily across the sagging green net, somehow annoyed him. One of the women had long, slender legs that disappeared into a pair of tight shorts.

He patted his pockets for another pack of cigarettes, cursing loud enough to draw a disapproving glance from the long-legged tennis player.

"*Pog mo thon,*" he yelled, causing her partner to miss-serve, the ball arcing over to the adjoining court. "Kiss my ass," he yelled louder, translating the curse to make sure they got the message.

The two women huddled at the net until Dunbar was out of sight.

Bitches, Dunbar fumed. They should be workin', or at home doing somethin' useful, cookin', cleanin', screwin' the bloody mailman, some bloody something—not playin' tennis.

He decided to give the merry-go-round a quick look, then hit a bar, get some smokes, and stake out the aquarium again.

He walked around the terrace of the two-story, red-stone Sharon building that overlooked the merry-go-round and children's playground.

The sun was bright and a light wind was ruffling the trees. The merry-go-round had a short queue of children and their mothers waiting to gain entry.

Dunbar took a slow, one-hundred-and-eighty-degree traverse of the area: a pair of two-story slides, swings made from rubber tires, sand-pits, all jammed with babbling kiddies and their hovering mothers.

Don't the bloody fathers ever get stuck with the buggers, he wondered, his head suddenly jerking to a halt.

It was her! Janna. Sitting alone on a bench near the swings, a tan canvas backpack lying on her lap. Jesus, Mary, and Joseph, she had Paulie Boy's little computer in her hands!

Oh, you sweet darlin', he cooed to himself, edging back into the shadows of the building. He slowly slipped the gun from his belt, resting the bulbous barrel on the crook of his arm.

Thirty yards, he estimated. He'd have to allow for the silencer. The bullet would tumble during flight, but he didn't know which way the tumble would go: left—right—high—wide.

He'd examined the gun thoroughly, while sitting on the toilet in the men's room at the aquarium—handling the weapon as if it were a fine piece of art, which, in Dunbar's mind, it certainly was. Slick as seal skin, no manufacturer's name, no serial number. It was patterned after a Walther PPKS 9mm. The gunsmith had gone to a great deal of trouble to improve on the Kraut pistol—the hammer spur had been removed so it could be unholstered quickly without snagging on a shirt or jacket. The silencer was part of the weapon, not just an add-on, and it had an extended fourteen-round clip.

Dunbar had extracted each and every one of the fourteen cartridges, slipping them like lozenges from the clip. He'd decided he'd have to fire it once, just to make sure the weapon's sound suppressor worked properly. He'd picked a spot on Fell Street, near the entrance to Golden Gate Park, where the vehicular traffic was heavy. There were many tempting targets to shoot out, but Dunbar had settled for the ground in front of his feet, quickly firing off one round, smiling at the result. The sound was no louder than a baby's cough.

Thirteen bullets in the clip. He could make a nice round grouping, circle her little body with shots—a half-dozen hits at the least, he estimated. Only one was necessary. But not here. He'd have to wait until she was away from the crowd. Kill her and get that computer.

Janna pushed herself to her feet, shoved the computer in the backpack, then strapped the backpack over her shoulders. What other treasures were in that backpack? he wondered. Some lovely little trinkets of the old whore's that he'd left behind?

The *cailin* didn't look too spritely. She was moving slowly, shuffling as if she was wantin' to leave a room without wakin' anyone.

What is it, darlin'? Are you missing Angela and your little whore friends? Sure'n you'll be joinin' them soon enough.

Chapter 33

Kordic cracked open the accordion door of the phone booth for some air. He had a good view of the lobby of the St. Mark Hotel and the elevator to the penthouse. Al Paramo had given Weeks ten minutes to search Philip Bovard's suite. Kordic glanced at the ornate lobby clock. Weeks was four minutes overdue.

He'd called the Homicide detail. Maureen Connah answered on the first ring. "How'd you make out at the morgue?" he asked her.

The brass elevator doors with the figure of a peacock in the middle spread open and the dejected figure of Anatoly Weeks appeared. He spotted Kordic and held out his hand, the thumb extended, then pointing downward like a Roman emperor pronouncing the death penalty.

"I think I've found Janna's mother. A Jane Doe, WFA, mid-to-late thirties, she was found in some bushes on Clement Street, out by the Veteran's Hospital, eleven days ago. No ID on her, but, according to Dr. Phillips, the dress she was wearing had a Russian label, and the morgue photo resembles the woman in the photographs at Cabrillo Street."

"She'd be about the right age," Kordic granted.

Weeks poked his head into the booth and raised his eyebrows at Kordic.

Kordic silently mouthed the word "Maureen."

Weeks bobbed his head, then said, "I want her when you're finished," then slipped into the adjoining phone booth.

"Who was that?" Maureen asked nervously.

"Anatoly Weeks. He says he wants to talk to you when we're through. What was the cause of death for the Jane Doe?"

"Get this," Maureen said, pausing for a few seconds as if marshaling her thoughts. "The woman died from an overdose of a drug called methaqualone. Dr. Phillips says that in his opinion the methaqualone was taken over a two- or three-week period, with a heavy dose at the end."

"So it could have been suicide."

"Could have been," Maureen said, "but Phillips doesn't think so. The woman had a brain tumor, Jack. Her prognosis wouldn't have been good—a few months maybe, if she didn't have an operation. Phillips says that there are a number of medications that could have been beneficial for the tumor, but methaqualone isn't one of them. Its main use is to relieve anxiety, tension, or insomnia."

"Which means what?" Kordic asked impatiently. "She knew she was dying and OD'd herself, or someone did it for her."

"I'm betting she didn't even know what she was taking," Maureen said. "Why wasn't she getting treatment for the tumor? And why the hell was she dumped in some bushes and left to wait for the city to ship out to a crematorium at taxpayer's expense, rather than having a decent burial?"

Kordic stood up in the narrow booth and massaged the small of his back. "No ID. She's an illegal. She doesn't know the score. She was probably afraid that she and her daughter Janna would be sent back to Russia if they were found. Somehow she got hooked up with Yuri Stoylar. We know from Angela Lolley's records that she paid him for Janna."

"Her mother could have been in on it," Maureen suggested sadly. "What's your opinion of Dr. Phillips, Jack?"

"He's tops. You can take whatever he says about an autopsy as gospel."

Maureen gave a sarcastic murmur. "He's a little strange though, don't you think? I saw him go to the refrigerator and take a slug from a bottle of embalming fluid."

Kordic laughed loudly. "That's his booze stash, Mo. Hold on."

Anatoly Weeks was rolling his hand impatiently, gesturing for Kordic to finish his conversation.

"Let me talk to her," he said, taking the receiver from Kordic's hand, then cupping it with his palm. "I just heard from my people. Word is that the nuclear reactors are on board a ship, en route to the Mediterranean, but we don't have a clue on the ship's name yet."

The Mossad agent pulled the phone booth door shut and turned his back on Kordic.

Janna had stuck to the pedestrian-clogged park paths for the past ten minutes, never giving Dunbar a clean shot. For a moment he thought she was headed back to the aquarium, but she had looped around the central bandstand, paused for a moment in front of the Japanese Tea Gardens, then started moving again.

Finally she stopped to rest on a park bench, near a sloping meadow that led down to a grove of pygmy cypress trees.

Janna leaned back on the bench tilting her head up to a dumpling of white clouds. Her neck was taut, the tendons visible beneath her pale skin. It was as if she were waiting for him to come down and run a knife across her throat. Was this a setup? Was she leading him to the cops? To that bastard Kordic?

Dunbar edged into a cluster of head-high shrubs and took out the silenced pistol, using the crook of his elbow as a tripod. Perfect! His finger started to tighten on the trigger guard when a sharp-featured man wearing gray slacks and a light blue sweater tied around his hips approached the bench.

Dunbar cursed violently as he looked at the man's shoes. Loafers, highly polished, with tassels. Not copper's shoes. The man sat down on the far end of the bench and said something to the girl.

Janna's head jerked down and she quickly clutched her backpack between her arms.

The man spoke again. His hand dropped to his lap and he raised the hem of his sweater. Janna leaped to her feet and started running.

Fucking pervert, Dunbar howled. The bloody dickey-shaker had scared her off. She disappeared into a grove of trees, running like a bloody deer. He started after her, but gave up after a few yards.

Dunbar wanted to scream. What was it with the wee *cailin*? Was there a snowy white guardian angel perched on her shoulder, guiding her out of troubles?

Dunbar decided he needed a drink. A bloody big drink. Janna would be back. Back to the aquarium, or the merry-go-round. It was just a matter of time.

He crossed Lincoln Avenue and spotted a neon sign on Irving Street, a lovely cocktail glass with a blinking bright red cherry. The bar was crowded, and none of the patrons were to Dunbar's liking. Suits-and-ties, half of them chinks. He settled on a bar stool and ordered a double bourbon.

There was a television set hanging from the ceiling at the end of the bar. Dunbar watched the screen while he waited impatiently for his drink. Suddenly his back stiffened. The face on the TV screen! It was the baby fucker!

"Turn that bloody thing up!" Dunbar shouted.

The bartender put the drink on the counter in front of Dunbar. "Hey, buddy, keep it down—"

"Turn the fuckin' sound up!"

The bartender looked at Dunbar for a moment, then shrugged his shoulders and adjusted the volume.

Dunbar heard the television newscaster say something about the federal government, then, with the baby fucker's face plastered across the screen, said: "Mr. Lynam was unavailable for comment."

The scene switched to a commercial. Dunbar leaned across the bar. "Did you catch that name? What was that about?"

The man sitting on Dunbar's left, a real estate broker celebrating a sale, twisted in his seat so that he was facing Dunbar. "What are you so excited about?"

"That fella. The one on the television, I think I know him," Dunbar explained. "What the hell was it about?"

The man handed Dunbar his newspaper. "Here. Take a look. Some financial district banker has been nominated to the Federal Reserve."

Dunbar held the newspaper in both hands. The baby fucker's picture. Patrick Lynam. A banker. A bloody banker! He started laughing so hard he slipped from the stool and almost fell to the floor.

The bartender had his hand on the phone, ready to call the cops if the red-nose drunk didn't quiet down. He pulled his hand away when Dunbar stopped laughing, slammed his wallet on the bar, and in a loud, boisterous voice hollered: "Drinks for everyone! I'm buyin'. Make it bloody doubles. Twice!"

Chapter 34

It was four twenty-five in the afternoon by the time Jack Kordic arrived back at the Homicide detail. There were two times a day when the office desks were fully manned by detectives: between nine and ten in the morning, and between four and five in the afternoon.

He knew that at the stroke of five, the place would be deserted, except for himself, and possibly Ray Tracey.

The detectives were finishing up their day on the phone, contacting witnesses, arranging appointments with the district attorney for future trial appearances.

Bill Swensen gave Kordic a wink, and Mary O'Grady, Swensen's partner, motioned with a friendly wave, then went back to their calls.

Vince Coleman glanced up and looked right through Kordic, his attention completely focused on the person on the other end of the line, who, Kordic could tell from the conversation, happened to be Coleman's bookie.

Coleman's partner, Marty Bastiani, the department's expert on organized crime, a handsome, curly-haired Italian with over thirty-five years of service, longer than any active inspector in the department, was deeply engrossed in a report and didn't respond when Kordic said, "Hi, Marty."

Barry Putman was nervously chewing on the end of a pencil while he clicked away at a computer keyboard.

Dave Grandanos was in Ray Tracey's office. The expression on Tracey's face was one of exasperation.

A slip of pink notepaper was centered on Kordic's desk blotter covered with Maureen's neat block printing: Your

Mossad friend is buying me a drink at his embassy. Page me when you get in, or come join us.

Something had been nibbling at the back of Kordic's brain all day. Sean Kelty, the Taraval Street bartender. According to Anatoly Weeks, the use of a kitchen iron was another IRA trademark. He flipped through the phone directory for the number and dialed the bar.

A sexy young voice answered: "Kelty's. Come on over and have some fun."

"This is Jack Kordic. Is your father in?"

"Hold on a minute, Jack."

Kordic could hear the phone being dropped onto something hard, and the hum of conversation and music in the background.

"You just missed him, Jack. Do you want to leave a message?"

"Yes. Tell him I'm coming in tonight, and if he's not there, I'm going to go looking for him."

Janna limped dejectedly down the street, her hands fingering her jacket pockets. Her money was gone. Money that could have lasted for years! All gone. She'd kept some of the cash, perhaps two hundred dollars, in her jacket, another hundred or so in her pants pocket, but the majority of the money had been taken from her. She examined the torn backpack. The compartment with her soiled clothes and the small computer hadn't been damaged.

She'd been in the restaurant bathroom, washing her face and arms when the husky waitress came in, all smiles, patting Janna lightly on the head.

"Where's your father? I thought you were going to bring him in. I bet he'd like our meat loaf."

Janna had quickly wiped her face with a paper towel.

Just as quickly the waitress had scooped up her backpack.

"What have you got in here?" the woman asked, hoisting the backpack up and down in one hand as if assaying its weight. "Schoolbooks? Which school do you go to?"

Janna grabbed for the backpack, but the waitress jerked it away, hoisting it above her head.

"It's heavy, honey. You must have a lot of books. I think I'll take a peek. Maybe I can help you with your homework."

"No!" Janna protested loudly. "Give it back to me!"

"My, my, there must be something good in here," the waitress taunted. "You think you've been fooling us, honey? Coming in here and washing up every day. Where are you sleeping? Who are you hiding from? You want me to call the cops?"

"Give me my property," Janna said firmly.

"I don't think so, I—"

Janna lashed out with her foot, caching the woman in the shin.

She dropped her arms and bent over at the waist. "You little brat! I'm going to—"

Janna jerked the backpack free, her wet hands slipping on the doorknob as she tried to turn the handle.

The waitress grabbed at her hair and Janna kicked backward, feeling contact and hearing another grunt.

Janna's frantic hands finally turned the knob. She rushed into the hallway leading to the front of the restaurant.

The woman screamed: "Get her, Leo! Get her!"

The bulky profile of the cook loomed in front of her. She quickly ducked through the first available door. It was the men's room.

A tall, stoop-shouldered man was standing at the urinal. He craned his neck around and gaped in disbelief at the frightened face of the young girl, then began fumbling with his zipper. "Hey, what the—"

Janna spotted the open window at the end of the room. She heard the door crash open and took a quick backward peek at the cook lumbering toward her, a knife in hand.

"Rape! Rape!" Janna screamed, then jumped on the window ledge. A hand grabbed at her foot.

"Leave that girl alone!" the stoop-shouldered man yelled as Janna shinnied through the window. Her progress stopped abruptly, and she was slowly dragged back into the room.

"Leave the girl alone, I said—"

"Fuck you!" Leo barked, wrapping a broad hand around Janna's ankle, another around the backpack.

"Let her go!" There was the smacking sound of a fist striking bone and Leo cried out in pain.

Janna was halfway out the window, her head and shoulders dangling over an alleyway garbage can, her free leg churning air.

She could feel the cook tugging at her backpack, then she heard a tearing noise as the pocket holding the money was slashed open. She twisted her head and saw packets of the currency, still rubber-banded together, the way she'd found them at Angela's house, tumble to the ground.

"No!" Janna screamed. "Give it back to me."

"Jesus Christ," The stoop-shouldered man said in a voice full of gravel.

The cook reached out a beefy hand to Janna's buttocks and shoved hard, sending her head first out the window. She bounced off a garbage can and tumbled onto the grimy alley floor.

She rose to her feet slowly, swung a leg up on the garbage can, and raised herself high enough to peer through the bathroom window. The two men were on the floor, sweeping up the money with their hands.

The waitress barged into the bathroom, her hands out, like a boxer's. She saw the money, then Janna's face peering through the window, and flashed a triumphant smile. "I knew you were a whore, you little bitch!"

Janna jumped back to the ground and began running. She was a full block from the restaurant before she realized that she'd lost a shoe. The cook must have pulled it from her foot when she was hanging out the window.

She spotted a small store on Irving Street that sold everything from cigarettes and soft drinks to inexpensive imported clothing.

She carefully checked the prices. There'd be no more

expensive shopping trips. No beautiful clothes. No meals where she could order anything she wanted without worrying about the cost. She selected a pair of chemically scented tennis shoes and carried them to the checkout counter.

The salesman was a dark-faced man with a small pearl imbedded in his left nostril. He gave Janna a sly smile and told her he had some special bargains in the back of the store that might interest her.

"My bill, please," Janna responded coldly, avoiding his eyes as she waited for her change, wondering how long the money would last now. The only thing she had of value was the computer. Paul's computer. How much was it worth?

Chapter 35

"This is it?" Maureen Connah asked, her lips forming a slight pout as she pirouetted slowly around the room, which consisted of a coffin-shaped table, a small desk with one telephone, and an awkward-looking piece of equipment that resembled a boxy old computer. "I'm a little disappointed. I expected a spy's lair to house banks of computers, secret cameras connected to spy satellites, and all those clever gadgets that Q supplies to James Bond." She ran her finger around the ashtray, which held a soggy cigar butt. "Or at the very least, air conditioning. Double-oh-seven would be very disappointed."

Weeks dumped the remains of his cigar into the wastebasket. "Even spies are on budgets nowadays, Maureen. I've got problems. Big problems. I need a little help. I've got to find this *momzer* blond guy you saw in the video of the Savoy Hotel. His boss, Philip Bovard, is here, in San Francisco. Or was, he has a room at the St. Mark Hotel. I've a feeling the blond guy's here, too."

"Why here?" Maureen asked. "Why are they in San Francisco?"

"That's the same question Jack asked." Weeks rummaged through a pile of documents on the coffin-shaped table. "My bosses just sent this to me. It's graded J-one. That means top secret. Top, top, top secret." He flashed his teeth. "Can you keep a secret?"

"I'm not sure I want to, Anatoly."

"I wasn't kidding about needing help."

Maureen uncrossed her legs and smoothed out her skirt. "Okay. I can keep a secret."

"I'll just give you the highlights. Four nuclear reactors were removed from two Russian submarines. They were supposed to be shipped to a waste site in Siberia. They never got there. Bovard was in Russia when the reactors were removed from the subs. I know he's involved in this. I've got to find those reactors." Weeks slapped his hand on his knee. "It's as simple as that."

"You're sure this Bovard has them?"

"Yep. And I know who he's selling them to."

Surprise showed on Maureen's face. "You know the buyer? Why don't you get him to—"

"It's not a him," Weeks said wearily. "It's a them. The Syrians. They're the buyers, they'll use the Hezbollah to do the dirty work."

"Hezbollah. The terrorist group that's always in the news?"

"Right. Hezbollah. Party of God." Weeks bared his white teeth in frustration. "The Syrians, the Iranians, the Albanians, they all use the Hezbollah. The son of the party chief was killed by one of our troops in a raid last year. It just added to the hate. It's tough for us to get any intelligence in that region, but what we have picked up is that something big is coming up. We don't have the exact date, yet. It could be any day, but it's going to be soon. Too damn soon. I'm sure it involves the reactors. I've got to intercept them before they're delivered to Hezbollah. Our best bet is that they'll come by ship. Delivered to a port somewhere in the Mediterranean: Spain, Italy, Greece, Turkey." Weeks sliced the air with his hand. "It could be anywhere. The Hezbollah will smuggle them into Beirut, or maybe directly into Israel."

"Why do you think they'll be delivered by ship. Why won't they just fly them in?"

"Well, for one reason, the time period. If they were being brought by plane, they'd already be at their destination. And getting the reactors out of Russia by plane would be difficult. They're monsters—each is twenty feet tall, half that in width. And they've been used on the subs for some time, so they're hot and dirty. The safe thing to do would be to package them in lead containers, truck them to a nearby port, and load them on a ship."

Maureen walked her fingertips across the desk. "If Hezbollah gets the reactors, what do you think they'll do with them?"

"They could be converted into a bomb. Or they could be dumped someplace where they'd contaminate our water canals, a seaport. They'll try to blame it on us, say it was from our stockpile." Weeks held the classified J-one document out to Maureen. "We've learned that the Syrians have been active in the precious metals market. They're disposing of a lot of their gold. We think it's to pay for the reactors."

"I'm still confused about why Bovard is in San Francisco," Maureen said.

"Me too. It's got to be the money. I'm betting that this 'Old Friend,' who's been calling Bovard from here, is Bovard's money man. I thought that you could—"

The phone chirped. Weeks picked it up, listened a moment, then said: "Send him back."

"Kordic's here," he explained. He gave her a lopsided smile. "I was kinda hoping that he might be too busy to join us for dinner."

Maureen's response was cut off by a knocking at the door.

Weeks opened the door for Kordic. "I'm trying to talk Maureen into becoming an Israeli agent," he joked. "Have you heard from Al Paramo?"

"Who's Al Paramo?" Maureen wanted to know.

"A retired SF cop," Kordic said, unbuttoning his sport coat. "He's the head security man at the St. Mark Hotel, where Philip Bovard is registered. He hasn't called."

Weeks fingered a humidor housing several Cuban cigars. "Maybe I should stop by the St. Mark for another drink."

Kordic pulled the three merry-go-round rings from his jacket pocket. "I found these at Cabrillo Street in one of Janna's shoes." He handed each of them a ring. "They're from the merry-go-round in Golden Gate Park, according to Ray Tracey. The flat on Cabrillo is only a few blocks from the park."

Maureen slid the ring up and down her finger, the one that once held a wedding band. "I should have thought of that. It would be natural for Janna to spend a lot of time in the park. It's so close to Cabrillo Street, where she lived with her mother." She checked her watch.

Kordic said, "The merry-go-round shuts down at five o'clock, Mo."

"What time does it open?"

"Eleven."

"I'll be there at nine." She dropped the ring into her purse. "I wonder if she's there now. In the park, I mean, sleeping. Where else would the poor kid go?"

"I don't know," Kordic admitted. "But you'd never find her at night. There're too many places to hide. We should get the full set of Janna's photos over to Park Station, and to the Horse detail at the stables in Golden Gate Park. I'm going to head out to Kelty's bar, on Taraval. Mike Divine in the Fraud detail says that the owner's a fence. The only Irish fence in town."

Weeks flipped the ring into the air and Kordic caught it in his palm.

"Do you want to meet later for something to eat?" Kordic asked Maureen, then turning to face Weeks, added: "You're invited too, of course."

Maureen smoothed her skirt, then caught Weeks's eye. "I had an early dinner, Jack."

"So did I," Weeks said quickly.

Kordic gestured impatiently toward Weeks. "Mossad should send you guys to acting school."

Chapter 36

Frank Dunbar lay on his bed, the pillows propped behind his neck, swigging directly from a bottle of Old Bushmills ten-year-old single malt Irish whiskey. His cell phone was ringing, vibrating on his lap. Patrick Lynam, gentleman, banker, baby-fucking pervert, had been calling for hours.

He was drunk, which was rare, despite his daily consumption of a six-pack of beer and at least a pint of whiskey. His drinking was spaced out over the course of the day. A beer or two with breakfast, then a couple of shots before lunch, followed by more beer, then several highballs before dinner, beer and more whiskey until it was time for bed. He might feel the effects of alcohol, but he never let himself lose control. Control was important to Dunbar. But tonight he wanted to be drunk.

"Patrick Lynam," he whispered in a soft slur. Dunbar had checked the local phone directories for a home number for Lynam, but found none. That didn't trouble Dunbar. A man that rich, with that many bad habits, wouldn't want his home address to be easily obtained.

But his bank. That was listed. In San Francisco. On Kearny Street. Kearny Street. Sure'n it had a nice, strong sound to it. A good street for a bank. For Patrick Lynam's bank.

He took a long pull on the whiskey bottle and decided it was time to do some celebrating. He dialed a familiar number.

"Kelty's. Come on over and have some fun."

"Debbie darlin'. It's me, Dunbar."

"Yeah? That cop called. Kordic. He's coming in tonight."

Dunbar slammed phone down, spilling half of the whiskey on the front of his shirt in the process.

Although Maureen Connah had been born and raised in San Francisco, she'd never been to the Palm Room of the St. Mark Hotel.

"Martini, okay?" Weeks asked.

"Shaken, not stirred?" Maureen chided.

"You're really into James Bond lore, aren't you? That's one of the few things Double-oh-seven had right. Shaking a martini gets them icy a lot quicker."

The bartender took their drink order and Maureen noticed a man standing under one of the twenty-foot palms gesturing toward Weeks.

"Someone's trying to get our attention."

"That's Al Paramo."

"Well, I'd just as soon he didn't know who I am," she said pointedly.

"Okay. I'll be right back."

"Your lady friend," Paramo said as he led Weeks down the steps to his office. "She looks damn familiar. I've seen her somewhere before." He held the door open. "Don't take offense, but she's not a working girl, is she?"

Weeks was thrown off balance for a moment. "A hooker? No. She's definitely not a hooker, Al. What have you got?"

Paramo switched on the radio. This time the music was loud, brassy jazz. He settled behind his desk, the leather chair groaning under his weight, and flipped on the computer. "Your buddy Bovard called and said he was checking out. We're forwarding his luggage back to London."

"When did he call?" Weeks asked stiffly.

"About four-thirty. There's more. The hotel switchboard operator is a friend of mine. Our guests don't know it, but it's standard procedure to record all incoming calls. So—"

"I already know what Philip Bovard sounds like," Weeks cut in.

"There was another call. For Bovard. It came in about a half hour before Bovard called. We have software sound cards hooked up to the switchboard computers, and they keep everything on-line for a week." Paramo clicked at the computer keyboard. "Cheaper than using recording tape, they say. Here's the call."

"Philip Bovard please."

Weeks's scalp started tingling. He recognized the voice immediately.

"One moment, sir."

There were a series of soft beeps and clicks, then the hotel operator's voice came back on-line. "There's no answer, sir. Do you care to leave a message."

"Yes. Tell him an old friend called. And that it's urgent."

Paramo clicked at the computer keyboard and frowned. "That's it. He didn't even say good-bye before he hung up." He gave Weeks an appraising glance. "It looks like you know that voice."

"Al, you just earned yourself a case of Cuban cigars."

Janna Drovana was crouched under the gnarly branches of a fica tree across the street from 1256 Cabrillo Street. A gust of wind rattled the tree—a sprinkling of soggy yellow leaves showered down onto her head and shoulders. A broken vodka bottle lay in the gutter, the fragmented glass sparkled like diamonds on the wet asphalt. She wondered if the bottle had belonged to Cousin Yuri, or his huge friend with the mustache.

Janna had lost count of the number of times she'd passed by the flat, always ready to run at the first sign of danger. But there were no signs of the police. Just the headlights of passing cars.

The lights to the upper flat, the one where the nice Chinese man and woman lived, had gone out a thousand ago. Janna did not have a watch, so she counted. One, two,

three, and on-and-on, until nine hundred and ninety-nine
had passed silently by.

The building was completely dark now. A strip of yellow tape crisscrossed the door to Cousin Yuri's flat. There
was printing across the tape. She could make out the
words SF POLICE, but not the rest.

Janna slipped into the alleyway, hopped up on the fence
bordering the building, and then leaned out to the drainpipe. The pipe was slick from the fog. It jutted out a half
inch or so from the wood siding, providing her a good
handhold. Her new tennis shoes made squishing noises
as she shinnied up the drainpipe to the small alcove outside the bathroom.

It was a journey she'd made many times in the past.
Sneaking in and out of the flat so that Cousin Yuri
wouldn't know. Mama would give her some money, tell
her to go to the store and bring back some candy. Candy
they shared in the small room, snuggling up together
under the sheets, laughing, like two good friends rather
than mother and daughter.

She knelt under the window and counted slowly to a
hundred, eyes half-closed, listening for any kind of sound.

Finally she stood up and reached for the window, emitting a sigh of relief as it slid noiselessly up the jamb.
Mama had rubbed the window jamb with a candle, so
that Cousin Yuri wouldn't hear it opening and closing
when she'd taken off on her secret trips.

Janna poked her head inside, like an animal sniffing out
his lair before entering. She nimbly jumped up, hooked a
leg over the sill, and dropped silently into the bathtub.

She went through the process of one more hundred
count before she felt safe in leaving the bathroom. There
was a pungent odor in the flat, a smell that she couldn't
quite place. Light from the streetlamps filtered in through
the windows, turning pieces of furniture into dark, threat-
ening shadows. Everything was turned upside down, furniture had been moved, kitchen cabinet doors were
unlatched, the sink was full of dishes and utensils. She
took a deep breath, consciously putting one foot in front

of the other, and approached the bedroom. Mama's bedroom. Her bedroom.

Her hand found the light switch. Her fingers rubbed alongside the switch. Should I, or shouldn't I? She could barely make out the room.

Now! She decided. She flicked the switch, blinking her eyes rapidly at the sudden light. She let out a sob. Her clothes, her mother's clothes, were all over the floor and the bed. She turned off the light and dropped to her knees, crawling on all fours, touching familiar articles of clothing and the television set.

Her books were still there. She brought one close to her face. It was too dark to see the title. Her knee bumped into another book. She kept groping until she found them all.

Her eyes were accustomed to the darkness now. She made a neat pile of the books. She found a box with some of her clothes, digging through piles of discarded garments until she found the one she wanted. Mama's thick black coat. Her father had bought it at one of St. Petersburg's finest stores, the day he had received his promotion. It was old now, the beautiful silk lining torn and faded. She buried her nose in the coat, inhaling the scent of her mother.

She wrapped the coat around her, like a blanket, and cuddled up on the bed. She was nauseous and perspiring profusely. If she didn't feel better by the morning, she would have to go to the Free Clinic. She tried to clear her mind. To think of nothing but happy thoughts. Their home in St. Petersburg. Her father riding a horse. Her mother humming while she made them breakfast. Within minutes, she was sound asleep.

Chapter 37

"Wouldn't you be better off somewhere else?" Patrick Lynam asked. "You could stay at my place or—"

"No," Bovard responded quickly. "This will suit my needs just fine for a day or two. I don't expect to be here longer than that." He sank down on the narrow bed, which was nothing more than a lumpish mattress covered by a stained brown corduroy spread. "They take cash, and ask no questions."

Although the Hotel Rio was just eight blocks from the St. Mark, it seemed to be in another country. A seedy, seven-story brick-front structure located in a neighborhood that catered to drug dealers and prostitutes. Lynam had felt uncomfortable entering the building. An aged, turkey-necked clerk had given him a toothless smile when he'd asked the directions to room 604. The room was hardly bigger than a closet: a bed, a single pressed-board dresser, a cracked mirror, one lone metal floor lamp with a scorched paper shade.

Bovard glared up at Lynam. "Have you been in contact with the girl? She still has the computer?"

"Yes. This morning anyway. She deleted a message. She won't respond to my messages, she just deletes them."

"Have you offered her money? She's on her own. She needs money. She may be tired of turning tricks." Bovard raked his hands through his hair. "That would be the end of it. Janna being arrested for whoring, while she still had your computer."

"I did mention money, but not a specific amount."

"Well do it, man. Do it!"

Lynam felt like sitting down, but there was no chair, and he didn't want to crowd Bovard. He pinched his nostrils against the heavy chemical smell, wondering if the disinfectant had been strong enough to kill the type of creatures that scuttled about in such a room. His right ankle was already itching. He scratched at it with his shoe. "Dunbar won't answer his phone. I'm worried, Philip."

"You should be," Bovard said in a voice heavy with regret. "The newspaper story and photograph. The television. That wasn't wise, Patrick. Not wise at all."

"It certainly wasn't my idea," Lynam protested bitterly. "I've done my best to avoid publicity." He scratched at his ankle again, glaring at the ragged, foul-smelling rug. He was sure it was infested with fleas. Or worse. "It must have been a slow news day." His photograph in the newspaper was a recent one. Taken a few months ago at a charity ball. He feared that his wife had sent the photo to her friend, a gossip columnist for *The Chronicle,* in anticipation of his appointment. It would be like Eleanor to do that. She probably had contacted the television stations, too. "The girl isn't likely to read the newspaper, Philip. Or watch a newscast. What about your man, Lancer? He won't answer his damn phone, either. Where the hell is he?"

"I'm afraid he's dead," Bovard disclosed.

"Dead? How?"

"My thought was that Dunbar killed him. But now, since you can't get in touch with Dunbar, I'm not so sure."

Lynam trapped his lower lip in his teeth. Bovard was acting strangely. He looked older, shorter, and . . . dirtier, as if he actually belonged in this loathsome room. His beautiful Savile Row suit had been replaced by baggy, wrinkled slacks and a scuffed black imitation leather jacket. Even his hair looked different, no longer neatly parted and combed close to his scalp. Unruly tufts of gray hair flapped over his ears. A forelock hung over one eye, revealing a bald spot Lynam hadn't noticed before. "Why would Dunbar kill your man? They're both after the girl."

"Because he no doubt correctly concluded that Lancer was going to kill him as soon as the girl was taken care of. Perhaps Dunbar was successful, and the child is dead," Bovard suggested. "If so, then he has your damn computer. I have to know where that computer is. I'm being pressured, by the Russians and the Syrians, Patrick. Time is running out. I must know what has happened to that computer. I can't have any last-minute fuckups. I was followed today. I'm sure it's the Jews."

Lynam's knees went rubbery. "Followed? Jews? What are you talking about?"

"Exactly that. A team of agents, inept agents, followed me from the hotel this morning. I lost them, but they're out there. Still looking. That's why I moved to this hovel. If Dunbar is alive, then he'll want his money. He won't forget about his money. You're sure that Dunbar doesn't know who you are?"

"Positive." Lynam's hand went to his crotch, and quickly retreated. "The money I've sent to him was by FedEx, to Kelty's bar."

"But you saw Dunbar? You can recognize him?"

"Yes. When he delivered the suitcases to the hotel. He's a short, fat, grubby old drunk. He won't be hard to spot."

"Really? Short, fat, and grubby." Bovard rolled onto his side and extricated a playing card-sized black-and-white photograph from his pocket. "Do you recognize this man?"

Lynam cocked his head and leaned down, squinting, then slipping on his reading glasses. "No. That's a police photograph, isn't it? Your man Lancer?"

"Hardly," Bovard said harshly. "Francis Aloysius Dunbar." He gazed at Lynam's humbled expression for a moment, then said: "Let me guess, Patrick. He's not the man who delivered the whore's luggage to you, is he?"

Lynam remained mannequin-still for several moments, then his face crumpled. "Oh, my God," he said in a voice full of pain.

"I wouldn't count on Him," Bovard counseled.

Lynam slumped down on the bed alongside Bovard.

"Maybe Dunbar is dead. And maybe," he added with a seasick look, "that's why he's not answering his phone."

"When did you last call him?"

"Forty minutes ago. From a bar near the office."

Bovard paused, breathing deeply, composing himself. It was partly his fault. He never should have let Lynam make direct contact with the IRA gunman. Lynam was an incredibly astute man when it came to numbers, accounting, stocks, bonds, international currency fluctuation. A dominating, take-no-prisoners businessman who could squeeze the last juicy dollar out of a deal, but an absolute bungler at anything else: his marriage, his disastrous sex life, and now this asinine encounter with Dunbar. "Dunbar is probably out celebrating the fact that he's killed Lancer, or that he now knows who you are, or perhaps both. Call him now."

Lynam withdrew a handkerchief from his pocket and blotted his forehead. "But what about Janna? We don't know if she's still alive."

Bovard glanced up, frowned, then made his forehead smooth again. "If she is, I'll take care of her. And Dunbar. My main concern is that computer. Call Dunbar. If he still doesn't answer, we begin the hunt."

Lynam rose unsteadily to his feet. "Hunt? Where? The only place I know of where Dunbar might be is that Irish bar, Kelty's."

"Then that's where we start."

Lynam's handkerchief whirled in circles across the lenses of his glasses as he nervously polished them. "If your scenario is right, then Dunbar will recognize me. I don't think I should go anywhere near Kelty's. We'll have to get someone else to handle him."

Bovard quickly rejected the proposal. "No. There's no time."

Lynam started to say something, but Bovard cut in quickly: "I've handled these things myself before." He dropped his hand onto Lynam's shoulder and tensed his fingers. "Four days, Patrick. Four days. That's all the time we have left."

* * *

Debbie Kelty was smiling, smacking her lips, and winking at a weathered-looking man wearing a corduroy jacket. She blew him a kiss as she slid a drink across the bar to him. The man said something that made her roar with laughter. She was wearing a scoop-necked black sweater, and she leaned over the bar to give the customer a better look at her cleavage.

Her eyes widened when she recognized Kordic. "Hello, again."

Kordic ordered a beer, then nodded toward the far end of the bar. "Is that your father?"

"Yeah, that's Pa." She bent over to get the beer out of the reefer. "I'll get him for you," she said, settling the bottle of Harp ale in front of Kordic before scurrying down to her father.

Sean Kelty was arguing with a middle-aged woman with disheveled gray hair and scaly, sunburned skin. Kelty reacted angrily when his daughter grabbed his shoulder.

Kordic watched as Kelty jerked his arm away. He tilted his head to the side, listening intently as Debbie whispered into his ear. His face wrinkled into a sneer as he turned to face Kordic.

"It's the Homicide copper, Pa. What you been up to?"

"Never you mind, just you take care of—"

"I told you, I'm takin' off." Debbie untied her apron and draped it casually on the bar.

Kelty's arm started to rise, as if he intended to strike the girl. "It better not be Dunbar you're seeing. I warned you about him."

"I can take care of myself, Pa. You better see what the cop wants."

Kelty watched his daughter prance down the plank, scoop some money from the cash register, then scoot under the bar counter and out the door. A whore, just like her mother. Worse than her mother. At least Margaret hadn't raided the till every night.

There were only six customers besides the copper. Kelty

pulled a bottle of whiskey from the well and set it in front of the woman who was trying to sell him a pair of diamond earrings she swore to God had belonged to her dear old ma, in Connemara. "Help yourself to a jar," he whispered into her sunburned ear, "and keep quiet 'til I've finished some important business."

Kelty ambled slowly down to Kordic. All he needed now was for the old biddy to flash some stolen earrings in front of the nosy copper.

"A beer," Kelty scoffed. "Let me fix you a real drink. I've got some—"

Kordic put his hand over the tip of the beer bottle. "I'm fine, Mr. Kelty." He let the silence drag on.

Sean Kelty folded his arms across his belly and gave a patronizing smile. "My daughter said you wanted to see me."

"Mr. Kelty, maybe you can help me out."

"Anything I can do. I like helping the police. You can ask anyone. I always—"

"What I want is the name of an Irish shooter. Late thirties, thin, wore a tweed hat when I saw him. He's got a red nose and talks with a brogue. He killed a woman, and two young girls. He used an old IRA trick. A potato for a silencer."

Kelty picked up a towel and began swabbing the bar in tight spiral strokes. "Why would you think I know anyone like that? This is a—"

"It I were an IRA hit man, this is the place I'd come for a drink." Kordic nodded at the flags on the wall. "It's well known that you've been a strong supporter of the Irish cause. The shooter took some items from his victims. Jewelry, rings, bracelets, watches. Expensive stuff. Heard anything about that?"

"I heard nothin'," Kelty said defiantly. "I'm a saloon keeper. Nothing more, nothing less."

Beads of sweat began popping out across Kelty's forehead. Kordic took a hit from the beer bottle, then said: "We figure the shooter fenced the jewelry. The victim kept a list of her jewelry, so we have detailed descriptions of every item." Kordic took another sip of the beer, then added, "And someone's been supplying the shooter with weapons. He used one gun to kill the woman and two young girls. Another to take a few shots at me, and—"

"You?" Kelty squeezed the damp bar rag between his hands, water dribbled down his apron. "He shot at you?"

"He used a revolver that time. Then there was a third gun. He killed a Russian with that one. We have the bullets. There'll be no trouble tracing them to the guns. So, whoever is selling them to the shooter is in real trouble, Mr. Kelty. Five murders and an assault on a police officer."

An old man in a plaid shirt slammed a glass on the bar and ordered another round for him and his companion.

Kordic watched Kelty fill the drink order. He moved in quick, hurried jerks, spilling half a shot of whiskey while filling a glass.

Kordic knew he had shaken the man. Kelty might have bluffed his way around the beat cops and the Fraud detail, but murder was different. Much different. He decided to push the knife in a little deeper when Kelty returned.

Kelty poured himself a shot, gulped it down, then walked back to Kordic. "You said this fella killed five people, Officer—"

"Kordic. Inspector Kordic. I gave my card to your daughter."

Kelty went back to wringing the bar towel with his massive fists. "I like to help the law. Anytime I can. A man like this. He's evil. A *madadh mire*—mad dog. The sooner you find him the better."

"The shooter is a pro, Mr. Kelty. My guess is he's a man who likes killing. He tortured one man with an iron." Kordic looked up suddenly and pinned Kelty's eyes. "Another IRA trick, according to the Irish police, then cut his throat. A man like that, he wouldn't want to take any chances. The man who sold him the guns. Who fenced the jewelry. I wouldn't want to be him."

Kelty let out a hollow laugh. "Indeed not, Inspector. Nor would I."

Kordic stood and reached for his wallet.

"It's on me, Inspector," Kelty said quickly, waving the money away.

Kordic slapped a five-dollar bill on the bar. "We're going to trace those guns he used. If you hear anything, get in touch with me, Mr. Kelty. I want this shooter, and I'm willing to make a deal."

Kelty ran the back of his hand across his mouth, as if wiping away a bad taste. "If I run into anyone who knows somethin', I'll have him give you a call." He watched Kordic go through the door, then called out, "Closin' time. Everyone out."

There was a chorus of protests. The woman with the earrings for sale had tucked away half of the bottle of whiskey.

"What about the earrings, Sean darlin'?" she slurred.

Kelty leaned over and slapped the glass from her hand. "Out, you ugly *baltai*. Out!"

The woman winced at the vulgarity, then slid from the stool with a noble attempt at acting sober, pausing at the door long enough to make sure Kelty saw her give him the finger. "And the horse you rode in on," she managed to say before ducking out the door just ahead of the glass Kelty threw at her.

Kelty started after her, then pulled to a stop. The old pussy would be back tomorrow, begging for a drink. He'd fix her then. But first he had to fix Dunbar. He pulled a bottle of Cork gin from the well and poured himself a double shot. He swilled the drink, a small river of the liquor coursing down his chin. Kordic. What the bloody hell kind of a name was that? Polish? Baltic? Some square-headed race of assholes.

He gulped down the rest of the drink, then staggered to his office, cursing as his fingers twirled the safe's combination lock. He grabbed a scratched old pistol that he'd picked up from a merchant marine that morning. It was one gun that Frank Dunbar would never get his hands on. If Dunbar came back, Kelty vowed to shoot the bastard himself.

Sweet Jesus. Kordic said he'd talked to the Irish police. They would know all about Frank Dunbar. Killin' women and children. With the bloody guns I sold him. Sweet Jesus.

Chapter 38

"A hooker?" Maureen Connah exclaimed. "Al Paramo thought I was a hooker?"

"Yep," Anatoly Weeks confirmed. "A *kurwa*." He rubbed his thumb and forefinger together. "But a high-class one. His estimate was a thousand dollars. He wondered how I could afford you."

Maureen raised her hands over her head and stretched, then, in that husky voice she'd used when working as a street decoy, said, "For all night? I am insulted."

"So was I," Weeks countered. "Imagine a good-looking guy like me having to pay for it."

Maureen laughed lightly and burrowed her head in her pillow. Anatoly Weeks was the first man she'd ever invited to her apartment, for dinner, and to her bed. The first kiss had been slow, lingering, then they were tearing each other's clothes off, Weeks struggling with his one good hand, while Maureen guided him to her bedroom.

The contrasts between their two bodies, discounting their genders, were striking.

Weeks's thin, wiry, tightly muscled body was nut-brown, except for a slim scarf of white from his bathing suit. There were dark maroon stitching wounds on his legs. A long, curving crescent-shaped scar journeyed down from his left shoulder to the small of his back. A purple-black scar contrasted with the pale skin by his left hip. A rough, still reddish pucker wound from the bullet was on his left shoulder, circled by dozens of scalpel incisions that stretched down to his forearm.

His left arm was flaccid, loose, while the right was heavily muscled. The knuckles on his right hand were extended, nearly double in size.

Maureen's milky white skin was dusted with freckles, her body sleek, smooth, unscarred, unblemished.

She trailed a finger over Weeks's disabled arm. "Does it hurt?"

"Like hell. The docs prescribed some pain medication, but if I take it, I can't drink, and I've found that booze does a lot better job at easing the pain. They say if I exercise hard, I'll get back about thirty to forty percent use of the arm, and the pain will go away, eventually. Eventually, of course, we're all dead."

Maureen scribbled her finger down to the scar by his hip. "How did you get this?"

"A Palestinian boy about thirteen. He walked right up to me on the street, pretended he was begging. Stuck his little gun right there and pulled the trigger."

"And these?" she asked, lightly, massaging the stitching on his leg.

"Sword fight with a midget," he joked. "Actually, it was a car bomb in Tel Aviv. I was lucky." He shifted on his side so he could see her better. "Three of my friends weren't." His eyes coasted up and down her body. "You seem to have lived a charmed life, so far."

"So far," she agreed, moving her hands over the taut, ropelike muscles of his right arm.

"Mother Nature's way of balancing things out," Weeks said. "You lose the use of one limb, the other picks up the slack."

"Do you have a code name? Or number? A license to kill?"

Weeks's lips twisted wryly. "Nope. And no machine guns hidden in the bumper of my car, no specially made cigarettes, no knives in the tips of my shoes like James Bond."

"It was Rosa Klebb in *From Russia With Love* who had the knives in her shoes."

"Jesus, you really are a Bond fan, aren't you?"

"Yeah. It drove my dad crazy. An English spy. He hates

the English." Maureen propped herself up on one elbow.
"I wonder what he'd say if he knew I was in bed with a
Jewish spy?" She gently fingered the scar on his hip. "Is
there a Mrs. Weeks?"

"No wife, Maureen. But there finally is one resemblance
between me and Bond."

"And that is?"

"I wound up in bed with the beautiful girl."

Maurren leaned back in bed and slowly stretched her
arms over her head.

Weeks murmured his approval. "I could watch you do
that all day, kid."

Maureen jackknifed into a sitting position. "When do
you have to go home? Back to Israel?"

Weeks plucked at the mattress buttons under the sheet.
"I've put a trace out on Bovard. Wherever he turns up, I
go. Are you gong to help me?"

"No. I'm going to find Janna."

"How, Maureen? Where?"

"Golden Gate Park. That's the only link we've got."

"Well, Inspector Connah, I wish you luck. Unfortunately, I may have to take off at any moment. This could
be the last time we see each other for some time."

Maureen extended her hand and grinned. "It's been a
pleasure to meet you, Mr. Weeks."

Weeks used his powerful right hand to drag her close.
He dropped his voice down to a threatrical baritone. "Call
me Bond, James Bond, just for the next hour."

The dispenser above the urinal was old and rusted. The
scratched and faded sign suggested that for fifty cents you
could take your choice of condom: Glow Body, Multi-Tip-
Ring, Duo-Delight Thriller, Fingers of Passion, or Black
Avenger.

Philip Bovard wondered when the last time any of the
customers of Kelty's saloon had actually put their purchase to good use.

The men he'd seen at the bar looked to be too old to
take advantage of a condom, and the women certainly

weren't appealing enough to spur anyone into buying one—except for the brazen young barmaid. Perhaps she was the reason for the condom dispenser, the men buying in hope, the prophylactic serving little purpose except to make an indentation in their wallets.

Bovard had been sitting with his back to the bar, monitoring the activity through a mirror mounted over the jukebox, and had picked up enough conversation to know that the big-bellied man working behind the bar was Sean Kelty, and the barmaid his daughter.

He'd known the tall, rugged-looking man was a policeman moments after he showed up at the bar. The aggressive, yet unhurried walk, the way his eyes swept the room, the obvious bulge of his weapon under his sport coat.

At first Bovard had thought the policeman was a regular customer, off-duty, but no, he had come on business, specifically to see Kelty.

Bovard had eased up as close as he'd dared, keeping his back to the policeman, sharing a drink with a wrinkle-faced woman whose whispered, whiskey-soaked breath informed him that she had some priceless earrings to sell.

Just after the policeman left, Kelty had shouted that the bar was closing. Bovard had immediately made his way to the men's room, locking himself in one of the foul-smelling stalls, his buttocks on the tank top, his feet resting on the toilet seat.

Five minutes later there'd been the sound of the men's room door banging open, Sean Kelty muttering a muffled curse as he made his lockup rounds.

Bovard studied his reflection in the mirror for a moment, tugging his navy English touring cap to a jaunty angle over his eye. There was no reason to suspect that the policeman had any idea who he was, but after realizing that he'd been tailed to the Bank of America Building, Bovard had altered his appearance. Nothing dramatic: the cap, slightly shabby clothes, a slump of the shoulders, a slight limp.

He approached Sean Kelty, who was behind the bar, a

bottle of gin in one hand, a half-filled tumbler in the other.
A pistol was lying on the bar top, within easy reach.

Kelty raised his head and stared at Bovard with red-rimmed eyes. "What the fuck are you doing here? I'm closed, you fuckin' *banrion*."

"Is docha nach bhfuil seans ar bith ann?" Bovard shot back in stilted Gaelic, responding to Kelty calling him a queer by saying that he supposed sex was out of the question.

Kelty slid his hand up the gin bottle, holding it like a club. "Get out of here, before I splatter your ugly face."

"Put the bottle down, Sean," Bovard said softly, "I'm a friend. I'm looking for the same man that policeman was. Francis Aloysius Dunbar."

Dunbar cocked the bottle over his shoulder. "You're no friend of mine and I don't know who the hell you're talking about."

Bovard had noticed the IRA flags and posters, when he first entered the bar. The policeman had mentioned Kelty's ties to the IRA. He rattled off a list of high-ranking Sinn Fein members. "Your good deeds were appreciated, Sean. But Dunbar. He's a renegade. You know that. I've got to find him."

Kelty lowered the gin bottle slowly. "They talked about me? Knew my name?"

"Certainly. Put that bottle to use," Bovard suggested. "Pour us both a drop."

Kelty reached back for two clean glasses and filled them to the brim. He slid one across the bar. *"Slainte."*

"Your health," Bovard agreed and tossed the drink down with one gulp. "That policeman? What was his name?"

"Kordic. Inspector Jack Kordic. Homicide."

"Dunbar's been sloppy again, hasn't he? We had him doing a job, but—"

"The copper said Frank killed five people, including a couple of children."

"Five people maybe, but not the one we ordered him to get, Sean. I sent someone looking for Dunbar. A tall man, with blond hair."

"He was here, all right, just that once," Kelty said excitedly. "Frank didn't look too pleased to see him." Kelty took a sip of his drink. "I just saw him that once."

"Where is Dunbar?"

Kelty slammed his drink on the counter, the liquor slopping over onto the bar. "Damn, I wish I knew. He's going to get me in deep shit, I don't mind telling you. That copper will be back. He's trouble, he is."

"You handled things for Dunbar, didn't you, Sean? I heard Kordic say he had a list of the jewelry he'd stolen. And the guns. You were supplying him with the guns, weren't you? If the police get to Dunbar before I do . . ." Bovard brought his hands together in a loud clap. "He'll turn you over. You know that."

Kelty ran his fingers down his cheek, hard enough to leave scrape marks. "I do! The miserable prick."

"Then tell me where I can find him, Sean. And I'll take care of him for you."

"I don't bloody know. I wish I did, I'd kill him myself, but God's truth, I don't know."

"Think, man, think." Bovard's voice had a steely insistence. "Where does he live?"

Kelty shook his head wildly. "I don't know."

Bovard slid his hand slowly down the bar, his fingers coming to rest on the gun. "Who are his friends?"

Another shake of the head. "I don't know. I doubt if he has any."

"A woman. Dunbar must have a woman, Sean, even if she's a *pucan*."

Kelty raised his head slowly, then cleared his throat like a man coming down with a cold. "He had one. My daughter. Debbie. My own flesh and blood." He looked down at his hand, twisting the thin gold wedding band slowly. "She's a whore all right. Just like her mother."

Bovard's lips spread into a toothy smile. "Your daughter. The girl who was working the bar tonight?"

Kelty's watery eyes rose to meet Bovard's. "I warned her. Told her I'd beat the livin' devil out of her if she let that scum touch her again. The bastard gave her a brace-

let. One that he took off a dead woman. I took it away
from her. If the copper had spotted that bracelet, I'd probably be in the slam now."

"Would Debbie know where Dunbar lives?"

"No. She told me she went to a motel with him. Once.
She promised she'd never see him again."

Bovard poked his finger into the pistol's trigger guard
and spun the weapon slowly in a circle. "You're not much
help to me, Sean."

Kelty let out a loud burp. "Dunbar. I curse the day I
met the man."

Bovard sighed reproachfully. The drunken slob was
right about one thing. The policeman would be back.
Somewhere in Kelty's alcohol-rotted brain there was information that might be of help to the police. Help them in
tracking down Dunbar. He picked up the gin bottle by its
throat, and in a whisper said, "Let me tell you a secret,
Sean."

Kelty leaned across the bar and Bovard brought the bottle down smartly alongside the man's head. There was a
cracking-ice sound as Kelty's head slammed into the bar.
Bovard calmly walked behind the plank, fished a fresh
bottle of whiskey from the well, and crashed it into the
back of Kelty's skull.

Chapter 39

April 7

J anna woke with a start and quickly scrambled to her
feet, her hands out in a defensive posture. It took her a
moment to identify the noise. It was only running water,
or a toilet flushing. She edged cautiously toward the window, then she heard footsteps from above. The flat upstairs where Mr. and Mrs. Lee lived. She sank back to the
floor and began gathering her things, wondering if she
could mend the rip in the backpack with tape. She took
the computer from the backpack. She was fascinated with
it, the chess games, the encyclopedia. It was all she had
now. The mailbox icon was blinking again. Another message from Paul, August eleven.

For the first time his message mentioned an amount
of money.

Janna. I know you must need money. Let me help you.
I will pay you a thousand dollars for the computer.
PLEASE respond.

Janna felt like crying. A thousand dollars. Yesterday
that wouldn't have sounded like very much. Not with all
she had then. She deleted the message, and touched her
forehead with her hand. It felt hot. A fever? Maybe she
should go to the Free Clinic, where her mother had gone.

Janna went to the window. The sky was light gray.
Morning gray. The streetlights were still on, forming halos
in the fog. The Lees were moving around upstairs. She
could hear the shower water running. She decided it was
time for her to go—but she wanted to take something

with her. A remembrance. Mama's coat? No, too bulky. Photographs. Certainly photographs. And the books. No, just one book. She had to travel light now. *Anna Karenina.* Her favorite. She ground her face into her mother's coat, inhaling deeply, then dropped the coat to the floor and took a final, mournful look at the room, knowing she would never be back. It wasn't safe. There was only one place she felt safe. The park. It had become her home.

It was standard procedure for all members of the Homicide detail to receive abbreviated reports, including morgue photos, of unidentified homicide victims.

Jack Kordic had been at his desk, straightening files, wondering if Maureen Connah was going to come into the office, or if she would go directly to Golden Gate Park to hunt for Janna.

He skimmed through the daily reports, until he came to the Polaroid of a blond man lying on a morgue slab. Case 20156—Grandanos and Putman. John Doe found in vehicle at Haight and Shrader. Stab wound to chest.

There was no doubt that it was the same man who Scotland Yard's video camera had picked up in the Savoy Hotel lobby and who Weeks had trailed to New York.

Kordic looked around for Grandanos. He was late as usual, but Barry Putman was at his desk. "This John Doe, Barry. Have you got anything more on him?"

"Nah. No witnesses. No ID. The guy had a fancy holster on him, but no gun. The car was a rental out of the airport. Dave's working on the car now."

"I think I can help you on this," Kordic said. "The John Doe is wanted by Israeli Intelligence."

Putman curled his tongue against his teeth and whistled softly. "Israeli Intelligence? What the hell was he? Some kind of spy?"

"Yeah. Some kind of spy."

Chapter 40

Dr. Susan Jacobs peeled the surgical gloves from her hands and dropped them into the disposal can. "You can get dressed now, Janna."

Janna's head emerged from behind a curtain in the back of the examination room. "Am I all right, Doctor? Am I going to die?"

"Not for about seventy years, if you're careful crossing streets, young lady."

Susan Jacobs was thirty-four years old: slim, dark, and pretty. She had been working at the City Free Clinic for eighteen months.

Janna's story, that she was a visitor from Russia, and that her mother and father were out of town for the day, was less inventive than most, but there was something about this girl—her manner, polite—not abusive. Defensive—not hostile. And none of the usual gutter language. And she was a virgin, both vaginally and anally, a real rarity at the clinic. Her body was in need of a good scrubbing; there were no needle marks, no scratches or scars. But she was sick, all right. A slight fever, sore throat, queasy stomach. Nothing more than a case of the flu and strep throat.

"Relax for a minute. I'll get you some medicine."

Duane Adams, the clinic's head nurse, was waiting for Dr. Jacobs at the door to her tiny office. At six feet four, Adams towered over the diminutive Jacobs. He slapped a clipboard against his thigh. "Another loser, Doctor. The Russian kid is going to be a no momma, no papa, no insurance ticket."

"I know, I know," Jacobs responded glumly. Duane Adams's duties at the clinic had gradually expanded from medical practice to handling the books, which included begging county, state, and private agencies for money. "She's a virgin, Duane."

Adams's eyebrows arched. "Really? Both ends?"

"Yes. Give her some antibiotics, Duane."

"Any particular antibiotics, Doctor?"

Dr. Jacobs shrugged her narrow shoulders. The clinic was, as usual, short of medical supplies. "What's available?"

Adams recited a short list, and when Jacobs made her decision, he nodded and said, "A virgin." He was silent for a moment, then added, "I wish that was contagious."

Patrick Lynam was at his office window when his secretary came into the room. She was in her fifties, square-chinned and long-faced. She'd been with Lynam for close to twenty years. Her glasses were hanging from a gold chain around her neck. The expression on her face was one of distaste.

"There's a very belligerent man on line three, sir. The gentleman wouldn't give a name, but says you're expecting his call. He insists on talking to you. He says it's about someone called Janna. I don't remember—"

"I'll take the call, Miss Perwak. And I'll be out the rest of the day, so move anything I have over to next week."

She paused at the door to look back at him. "You have that appointment with Doctor Winquest and—"

"Cancel it," he instructed irritably. "Cancel everything for the rest of the day."

Lynam waited until the door had clicked solidly shut, then settled behind his desk and gingerly picked up the phone.

"That was rather foolish, Mr. Dunbar, using Janna's name."

"No more foolish than you using mine," Dunbar said defiantly. "You're a popular man, you are. I saw you in the papers. And on the television."

Lynam wheeled his chair around so he was facing the

window. The sun had burned off the fog earlier than usual. There were just a few whiskers of clouds, the bay was a flawless blue enamel dotted with pocket handkerchief sailboats.

Lynam saw none of this. "Did you complete the job?"

"The girl. She's all you worry about, Patrick. Forget Janna. Put her out of your mind. It's me you should be thinking about."

"You didn't complete the job," Lynam accused.

"Forget the bitch! You've me to deal with. And I want some of your money. A damn high pile of it."

Lynam involuntarily sat up straight and squared his shoulders. "And what do you think you are worth, Mr. Dunbar?"

"I was thinking of, oh, five million. Dollars, not pounds. I wouldn't want to take advantage of you, would I?"

"Use your head, Dunbar. We can come to a financial arrangement. Not the one you mentioned. And there's no sense talking about any kind of money until the girl is killed and we've got the computer. Because if either lands in the hands of the police, I'm screwed. And you won't get a fucking dime."

Dunbar dropped his cigarette to the phone booth floor and ground it out with the heel of his shoe. "All right, I'll take care of your darlin'. I nearly had her, don't ya know. She was sittin' on a bench, near the merry-go-round, playin' with your bloody computer, Patrick, then—"

"You had her and you let—"

"I let nothin'. There were too many people around. Don't worry, she won't get away again. I'll call—"

"Not here," Lynam said quickly. He gave Dunbar his cellular number, then said, "Finish the job. Then we'll talk money."

Chapter 41

"Thanks," Jack Kordic said to the morgue attendant after he'd wheeled out the refrigerated drawer containing the corpse of John Doe #7421.

Kordic pulled back the stiff, mottled gray sheet. It made a crackling sound, like an envelope being peeled open.

Anatoly Weeks stared down at the body of the man who'd used the name John David when he'd flown from London to New York. He carefully examined the coagulated cavity under the dead man's chest. "Nice job. A pro, Jack. This guy's what? Six two? Two hundred twenty pounds. He looks like he was a tough piece of meat. I wouldn't want to go after him with just a knife."

Weeks picked up the dead man's clammy right hand. The knuckles were extended, a rind of callused gristle ridged the palm. "Let's look at his stuff."

Kordic nodded his agreement. The sound of the drawer closing—the soft scraping, the light squeak of the rollers on casters, followed by a clash of metal on metal as the locks slipped into place—was like no other to Kordic.

Both men were silent with their own thoughts as they exited the morgue and made their way to the property clerk's office in the basement of the Hall of Justice.

Kordic filled out the proper request form and the clerk released a pillow-sized, clear plastic bag containing the possessions found on John Doe #7421. They went through the clothing in a quick, methodical manner. The herringbone sport jacket was well made, the material felt like cashmere to Kordic, but bore no manufacturer's markings. The shirt was light blue, with a spread collar. The pants were dark blue wool and, like the jacket and shirt, of superior quality, and bore no labels. Weeks held the shirt up to the ceiling fluorescents. "No visible laundry marks, Jack. Are you going to have the lab scope this stuff?"

"I guess," Kordic said with little enthusiasm. It was standard procedure for laundries to stamp clothing with a colorless dye that is invisible to the naked eye, but which shows up in filtered ultraviolet light.

The wristwatch found on the deceased was a cheap plastic digital model, the brand name unfamiliar to Kordic or Weeks.

His shoes were expensive Italian leather models.

Weeks folded the shirt and slid it back into the bag. "Our dead friend spent some good dough on his clothes, but the watch looks like a ten-dollar special."

"Want to bet that there's not a solid gold Rolex somewhere waiting for his return?"

"Yeah. And a half-dozen passports."

Kordic picked up the black nylon shoulder holster. He'd never seen one like it, a confusing web of crisscrossed Velcro straps. The molded nylon holster itself was sealed with Velcro, and was long, narrow, and bulbed at the bottom. Kordic slipped it around his shoulder, positioned the holster under his arm, and simulated going for a gun.

Weeks held up three lengths of nylon strips similar to the holster webbing, each end was tipped with Velcro. One was approximately eighteen inches in length, the other two a foot longer. The shorter strip had been wrapped around a knife on the dead man's left forearm, the second was wrapped around his left calf and held a clip for an automatic weapon, twenty-four shells in the clip. The third was around his right calf and held several metal capsules, identical to the ones found at the Cabrillo Street homicide scene.

Kordic opened a zip-top sandwich bag that was labeled FOUND IN CAR. He carefully sprinkled the contents onto a tabletop. "Ticket stubs. To the aquarium at Golden Gate Park. There must be over a dozen. I found the Golden Gate Park merry-go-round rings at the Cabrillo Street flat, now these ticket stubs. You realize what those ticket stubs and the blasting caps mean, Anatoly. They're a definite link. Somehow Bovard's henchman was involved in my case. The Cabrillo Street murders are connected to the homicides on Tara Street. But your John Doe wasn't in San Francisco when Angela Lolley and the two girls were killed."

"*Shtup,*" Weeks cursed. "I wish there was a bar in this joint."

"You're in luck," Kordic informed him. "Follow me."

Dr. Phillips was off-duty, but the door to his office was unlocked. Kordic closed the door behind Weeks, pulled down the shade, went to the refrigerator, and took out the embalming fluid bottle.

"Relax," he told Weeks. "It's bourbon and vermouth. A manhattan." He poured a hefty shot into a paper cup. Weeks ran it cautiously under his nose before taking a sip. "You're not joining me?"

"It's a little early."

Weeks swilled the liquor around the paper cup. "None of this makes any sense, Jack. That knife wasn't made for peeling apples, it's a real weapon. And the holster. Custom-made. For a custom-made gun. One with a silencer. One that accepts an extended clip. I can give you a list of three guys, one in Tel Aviv, one in Marseilles, and another *ben zsona* in Modica who probably did the whole package, gun, silencer, and holster."

"What's a *ben zsona*, and where the hell is Modica?"

"Son of a bitch, and Sicily." Weeks drained the remains of the manhattan. "Those bullets. Nine-millimeters, and I'd bet my tush they're subsonic, to go along with the silencer. There's not a mark on the clip or the cartridges. All custom-made, Jack."

Kordic said, "The lab results showed that the bullets that killed the big Russian were from a twenty-five caliber so that leaves out the fancy gun. Which means what? That the John Doe in the morgue didn't shoot that big weight lifter, and I'm betting that the knife he had strapped to his forearm won't match up to the knife wounds on Stoylar's neck. So they were already dead when John Doe got to the flat."

"I can live with that," Weeks accepted. "He gets there, sees the two stiffs, then booby traps the place, so that a fire will help cover up the mess the killer made. I can live with the theory, but I can't figure out why."

"Let's try and connect the dots," Kordic suggested. "We know Yuri Stoylar is linked to Angela Lolley—he sold the girl, Janna, to her. Lolley and two girls are killed by what we figure to be a professional hit man. Janna was there, but somehow she escaped. So, maybe this guy is not as professional as John Doe appears to have been. He uses a potato for a silencer, he returns to Lolley's house and ends up shooting at me. He does a sloppy job killing Stoylar and his roommate."

Weeks went to the refrigerator, picked up the embalming fluid bottle, and shook it vigorously. "Which means what? Philip Bovard sends John David-John Doe to eliminate the girl that got away? Why does Bovard care about the girl? What's so important about Janna to involve two hit men? One who flew in all the way from Europe."

Kordic brought Weeks up-to-date on his meeting with Sean Kelty at Kelty's bar. "He's dirty, Anatoly. He knows who this hit man is."

Weeks held the embalming fluid bottle up to the light, slowly sloshing the liquid back and forth. "What a *tembel* I've been. Bovard hired an ex-IRA man, Mouse Fennesy, to plant the bomb in the Savoy. John David-John Doe in the morgue there couldn't come to America, because of the Savoy Hotel job. So what does Bovard do? He finds someone local, here in your town. Another ex-IRA killer to take care of Old Friend's problems."

"Angela Lolley was the problem," Kordic said with grim satisfaction. "And her girls. Old Friend was a client. He must have ordered the killings. He needed Bovard's help to find a hit man. But the killer missed one girl. Janna. The notebook computer case we found on the floor in Lolley's bedroom. Maybe Janna took it with her."

"Notebook computer. You didn't tell me about a computer."

"We found the leather case for a Helmut-Victor 2500 notebook computer. Right next to a metal box, some hundred-dollar bills, and three computer disks. The killer took everything connected to Lolley's computer except the screen, yet he missed those disks, and maybe the notebook computer."

"Whoa, Jack. Why the hell didn't you tell me about the computer before? That's a powerful little machine."

"Too powerful for Lolley. Her computer repairman said that she would never have spent the money for one. So, it had to belong to one of her clients."

"Hell, yes, one of her clients! That's the connection. Old Friend leaves the notebook at the whorehouse. He's in a panic. He calls on Bovard to send someone to get it back. And kill anyone who has had any connection with it. You should have told me about the damn computer."

"Is Bovard back in London?" Kordic asked.

"Not according to Her Majesty's Customs people. He checked out of the St. Mark. By phone. He could be anywhere." Weeks shook the bottle once more, then replenished his cup.

"Finish it quick and let's go."

Weeks followed instructions, then asked, "Where to?"

"Sean Kelty's. He's the only link we've got to this Irish hit man."

Chapter 42

"Yeah, I recognize her. The monkey, that's her."

"You're *sure* it's the same girl, Mr. Gerber?" Maureen Connah questioned. "It's important."

David Gerber, the merry-go-round operator, had a narrow face, with pointy, foxlike features and a wattled neck. He ran his hands down the front of his coveralls and said, "Let me take a closer look."

Maureen glanced at the children on the merry-go-round while the man studied the photograph of Janna. A fifty-fifty mixture of boys and girls, most of them were younger than Janna by several years.

"Yeah, that's the monkey all right. I haven't seen her for a while. I guess I scared her off."

Maureen tried to keep the disappointment from showing in her voice. "Why would you want to scare her off," she asked stiffly, "and why do you call her the monkey?"

Gerber pointed to a curved iron bar standing alongside the revolving merry-go-round. "That's what she was like. A monkey. She'd hang off the horse and grab the rings for a free ride." He shook his head at the photograph before returning it to Maureen. "It wasn't fair. The other little brats didn't have a chance to get a ring. She'd get them all. It got so I stopped putting the free-ride rings out when she was around."

The clinky-clank music was getting on Maureen's nerves. She wondered how the operator could stand listening to it all day. "Do you think she'll come back?"

Gerber hooked his thumbs in his coverall pockets. "The

monkey? Yeah, she'll be back. She loved this damn machine. I kept telling her she was too old for it. She should be out chasing boys or something, you know. But the monkey wouldn't listen. Yeah, she'll be back."

Maureen thanked the man for his time. "I'll be around. If she shows up, be sure and let me know. It's important." She circled the merry-go-round, then leaned against the railing guarding an algae-streaked fountain. A graceful sculptured dolphin was hovering above the dry fountain bed, seemingly caught in mid-dive with nowhere to go.

There was a queue of young children in line to buy tickets for the merry-go-round, most with their small hands firmly gripped by their mothers.

Maureen had shown Janna's photograph to the lot of them, but no one had recognized her.

Maureen raised her coat collar as a gust of wind rattled through the towering pine trees, then headed over to the concession stand for a cup of coffee and, perhaps because of Anatoly Weeks's bad influence, ordered a jelly doughnut to go with it.

The squeal of brakes, followed by a chorus of shouts, caused her to turn around. Two yellow school buses had arrived in the parking lot. The bus doors opened and a swarm of children spilled out, quickly running off in all directions. Maureen dropped her uneaten doughnut into a garbage can. The children were all girls, and appeared to be eleven or twelve years old. Janna's age.

"You're late," Philip Bovard protested as he slid into the front seat of Lynam's Lincoln Town Car.

Lynam turned onto Fulton Street, heading west toward Golden Gate Park. "I really don't think that I should be a part of this, Philip. Janna might recognize me."

"I want you to recognize her first," Bovard said, zipping up his jacket. In the right pocket was the pistol he'd taken from Sean Kelty. He'd wired a baby bottle nipple to the end of the gun's barrel. It was a makeshift silencer he had used before. The escaping gases generated by the muzzle blast blew the nipple up like a balloon and escaped through the bullet hole. The nipple would not completely silence the bullet, but would muffle the sound by some seventy percent. The jacket's left pocket contained the items he'd purchased for the makings for a garrote: strong cable used for hanging pictures and two rubber bicycle grips, and an old favorite—an ice pick.

Bovard scrutinized Lynam. He was wearing a banker's gray suit, white shirt, and dark tie. "You should have dressed for the occasion, Patrick. We'll have to stop and get you something more appropriate."

Lynam waved away the offer. "I've some things in the trunk, and there are dark glasses in the glove compartment." Lynam accelerated into the next lane, gliding around a pickup truck loaded with lumber. "What if Janna isn't there?" he protested, his whining voice beginning to grate on Bovard's nerves.

"Dunbar says she almost lives in this damn park. And Dunbar will be there, we know that. You handled Dunbar well, Patrick, insisted that he kill the girl and get the computer before you'd negotiate with him. Now, we have to finish it, as quickly as possible."

"Yes, yes, I understand," Lynam said hurriedly. "It's just that I never . . ." His voice trailed off into a muffled cough.

"I have. So relax. This Golden Gate Park. It is large, no?"

"Quite large. Miles and miles of it."

"Good. If Dunbar spots you, try to take him somewhere away from the crowd. Some bushes, trees. He will no doubt want to talk to you in a private place. Let him lead, I'll follow."

They stopped at a red light. The only sound was that of the engine ticking away its heat. Lynam turned to look at Bovard, his face slowly turning red. "By God, you're using me, aren't you? I'm . . . I'm a Judas's goat. That's it, isn't it?"

Bovard shrugged his shoulders and pursed his lips in

an exaggerated Gaelic gesture. "When you hunt for sharks, Patrick, you have to churn the waters. Dunbar has to come to you for the money. Hopefully he will have already killed Janna by the time we find him."

Chapter 43

An all-too-familiar sight greeted Jack Kordic as he turned onto Taraval Street. Two radio cars and an ambulance were nosed into the curb in front of Kelty's bar.

"We're too late, Jack," Weeks told him. "I'm betting the bar owner is room temperature."

Kordic parked alongside the ambulance. "You like to gamble on sure things, don't you?"

A uniformed sergeant was at the bar door, gabbing with a half circle of middle-aged men. "Make way," the sergeant ordered when he saw Kordic approaching. "You got here quick, Jack."

"I was just driving by, Sarg. What have we got?"

The sergeant jerked a gnarly thumb toward the bar doors. "Sean Kelty. Someone bashed in his head. Too bad. The man poured a pretty good drink. Cash register looks like it had a night's take, so it wasn't robbery. His daughter found him and called us, that's all I know, Jack."

The paramedics were bent over Kelty's corpse. Kordic took a quick look. Kelty was lying on his stomach. The back of his head was a pulpy mass of coagulated blood. Pieces of broken glass were littered across the top of the bar and on the floor.

A young uniformed officer was leaning against the bar trying to look casual.

"Where's Debbie Kelty?" Kordic asked.

"My partner's in the office with her. Back there."

Kordic and Weeks marched to the back of the bar side by side.

The door to the office was closed. Kordic opened the door without knocking. The uniform was sitting in a chair across from Debbie. An open bottle of whiskey was centered in the middle of the desk. The officer rose quickly to his feet when Kordic introduced himself.

"Wait outside," Kordic advised him, his eyes never leaving Debbie. Her hair was tangled, her makeup blotched, her eyes dry. She hadn't cried for her father yet. He wondered if she ever would. A half-filled old-fashioned glass was clutched in one hand. She brushed away a coil of hair from her forehead. She pointed her chin at the one-way mirror. "I found him like that. Not an hour ago. The front door was locked. I had to use my key to get in."

"The cash register's full. It wasn't a robbery," Kordic said. "You know who did it."

"I don't know! Pa didn't have an enemy in the world."

"Come on, Debbie," Kordic pressed. "The man I asked you about. With the tweed hat, and red nose. You know who it is, don't you?"

She tipped the glass and drained the last droplets of the whiskey, then looked at Weeks. "Who are you?"

Weeks ignored her question, and Kordic dragged the bottle away when she reached for it.

"If he killed your father, there's no reason to think that he won't come after you. He's already killed a woman and two little girls, Debbie. Who is he?"

Debbie sucked in her lips so that they virtually disappeared. "Dunbar. Frank Dunbar."

"Where can I find him?"

Debbie cleared her throat, then hiccuped a few times before responding. "I don't know. I was with Dunbar just once. That night that you first came in." She patted the arms of the chair. "Here, with Pa. He went crazy when he saw you."

She leaned across the desk and tried to tug the bottle of whiskey free from Kordic's hand. "I don't know where you can find him. I really don't."

Weeks grabbed Kordic by the elbow. "We're wasting

time. Let's go. Dunbar's cleaning up shop, Jack. He'll want to get rid of Janna, too. Mo's out there in the park looking for her. All alone."

Kordic nodded his agreement and let go of the whiskey bottle.

Philip Bovard chewed unenthusiastically on something called Milk Duds that he'd purchased at the concession stand across from the merry-go-round. The candy tasted artificial: mass-produced mediocrity. Like so much of America. He finally gave up and spat out the offending pellet. He was positioned in a thick cove of shrubs, so that he could observe the merry-go-round, the swings, slides, and Patrick Lynam, who was seated on a bench some fifty meters away, directly across from the merry-go-round ticket counter.

Bovard thought that the casual clothes that Lynam had procured from his car trunk suited him perfectly: a hooded, dark green, oil-skinned parka, of the same type worn by the British royal family. The hood was snugged over Lynam's head and latched at his throat. His eyes were hidden behind amber-lensed shooting glasses. He looked exactly like a banker trying not to look like a banker. Dunbar would have no trouble spotting Lynam. The question that concerned Bovard was, would Dunbar approach Lynam?

Lynam's head pivoted slowly from side to side, like someone watching a tennis match in slow motion, stopping every so often to study a passing young girl.

That was one thing Bovard had failed to take into consideration. Lynam's attention being drawn to one of the dozens of young girls in the park. This particular girl was very pretty, and had been running back and forth, pushing younger, smaller children out of her way so she could use the slides, the swings. Her skirt billowed up over her thighs as she skimmed down the slide. She had certainly caught Lynam's interest.

The area was awash with women and children. Women

looking for their children. Women chasing after their children, screaming at their children.

Bovard spotted a man heading toward the merry-go-round. He was too short and heavy to be Dunbar. Gray uniform and peaked cap. The school bus driver. He turned his attention back to Patrick Lynam. It would be a shame to kill a man with that much potential, but if the girl or Dunbar didn't turn up soon, that's exactly what he planned to do.

Janna slid a dollar bill across the ticket counter. One ride. She knew she could grab a couple of the free-ride rings.

The sight of the children with their mothers cheered her up at first, then she felt a sudden stab of sadness, a vision of her mother flashing through her mind. A group of girls were standing in a circle by the entrance to the merry-go-round. They were wearing school uniforms, short skirts, white blouses. Like the uniforms Angela had made her wear when that man came and—

She felt a sharp prod in her back and turned to look down at a young boy, with hay-colored hair and a ring of pink cotton candy smeared around his mouth.

"Get going," the boy said belligerently. "Or get out of line."

She moved forward and handed her ticket to the mean-faced operator. He gave her a funny look, then said, "I knew you'd be back."

Janna hurried onto the merry-go-round, searching out her favorite horse. She swung up onto the seat, and for several moments sat there, feeling odd and somehow out of place. She *was* too old for silly children's horses.

The music started and the merry-go-round operator pushed the big brass-handled winch that set the machinery in motion. Janna craned her neck to look for the pole with the free-ride rings.

Maureen Connah recognized the unmarked police car as it rolled to a stop alongside a privet hedge bordering the concession stand across from the merry-go-round.

She gave Kordic a wave and Anatoly Weeks a wane smile. "No luck yet," she said when the two of them were out of the car. "I haven't spotted Janna."

Kordic's lips twisted wryly. "We've had some luck, not all of it good. We've ID'd the shooter. Frank Dunbar. Sean Kelty's dead."

Weeks scanned the area. "I'm going to take a look around."

Kordic brought Maureen up-to-date on the Kelty murder, and the John Doe in the morgue. "The John Doe had a handful of ticket stubs to the aquarium, Mo. It must be another favorite spot of Janna's."

"But how could—" Maureen's face froze. The merry-go-round operator was waving his hands at her. She could barely hear his voice. "The monkey! She's back."

"It's Janna!" Maureen shouted as she started running. "In the merry-go-round."

Frank Dunbar winced at the sound of the tinkling merry-go-round music. Drive you to bloody drink listenin' to that all day, it would.

Dunbar needed a drink, now. Needed it badly. He strolled up to the merry-go-round entrance and scanned the children, not expecting to see his quarry, then he spotted Janna on the silver horse. "Sweet Lamb of God," he murmured, "it's really you!"

Chapter 44

Janna jingled the free-ride rings on her finger. Grabbing the first ring had been easy. The second a little harder, the third harder still. They'd been clipped on a post, some six inches apart. Four of them. She'd never gotten all four. One more. Just one more. She leaned out over the saddle, one fist clamped onto the hand-carved horse's mane, her right hand ready to snatch the ring once the merry-go-round made its full circle back to the post. She paid no attention to the man standing near the post. There were always a group of mothers, and sometimes fathers, standing alongside the carousel, watching their children.

She kept her eyes focused on the last ring, then something drew her attention to the man as she came closer. He was smiling directly at her. It was him! The man who'd killed Amber and Tina!

Dunbar rested the barrel of the silenced semiautomatic on the crook of his elbow. He was taking no chances of losing her this time. Kill Janna, and grab that bloody backpack. He sighted in on her face, smiling as his finger tightened on the trigger.

Kordic scanned the band of parents circling the interior of the merry-go-round, all women, except for a lone man. Thin, wearing a baseball hat. He had a gun in his hand. Dunbar! It was too risky to take a shot at him. Kordic shouted "Freeze" as he pointed his gun straight up in the air and fired off a round.

The gunshot startled Dunbar, causing him to yank his

trigger finger. Janna screamed and sailed through the air, right at him. He felt her impact his chest, and he wobbled awkwardly, trying to regain his balance. More gunshots. The copper. Kordic was running toward him! He snapped off a volley of a half-dozen rounds, then turned on his heel and ran.

A woman clutching a child and screaming veered directly into Kordic's path. He twisted to avoid her, their shoulders made contact, and he stumbled several steps before crashing into the side of the rotating merry-go-round. He heard his knee make a cracking sound over the pandemonium of the music and screaming.

Maureen saw Kordic fall, but she kept moving toward the girl on the floor. "Janna," she called out, dropping to her knees, her fingers going to the girl's neck. There was a pulse.

Janna opened her eyes, they were dazed, but she recognized the redheaded woman hovering over her.

"Are you okay?" Mo asked, her hands searching Janna for wounds.

Kordic limped over to them, his face a gargoyle of pain. "Get Dunbar, Mo. I'll stay with Janna. Get Dunbar!"

Philip Bovard stood on his tip-toes to look over the crowd. A redheaded woman with a gun in hand was kneeling over the supine body of a young girl. The girl was struggling to get to her feet. Bovard saw her face. Janna. Still alive. A tan backpack strapped to her body.

A tall man with a gun in hand limped over to them, then collapsed to the floor. Kordic. The policeman who had come into Kelty's saloon.

"It's her," Patrick Lynam hissed. "Janna."

Bovard grabbed Lynam's sleeve to keep him from running away. "Slowly, Patrick. Walk very slowly."

Every time Lynam opened his mouth to say something, Bovard would hush him. "Quiet! Wait until we get to the car."

The Lincoln symbolized a lifeboat to Lynam. He quickened his pace when the big car came into sight.

Bovard waited until Lynam had his key in the car's

door and had heard the click of the lock sliding free before slipping the gun from his waistband. He jammed the baby-nippled barrel into the base of Lynam's neck and fired, his left hand fanned in front of his face in case there was a spray of blood.

Dunbar's mouth was wide open, gasping for air. He slowed down and tossed his baseball hat into a cluster of shrubs. Out, he vowed. I'm getting out of this bloody place for good. The big money was gone. But there was always work for a man of his talents.

There was a garbage can standing near a park bench. He slipped out of his jacket, wrapped the silenced weapon in it, and thrust it into the can, covering it with a mashing of newspapers. He hated losing a gun that good, but one of the first lessons he'd learned was to get rid of the weapon as soon as possible. "It's not your prick," the foghorn-voiced Sinn Fein commander had advised him after Dunbar's first kill. "It's just a gun, and they're like women. There are more than enough to go around."

A whining, staccato chorus of police, fire, and ambulance sirens filled the air.

He looked over his shoulder. No one was coming. No one was chasing him. They'd be lookin' for a man in a baseball hat and brown jacket. He hoped he'd hit the bloody copper. Hoped he'd killed him.

Maureen had no idea where the shooter was. He could have gone in any direction after he left the merry-go-round. She'd taken three shots at him, none coming close, then her attention had been focused on Janna. Thank God Janna was alive. Maureen had no idea if the gunman's shots had hit any of the other children or their mothers.

The nearest trail led west. Toward the Pacific Ocean. She decided to take it.

Anatoly Weeks skidded to a halt alongside Kordic, who had his arms wrapped protectively around Janna. "Are you okay?"

"I think I broke something," Kordic said between clenched teeth.

Weeks patted Janna lightly on the head. She looked up at him with frightened, tear-smeared eyes. "You are in good hands," he said in Russian. "You will be treated well. Do not fear this man, or the police."

Janna's eyes brightened. "They will not send me home? Or to prison?"

"No. Never."

"Are you the police? Russian police?"

Weeks couldn't hold back a smile. "No. I'm a friend, too." He reached out his hand. "Do you have a small computer in that bag?"

It seemed hopeless. The picnic grounds were filled with families enjoying a meal, playing baseball, tossing Frisbees. Maureen estimated she'd gone over a mile, and hadn't spotted anyone resembling the man at the merry-go-round.

A man in a white shirt hurriedly threading his way through the party of picnickers caught her attention. His hands were clutched across his chest, as if he was trying to keep himself warm. Everyone else was wearing a sweater or jacket. It was a typical San Francisco afternoon—the sky a gray smear of light fog, a crisp wind rattling the tree branches.

The name that Kordic had developed for the shooter. What the hell was it? Frank . . . Frank something . . . Dunbar.

Maureen cupped her hands around her mouth, took a deep breath, and yelled, "Hey, Dunbar!"

The man in the white shirt pivoted around, almost falling down, then he started running.

Mo went after him. He was laboring as he ran, arms grasping out, as if pulling himself forward. There was no sign that he had his gun. Her own weapon was a Smith & Wesson forged aluminum Airweight revolver, with a five-shot cylinder, and, for safety, Maureen kept the chamber under the hammer empty, leaving her just four cartridges.

She'd fired three times at the merry-go-round. Only one bullet left. She'd have to make it count.

Dunbar cursed himself for getting rid of the gun so soon. All he had now was the knife. He'd have to do something soon. The woman was gaining on him. A woman copper! He ducked into a grove of pygmy cypress, careened across a cobbled road and into a dark, narrow pedestrian tunnel leading toward Nineteenth Avenue.

He stopped in the darkness, leaning against the cold, weeping cement tunnel wall. He couldn't run any farther. He'd have to make a stand. He crouched down, picked up a jagged, baseball-sized hunk of concrete, and waited.

Maureen was barely into the tunnel when Dunbar fired the rock at her head. Her hair absorbed part of the impact. As she fell forward, she swiveled around and fired at the dark silhouette against the wall. As she hit the packed-earth floor, the gun skittered from her hand.

Dunbar pounced on the gun, snarling as he pointed it directly at Maureen's head. He pulled the trigger several times, the sound of the hammer hitting an empty chamber causing him to roar in frustration. He threw the gun at Maureen who was scrambling to her feet.

"Lamb of God," Dunbar wheezed, his hand searching for his knife. "It's a wonderful gift you're leaving me. A copper with an empty gun. A big, beautiful woman copper."

"Stay where you are!" Maureen ordered.

Dunbar straightened up. "What are ya gonna do to me, Red?" He passed the knife from hand to hand. "You know the difference between us, Red. You're afraid to die, and I'm not. You probably pray to some Christian God. Confess to him, too, eh, Red. Have you been a naughty girl? Fuckin' all the boy coppers." He wiped the blade of the knife across his pants leg. "I'm gonna gut you like a pig, Red. You never should have been a copper. Ya should have stayed home, with your legs in the air, givin' the boys a good time."

Maureen struggled out of her coat, then waved it in front of her like a bullfighter. "This isn't going to be like killing an old woman. Or helpless little girls."

Dunbar thrust forward, the knife slicing through the coat and slashing across Maureen's arm.

"That's just a taste of the steel, Red. My, my. You've got big tits under that sweater. I think I'll cut one of them off as a sourvenir."

He slashed out again, this time the knife blade momentarily became tangled in the lining of the coat. Dunbar shuffled backward, his feet sliding on the slick, moss-coated flooring, then lunged forward.

Maureen flung the coat at Dunbar's face. Suddenly his legs went out from under him and he fell backward, arms flaying, the back of his head making a thwacking sound when he hit the ground. The woman copper was straddling his chest, her hands in a viselike grip around his hand. Squeezing it, trying to get him to let go of the knife. Dunbar used his free hand to claw at her face, searching for her eyes. God Almighty she was strong. He felt his strength ebbing. Too much drinkin', too much smokin'. Get me away from this bloody amazon, sweet Jesus, and I'll give them all up!

Dunbar took a desperate swing, catching Maureen on the side of her jaw, stunning her momentarily. He bucked his hips, in a futile attempt to drive his knees into her back.

Maureen dug her nails into his hand. "Drop the knife. Let go of it!" she demanded.

Dunbar struggled to raise his head, his lips peeled back, teeth snapping, trying to reach her nose, to bite the bloody thing off.

There was a cracking noise and Dunbar cried out in pain. His wrist had been broken. The knife's blade hovered over his face.

His grip loosened, his fingers unfurled as Maureen's body weight inadvertently drove the blade into Dunbar's throat.

There was an eruption of blood. She pulled the knife

free, then quickly slipped out of her sweater, rolled it into a ball, and jammed it into the wound.

Dunbar stared at her with hate-filled eyes. Blood foamed between his teeth. "Hang on," Maureen urged. "I'll call for an ambulance. Hang on."

Dunbar mumbled something. Blood pooled in his mouth and he gagged as he swallowed.

Maureen's white sweater was now saturated with blood.

Dunbar's lips were moving slowly. The hate was gone from his eyes, replaced by fear.

"You'll be all right," Maureen said softly.

She leaned down to hear what Dunbar was saying. She could barely make it out. "Fuck you, Red."

Chapter 45

The Mediterranean
April 10

The Israeli Sea Corps has long been overshadowed by the army, navy, and commando units, but their presence was still a powerful force in the Mediterranean.

Captain Eric Nordeman ordered the helmsman to follow the orders that had been communicated by the Israeli captain of the Israeli destroyer: "Stop engines and prepare to be boarded."

As the *Sjogang* rolled in the wake of the destroyer, Nordeman raised the binoculars hanging from a cord around his neck and focused in on the hazy green-and-brown outline of Cyprus. An hour, he estimated. Two hours at the most, and he would have made it to Limassol. He leaned over the railing and stared down at the sleek, needle-nosed Israeli warship, rolling in the azure blue water. Seventy-two meters in length, with a top speed of thirty-three knots. A squad of black-garbed commandos were standing amidships, staring up at him. They looked anxious.

"Lower the boarding ladders," Nordeman hollered to his boatswain mate, knowing full well that if he didn't, the Jews would use grappling hooks. There was no sense in damaging the *Sjogang* any more than was necessary.

Captain Nordeman was fully prepared to play dumb. The cargo Gregor Zinovsky had delivered was deep in the ship's hold, buried under legitimate ladings of freight containers holding electrical motors, plumbing fixtures, and a number of Volvo station wagons, all bound for the city of Izmir, Turkey. He'd rehearsed his speech: "Those containers were delivered to me as tractors. I have the invoices to prove it." Then he'd do some ranting and raving, threaten to sue, threaten to go to the authorities, whichever authorities had jurisdiction for this particular latitude and longitude of the Mediterranean they were sailing on.

He hoped the Jews wouldn't concern themselves with him. All of his money had been paid up-front. He wondered if the Russian's cargo would be unloaded at sea, or if he'd be forced to take the *Sjogang* into Israel, most likely the port at Haifa.

Captain Nordeman turned his attention back to the boarding party. Most were young toughs, with machine guns strapped to their backs, their faces blackened to blend in with their helmets and uniforms, scrambling up the rope ladders like monkeys. Except for one man with woolly gray hair who was noticeably older than the others, slowly, awkwardly making the climb with the use of just one hand. He'd be the one to deal with, Nordeman knew.

San Francisco
April 12

Someone was leaning on his doorbell. Jack Kordic caned his way over to the kitchen door. "Come on in," he shouted.

The door swung open and Maureen Connah strode into his apartment, with Janna Drovana in tow. "Janna. You remember Inspector Kordic, don't you?"

Janna walked shyly over to Kordic and extended her hand. "I want to thank you very much, sir."

Kordic accepted her small hand in his. Janna had fared much better than he had. She'd suffered only bruises on her arms and legs when she fell from the merry-go-round. The crime lab estimated that Dunbar's bullet had missed her by a matter of inches, plowing harmlessly into the

neck of the wooden horse she'd been riding. Falling right
into the Irish gunman had cushioned her fall and saved
her from further injuries.

Others hadn't been as lucky. The wild barrage of shots
Dunbar had fired before fleeing the merry-go-round had
killed one thirty-four-year-old woman and crippled her
daughter. Kordic had a fractured left kneecap resulting
from crashing into the merry-go-round. His cast stretched
from his hip to his ankle.

Kordic smiled at Janna. She looked good. Clean, fresh-
faced. There was a sparkle in her eyes. "I don't have much
to offer, but I think there's the makings of hot chocolate
around here somewhere."

Maureen held up a pink box and said: "I brought
some doughnuts."

"You hung around Anatoly Weeks too long," Kordic
mocked.

Maureen volunteered to make the chocolate and some
coffee and Kordic gave Janna a brief tour of his apartment,
leading her over to a bookcase. The top shelves were
jammed with books, police procedural nonfiction works,
then a mixture of fiction from classics to pulp: *Moby Dick,
The Three Musketeers, For Whom the Bell Tolls,* Louis L'A-
mour, Le Carré, Wambaugh, paperback westerns, and a
large collection representing the various Peanuts characters and Calvin and Hobbs that had belonged to his son,
Danny.

Kordic figured Janna was probably too old for Peanuts
and Calvin, so he pointed to the shelf holding a half-dozen
videocassettes that spanned the generation gap, and that
he had watched over and over with Danny: *Casablanca,
North by Northwest, The Pink Panther, Gunga Din, The Ad-
ventures of Robin Hood,* and *The Quiet Man.*

"How about a movie?" he suggested. "Have you ever
seen *The Pink Panther*?"

Kordic set up the movie and showed Janna how to operate the TV remote control.

Maureen was waiting for him in the kitchen. "That's a
nice kid," he said, reaching for his coffee.

"The immigration department is screwing us around, Jack. They want to put Janna in a holding house. I'm fighting them."

"Where's she staying now?"

"At the Juvenile Ward," Mo said, using a kitchen knife to cut through the string wrapped around the pink bakery box. "I'm trying to get them to release her to me. Wish me luck. Anatoly called. They found the ship. The nuclear reactors were there all right."

"Yeah, he called me, too." Kordic sipped at the hot coffee. Anatoly Weeks had worked feverishly on the HV2500 computer he'd found in Janna's backpack, accessing the information he needed to trace the money transfers from Philip Bovard's numbered Swiss accounts to like accounts in South and Central American banks; the Syrian's accounts in Beirut, one very rich Russian bureaucrat's account in southern France, and an unknown character by the name of Eric Nordeman.

The grand prize had been the date and place of delivery of the Russian nuclear reactors and, eventually, the name of the ship. Patrick Lynam had logged in the notation High Seas and Eric Nordeman alongside the port of Limassol, in Cyprus. The High Seas notation drove Weeks crazy, until a Mossad cipher clerk hit on the translation for the Swedish freighter *Sjogang*. A check with the shipping line confirmed that the captain's name was Eric Nordeman.

Weeks had chased shadows all over the isle of Cyprus, reported sightings of men who matched Bovard's description, but none of them had panned out. Bovard had somehow slipped away.

The serial number on the HV2500 notebook computer had led Maureen directly to Patrick Lynam. Lynam had registered the computer in his name on the date of purchase. Kordic had been in the hospital, being fitted for his leg cast, when Maureen learned that Lynam had been found shot to death in Golden Gate Park, less than a quarter of a mile from the merry-go-round.

Maureen rattled the box of doughnuts at Kordic. "The chocolate ones are good."

"How good are you?" Kordic wanted to know. Her face looked puffy, her eyes dull, yet restless, flicking around the room every few seconds. He remembered how he'd felt after killing a man. Even though the man was a mass murderer, and had nearly killed him, Kordic had gone through months of depression. He wondered how Mo would react if he suggested that she talk to Barney Ford, the psychiatrist who had helped him.

The question hung in the air for several seconds. "I'm fine, Jack. There's something I want to tell you about Dunbar. In the tunnel . . . there . . . I—"

The musical sound of a young girl's laughter interrupted Maureen. She got to her feet and leaned against the door frame, watching Janna happily sipping a cup of hot chocolate and chuckling at the antics of Peter Sellers's inept policeman, Inspector Clouseau, on the television set.

She turned back to face Kordic. "I'm fine, Jack. Just fine. I wonder when Anatoly will come back?"

"Not until he's found Philip Bovard." And eliminated him, Kordic said silently. Anatoly Weeks was not the type who would have to lean on psychiatric counseling after killing a man.

Chapter 46

Cornwall, England
Three Weeks Later

Philip Bovard kept a list of his favorite restaurants worldwide. It was a small list, twenty-two in all: two in Austria, two in Switzerland, seven in France, three in Germany, two in Belgium, a single entry each for Ireland and Sweden, and four in England.

It was a personal list, not one he shared with friends. Bovard more often than not dined alone, and tonight was no exception. He'd be dining alone for the foreseeable future.

He liked Cornwall, the so-called English Riviera. Liked it now. He feared that in another few years the tourists would turn it into another gaudy, seaside amusement park.

From his veranda table at the Seafood Restaurant, he could observe the quay where the lobster boats and trawlers docked and unloaded the marvelous fish, the best of which was carted directly over to the kitchen door of the restaurant. The name annoyed him, it didn't do the establishment justice. Seafood Restaurant. It sounded like a cheap fish and chips establishment. But cheap it was not. His marvelous fish soup, fresh oysters, and grilled dover sole with lime, along with a bottle of Batard-Montrachet, ticketed out at over seventy-four pounds.

Bovard sipped at his coffee, while the end of his cigar marinated in a snifter of Quinta do Vesuvio Port. His plans were to hide out, in comfort, for a month or two.

Let things settle down. He couldn't risk touching the money he had in the accounts that Patrick Lynam had been monitoring, but there were enough dollars, pounds, and francs tucked away in accounts Lynam never knew of to keep him going for some time.

Somehow he'd have to mend fences with the Syrians. They were unforgiving bastards. But they needed the Philip Bovards of the world, and, Bovard thought with some pride, there weren't many of his kind around.

He retrieved the cigar from the snifter, placed the now soggy end in his mouth, and lit up, ignoring the look of disapproval from the horse-faced woman in tweeds at the adjoining table.

Bovard drained the remains of the port, left a sheaf of pound notes to cover the bill and an overly generous tip, blowing a cloud of cigar smoke as he passed the woman's chair.

The night was warm, the sky a velvet black, twilight crowded the horizon. Bovard crossed the cobblestone road to the quay. Gulls wheeled in circles around the rows of moored fishing boats.

He leaned against a warped wooden dock railing, puffing at his cigar, enjoying the view. He was booked into the Tredagon Hotel, a few miles away. Three days, four at the most, then perhaps he'd journey over to France. It was time he found a new restaurant for his list.

A fisherman, his face a stubble of gray beard, wearing a shapeless, dark blue pea coat and long-billed cap, a thick dark cigar clamped between his teeth, leaped from one of the boats and trudged up the gangplank. He looked like a man who'd put in a hard day's work. If that work had included delivering the fish he'd had for dinner, then Bovard considered it a worthy effort.

Bovard gave the man a small nod, one cigar smoker to another. The fisherman responded with a plume of smoke. The man was directly behind him when Bovard's nostrils twitched and it dawned on him that the cigar smoke was too rich to be coming from a Cornish fisherman.

Bovard felt a cold circle of steel pinch into his back.

"Who are you?" Bovard demanded.

"Not a friend," Anatoly Weeks assured him.

"Who? Mukhabarat? Don't do anything foolish. There must be some way we can come to an understanding, you don't want to—"

"I worked for Ira Heiser."

Bovard took a long draw on his cigar, figuring it might be his last. "Ah. Mossad. I can be very helpful to you. I know a lot about the Syrians. About the Libyans. All of them, I can tell you things you'll never learn in any other way. And the Russians, I know about—"

Weeks jammed the gun barrel into Bovard's back to silence him, then leaned close and whispered into his ear. "No deals, Bovard. Did you notice a black Mercedes with smoked windows parked outside the restaurant while you were enjoying dinner?"

Bovard's heart thudded painfully against his rib cage. He had noticed a Mercedes. The Jew was going to transport him somewhere. Interrogate him. "Yes, but—"

"Mukhabarat. I tipped them that you'd be here. Colonel Rashid Awad is in the backseat of the Mercedes. When I last saw him, he was sharpening his knives."

"*Momzer*," Bovard hissed. "You can't turn me over to them."

"I can and will. The deal's been made. So long."

"Wait!" Bovard pleaded. He took a deep breath. "Do it. Please."

"Do what?" Weeks asked.

"Kill me, you fucking Jew! Do it!"

Weeks augered the barrel of his gun into Bovard's back. "I thought you'd never ask," he said, then pulled the trigger.

Bovard slumped forward, his cigar slipping from his hands and falling into the harbor.

Weeks tossed the gun into the water, wheeled around, and circled his hand over his head. The Mercedes made a decorous U-turn and pulled up alongside him. He jumped in the backseat and told the driver, "Let's go home, Jacob."

The driver punched the accelerator, throwing a fountain of dust into the air. When they reached a straightaway he glanced back at Weeks and smiled widely. "Nice job, boss."

Weeks grunted an acknowledgment. Jacob was a new recruit. Straight out of the army. The new breed. Twenty-six years old, and he actually smiled. Showed his teeth. Maybe there was hope for Mossad yet.